STORM
AND THE
HURRICANE LADY

Mermaid's Knot Books

Storm and the Mermaid's Knot

Storm and the Hurricane Lady

STORM
AND THE
HURRICANE LADY

MEGHAN RICHARDSON
AND
TINA VERDUZCO

LunaSea Publishing
ST. AUGUSTINE, FLORIDA

STORM AND THE HURRICANE LADY

Copyright © 2022 by Meghan Richardson and Tina Verduzco

All rights reserved. No part of this book may be reproduced, distributed or transmitted in any form or by any means without the prior written permission from the publisher, except in the case of brief quotations in a book review or as otherwise permitted by copyright law. For information, please write to the publisher at the address below.

This book is a work of fiction. Any references to historical events, real people, or real places are used fictitiously. Other names, characters, places, and events are the product of the authors' imaginations, and any resemblance to actual events or places or persons, living or dead, is entirely coincidental.

Published by LunaSea Publishing, 497 Florida Ave, St. Augustine, FL 32080 USA
Visit us at LunaSeaPublishing.com

Cover artwork by Dean Richardson
Typeset in EB Garamond and Cinzel Decorative

First Edition, October 2022

ISBN 978-0-9985495-3-8 (hardback)
ISBN 978-0-9985495-4-5 (trade paperback)
ISBN 978-0-9985495-5-2 (ebook)

Dedication

To Dad, yes, book 2 is finished! Love, your little girl. ~Meghan

For my son, Nick, for believing. For my Auntie Karen, AKA Momma Lite, for the love and support. ~Tina

CHAPTER ONE
Jon

Oh, Jon. We need to talk.

Talk? Storm... Storm!

Shh, I thought to Jon. I lay at the bottom of the inlet in the dark, still water. My fingertips moved slowly through the silky sand beside me, leaving small furrows in their wake. I felt at peace. *It's okay now. You're a water spirit. I found you. Lilli couldn't find you.* That felt important, but I couldn't remember why. I was so comfortable. I closed my eyes.

The girls chattered and giggled nearby.

Hide-and-seek! one said excitedly.

They wanted me to play with them.

Please, please, please? another squealed.

Sure, I answered through my mental fog.

Yay! they shouted in unison.

Storm? Jon asked.

Yes, Jon? I answered, finding it hard to focus. A little voice inside my head tried to tell me about something I was doing or was supposed to do or had forgotten to do. *Hang on, girls. I have to... do something... oh, right. Lilli. I need to get Lilli. She's just over there.* I meant to point with my right arm but wasn't sure it actually moved.

Storm, get up! Jon shouted.

We'll hide, and you'll seek! the girls called out.

What? I asked them. *Oh right, hide-and-seek. Okay.* I yawned and snuggled deeper into the velvety sand. *I'll count. One... two...*

I wasn't sure how much time had passed, but I realized I had forgotten to keep counting. My mind was quiet—no giggling little girls and no...

Oh God! Jon! My eyes popped open, and I looked around. Nothing but the silent dark water. *Why am I still lying here? I have to tell the others about Jon. His soul... I found him.* I pushed off from the bottom and swam as fast as I could to shore.

I lifted my head above the waterline. I was about ten yards from shore. The night air seemed to match the water temperature, and not an ounce of breeze disturbed it.

Lilli was in the shallows with someone in her arms. Rowan hovered over her right shoulder, his back to me. Lilli's white hair blew around her head wildly.

But there's no wind, I thought with some confusion.

She looked up at Rowan. "How long has it been?"

Rowan replied, slightly out of breath, "Only a few minutes, I think."

I hovered in the water and watched Z and Sara rush from the beach and join Rowan and Lilli in the water. Sara brushed her dancing hair away impatiently.

But there isn't any wind, I thought again.

I did the breaststroke closer to the shore and shouted, "Hey!"

Nobody turned.

Come on. I swam closer.

"Hey!" I tried again. "I found Jon's soul! Guys!"

Still no response. The palm trees and large oaks bent and buckled with sharp gusts of wind. But I still felt nothing.

Something's wrong. Is it Pearl? Did the braid not work? I swam with larger strokes. *Please be okay, Pearl. And I have to tell them... Jon...*

As soon as my feet could touch the bottom, I stood and rushed with clumsy, sloshing steps toward the group. No one turned despite my splashes and calls. I half jumped, half dove the final feet and landed next to Lilli.

"Lilli!" I screamed, and then I screamed again in terror.

I did an awkward crab-walking scoot backward, away from the vision in front of me. The body in Lilli's embrace had one arm extended, floating lightly on the water's surface. The hand wore a moonstone ring on the middle finger.

The hand... the body in Lilli's arms was *mine*.

Impossible. How am I...? I'm right here... I'm... not feeling any wind. The water and air aren't the same temperature—I'm just not feeling anything. Nobody can see or hear me. I'm... noooooo.

"Everybody, shh," Lilli said softly. I looked at her, wide-eyed and scared, but like everybody else, I listened to her directions.

"She's near, and I need her to stay calm."

I nodded. *Right, calm.*

"Help me!" I shouted to Lilli. *No, not calm.*

Lilli softly hummed a beautiful tune. The soulful music touched deep inside me and felt warm and inviting, as if giving me a hug from the inside out.

Vibrations tickled behind my belly button and spread to my chest. A glow lit Lilli's face from below as she leaned over my body. Goose bumps rose on my arms, and my teeth chattered with the sudden cold. I slid closer to Lilli. I kept my eyes on the top of Lilli's downturned head. I placed a hand on soft, warm skin. A part of me knew it rested on my own forehead, but I didn't want to look. The warmth radiated up my arm, and the goose bumps receded. I placed my other hand next to my first.

I closed my eyes. The heat filled my body, and so did Lilli's beautiful song. I crawled on top of my body into Lilli's arms. I sank down. This felt so nice, so safe, so...

Ouch. Pins and needles, pins and needles, not okay. Need to breathe.

I gasped. "Huuuh!" Then I mumbled, "Help."

Z whispered, "Rowan, take Storm to the house and give her this."

"Help..." My tongue wouldn't cooperate. Searing pain spread through my body. But I had to get them to understand. "Jon," I finally pushed out through thick, unyielding lips.

"Shh," Rowan's deep voice said, reassuring me. "You're okay now. I shouldn't have left you. I'm so sorry, my rainbow fish." He hugged me to his chest and lifted me from the water. "I'm going to get you home, m'love."

I shook my head from side to side. Trapped inside my broken body, I realized I'd lost Jon forever. I never got to tell anybody about where he was.

I failed my best friend... twice.

CHAPTER TWO
A Stranger among Us

That tall red-haired mermaid and the dark-haired one don't seem to like each other very much. The woman chuckled and slowly ventured out from the protection of the dense canopy behind the lighthouse.

The small white bird perched on her shoulder cocked its head.

I think they're done with their childish fights for tonight. She winked at the bird.

Her willowy frame wove between the low-hanging Spanish moss and vines as she stepped carefully over the debris piles that littered the brick patio. The silence was in stark contrast to the booming of thunder and explosions of glass and stone just moments before. She and her feathered partner didn't know the whole plot, but the gathering at the water's edge piqued her interest enough to make her move closer. The group didn't notice her hovering at the edge of the shadows.

A tall merman hurried past her with a limp body in his arms. An old woman and an old man followed him. The red-haired mermaid, a tiny white-haired girl, and a man walked slowly with a boy who had been sitting on the grass. The remaining two mermaids waded into the dark water and disappeared beneath the surface.

The woman had never seen so many types intermingling. Mermaids, a merman, humans, and the tiny one, who was most definitely a sprite. She shivered, despite the warm night air, upon realizing she might have to deal with sprites.

"We must be very careful as we tread among this foul mix of creatures," she whispered. The bird fluffed and gave a shake of its body. "I know we've been searching for so long only to be one step behind. But now we've caught up to our prize. Once I get them back, we will reclaim the tale that is rightfully ours, and I will finally be free of this vile form." She gave a hushed laugh as if the cleverest thought had made itself clear. "Do you know what I think?"

The bird looked at her with one dark eye.

"I think I will make them help us. That's the least they can do after what they have put me—us—through. And the best part is they won't even know until it's too late, stupid creatures that they are."

The bird watched her intently and nudged its beak into her cheek.

"Well, the sprite is a different matter, but even they have weaknesses to exploit. This really will be a fun turn of events." She giggled.

The tern nipped lightly at her ear.

She gave a crooked half smile. "No pun intended."

She began the trek back. Walking was an effort. She was tired and needed to rest. She had just reached the small forest when her companion tilted its head quickly from side to side. She froze, listened, and then backed slowly toward the nearest tree for cover. The bird flew up to a twisted limb. They watched silently as two of the mermaids from earlier, the ones who had taken to the water, walked toward them.

"Do you really think that's an appropriate outfit to wear for this?" the blond mermaid said to the dark-haired one. Each held a bucket in one hand and a long-handled mop in the other, and each had towels tucked under one arm. The blonde wore khaki shorts and a tank top, the brunette a spaghetti-strapped black sequin dress that glittered like tiny stars with each passing of the lighthouse beam.

The tern shifted his head so his left eye faced the mermaids and then glanced at his companion.

She cocked her head to look up at him with her right eye. *Yes, she was the one who was so pale on the lawn,* she thought in a silent response and gave a nod.

"Yes, I do, dearest sister. You know, I liked you more before you got your braid back," the dark-haired mermaid replied with a sigh.

The blonde elbowed her.

The brunette laughed lightly. "Just kidding."

The blond mermaid stopped suddenly. The tern and his companion remained motionless.

"What?" the brunette asked. "I said I was kidding."

"Sara! Are you wearing my new Fluevogs?"

"Honestly, Pearl, they were on the floor and—"

"They were on the floor, *in the box*, because I just bought them!"

"It was you who told me I had to hurry." In a mocking tone, she said, "Hurry up, Sara. We have to get back to Storm. Sara, aren't you ready yet? Sara!" Sara shrugged and returned to her normal voice. "Plus, they match my dress."

"I swear, if you mess them up..."

Sara flashed a coy smile and gave Pearl a friendly shove. "Don't worry so much, sis."

The observers remained motionless as the sisters passed closer than a wing's distance. Busy arguing, the sisters failed to notice the slight frame of the woman pressed tightly against the trunk of the oak. This solidified what she had already known—that mermaids got easily wrapped up in stupid things. They really were silly creatures, which made their stealing of her tale all the more insulting.

While she could probably follow them, she had to admit her legs were tired, and she feared one wrong stumble would betray her location. And even though mers were not all that bright, their hearing was remarkable, and their fighting skills were strong. Her success depended on her staying unseen, at least until she chose to be seen.

Follow, she thought to her companion.

The tern took flight while she slowly slid down to a sitting position with her aching legs bent to her side and her back still pressed against the rough bark. With closed eyes, she relaxed and waited. The image formed slowly, its edges distorted around a bulging center. It made her long for the old days. But now wasn't the time for memories—now was the time to gather information. She watched the scene from above, connected to her companion's bird's-eye view.

"This won't take all night, will it?" Sara whined.

"No, it'll be quick." Pearl held a branch back for her sister to pass under. "We *have* to be quick. I need to get back—"

"To Stormy, I know. You've told me a hundred times."

The sisters crossed the patio and made their way to the two-story brick building. The tern landed on the second-story railing, lowered his body so his belly nestled on his legs, and watched them approach.

Pearl replied, "Let's get in, get it cleaned up, and get home."

"I agree with the first two parts, sister, but I'm not planning on heading home. It *is* still Saturday night!"

"Technically, it's Sunday morning, but fine, Sara. Wherever you choose to go after here is fine by me. Let's just get started."

The ground-level door hung at an odd angle. Sara pulled its handle, and the entire door came away from the building. She let it go and laughed as it fell heavily to the ground. "Yup, this will be a piece of cake." She disappeared into the darkness of the building. Pearl followed.

The woman opened her eyes and was back at the base of the tree. With a soft moan, she pushed herself back to standing on her reluctant legs. The pain was excruciating, but this was her chance to find out more, so she clenched her jaw against the stabbing sensations and crept quietly to the building. She could no longer hear them, which meant they most likely couldn't hear her. She was pretty sure mer hearing had limits, like her eyesight, but she was mindful of staying as silent as possible. *Better to be safe than to be surprised.* And she was in no shape to take on two healthy mermaids.

She glanced up at her companion still snuggled down on the railing. It was late for both of them, but they needed just a little more time, and then they could rest. She stepped around the downed door and slid through the doorway, hugging one side and willing herself to appear as nothing more than a shadow.

The battle had indeed been fierce, and the destruction was impressive. The bottom two steps to an interior set of spiral stairs were missing, and the ground was covered in what looked like diamonds. On the far wall, two words remained on a broken brass plaque: Fresnel Lens.

Not diamonds, then, she thought.

Pearl's voice echoed softly in the distance. "Well, that's not bad. We can put it back into place."

"Good news! I found the missing steps," Sara said.

"Awesome," Pearl said.

Sara laughed. Pearl sighed. "Oh, not as awesome."

The woman ventured into a narrow hall and kept her back to the damp wall. Even though she padded lightly on the cement floor, she had to clench her jaw to stifle her cries from the pain in her legs. The hall opened to a larger room with littered glass, a cannon at an odd angle, a gaping hole in the floor and... the missing stairs, which were embedded in the far wall.

These creatures are more barbaric than even the tales made them out to be.

Both girls had their backs to her as they studied the misplaced stairs. Sara glanced at her sister and then back at the stairs and laughed again.

"Why are you laughing?" Pearl asked angrily.

"This is hilarious!" Sara exclaimed in a loud whisper. "There isn't one thing *not* destroyed in here. And you made me carry a bucket and a mop! What are we going to do with these?"

"Okay." Pearl placed her bucket on the ground. "Plan B."

"What's that? Should I run and grab the Swiffer too?" Sara snorted.

"No, Sara. There's no way we can fix this mess, so we have to make a new mess to hide our mess. Get it?"

"I can do messes," Sara responded with an enthusiastic nod.

"We'll have to hide the tunnel, obviously, but then let's just make it look like vandals have been here."

"Vandals?"

"Protesters making a point."

"Protesters? Like fighting against the cruel display of artifacts?" Sara asked.

"Okay, you may be right. Protesters might not fly. Tornado?"

"A tornado in a basement? Pearl, I think that braid got tied back on a bit too tightly." Sara snickered.

Pearl sighed. "Fair point about the tornado. Okay, let's stick with protesters. The humans in town are always angry about something happening. I could see a group believing that these artifacts are not being respected." Pearl reached into her bucket, pulled out two cans of spray paint, and shook them. She handed one to Sara.

"Ooh, fun!" Sara grinned as she took the cap off and aimed.

"Wait!" Pearl held her arm out to block the spray.

"What?" Sara pouted as her arm sagged down.

"Tornado. We should do a storm. If we could get these windows to blow out, maybe just a touch of the wall, a tornado could easily rip through here and cause massive damage."

"Ooh! Can we take the roof? Then the floor could fall in a bit."

Pearl thought. "Okay, but just a bit of the roof."

Sara gave a wink. Thunder rumbled.

"Wait!" Pearl held her hand up again.

"Oh my God! Make up your mind." Sara tapped her foot impatiently.

"Protesters." Pearl nodded confidently. "We will stick to protesters."

Sara lifted her spray paint but paused. "Are you sure?"

"Yes."

"Okay." Sara smiled, shook her can, and pointed to the damp gray stones. "Let the games begin." She depressed the trigger. Red canvased the wall in front of her. Pearl joined in, and the two were quickly lost in the art of destruction.

The lurker's head felt dizzy with the fumes, so she left the girls to their art and crept away. Her small shoulder companion rejoined her, and the two made their way to the shelter and comfort the woods would provide.

CHAPTER THREE
Reality Check

"Jon!" I shouted and sat up in a panic in the darkness. The jolt wracked my body with agony. My breathing came in short gasps. I coughed.

"Ouch, ugh." I moaned in pain and swiped at the sticky wet veil of hair plastered to my face. "Where...?" I whispered.

The glass panes of my bedroom window rattled, answering my question.

"How...?" I looked into the night and heard the angry waves crashing onto the shore, matching the pulse beating too loudly behind my temples.

I tried to remember what had happened. Every inch of me hurt. My pinkie toenail even seemed to scream at me.

I rested back on my pillow and searched my mind for memories. All that I could scrounge up were short flashes of images that played like an old black-and-white movie, all scratched and distorted. In one scene, I looked up from the bottom of Jack's pool at the rippling clear water. Another had me biting a hand underwater. A third and fourth were more pleasant with a close-up of a beautiful man's chest and a hug from my mom. But they faded in an instant.

Are these memories or dreams? If memories, are they recent or are they from years ago?

A single hot tear slid down my cheek and plopped onto my lip. My tongue darted out and drew the tear into my mouth. "Ah, salt." I sighed.

Then it happened. That one salty tear was the key needed to unlock the vault of memories. They started out slow and steady, details filling in the missing pieces from the first memories. I had fallen into Jack's pool before I knew I was a mermaid. I had bitten Daniel's hand. Rowan's chest was the most beautiful in the world, and Pearl had given me a huge hug after the solstice ceremony. These were nice memories, but then others followed. They accelerated and wouldn't stop once they had momentum, like a tidal wave that tricked you into thinking the beach was safe until it was too late to run and you were drowning in the unrelenting current. The mood changed to horror and sadness. Fighting, water, hitting my head on the cave ceiling, leaving... returning to... Jon.

"Oh my God!" I inhaled sharply and sat back up. "I found Jon," I cried out weakly. "Lilli... I never told Lilli."

I leaned over the edge of the bed and threw up.

"Stormy," a hushed voice said to me.

I looked up from my half-off-the bed position. Hot tears slid in rivulets down my cheeks. I thought of the word-of-the-day calendar Nana had gotten me. *Ugh, what is happening?*

Pearl climbed onto the bed next to me and helped me back to the pillow, "Oh, Stormy, you threw up. Of course you did. Reentering your body is traumatic. Lie back, baby girl. I'll clean this all up."

In the dark, she bustled in and out of the bathroom and around my bed. I tracked her with my ears rather than my eyes. Eventually, her body slid in next to mine again. She smelled like the ocean... salt, brine, sweet sun-warmed skin, and... *spray paint?*

"Drink this." She pressed a cup to my lips. The thick, cold liquid coated my throat.

Pearl brushed my hair off my forehead as I drank. Her lightest of touches continued, and I relaxed despite wanting to find out what had happened. The hands were so soft and relaxing. I gave up fighting and drifted off into blissful darkness.

******

The brightness of my room lit up my eyes from behind my closed lids.

I pried them open and blinked like crazy against the onslaught of light. I shoved the damp sheet away and lay like a starfish in a heat coma. My head pounded, and my limbs were too heavy to lift.

Memories of Pearl with me last night surfaced. I sighed and didn't even try to hold back the tears. *Jon is dead. I couldn't save him. I left him. I said I'd be back. I couldn't even save his soul.*

"I'm such an idiot," I whimpered and crashed my head up and down onto my pillow as hard as I could. My head spun and pounded.

"Here are the eggs," he said from the porch below.

I froze in my verbal and physical abuse.

"Awesome, Jon. Thanks!" Pearl replied.

"What'd I miss?" Jon asked.

"Well, Rowan was just filling us in on how Sara's been doing at Paige's store. She apparently is a true favorite among the clients." Pearl laughed lightly.

I fell out of bed in my rush to get to the window. *This can't be true. I'm dreaming. He's dead. He's not...*

I pressed to all fours and reached for the windowsill to pull myself up high enough to see out. Down below on the deck, Rowan and Sara sat at the round table and Pearl in a lounge chair. I couldn't see Jon—if it really was him—because of the angle of the umbrella. I pressed the left side of my face to the glass and then my right, like a bird, to try to get a better angle, but it was still no good.

"Come on, man," I whined in frustration.

"It's not a matter of what she said—it's a matter of how she said it," Rowan said.

"Oh, stop trying to get me in trouble. You always do that. And that was so last week," Sara sneered.

"I do not. I'm just saying that it was pretty embarrassing."

"And when did you become so prim and proper?"

"Well, obviously, many decades before you."

"Sara and Rowan, please."

"Pearl, I'm just saying Sara didn't need to tell that woman she was fat."

"I didn't say that at all!" Sara put her hands on her hips and swiveled her chair to face Pearl. "I just said there was no way she would fit into that dress. I mean, come on—it was an extra small, and she was *not* extra small. Why is that wrong?"

"Like I said at the store, it wasn't wrong to give advice, but to grab the dress from her hand as you laughed, saying that she'd 'be lucky if her right leg fit into it' seemed a tad harsh."

"I think women appreciate my honesty," Sara said.

"Ha! She used some funny words to show her gratitude, then," Rowan replied.

"What, Rowan—should I have been more like you and offered to help them try things on?"

"Seriously, you two?" Pearl interjected between her giggles. "Sara, please keep your advice to good color choices, and, Rowan, get the smug look off your face. Sara, really? Sticking out your tongue?" Pearl laughed. "Come on. Last night was freakin' long. I haven't even slept yet, and you two have the energy to argue."

"Well, Paige can find another assistant after what Laverna pulled last night. And I haven't slept yet either. Pearl, when did you get old?" Sara glanced up at my window.

"Last night," Pearl replied.

Sara winked. "Well, old Mama, don't look now, but I believe someone woke up."

Pearl looked up at me, and her face lit up with a beautiful smile. "Stay right there. I'll be up to help you."

Rowan also turned his head, and he blew me a kiss. The other person remained stubbornly hidden by the umbrella. I lowered myself gingerly back to the wood floor, sat with my back propped against the wall, and waited impatiently for Pearl.

Is he, or isn't he? Is he, or isn't he? Is he, or isn't he? Is he, or isn't he?

"Hi, baby girl!" Pearl's smocked pink dress flowed around her like cotton candy. "How ya feeling?"

"Is he, or isn't he?" I croaked in a voice I didn't recognize.

"Oh gosh. Hang on, Stormy. You need some more salted cream. No no no—please don't cry. That will only make you weaker." She crouched next to me and wiped the tear from my cheek. She then pressed her damp finger lightly against my lips.

My tongue grabbed at the salty gift. "Is he, or isn't he?" I repeated quietly, pleading.

"Is who what or not what?" she asked with kind eyes as she handed me a glass with thick blue liquid.

I took a sip. It was the same stuff she'd given me the night before. I felt some relief to the fire in my throat. I swallowed another sip, took a breath, and tried again. "Jon. Is he, or isn't he?"

"Downstairs?" she asked, her eyes wide in genuine confusion.

"Dead or alive," I clarified.

"Well, most definitely alive! It would be awkward to have him downstairs otherwise." She giggled.

It was my turn to feel genuinely confused.

"Stormy, look." She lifted me up to the edge of my bed with ease then held me as I faced the window. "On three. One... two..." She put her arm around my back, hooked it under my armpit, and on "Three," she stood us up.

We took two steps to the window together.

"Look," she said.

A boy sat in the lounge chair Pearl had vacated. He wore ripped khaki shorts and a wrinkled T-shirt, and as I watched, he brushed an errant dirty-blond curl from his forehead.

My legs weakened, but Pearl was ready. She supported my deadweight and guided me back to the edge of the bed. Taking her place next to me, she smiled. "Jon's just fine, Stormy. You saved him."

I shook my head in disbelief. *No, I killed him!* my mind yelled. No words escaped my dry lips, though. I just looked from the window to Pearl and back again. A tear rolled down my cheek.

She handed me the glass again. "Drink, and I'll tell you a tale," she said as she guided me back toward the pillow. "But only if you promise no more tears for now."

I just looked at her.

"Promise?"

I nodded weakly and sniffled. I wiped my nose with the back of my hand and took another sip of the shake. Pearl snuggled next to me, and I laid my head against her chest.

She stroked my hair. "After you ran off..." She paused as I stiffened at hearing those words, and my eyes filled. "No, Stormy, relax. Just listen."

I took a deep breath.

"After you ran off, Lilli said we needed to take Jon down to the water because the building or land or something was preventing her from finding his soul. Too many vibrations, she said. So Matthew carried him down."

"But Rowan said Lilli couldn't find him."

"He didn't know. He ran after you as soon as you left."

"I thought Jon couldn't be saved," I said.

"Me too! But Lilli held some hope, I guess. And not wanting to disagree with a sprite, we all gathered at the water just as Rowan emerged from it. What was strange was he saw us and then looked back at the inlet, but before we could even talk to him, he dove back in. Matthew handed Jon's body to Lilli, who crouched in the water with him. Within seconds, she started to hum quietly. She slowly rocked him in the water. Her hair turned brighter white than usual, and her skin nearly glowed. And then, all of a sudden, Jon gasped for air!

"Z told Matthew to take Jon immediately to dry land, which he did.

Nana stayed with him as he recovered. Just as Jon got settled, Rowan emerged from the water, carrying you! He said he found you lifeless by the cave, and Jon's soul had spoken to him. He told the soul to get to the water's edge immediately, and then he proceeded to rescue your body. While Lilli worked on you, Jon recovered quickly."

I had no words. I was working hard to not cry. These were tears of happiness. But still, I'd promised I wouldn't.

"You really scared us, Stormy. Mers don't often recover from being separated from their bodies because our souls aren't the same as humans'. It's harder to get ours back once we've separated. But you saved Jon, because when Rowan went to find you, he found Jon's soul!"

She gave me a squeeze and then looked at me sternly. "Please don't do that again, though. I only just got you back! I certainly don't want to lose you again."

I nodded and leaned in for a hug. After a minute, I sat back. "Can I see him?" I whispered. "Jon?"

"Yes, tonight. After you sleep. We're all meeting here. Z wants to talk with all of us, human, mer, sprite, and everything in between." She gave me a little squeeze. "So you need to build some strength before then."

She pushed the glass to my lips. I sipped.

"Close your eyes now. I'll wake you in a few hours." Pearl smiled and stood up to leave.

The heavy veil of sleep covered me before she left the room.

CHAPTER FOUR
Reunion

I stood just inside the screen door and heard Mr. Humpphrey ask, "When is the move planned again?"

"End of the month most likely," Nana replied. "To have it on display in September."

"And you think she'll plan something during that time?"

"Most definitely. The time spans the equinox, which is also a new moon this year."

Mr. Humpphrey shook his head. "Mers and their obsession with seasons and moons."

Nana gave a half laugh. "Well, at least it gives us a target to prepare for."

"Great. We know *when* to prepare, but we don't know *what* we're preparing for." Mr. Humpphrey sighed.

"Well, Miles, if we knew all the answers, we'd be bored," Nana replied with a sly grin.

"I'm an old man, Rean. I relish a life of boredom." Mr. Humpphrey lifted his glass. "Here's to a future of boredom."

I gently pushed open the screen door, and Mr. Humpphrey and Nana paused in midtoast.

"Oh, hey, Stormy. Let me help you!" Mr. Humpphrey got up and met me at the door. Nana joined him on my other side.

"I didn't know you were up. You should have called for some help," Nana chided.

"I've got it," I replied hoarsely. "I'm feeling better."

Which wasn't really true. Each step—more of a shuffle really—from my bed to this door had taken total concentration. Objects around me seemed to sway and tilt, like I was on a boat in rough seas. My legs also hurt super badly with every step. But I didn't want Nana and Mr. Humpphrey to worry.

"You sit here," Nana said as she and Mr. Humpphrey guided me into a lounge chair. The sun had dropped behind the house, and the sky over the ocean turned orange.

"Z and the others should be here soon. Let me get you the drink Z left for you," Nana said, fussing around me.

"It's okay," I mumbled with a thick tongue, but Nana was already inside.

"You gave us quite the scare, kiddo," Mr. Humpphrey said with a kind smile.

"You sure did!" Dad echoed as he came up the stairs. He walked with a limp and held two boxes that, if I wasn't mistaken, contained... "I see that smile starting on your lips. And you're right, Stormy!" He leaned down and gave me a kiss on my forehead as he lowered the top box so I could see through its window. "Brownies topped with bacon and sea salt. I'm pretty sure the bakery thinks I'm crazy for ordering this."

I smiled bigger. "Extra... raac... chaah..." A painful fit of coughing made me stop talking.

"Bacon? Yes," Dad finished. "Now, shh. Let that voice and those lungs recover." He gave me another kiss on the head. I caught a concerned glance from Mr. Humpphrey.

"Perfect timing, Matthew." Nana held the door for him to go inside. "How's the leg?"

Dad replied casually, "It'll heal."

Nana handed me a glass containing the same thick blue shake. The tightness in my chest relaxed as I drank it, and fortunately, the pain dulled.

"And then they all raced and leapt off the waterfall, so he couldn't catch them!" Lilli said excitedly as she and Pearl rounded the corner from the stairs to the deck. Pearl laughed at what I was guessing was a funny story told by our favorite sprite.

"Hiya!" Pearl smiled at us and put down a small gold bag. "Oh, Stormy, you are looking so much better!"

"Storm!" Lilli exclaimed. She jumped three times and clapped excitedly. "Storm! Storm! Storm! Storm! Oh my goshes!" She bounced toward me but tripped in midskip. She bounced right back up, though, and then wrapped me in a beautiful hug.

"Oh, to harness a tiny speck of that energy." Dad laughed.

"Oomph." All air was squashed out of my lungs by the deceptively strong little creature. "Hi," I managed to whisper when she released her hold.

She stared into my eyes for an awkward amount of time. Finally, her face filled with a smile, and her bright-green eyes released their hold on me.

"Two for two. Storm's also completely settled back into herself," she announced with a giant grin.

"I'm what?" I asked through a cough and tensed against the pain. Pearl mimed drinking from a glass. I took a slow sip, and the coughing and discomfort abated.

"Settled back in, of course. Your soul." Lilli then popped into an empty chair, tucking her legs up under her. She continued with excitement, "Your soul is exactly back where it's supposed to be. Doesn't always work that way—oh no, it does *not*. Sometimes, they can go in crooked or get stuck part in and part out! There was one time it never really settled in at all, and it just took off with no warning!" Her face wrinkled with concern, but then she smiled again. "But you. Are. Perfect!"

Glad my soul is settled in for the long haul, I thought sarcastically.

"And I wasn't so sure with you because I've never put two souls back in on the same night, and with you being the second one, I mean, so much could have gone wrong, but it didn't. So much went right, and so much is so right now, and I'm just so happy!" Lilli bounced in her seat then absently brushed away a lock of hair that had fallen in front of her forehead.

"Two?" I whispered and smiled slightly.

"Yes, of course, two!" Lilli giggled. "Before it was your turn it was—"

"Mine," Jon answered from the beach.

I spun so quickly toward his voice that I got vertigo. I gripped the edge of the chair and waited for the world to stop spinning. When it did, I was rewarded with *him*. There he stood in the flesh, in his khaki shorts with a ripped hem and a white T-shirt. His curly blond hair was windblown, and his face was a touch pale, but other than that, he was most definitely alive. He hopped up the stairs two at a time, brushing a curl off of his forehead. He leaned in and gave me a hug. I hugged back with all the strength I had, so glad to hold my best friend.

"Ahem. That's quite enough there, Manistar," Rowan joked as he joined the growing party from the other direction.

Jon stood back up and laughed. "Sorry, man. Had to give proper thanks to my rescuer."

"Yeah, yeah. How ya feeling, beautiful?" Rowan leaned in and kissed me.

"Eh." I shrugged.

I looked around at everybody, and a smile broke through my dry lips. They all looked so great, even Jon. *I'm the only one who looks like they died.*

"How come I'm—" Coughing stopped me short again. I sipped the drink, untensed and tried again. "How come," I began, taking cautious, shallow breaths, "I'm super hurt and…" *Don't cough, don't cough.* "Jon looks—"

Coughs broke through. It was as if knives bounced around my inside. Rowan held me until I finished.

"Ouch," I whined, defeated.

Pearl completed my question. "How come you're in so much pain and Jon isn't?"

I nodded.

"Jon's just a human," she replied.

"I'm strangely starting to become more okay with that phrase... once the old ego is taken out of it," Jon replied with a laugh.

I mouthed, "Sorry."

Pearl continued. "Sorry, Jon. I just meant that human souls have much simpler connections than mer souls. They aren't as sticky because they don't need to stay together with the body as long."

"Yeah, that makes me feel better," Jon replied with a lifted eyebrow.

"And he also got a bit of Lilli's energy when she put him back together."

"Now that *does* make me feel better." Jon smiled. "Thanks, Lil."

Lilli giggled.

"Couldn't you have given me a little also?" I whispered.

"Oh no! That wouldn't have worked. Can't mix sprite energy with mer energy. It's like mixing oil and water. No, I had to be very careful with what you took."

"I took?"

"Yes. Sprite energy in a mer body would have made everything inside all sorts of slippery. No, I made sure you got something that would stay on the outside."

"What is it?" I asked after taking another long drink of the shake.

"You haven't looked in the mirror yet?" Lilli asked.

I shook my head. Everybody else just smiled at me.

"I think you'll like it," Pearl said.

"I love it," Rowan added with a wink.

Dad, Mr. Humpphrey, and Nana nodded.

"I didn't even notice until I got up close," Jon shrugged. "It's cool."

"Seriously, nobody's gonna tell me?" I looked around in astonishment and then assessed all the parts of me I could see. Nothing seemed different. Fingers and toes—all accounted for. Arms, legs...

"Hello, my beautiful family," Z said, her rich tones filling the air.

Like Jon, she approached from the beach, barefoot and fabulous as ever in her flowing blush-pink dress and her fire-colored mane, loosely tied back. Sara was a few steps behind her in a bikini and wrap skirt. Her dark hair hung heavily down her back and dripped water onto the sand. She set the surfboard she carried at the bottom of the steps and followed Z up to the deck. They went around with greetings and hugs and ended with me.

"Looks like we let any old riffraff in nowadays," Sara said jokingly and winked at Jon. "Good to have you back with us, Stormy." She leaned in close to me, stared a moment, then stood back up and turned to Pearl. "You're right, Pearl. It works on her."

Seriously? What is it? I wanted to scream.

"Yes, your eye is quite astounding." Z turned to Lilli. "Good choice."

Lilli bounced a little in her chair. "Thanks!"

My eye? I looked frantically at each person on the deck, but they were just talking to each other.

"So as not to waste any more time..." Z began. "Unfortunately, Laverna doesn't like to lose."

What? No. My eye. I shook my head and tried to speak but immediately felt a cough rise. *No no no no*, I pleaded with my body as I calmed down. Then I resorted to the only thing I instinctively knew to do when needing attention.

Sara laughed. "Uh, Stormy? Why are you raising your hand?"

All eyes turned to me.

Taking a shallow breath for each word, I said carefully but firmly, "Could. Somebody. Please. Tell. Me. About. My. Eye."

"Pearl, run inside and grab the small mirror out of the bathroom," Nana said.

Pearl returned with a mirror. "It's really not even that noticeable," she said with a smile.

I took the mirror. *Oh...* "Lilli?" I whispered.

"Yes?" she replied.

"My right eye is bright purple."

"Well, technically, it's violet, but I suppose purple…"

"Lilli!"

"Sorry, yeah, it's purple." She smiled.

"Lilli?" I asked.

"Yes?"

"Why is my right eye bright purple?"

"Well, you see, Stormy, it's like I said." Lilli spoke quickly. "As you were settling back into your body, you were trying to take a little piece of me, and I had to make sure you didn't take my energy, so I had to redirect you to something safe, and at first, I thought maybe my hair, but then, what good would it be to you to have some of my hair, and truth be told, you really weren't that interested in my hair, which I understand because, I mean, your hair is already so pretty, and I love your hair, and anyway, I had to think quickly, and so I came up with my purple eye color. I thought briefly about the red or the yellow, but really, you seemed most eager for the purple. I don't know why, but it kept you away from my energy, so I let you have the purple. So, yay!" She clapped three times and bounced in her chair.

"Thank you, Lilli. I love it."

"Oh goody!"

"Okay, now that we have that sorted…" Rowan said.

"We'll talk more later." Pearl winked, took the mirror back, and smiled at Z.

Z began again. "Unfortunately Laverna doesn't like to lose."

"What's she up to—like, really up to?" Jon asked.

"Well, therein lies the problem. We really don't know what she has planned, but I believe it will be tied to the Hurricane Lady moving to the lighthouse."

"What could she possibly do? And what right does she have? Pearl has her braid. The clan has an heir," Rowan said.

"Two heirs actually," Z said calmly. "As for the first question, she can be quite clever. For the second, in her mind, this territory has *always* belonged to her. Our clan has been in the wrong ever since our mother perished and willed it to me for safekeeping of the statue. She never saw me as the rightful ruler and never saw Pearl as a rightful heir."

I whispered, "Her next move is the statue, then?"

"Seems the most logical. No statue, no need for us to be here. It was never really about the town or the braid or even you, Storm. It was always about getting rid of me. She hated my mother giving this territory to me."

"But you said yourself that you've protected our town and its people from Laverna," Dad said.

"Yes, we have. But that was merely a by-product of our mission to protect the statue."

"So if the statue is gone, our clan would have to leave," Pearl added. "Then..."

"St. Augustine would be at the mercy of Laverna," Z said.

"Then we just have to protect the statue, right?" Jon asked.

"*Just* and *have to* are not quite right placed together like that. *Have to*, yes. *Just* is the challenge, as the statue has some unique properties that will make it quite difficult for us."

"You mean the power over mers is real?" I quietly scoffed. "I thought Sara was just messing with me."

"Me?" Sara feigned surprise.

I rolled my eyes and took a sip of my shake to calm the tickle that threatened to turn into a cough.

"Oh no, Storm. It is real, and it is dangerous to our kind," Z said.

"Okay, but then, it's also dangerous to Laverna, right?" Dad asked.

"Yes, it is. But there is one very big difference."

"What?" I asked.

"We care about the lives of those we love. Laverna neither loves nor cares. It's much easier to destroy things when you are unconcerned about the cost."

Z's words hung heavily in the stillness of the descending evening.

"What would she get out of it?" Jon asked.

"She gets to win, Jon. And that is what she cares about the most."

"Do you have a plan to stop her?"

"Sadly, yes, but it is not ideal," Z said.

"But we will not have it any other way," Rean said.

"Nana? Mr. Humpphrey? What do you mean?" I asked.

"Mers can't get near the statue, but humans can."

"Nana, I can't believe you!" My anger rose. I felt the beginning of a cough, but I didn't care. "You guys are going to try to stop Laverna? *Laverna*? She'll totally kill you just for sport! Z..." I spun to face her. "You can't..."

A gust of wind toppled over an empty glass, and my hair swirled around my head. My stomach did a tumble, and my head threatened to crack open just behind my eyes. I doubled over as the coughing fit took hold. Pearl and Rowan came to my sides.

I looked up with liquid-filled eyes. "I just got all of my family and friends back," I whispered through the pain. One hot tear spilled over the edge of my lid.

"Stormy, no." Pearl hushed me. "No tears." She held my face gently in her palms. The wind calmed, and my stomach settled.

"Before we make vows of action or worry, I am not going into this decision lightly," Z said. "I owe all of you a tale. This is a tale known only by three others, one of whom is no longer with us and who also happened to be Laverna's and my mother." Z sighed then looked at each of us in slow succession. A wry smile formed on her lips. "This is the tale of the Hurricane Lady."

"Oh wow," Rowan whispered.

Pearl and Sara glanced at each other and sat back in their chairs.

"It's time you all knew," Z continued with a sigh. "While I had hoped to never have to share this painful tale, I believe now is the time for us all to know what we may be up against and why."

She looked around and then started in a low and steady voice. "The Hurricane Lady was never meant to be what it became. She started as little more than a token of a father's love for his eldest son. The gentleman who commissioned the statue did so with the intention that the likeness of Saint Barbara would protect the journey his son was about to take from Spain to the Americas. It's not without its risks even today, but back in the early 1800s, the obstacles against a safe and successful journey were enormous. So he decided to draw upon the favors of the patron saint of sailors and the protector against sudden death from lightning, fire, or flood. He also knew two additional things. First was that his son would never know it was he who had commissioned the statue. Second, nobody could know it was for the son, so as to avoid undue attention paid to the young sailing apprentice."

"This is better than most plots in novels," Nana whispered to Dad and Mr. Humpphrey.

Z chuckled. "Yes, and I only wish, for all of our sakes, that it was fiction. But as is often said about life imitating art, in this case, life far outdid even the wildest of imaginations." She strolled away from the railing and took a seat by the table. Z took a sip of salt ale and then continued. "To answer the reason of why the son should never know his father commissioned the statue, it was because the son didn't know this gentleman was his father. In fact, the son was an orphan for all intents and purposes since his mother was unable to take care of him. But through the years, while understanding that he could never acknowledge his son openly, the man made sure the boy's life was as comfortable as possible with the best care given to him at the orphanage, and as soon as the boy turned fifteen, the father arranged for this apprenticeship on the journey to the Americas. He confided none of these details to the artist, but he did request that the statue contain a small painted likeness of the boy's mother for added protection on the journey. He provided the porcelain miniature to the artist just prior to the completion of the statue."

"Was the mom dead?" I asked.

"Many thought that was the case, but no, she was quite alive," Z replied. "The boy's mother also kept a secret interest in the boy over the years. She was so secretive that not even her own family knew or suspected anything.

"I suppose the story could have ended there, with a young orphan secretly protected by his parents and sent to America to start his life. But that is not the ending. I take you now to our talented artist, the one commissioned to create an object of protection. His sculpture was beautiful! It was the perfect honor to Saint Barbara. All that remained was to place the miniature inside as directed by the buyer. The artist unwrapped the delicate oval piece and looked at the picture. As he later relayed this moment at the local tavern, his shock nearly caused him to drop it. He steadied his shaking hands and held his workbench for support. He had to be mistaken, he thought. He slowly unclenched his fist and gazed again at the tiny painting. Rage and confusion rose simultaneously. In his hand was the likeness of the woman he was madly in love with. But the buyer was very much the artist's senior, and the woman the buyer had spoken of would have had a fifteen-year-old son, but she hardly looked older than twenty years."

"She was a mermaid," Dad said.

Z gave a little nod. "She was a mermaid."

"So the son, he was a half mer! Like me! What happened to him?"

"He should have set sail for the Americas and started a new life guided by both a beautiful statue and the safety of his mother's currents. However, the artist confronted his lover that night. She told him the truth—she was a mermaid, and she'd had many lovers over the centuries. This hurt his ego, and as many can attest, the most dangerous person is the one with a hurt ego. He flew into a rage and swiped at her with one of his carving knives, striking her arm and making her bleed. Immediately filled with remorse, he rushed toward her with a bandana and sought to wrap the wound. She laughed at him, pushed him down, and threw the bloody bandana on the floor. She called him pathetic and walked out of the workshop, saying she had no time to cajole the hurt feelings of little boys. She had a ship to catch, and he had a statue to finish."

Z frowned. "And again, the story could have ended there. But the artist was putting it all together in his mind. The mer—*his* mer—was choosing some bastard son over him, an up-and-coming artist well-known for carvings that were ahead of their time in detail and design and now breaking away from only doing commissioned pieces and embracing his love of oil paintings. Sure, he had been madly in love before and sometimes simultaneously with multiple women. He had, in fact, had a beautiful muse over the previous year who was the subject of new paintings, but he'd never been rebuffed before and certainly never laughed at. That sent his mind reeling farther down a dark path. He held the blood-soaked bandana so tightly in one hand that his knuckles turned white. He searched frantically around his workshop until he found the item he searched for, a withered set of bird's feet that had been given to him by a passing medicine man years before. They were, so he was told, to protect him from evil and also could be used to destroy his enemies. He'd never had enemies until now. He wanted nothing more at that moment than to destroy the whore who'd hurt him. And how better to do that than curse her bastard son. The artist wrapped the feet and the likeness in the bloody rag and placed the small satchel inside the statue. His commission complete, he wrapped the statue in a black cloth and walked down to the docks. The man met him, paid him, and then brought the statue on board the ship. The artist watched with darkness in his heart as the ship dropped its lines and exited the harbor."

"Z," Rowan asked, "this sounds a bit like wishful thinking on the artist's side that he could successfully curse someone. I know mer blood is powerful, but chicken feet? Never heard of that in the old magic ways."

Z nodded. "And you would be correct, Rowan, if the feet were chicken feet. Unfortunately, the artist created a true curse because what he had in his possession were no ordinary bird feet. They were bird-of-paradise feet, and they were magic because of the particular bird they'd been removed from. But that is something I only found out later. At this point in my tale, I only knew mother was accompanying a small band of mers on the ship's crossing. It wasn't unusual for mers to accompany ships. Some liked driving the sailors mad and meeting them in the sea if they could get them to jump. Others enjoyed the waves produced by the powerful wooden hulls cutting through the deep waters. Still others did take an interest in helping with safe journeys by thwarting weather hiccups or other obstacles, such as pirate ships. I had no reason to be concerned or curious as to my mother's interest in this vessel. Only when some mers returned to our port with stories of illness did I think something was not right."

"Why?" Lilli asked.

"Why indeed," Z answered. "When the first mers returned to port, sharing their tales, they mentioned feeling dizzy and faint. Some sank lower in the water and then got weaker from lack of sunlight, but they were able to keep their direction about them and return. I didn't think too much of it until a week later when others returned looking ill. Of the mers I saw, all had sunken cheeks and darkness under their eyes. They were all exhausted, and some had to be helped from the water. As I helped one inflicted mermaid, I noticed a man sitting on the seawall. I recognized him as one of the local artists. He watched and smiled."

Z sighed. "Soon after, other trading ships limped into the harbor. The sailors told tales of massive seas and unusual storms wreaking havoc on their journeys. They felt lucky to have made it to shore alive and said prayers for any sailing vessel out in the waters. It was as if the oceans had turned against them."

"Were mers doing this?" Nana asked.

"Quite the contrary, Rean," Z answered. "While Mers may have held differing opinions of humans and their value, many of us had developed friendships with the sailors. Ships carrying these friends were often afforded extra protection by the mers. Among the sailors kissing land were many familiar faces. These were our friends, which made me wonder where their usual protectors were. What was happening beyond the horizon?

"After witnessing both mers and humans suffering, I went to Laverna, at the local tavern, to discuss my concern. On the way, I happened to cross paths with the same gentleman who I'd seen on the rocks, the artist. He appeared quite drunk as he staggered along the uneven brick streets, and he rambled to the wind that he didn't mean to hurt so many but damn it if he would be treated that way. He prayed to his god to forgive him, swearing he hadn't known the curse would work. I decided to delay speaking to Laverna and instead followed the fellow back to his studio. Unfortunately, once he arrived, he staggered inside, letting out his pet bird, who flew past me. The man promptly fell on his face and began snoring. I gave a brief look around his studio, which was filled with half-completed statues and some paintings, and went to find Laverna.

"She was holding an audience of men, as usual. She was the barmaid, and the place, as you may imagine, was wildly successful. Most importantly, nobody raised alarms when patrons would occasionally disappear, undoubtedly ones who were rude to the ladies. But after hearing my tale, she agreed to join me to find our mother and try to find out what was happening in our waters. She filled me in on the artist's ramblings as he had warmed a barstool for many hours that afternoon. He'd spoken about a statue, a curse, and a siren's call, none of which made much sense.

"We chased the entrails of the ship for days, guided mostly by returning mers who had fallen ill. On the eighth day, we finally encountered the pathetic and beleaguered ship, caught in the middle of a raging Atlantic storm.

"I called to Mama as we approached. She told us to stay back. Laverna rushed forward despite her warning. I followed. We found Mama forty feet beneath the churning surface waters. She held what looked like a human body wrapped in linen. Her eyes were burning with anger, glowing brightly in the murky green water. She said, *There is evil aboard the ship, evil more powerful than we've seen.* Objects from the ship sank past us. The sailors were jettisoning their stores to help the ship stay afloat in the raging waters. How much of the rage was due to the storm and how much to Mama, I'll never be sure. She told us, *These waters will be yours, my daughters, once I am gone, and I must know that you will be fair and true.*

"Her words were no more than whispers in my mind, and as we floated, we also drifted deeper into the cold darkness. *Laverna, my bold beauty, you will protect the powerful north, and Z, my fiery likeness, will have power in the south. But hear me, Z—to you, I order the passage of this devil ship to the nearest port, and once there, you must take command of whatever is causing this evil to our kind.*

"*But, Mother,* Laverna protested, *the north is my territory.*

"*No, this is for Z, and you will respect my decree.*

"Thinking that this was not much more than words, I listened and agreed. Only when I realized that even I was feeling weaker than usual, with the immense darkness and coldness surrounding us for so long, did I see the truth in her words. Mama wasn't coming back up. My last view of her was her beautiful pale skin, her auburn hair floating freely around her as a veil, and her body wrapped tightly around the linen-shrouded form.

"*Mama!* I called. *Mama, I can't follow. I have to go back. Please, come back!* I felt a slight touch on my arm. It was Laverna. She beckoned me upward. I followed slowly.

"We reached the churning surface. I was drained. We both gave ourselves to the violence of the waters as we struggled to regain some energy. Floating in the froth, I replayed our final conversation with Mama. Only one thing had to be done at this moment—we had to get that ship to the closest land. We would figure out what to do next only after whatever evil was aboard the ship was removed from our waters.

"And that, my friends and children, is what we did. We argued the entire way, as was—and still is—Laverna's and my preferred method of conversation. Protecting our kind from the Hurricane Lady has been my task ever since we discovered that was the cause. This evil not only destroyed our mother but irreparably broke whatever tenuous bond Laverna and I might have created under a more natural succession."

Ice shifted in glasses. An angry seagull, late to roost, shouted in petulant defiance overhead, and Zelda stretched and yawned beneath the table. These noises seemed amplified in the silence between us. We were all completely entranced by the tale.

Z finally spoke, breaking the tension. "So, I appreciate everybody for their desire to help, but I need you all to be clear on just how immense a challenge this could be. Storm, first we need you to heal because, unfortunately, your convalescence will be cut short if what I am hearing from the Lionfish is true. Rean, Miles, Matthew, and Jon, I need you to find out more about the planned timing and location for the move of the statue. Pearl, Sara, and Rowan, you will need to get Storm strong and ready."

"Z?" Lilli asked.

"Yes, little one?"

"You didn't give me a job." Her eyes glowed amber.

"Lilli, you have a visitor to attend to."

"What?" the sprite said.

An angry storm cloud over the ocean rumbled, followed by a flash across the sky of the strangest blue-white lightning bolt I'd ever seen.

"Oh!" Lilli, shocked, immediately bounced out of her chair, ran to the beach, and disappeared in the night.

"What just happened?" Rowan asked, looking around.

"Now, that tale *isn't* mine to tell." Z stood. "Till the morrow."

"Well, kids, on that note, how about we let Storm get a good rest so she's ready for whatever craziness tomorrow brings," Dad said to the remaining group.

Sara snickered. I wasn't sure if it was about my dad treating me like a kid or about what awaited us the next day. Either way, I was too tired to care.

"Shall I carry you to your bed?" Rowan approached me, but Dad's glare brought him to a halt. "I am, of course, kidding, sir." He cautiously leaned in and settled for a kiss good night... on my forehead. "Sweet dreams, m'love." Then, in a voice so low only mers could hear, he whispered, "I'll check in on you later tonight."

I smiled. Sara laughed. Pearl punched Rowan's arm.

"Ouch." He fake rubbed the spot. "Mermaids are so strong," he whined.

"Come on, lover boy." Sara took his arm. "I'm sure there is some kind of mischief we can get up to while little Stormy, here, gets her beauty rest. We need her ready to roll tomorrow if we plan to train, hit the drum circle, *and* go to the lighthouse."

"We'll see you *tomorrow*, Stormy," Pearl said a little too emphatically as she leaned down to kiss my head. "You will feel much better—I promise. And here, open this when you get upstairs." She handed me the small bag she'd brought in with her.

"Jon?" Sara motioned to him to join them.

"Eh, not tonight. Still have some work to do at the lighthouse to get it ready for tomorrow night. But thanks." Then Jon turned to me. "See ya tomorrow, Storm. Glad we're, uh, both alive."

I chuckled. "Yeah, me too. See ya tomorrow for whatever they were talking about."

And with that, Nana and Dad helped me back to my room. I did feel stronger, and my chest didn't pain me as much.

"Good night, Stormy," Nana whispered as she tucked me in.

"Sweet dreams." Dad gave me a kiss on the forehead.

That night, I was happy to pretend to be just a girl who needed help feeling better. I snuggled into my bed. Then I remembered Pearl's present. I picked up the gold bag from where it sat next to my bed. Inside was a gorgeous green shawl with an intricately embroidered peacock on the back.

The purple-and-gold threads shimmered even in the dim light filtering in from the window.

"Beyond the Veil," I whispered, reading the name printed on the bag. I wrapped the shawl around me and tucked myself back in for sleep.

CHAPTER FIVE
Dreams and Reality

"Storm, come on. I want to show you something really cool!"

"I'm coming, Jon. Don't run so fast!"

The damp air chilled my skin. Walls of roughly cut coquina flanked each side of the narrow passage. *Where am I?*

I tried to run, but my feet felt glued to the ground. Every step was painfully slow.

"Slowpoke! It's just a little farther," Jon's voice taunted me.

Adding insult to injury, when I looked to where Jon had run, I was blinded by a bright light shining directly in my eyes. I shut my eyes tightly and then blinked uncontrollably to get rid of the black blobs floating in my vision. I tried to look again, but it was as if I stared directly into the sun. *Is this because of my new eye?* I wondered, trying to blink the spots away again. In between blinks, I caught a glimpse of Jon darting around the corner.

I gazed down at my feet, and my eyes relaxed. Then I looked back up. Uncontrollable blinking. Down to the floor—better. This reminded me of my old underwater dream where I could never keep my eyes open. But I wasn't underwater.

"This is so freakin' stupid," I called to no one because Jon had obviously not waited. "Jerk!" My voice echoed down the long corridor.

At my snail's pace, and only being able to look down, I should catch him... umm... never. I'd be able to walk faster on my hands, I thought angrily. *Huh. Maybe that isn't so far-fetched.*

I placed my palms on the dirt floor and kicked my feet up behind me.

In a handstand, I "ran" a few paces forward on my hands before losing my balance and crashing down in a heap.

Well, that was farther than I made it on my feet. Back up we go, Storm.

Up I went and ran again on my hands. This time, I made even more progress. Though this technique was weird, it was also fun. I kept hand-running until I noticed a passageway on my left.

I lowered to all fours and called, "Jon! Are you down here? You left me behind!"

Jon's voice drifted from the far end of the new passage. "I'd never leave you behind, Storm! I'm just down here. Come on, a little farther."

"My legs aren't working well! I've been having to walk on my hands!" I cried.

"Have you tried flying?" Jon called back.

"I... what? No, Jon—what?" I hung my head, super frustrated.

"Fly, Storm!" Jon called again.

"I'm a mermaid, not a bird," I mumbled.

"You stole their tale. You can steal their wings!" Jon called, his voice reverberating back to me.

What are you talking about?

"Fly!" he repeated.

I stood up, looked down, forced two long strides, and pushed from my back foot. At the same time, I spread my arms wide and lay horizontally, not touching the ground, which passed inches below my body at breakneck speed. My fingertips lightly grazed the coquina walls. I dared to face forward and, to my added joy, saw no bright light.

Why didn't anybody tell me I could do this? This is crazy. I dipped and rose and smiled. I landed on my feet at the end of the hall. In front of me was an oak-paneled door.

I knocked lightly. "Jon?"

"Storm, in here!" he replied from the other side.

The heavy door creaked as I pushed it open a few inches. I slid through the narrow gap into the room and let the door close behind me. The large dark room had a wooden table along one wall, a fireplace on another, and an entrance into a side room.

"Jon?" I repeated.

"In here," he replied from the side room. "Come on in. We're waiting!"

"We? Jon, who...?" I walked toward his voice, turned into the room, and stopped.

"Thank you for doing this, Storm," Jon said. Or at least, something that looked like Jon spoke to me. His body was visible but also kind of see-through. He stood next to a beautiful four-foot-tall statue of a woman in a long, intricately embroidered white dress.

"Jon, what's going on?"

"I knew you'd do this for me." Jon smiled.

"Do what?" I felt the room tilt slightly. I looked back at Jon, who just kept smiling at me. I plopped heavily onto the stone ground as the world spun too quickly.

"Jon? Waz hapnin..." I slurred.

"Well, Storm, it's only fair. I gave my life for your clan, and now you can give your life for my clan."

"Clan?" I mumbled in confusion. I leaned heavily on both hands. I turned back to Jon. He wasn't Jon anymore. He was a giant white bird with beady black eyes.

"Come closer, my child. Do not fear," the bird said.

"Join me," the statue whispered.

"Idonundetaaand," I moaned. "Jonwhere'sjon..."

"Someone has to join me," the statue replied coolly.

"You stole her wings," the bird cawed.

"No... Jon... no! No no no!" I shook my head violently. "No!" I shouted and woke with a start.

I sighed and let the final images melt away like waves washing the shoreline clean.

"God, I hate dreams." I rolled my legs off the bed and sat up.

I took a tentative breath and was pleasantly surprised that I didn't cough. I walked to my mirror and was happy to find that my legs also felt normal again. A shake of my mane made the soft chime of the bells on my mermaid's knot sing to me. I smiled and then sighed at the vision before me.

"My right eye is completely bright purple."

I leaned in a little, then back, then back in again. *Yup, definitely purple.* And while turning left to right to see it from different angles and lights, I noticed my depth perception was strange.

I walked back to the window. I covered my left eye with my hand and then my right as I looked at the ocean. Back to the left... then right.

My purple eye isn't nearsighted! I thought in amazement. With the right eye, I could make out every little detail all the way out to the horizon. No glasses, no contacts.

My left eye was just as nearsighted as ever. Nearsightedness was great in the water, which was why all mers were very nearsighted and needed help seeing on land with glasses or, in recent decades, contacts—disposable ones, obviously, and we always had dozens of pairs on hand to replace the ones that washed away.

But back to my right eye... *It's, like, bionic. Wow! Thanks, Lilli.* I smiled.

"Good morning, sunshine!" Pearl bounced into the room and hopped onto my bed. "Feeling better?"

Turning from the window I answered, "I actually am!"

"Good! Because we have a big day today. Take this." She handed me a glass of the blue shake. I drank it happily. "This morning is training on new skills, sunset is the drum circle at the fort, and then we have the Dark of the Moon Tour at the lighthouse!" Pearl absently brushed her silken hair, looking in the mirror as she spoke.

Rowan called up from downstairs, "Pearl, did you ask her?"

Pearl rolled her eyes and called back, "I already told you the answer, Rowan!"

"But did you *ask* her?"

"Storm." Pearl turned back to me. "Rowan would like to know if you need his help putting on your bathing suit."

I laughed. *Of course he's asking that.* "No, I'm good," I replied with a smile and finished my shake.

Pearl turned back toward the door. "She's good!"

"Is she...?"

"She's *good!*" Pearl repeated and motioned me to the bathroom to get ready. "Hurry up before he decides to come up and check for himself." Pearl laughed then stood and gave a luxurious feline-worthy stretch toward the ceiling. "Come on down when you're set."

I met Rowan, Sara, and Pearl on the porch a few minutes later.

"It'll be fine," Pearl was saying to Rowan and Sara when I went outside to meet them.

"Only if we can get her—" Sara stopped short when she saw me. "Hey, Stormy."

"Hey! What's up?"

"Nothing, m'dear. You are looking beautiful, my emerald princess," Rowan said, glancing at my green bikini, and gave me a kiss. "Ready for a wee swim?"

"I guess."

He gave me a wink. My stomach jumped.

How does he always make that happen?

"Where's Dad and Nana? I didn't tell them I was heading out."

"They had to go to an appointment," Pearl replied. "But Matthew promised he'd be back in time for the drum circle!"

"Dad's going to the drum circle?"

"Oh yeah, Stormy. He's amazing at playing drums. Back in the day, he had all the girls— humans and mers—eyeing him." She giggled with a private memory.

"If we're done with the chatter, I'd love to get this training on so we can finish at some point this century." Sara sighed.

"Aren't you an impatient mermaid." Pearl nudged her.

"Well, some of us have other things to do, my dear sister," Sara quipped and picked up the scuffed blue surfboard that had been leaning against the deck railing.

"Did you bring it?" Pearl asked her.

Sara reached into a knit purse on the table and pulled out a metallic silver rock.

Pearl wrapped it in her left hand for a moment and stood still and then smiled. "Perfect. Let's go."

"What're we doin'?" I asked as Rowan waved me ahead of him down the stairs.

"Working on getting your strength back and then teaching manipulations," Rowan replied.

"Manipulations?"

"Yeah. Water, air, weather, that sort of thing." Rowan smiled and gave me a light smack on my bottom.

"Hey!" I said, pretending to protest.

"Sorry," he said.

Pearl and Sara chatted lightly as we walked across the beach. I heard Paige's name mentioned a few times. The surf was calm, and the water shimmered like mercury in the morning light. Sara tossed her board ahead of her into the rolling surf, gracefully slid onto it, and paddled away with strong strokes of her arms. Pearl, by contrast, dove headfirst into a low swell.

"Ready, rainbow fish?"

"I guess .I still don't know what—" I stopped speaking as Rowan dove into the oncoming wave with my hand still in his. We submerged ourselves in the warm Atlantic water, and I let my mer instincts take over.

When I opened my eyes, I noticed a second strange vision change. Lilli's purple eye—well, *my* purple eye—was bird's-eye great on land but awful underwater. I saw clearly out of my normal eye but saw nothing but blurry shapes from my purple one.

That sucks, I thought.

What does? Rowan asked.

My purple eye can't focus underwater.

Let me see. With his face an inch from mine, he hovered with me in about twenty feet of water. *Can you see me now?*

I giggled. *Of course.*

Well, not so bad, then. He smiled and leaned in for a kiss.

Ahem. Ticktock, guys, Sara said.

Where is she? I looked around with my good eye and kept the other one closed.

Pearl glided by. *Look up.*

Overhead, I saw Sara's legs dangling on either side of the silhouetted surfboard.

The name of the game is topple Sara, Pearl said.

I had a quick memory of one of my first sightings of Pearl, Sara, and Rowan. He'd been knocked off his board by a wave, and as I waited for him to reemerge, Pearl and Sara both flew from their boards into the air. At the time, I'd thought it was another rogue wave. Now I knew it was Rowan, but I didn't know how he'd done it.

Energy, Pearl answered.

Of course. I mean... I knew that.

Pearl's laughter was a beautiful sound in my mind, even though she was laughing at me. She swam in slow, graceful circles around Rowan and me. *You know by now that we are different from humans in many ways, but one important difference is our energetic connection to the world around us. We are made of salt, and salt has polarity. With that polarity, we're able to manipulate other polar items, like...*

Seawater, I replied.

Like seawater, Pearl repeated and smiled. *Very good, Stormy. But beyond simple polarity manipulations, our positives and negatives can produce powerful physical actions to even nonpolarized objects if...*

If... I repeated.

Pearl raised one perfect eyebrow as she drifted by. I shrugged. I didn't know the answer.

If the positives and negatives can align! she finished.

Of course—yeah, that makes no sense, I thought.

Ripples of water surrounded Pearl as she laughed with her whole body and not just in her mind. *Let me show you.*

Aw, can't I? Rowan asked.

Not yet, Rowan.

Anytime we want to get this show on the road, that would be great, Sara said with obvious impatience. Her one dangling leg swooshed back and forth underwater like the flicking of an angry cat's tail.

You sure you don't want me to demonstrate? Rowan asked again with a glance toward Sara at the surface.

Pearl smiled. *Tempting, but give me just a moment, Rowan. Now, Storm, the first step is to align your positives and negatives. Eventually, you'll do this with your mind, but to start, use this.* She handed me the shiny metal rock. *This is already negatively charged. Rub it slowly down each arm. The positives within you will be attracted and the negatives repulsed.*

Water rippled around the smooth rock as I slid it down my left arm and then my right. *Am I doing it right? I don't feel any different.*

Let's do a test to see. Lie horizontally. Pearl shifted her position to float just underneath me. *Now, put your arms out to the side, like you're flying. Palms down. Check!* She brought the rock close to my down-facing hands. It flew upward through the water and stuck to my open palm.

Well done, Storm! You're charged! Rowan floated a few feet to the side of us.

Whoa, I thought. *That's super cool!*

Now, roll onto your back, Pearl instructed.

I did as asked. Rowan circled lazily around us. Pearl tugged the rock away from me. *Turn your palms down again. Good.* She brought the rock over the back of my hand. This time, it didn't stick to me but rather flew up in the water column a few inches. *Move your hand below it. Keep it hovering above you.*

This is awesome! I told her.

Awesome indeed. Sara sighed. One of her hands now drifted back and forth.

Watching Pearl give a frustrated glance upward at the floating Sara, Rowan asked with an impish smile, *Can I do it now?*

Pearl shook her head. *Just a few more moments.* She turned back to me. *Now, flip your palm.*

As soon as I turned my hand, the rock flew with force back to my palm. I closed my fingers around it and smiled as I righted myself. *Will I stay magnetized forever now?*

No. Without your will on your ions or constant influence by the external negative charge, your polarity will gradually move closer to neutral again.

Does it only work in the water? I shuddered as a chill ran down my body.

No, but it's easier to train here, away from curious eyes, Pearl answered.

Yeah, because so very much is happening right now, Sara added sarcastically.

Now? Rowan asked for a third time.

Pearl nodded. Rowan's eyebrows rose high with excitement. Pearl tipped her head slightly. I watched with anticipation.

Rowan flashed a Cheshire cat grin. He looked up at the surfboard above us. His arms straightened by his sides, and he gradually floated higher in the water column. The water by his stiff arms and splayed fingers rippled out and away. When he was about three feet from the board, he shot his arms forward with his palms up. The water welled out, and the board disappeared.

A second later, the board splashed partway under, and Sara splashed entirely under. She did a graceful flip and came face-to-face with Pearl. *That. Was. Not. Stormy.*

It was for demonstration purposes only, dearest sister.

We all laughed—well, all except Sara. She just glared at each of us in turn. *Well, if we're done now, I have many other things I could be doing.*

Yes. Pearl winked at me. *We're done now. Thank you, Sara.*

Yeah, yeah, she scoffed as she swam back to the surface and climbed on her board. She paddled back to shore.

Come on—enough for today, Pearl said to Rowan and me.

My teeth chattered.

Let's get Stormy into the sun and then get ready for the drum circle.

Back on shore, we trudged back to the house. "I'll meet you both at the fort in a couple hours," Pearl told us. "We'll have the drums, so all you need to bring is yourselves!"

"Oh, here!" I realized I was still holding the silver rock and went to give it back to Pearl. My hand shook with the continued chills.

"No, Stormy, you keep it for now." She smiled and kissed my head.

"I trust you'll help Stormy warm up?" Pearl asked Rowan.

"I'm here to serve." Rowan winked.

Pearl shook her head. "Keep it G-rated, Casanova."

Rowan gave a play bow. "That was a lot for your first day back at it," he said as we settled onto the lounge chairs in the sun.

"I barely did anything."

"Energy work is draining on the best of days. You did great."

"Really?" My teeth chattered.

"Yes, really. Here, hang on." Rowan came over to my lounge chair and slid in behind me, his legs on either side of me. I nestled back into him, and he wrapped the towel around me and rubbed on my arms. "Better?"

"Yes." I sighed and closed my eyes.

I think this may be more PG than G, but who am I to argue? I looked back at him, and he leaned in for a kiss. *Definitely PG,* I thought happily as I lost myself in the moment.

CHAPTER SIX
Drum Circle and Rumors

"And I thought Sara was an insane driver." Rowan stepped off the back of the scooter.

"What?" I put down the kickstand. I had won the rock-paper-scissors competition against Rowan, so I got to drive us to the fort.

"I just didn't realize you only went one speed—fast." He leaned in and kissed me.

I smiled. "I learned from the best!"

"Me?"

I laughed. "No, Sara."

"Ooh, that's low, Storm."

I laughed again and handed the green bottle of lotion to him after I was done with it.

"Perfect!" he announced with a quick sniff and tucked the lotion under the seat. "Let's go, m'love."

Up the hill, we went. Drum sounds drifted in the air.

"I can't believe my dad does this."

"Well, the Harns are well-known for their secrets," Rowan replied, squeezing my hand.

We dropped down to the moat and continued past the cannons facing the moored sailboats. As we rounded the corner, I saw about twenty people scattered between the lower moat and the upper grass ledge. They talked and laughed in small groups, played riffs on their drums, or just sat watching and snacking from picnic baskets. Eyes shifted to us as we joined them.

I stopped suddenly.

"What's up?" Rowan asked.

"Him." I glanced to the side.

Rowan followed my glare. "Ah, don't worry. Daniel's nothing to be concerned over."

I met Daniel's eyes, and he met mine. He gave a crafty half smile and leaned over to the mermaid next to him.

"Why are they staring at us?" I asked, feeling self-conscious.

"Maybe they never saw such a good-looking couple before." Rowan winked.

I snorted.

"Come on. Don't waste energy on that." Rowan nudged me, and we kept walking.

Pearl and Dad waved us over to them up on the grass hill. Sara, Lilli, and Jon were there also.

"Hiya!" Pearl said.

"It's about time you got here," Sara said.

"You know, for a nearly immortal being, you are really impatient," Jon quipped.

"Oh, look who's taken the pacifier out long enough to speak," Sara shot back.

"Really, guys?" I asked with a shake of my head.

"Whaaat?" Jon and Sara said simultaneously with raised eyebrows and false innocence.

"Just so you know, Sara, I think Stormy, here, beat your record for getting from the beach to town," Rowan said.

Her eyes narrowed and, with a slight smirk, she said, "Well, at least someone's a good teacher." She shot a glance at Pearl.

"I thought you said sprites were generally reclusive?" Jon said, wisely changing the subject. He pointed at Lilli, who was dancing in happy little circles by a group of drummers.

"*Generally* is the key word. Music tends to bring out their gregarious side." Pearl laughed.

"What was up with her before?" I asked. "Who did she have to go see?"

"No idea." Pearl shrugged.

Lilli bounced and spun over to us, clapping. "Ooh, ohh, ohh! It's getting started! Come on, come on, *come on!*" she squealed then grabbed Jon's arm and pulled him over to the loose circle of bodies and drums.

"Pick a drum, everyone!" Pearl said with a giggle and went over to Dad.

They both chose the large drums, leaving the three smaller ones for Rowan, Sara, and me. With drums in hand, we followed Lilli toward the growing crowd in front of the seawall. Some people sat on it, straddling their drums. Some crouched on the grass, and others stood behind taller drums. We wandered past them and found a space to slip into. Eyes followed us. A few people mumbled to each other. I saw Daniel again, lingering at the edge of the group.

Seriously, what are they looking at? Jeezus. Mean girls anyone?

When the sun slipped behind the buildings and the thin, high clouds turned red and orange, a coordinated beat started. The circle filled in with more bodies and drums. Dad and Pearl stood behind their large drums. Sara, Rowan, and I sat with our smaller ones. Drummers ranged in age, and mers were mixed in with humans.

Hiding in plain sight, I thought with intrigue.

As I watched the crowd, I realized that the mers, not the humans, were the ones taking an interest in us. Some stole glances our way, and others blatantly stared until it was uncomfortable. I looked at Rowan and Sara, but they were just drumming away happily.

Am I the only one noticing this? I looked around again and made eye contact with Daniel.

He winked. I scowled.

"Of all the stupid things humans do," Sara said above the escalating beat, "I've always felt like they got this one right."

"Join in, Stormy." Rowan nudged my shoulder.

"Huh?"

"Just feel the beat and join in whenever." His hands alternated with heel to fingertip strikes on the drumhead. He leaned over and kissed the side of my head without missing a beat.

I'd never been overly musical, although I'd always loved music. I sighed and pushed Daniel from my mind. He was probably just messing with me as usual.

Lilli danced with Jon, and others joined them. Her white hair bounced and twirled around her as she circled with him. His mop of blond hair was also extra wild. The smiles on their faces were infectious. They appeared so happy and carefree.

I felt glad for the two of them, but then nervousness set in. *Jon needs protecting... all of my human family needs protecting.*

An onset of bad memories flooded my mind. A burst of wind tore through the circle. Humans giggled and guffawed at having their hair blowing everywhere. Mers looked around slyly as if trying to figure out who was doing it.

Big breath. Calm down, I told myself. With a quick shake of the memories and a reminder that everyone was okay, I gave a slow exhalation. *Okay, better.* The wind calmed.

Pearl caught my eye and raised a questioning eyebrow.

I gave her a subtle nod and a smile. *Yes, I'm okay now. Thanks, Mom.*

I considered the drum straddled between my legs. My hands rested lightly on the taut leather top. I waited for the return of the beat and then slapped my right hand down on the drum... and boy, did it feel wonderful.

The fort's towering coquina wall provided the perfect acoustics. The harbor was alive with music, and the grassy moat held a symphony of beats, with feet spinning and hopping in time. The music ebbed and flowed as old beats dropped out and new ones took over, ever-changing, flowing, and shifting, like the ocean itself. I closed my eyes and let the rhythm fill me.

Darkness cloaked us all, and the moon rose above the horizon. The drums quieted one, two, three at a time. The final minutes ended with only two hypnotic beats calling and responding only to each other—Dad and Pearl. The final heavy, coordinated *wump* by both their right hands hung in the heady night air, reverberated off the coquina, and then drifted out to sea. Clapping filled the void left behind, quickly followed by little shouts and whoops of delight. Conversations resumed, and the single circle dissolved into small groups.

"I can't believe I've never done that before!" I exclaimed as we wandered toward the parking lot.

"I'm sorry I never took you to one in Indiana. I guess it was always a painful memory for me after we left here." Dad gave me a one-arm squeeze. In the other, he carried the large drum.

"Yeah, Dad. You were awesome!"

"Not bad. Nowhere as good as your mom."

Pearl giggled. "That is always so energizing. I wish they did it more often than every couple of months."

Two beautiful mers strode past. One of them glanced back and then whispered to her friend, "I think she'll drop out."

The friend shook her head, "I'm still keeping my bet as it is."

I followed them with my eyes until they disappeared around the curve of Charlotte Street. "Guys? Why is everyone whispering about me?" I asked.

"Who is?" Dad asked, looking around.

"Other mers. I thought I was just making it up at first, but those two mers totally commented on me. Like they had a bet. And Daniel was here, and he was looking all annoying."

"Daniel doesn't look anything other than annoying," Rowan said.

"It's nothing to worry about, Storm," Pearl said.

"Who's up for ice cream?" Dad said, changing the subject.

"Yes yes yes!" Lilli bounced excitedly.

"Sure, Mr. Harn." Jon's hand, holding Lilli's, went up and down as she bounced. "But then I have to go to the lighthouse to check that everything's good for the Dark of the Moon."

"Thanks, Matty, but I'm meeting up with Paige in a few at the Cigar Bar," Sara replied with a wink.

"Cigar Bar?" Rowan asked.

Pearl replied with a little head shake. "Paige has a morbid fascination with humans who smoke because they're killing themselves even faster than they're already going to die. She loves just watching them and counting back the years they have left. But, Sara, I thought you weren't hanging with Paige much these days."

"Eh, sins of the parents and all. Anyway, she may be able to spill the tea on Laverna's plan a bit, at least as far as the best way to train up the little one." Sara tilted her head at me.

"So they *are* making bets on me?" I asked, finally putting together the bits of conversations I'd overheard.

"If it makes you feel better, I bet *for* you!" Sara responded.

"Doesn't really," I whined.

"It doesn't matter, Stormy. Everything will be great." Rowan kissed my head.

"It's just mers being mers. Everything's a game, even your rematch," Pearl added.

"Catch you all at the lighthouse. Don't be boring." Sara blew us an air kiss and strolled away toward Charlotte and Cuna Streets.

A distant rumble of thunder punctuated our departure. A small white bird flew past us from its perch on the streetlight.

CHAPTER SEVEN
Observations

The tern flew past the departing group of humans and mers, circled high above them, and coasted back toward the fort. It perched next to a crumbling turret on top of the fort. Thunder rumbled.

She emerged like an apparition from the turret. The ghostly illusion was emphasized by her white gossamer tunic and pants, which flowed weightlessly in the presquall breeze.

"Yes, I'm sure we are in the right place," she stated calmly as she leaned on the wall next to her feathered companion.

The tern tilted its head to keep one eye on the departing group on the ground and one eye on her.

"I know we've been steered off course before, but we always find our way eventually. This place is strange, and some areas turn me around, but I feel that it's here even through the confusion. Also, I saw the red-haired one. If she's here, it's here as well."

The bird clacked its beak.

"Yes, I'll get going on it. Mers are simple creatures, and I shouldn't have trouble getting what I need from them. But they can also be very dangerous. So we must pick our targets smartly."

The tern's feathers fluffed and smoothed.

She glanced at the sky over the harbor, which was navy blue with the thinnest of deep red at the horizon. "Red sky at night, sirens' delight. Red sky in the morning, mers take warning."

She placed her upturned palm in front of the bird. It immediately hopped into her hand, which she lifted to her shoulder. The bird snuggled down against her neck.

She turned and made her way across the fort's roof. Her progress was slow, and her light clothing whipped around her with every step. From an outside vantage point, one might have thought she was carried along by the wind rather than by her legs.

CHAPTER EIGHT
Dark of the Moon and Sprite Lightning

The base of the lighthouse was surrounded by people by the time we arrived. Lilli and Jon were easy to spot in the crowd. Pearl, Rowan, and I wove our way through to them.

"Hiya, guys," Pearl said. "Any news?"

"So far, so good," Jon answered. "Dad says the police are still reviewing evidence, but he seems convinced, and *angry*, that people broke in and destroyed stuff to make a statement."

"What are you talking about?" I asked.

Jon cleared his throat. "Apparently, the Lighthouse Historical Society is being blamed by a radical group of activists for desecrating sacred land. They, umm, *broke in* the other night and destroyed the basement. Dad's trying to figure out what can be done."

"They broke in?" I asked, looking at Pearl.

"Yes. A shame really. There's no proof that the Historical Society did anything of that nature, but... radicals. What can you do?" She shrugged.

Sara sauntered up next to me. "And they may have spray-painted 'St sells out Native Americans for the price of admission' on the walls." She chuckled, motioning to the words on an invisible wall.

"Ah." I now understood the scent of spray paint I'd detected when Pearl came into my room the night I woke up.

"It was the best we could come up with. We're hoping it passes as a horrible but believable event."

"What did the others say?" I asked, worried about what our clan would think.

"They understood the need to cover things up. It should be fine," Pearl reassured me.

"Ooh, ooh! The tour is starting!" Lilli jumped up and down.

"Lilli, we don't really care about the tour. We were just checking on our story. You've been coming to this lighthouse for centuries," Sara said.

"Some of the stories they tell are even about stuff *you* did," Paige added as she joined our circle.

"Aren't these gorgeous, Pearl?" Sara lifted Paige's long embroidered skirt to show Pearl her ankle booties.

Paige turned her right foot from side to side. The spotlights caught a shimmer of the purple patent leather as she turned. "New shipment. You must come to the store soon. Now that *this*"—she waved her hand absently toward the lighthouse—"is all behind us."

"Is it?" I asked without disguising my anger. "I'm pretty sure Laverna has more in store."

"Whoa, little one, retract the claws," Paige said, a sly grin on her face. "If you haven't guessed by now, our clans have some issues, but when Mummy and Auntie Z aren't at war, the rest of us get on just fine."

I just stared in disbelief. Everybody was just acting like things were fine, maybe because they weren't the ones being questioned about their right to belong. Or having to prove themselves... again.

"It's true," Pearl replied. "We didn't start the problems, but we have to live with them. Mers don't really like conflict in general."

"But your braid... Tressman... Daniel..." My confusion rose.

"Yeah, that got pretty out of hand. But it's all good now." Pearl smiled.

"It's all good now. Cool. Yeah. So Laverna's new something that has to do with me—is that also all cool?" I asked incredulously.

"Not at all, Stormy. But we can't do anything about it until it's a thing to do something about. So we'll make sure you're ready!"

"And then you'll win," Sara added.

"Again." Rowan winked.

"Maybe, or maybe not," Paige added, unbothered.

I looked at each face in turn. I was so confused and angry.

"Are you guys done?" Lilli interrupted. "We're going to be late for the tour, and I love the story of Smokey. Come on!"

We followed the crowd into the tower.

"No, Sara, I'm not exaggerating. Something isn't right with that woman," Paige whispered intently on our way to the tower entrance.

"Do I sense a bit of jealousy?" Sara asked.

"Most definitely *not*," Paige replied indignantly. "That store is just not normal. *She* isn't normal."

"Shh," Lilli said to the two of them. We'd just gotten inside. Black spiral stairs loomed in front of us. The guide was discussing the carrying of the oil up to the top.

"We'll talk later," Paige whispered to Sara and gave Lilli the side-eye.

After a brief accounting of the hauntings of the lighthouse—most likely sensationalized, Lilli's huffs and sighs implied—the tour began its dizzying journey up the two hundred nineteen stairs. People lined the railing of the balcony at the top, taking in the panoramic view of Matanzas.

Photos were interrupted by a flash of lightning that streaked across the sky. "Ba-ba-*boom!*" A loud crack of thunder split the air. One woman shrieked.

"No one panic," the tour guide said loudly over the excited and nervous chatter. "Please walk back into the tower. No pushing, please. Yes, that's right—follow the person in front of you. When you reach the base, a guide will lead you to the Coast Guard barracks to wait out the storm."

Lightning flashed a full zigzag from sky to water. The hairs on my arms stood up. Before the sky was fully dark again, thunder cracked again. "Ba-ba-*boom!*"

Nervous screams echoed up from the stairs.

Our guide continued to reassure us as he ushered us off the balcony. "Everybody will be fine. Just carefully make your way down. Thank you."

I was the last to step back into the tower. The guide gave me a small smile, but his eyes betrayed his nerves.

His radio chirped to life, and a voice distorted by static said, "When did that storm come up? It was clear a few minutes ago. Is everyone back inside?"

"Roger that. Everyone's in. I directed them to the barracks and am securing the observation deck now." The metal deadbolt on the observation-deck door slid into place with a resounding echo.

But he was incorrect about having everybody inside. Our single-file line down the spiral staircase was one person shy. Specifically by one petite white-haired sprite.

Pearl feigned taking a rest on the fifth-floor landing.

"Are you okay, miss?" the guide asked as he reached her.

"Oh, yes. I just need a quick stop to catch my breath." Pearl smiled. He melted slightly in front of her. I swallowed a giggle.

"Well..." He cleared his throat. "We must get everybody down and out of the tower."

"I'll be right along, but it's okay if my friends and I just take a moment here, *isn't it*?" She looked with wide eyes and gave a tilt of her head.

"It's, well, yes, that will, umm, yes, it's okay." His eyes glazed. "Is there anything I can bring you?"

"Oh no, we aren't going to be a bother." Pearl smiled brilliantly.

He melted a little more. I shook my head in disbelief. I'd seen Sara do this but never Pearl. It was so simple for her. I could tell she wasn't even trying with a tenth of her will. It made my stomach lurch.

"You can run along now," she added.

"Okay." He moved away from us and robotically continued his spiral descent.

Once the guide rounded the next landing, Pearl stood up. She scanned the horizon from the narrow window. After another crash and flash of bright white, I blinked, and flashes replayed behind my eyelids. A gust of wind broke the metal clip that held the window's shutter open. The shutter banged open and closed with each gust.

"What's going on?" Jon asked after a fourth brilliant display of light flashed across the dark sky before the follow-up stomach-pounding rumbles ended.

Lilli whispered, "Papa."

We all turned to see what might as well have been an apparition standing on the stairs leading to our landing.

"Lilli, how did you get inside?" I asked, remembering the sound of the deadbolt.

She didn't answer. She just pushed past us and raced down the stairs. Her white hair trailed like a veil.

"Come on," Pearl said.

We continued down after Lilli. Outside, we found her snuggled next to Z, who stood tall with red hair flying about like flames in the confused wind.

Our guide locked the heavy metal tower door after we exited. "You folks coming in?" he asked us as he walked toward the barracks.

Z smiled. "Not at this time." The guide shrugged and disappeared inside.

As soon as the doors to the barracks were shut, Z said calmly to the darkness, "Vincent, stop with the theatrics and make yourself known!"

A small, handsome man stepped forward from the tree line. His vibrant green eyes, surrounded by long bright-white hair and a full beard, displayed no warmth. He kept those cold eyes trained on Z as he approached us. As he got closer, he tilted his head up. He was much shorter than she was.

"How could you let this happen to my daughter?" Despite his stature, his presence was anything but small. He spoke in a low, ominous tone.

Z's face betrayed no feelings. "Vincent, you know I take the safekeeping of Lilli very seriously. But I also respect her choices."

Lilli said from behind Z's fluttering dress, "Papa, they *are* my family, and I—"

"No, Lilli, they are not." He held out his arm in Jon's direction and spat through clenched teeth. "Especially not *that* one."

"But, Papa, Jon is..." Lilli whispered.

"Is *what*?" His face contorted in hatred and rage. "A creature that has no depth to even understand the greatness of you? You are a free spirit, a nymph of the rivers, an untamable soul of energy. He is base, mundane, and despicable."

Vincent shot each of us a glare that made me happy shooting lasers from their eyes was *not* a magical skill that sprites had. At least, I really hoped it wasn't.

I should really ask Lilli about that.

He ended back on Z and, in a growling tenor, said, "It's time to find a better-suited mentor for you because consorting with *these* types of mers, who see nothing wrong with befriending mixed breeds *and* pure humans, is obviously destroying your higher perspective." He reached around Z, grabbed Lilli by the wrist, and pulled her toward him. He turned to leave, but Lilli shrugged free of his grasp, planted her tiny feet, and squared up to her father.

"No," she squeaked. The air around her petite form shimmered with energy. Bright-blue streaks danced across the sky.

"Lillianna Tabatha Cerulean James. You dare to defy me?" Vincent said menacingly.

"I, uh, I..." Lilli stammered, but she inhaled and renewed her resolve. "I am *not* leaving, Papa."

"Yes. You are. Now, come."

Lilli vanished as Vincent reached for her. I let out an involuntary gasp. Vincent looked at us.

Uh-oh. I sure wish I had Lilli's vanishing talents right now. His eyes changed from green to red. His hair lifted from his scalp, energized.

"Uh, guys, this can't be good," Rowan whispered.

Vincent walked to us. Each step buzzed with audible current.

"Hey, guy, we really aren't..." Rowan stood in front of us with his hands held out in a sign of peacemaking.

"Quiet," Vincent growled and pushed past Rowan, past me, Sara, Paige, and Pearl. He stopped directly in front of Jon and remained an arm's length from him. And although Jon towered over the sprite, there was no question of who was in charge of this interaction.

"Vincent, leave him be." Z walked toward the pair.

"You. Stay. Away. From. My. Daughter," Vincent said slowly.

"But—" Jon started.

"Or you will die," Vincent finished.

"Again?" Sara whispered. I shot her a glare. "Too soon?"

"Oh my God," I mouthed at her in disgust then returned to the horrible showdown.

Z moved to Jon's side. "Vincent, do not do something you will regret."

Like a defiant child, Vincent glanced at Z and then back at Jon. Before any of us even knew what happened, he darted his finger out and hit Jon's chest. Blue light arched between his finger and Jon, who flew backward off his feet. He landed on his back and gasped for breath.

"Hey!" I shouted at Vincent and ran toward Jon.

Z towered in front of Vincent and hissed, "You have overstayed your extended welcome to my territory. We all know what happens to sprites who aren't invited."

"You have betrayed my trust, Z, and I will get my daughter back. And I believe we all agree it will be much better for everyone if she comes on her own," Vincent replied. With a loud crack, he disappeared in a flash of blue light.

Rowan helped me get Jon to his feet. Jon held his hands to his chest and took slow, deep breaths.

Z placed a hand on Jon's heart. After a few seconds, she seemed satisfied. "You'll be okay."

"Uh-huh." Jon nodded but didn't look so sure.

"He just tapped you. He was making a point but wouldn't have dared to truly harm you, or anyone, tonight. Not while I was here."

"Tapped, yeah, he tapped me, all right," Jon said as he struggled to regain his breath.

"Z, how did you know to show up here?" I asked.

"Sprite lightning."

"Sprite what?" I asked.

"Sprite lightning, little one. Sprites are very old magic and tied directly to the earth's energy and natural freshwater features. As a result, they are more or less pure energy packed into tiny little capsules fueled and energized by the constant motion of the waters that run deep below the earth's surface. When sprites are on the move, you can observe them by the release of some of that energy. A special kind of high-atmospheric lightning, easily confused with terrestrial lightning unless you know what you're looking for, is called sprite lightning. Humans, ironically, named it that. Unbeknownst to them, it is caused by actual sprites. I swear that over the millennia, humans have become more intuitive than they give themselves credit for. I've always said if they were to begin to believe with their hearts rather than only with their eyes, they would be quite the formidable force. But..." She chuckled. "That will never be, so we're safe from their possible enlightenment. To answer you, I saw sprite lightning tonight over the lighthouse and thought I should make an appearance to greet whoever decided to appear. In this case, it was Vincent, and I'm sorry to say he isn't going to make life easy for any of us if we can't resolve this Lilli issue."

"What is so wrong, all of a sudden, with Lilli hanging out with us? She's been with us for decades," Pearl said.

"I'm not sure what sparked his sudden outrage. Sprites are closed-minded when it comes to the mixing of kinds, but something has certainly set him off... more than usual," Z said, mulling.

"So he's angry and decided to electrocute Jon?" I asked.

"A minor electrocution, low voltage. But there is a more troubling item," Z replied.

"More troubling than being electrocuted?" Jon asked with raised eyebrows, still rubbing his chest.

"There are only two reasons sprites use that particular energy. The first is self-defense, and it is quite effective because at full power the attacker ends up dead."

"Okaaay." Jon sighed. "I'm not dead, and for the record, I certainly didn't attack him. So what's the second?"

"To connect with your energy."

"Ooh," Sara replied.

"That sucks, Jon," Paige added.

Pearl just shook her head slowly.

"What? What sucks?" Jon scanned the group as if trying to get the punch line to a joke that was on him.

"That's the tap. He's onto you now," Pearl answered.

"Like a GPS locator. He can tell exactly where you are at any time just by tuning into your specific energy frequency," Rowan added.

"Seriously?" Jon asked.

"Has Laverna ever mentioned Vincent?" Z asked Paige.

"No. Not that I recall. Although she's been rather flipped out since you guys beat her to the braid. Like, I'm thinking you really pissed her off this time."

"Well, Paige, I'm sure I have *pissed her off*, as you say, many times." Z turned toward Salt Run, but her eyes seemed to be gazing much farther away.

"Well, all," she said, her eyes focusing back on us, "please behave yourselves for the rest of this rather eventful evening."

"Z, really, you have to ask?" Sara replied with a smirk.

"Ask, beg, demand—I'm sure they all have the same effect on you, my dear Sara," Z replied with a warm smile.

"So, home time?" Pearl said.

"Oh, sister, not up for one more adventure?" Sara said, goading her.

"I think I'm good for one evening."

"Where did Lilli go?" I asked.

"Only she knows, and I think it's best that way for now," Pearl answered. "Come on, Jon. We'll give you a lift."

"Will it be safe for him?" I asked. "To go home, I mean."

"It should be, at least as long as Lilli doesn't show up there."

"Or her dad," Sara added.

"Come on, Paige, let's head to Ripley's and enjoy the artistic renditions because last I checked, it wasn't past *my* bedtime." Sara winked at me and linked her arm with Paige's. The two strolled behind the lighthouse and disappeared into the woods.

I asked Pearl and Rowan, "So, really, does Jon need to worry?"

"Between Z removing her invite to be in her territory and that little show, which would have substantially drained his energy, I doubt Vincent will return tonight," Rowan replied.

"Are you sure you're okay?" I asked Jon. He still looked pale.

"Yeah, totally fine. I mean, it was no dying or anything. Ouch! I was kidding—geez, Storm. You hit the same spot every time," Jon whined as he rubbed his arm.

"Come on, kids—let's go," Pearl said, and we walked back toward the lot where the scooters were parked.

CHAPTER NINE
Maneuvering Pieces into Place

Bird and woman watched the group split into two as they departed the lighthouse grounds.

"Yes, my love," she whispered to the tern. "Sprites are untrustworthy, but in this case, I think he is useful to us, and I'm glad we contacted him."

The tern tilted his head.

The woman stroked the bird's soft feathers with her index finger. "No, I didn't know the small one was his daughter, but all the better! Did you see his anger at the mers? *And* the human? If we're lucky, he will take care of most of our foes, and we will be free to concentrate on finding our prize."

Once the area was quiet, they stepped out from the shadows and meandered along the brick path.

"The dark-haired leader was more than happy to meet with the sprite. Quite a clever idea on your part. You were right—having a territory war makes it easy to ruffle feathers." She chuckled softly, and the tern fluffed with pride.

"But while that one was manipulated by jealousy, these others will require more creativity, especially the ginger. She doesn't seem motivated by jealousy or revenge. Like mother, like daughter, I suppose. But this time, I won't let them mess it up for us. We were so close last time. If only that mermaid hadn't pushed the dumb human to react so strongly. If only we'd acted more quickly once we realized he had them."

She gave a side glance up at the revolving beacon of light and furrowed her brow in thought. "We've come so far, and I mustn't rush this final leg, but I also mustn't be caught one step behind again. I believe I'll start with the young one as soon as possible. We will work our way in slowly. We'll gain trust and destroy this nest from the inside out."

She leaned into the bird's head, and he lovingly preened some loose hairs.

"Go and follow her movements. I'd like to find out more about that one. I do believe we will become exceptional friends." She grinned broadly.

The bird took flight into the night, and the woman was left alone. She continued carefully down the path. Her pain was less when she went slowly, which made her less angry that she had trouble walking in the first place.

CHAPTER TEN
School Days

Bleary-eyed but at least not late... yet.

The summer class had moved to a new location downtown. I lucked out and snagged the last open seawall parking spot for the scooter. I hurried up the street flanked with historic homes, bed-and-breakfasts, and a museum. From Bridge Street, I turned right onto Aviles.

I read the address again from the paper Nana had given me before I left the house. "Twenty Aviles. I've got this!"

The street was unusually quiet. Just one woman walked a bit ahead of me.

I wish I could wear white, I thought, observing the woman's flowing white top and pants. *But white on me quickly becomes* not *white after I spill stuff on myself. Okay, refocus, Storm.*

"If I cut up here, it should be just left, past—*oomph.*" I landed heavily on my right hand. "Ouch, ouch, ouch." I squeezed my wrist to make the pain stop then lowered myself slowly the rest of the way, sat on the warm bricks, and held my palm, mumbling, "I hate these stupid brick streets."

Being a mermaid had the advantage of having better reflexes underwater, but my coordination had not improved much on land. My hand was scraped up, and a mixture of clear liquid and blood rose to the surface and oozed out. *Ouch.* I grimaced and shook my hand to try to make the stinging stop. I got back up, still cradling my hurt hand, and tried to keep walking down Aviles. I only made it a few more steps.

My head swam, and beads of sweat rolled down my forehead and from my armpits. My stomach lurched. I sat down heavily next to a small grassy park on the corner and held my head in my good hand.

What the hell? I thought as I waited for this horrible feeling, which was somewhere between light-headed and seasick, to pass. I stole a glance between my fingers and noticed the sign of the Father Miguel O'Reilly House.

Is it swaying? Maybe I'm swaying. Maybe the world's swaying... spinning. Get me off this horrible ride.

My breath caught, and my stomach lurched. I flung myself on all fours and threw up... water. It just poured out of me. I gasped for breath in between gags.

I'm drowning, I thought deliriously.

"Well, well, little one." A woman's voice broke into my spiraling thoughts. "You can't stay here." Cool hands gripped me under my armpits and hauled me onto my unresponsive legs. My head was too heavy to lift, but I saw ornately painted fingernails.

I stumbled forward with the mystery woman's help.

"Storm?" A distant voice cut through the loud ringing in my ears. "Storm?" The voice was closer this time.

"You're the Manistar boy?" the woman asked.

"Yes. What's happening?"

"She needs salt. I trust you can provide for her from here?" She settled me onto a cement bench.

My breath came in short gasps. I felt like a fish out of water. I opened my panicked eyes and saw a slim figure retreating down the street. Her white-blond hair was woven into a single braid down her back.

"Are you okay? What's going on?" Jon asked with just as much panic in his eyes as I was feeling.

I could only shake my head in fear. I couldn't catch my breath.

"Are you choking?"

I shook my head.

"Are you in pain?"

I shook my head, still gasping.

"Just sit here a second," Jon said, staying by my side.

I closed my eyes and focused on breathing slowly. I opened my eyes again. "What the heck?" I asked weakly.

"What happened?"

"One minute, I'm picking myself up from tripping on a stupid uneven brick, and the next, it felt like I was drowning and couldn't catch my breath."

"How can you, like, you know…" Jon made a motion with his hand, imitating a dolphin swimming. "Drown?"

"I have no idea." I shook my head. "Who was the woman who helped me?"

"Never saw her before, but she knew me and, I guess, you too. Here." Jon held out a bag with pretzel sticks.

I took a pretzel out and nibbled on it. I immediately started to feel better, which made the whole thing weirder.

"Let's go inside, so we're not late," I said after I finished chewing.

"You sure? We still have a few minutes."

"Nah. I'm good, really." I stood up and nearly believed myself.

"Okay." He got up, too, and we walked through the white picket fence, down the stone path, and around to the back of the historic Ximenez-Fatio House.

"Hey, maybe you'll finally get a tail!" he whispered excitedly as we approached the house.

I gave him a shove with my shoulder. "Really? That's what you think that was? A tail-growing exercise?"

He held out the pretzel bag, and I happily took a few more. "Well, I would think growing a tail would be traumatic, so…"

"No, Jon, no tail. Sorry to disappoint."

"Well, okay, but—"

"No."

"Okay, fine." He rolled his eyes and swiped away a stray tuft of hair. "But it'd be cool," he muttered.

I shook my head at him with a little laugh. All sense of awkwardness was gone with one simple joke... at my expense, but still, Jon was a true friend to the end and back again.

"Hey! Jon! Storm! Over here!" a girl's voice shouted. We looked to the left of the house, where the grounds opened up into a grassy grotto surrounded by towering oak trees.

"Samantha's early," Jon remarked. "How odd."

This time, I laughed fully out loud. Seeing Jon tap next to his eye, I remembered my new and improved eye color. I pulled out a pair of sunglasses from my bag and put them on. We walked toward the waving arms of Samantha as she stood in the shade of one of the ancient oaks.

"I worried you guys were going to be late. It's okay. I saved the three of us seats."

"Thanks, Samantha," Jon said with a smile.

"Oh, you're welcome. I figured you'd be pretty upset about what happened at the lighthouse. I mean that's super crazy."

"Yeah, it was pretty horrible. The... uh... the..."

"Vandalism," I said, finishing Jon's sentence.

"Yeah, the vandalism." He looked appropriately upset.

"Well, anyway, I'm sure they'll be caught. And I guess now we get to have class out here, which is really pretty, but I'm not sure how the professors will be able to keep the class to its high standards or how this place has anything to do with marine life. I researched the history of this house, and did you know that it's made of coquina and was part of the first tourist boom in St. Augustine in the early 1800s? And it's been owned and managed by women since the 1830s. How cool is that?"

"Actually, Samantha, that *is* cool," I replied. *That seems strange for the 1830s. I'm pretty sure women couldn't do very much back then.*

My eyes traced the lines of the restored main house, and I wondered if a certain group of *unique* women might have helped the human women with that. The lawn extended behind the main house, and folding wooden chairs had been set in a loose circle near one of the trees. Four of our classmates were already seated. Owen had his earphones in but gave us a little nod and half smile. Shannon sat next to him and rummaged through her backpack. Kendall, on Shannon's left, swatted absently at a bug after saying hello to us, and Hayden, flipping through a pamphlet, rounded out the semicircle of filled seats.

Hayden smiled up at us. "What's up?"

"Nothing much," I replied. He went back to reading his pamphlet.

Just as Samantha had said, three seats were marked as occupied, one with her backpack, one with a notebook, and the third with a pen.

"Thanks," I said as I sat down.

"Yeah, thanks," Jon parroted and took the notebook chair.

We handed both items back to Samantha as she took her seat. Today promised, like every day during St. Augustine summer, to be a scorcher. I looked around at the deadly still branches above us—not a touch of breeze. A small white bird sat quietly among them. I attempted to move some air, but a pain behind my eye stopped me.

Great, now I can't even take advantage of my ability to control the weather because of a headache. I closed my eyes for a long moment and reopened them. It did nothing for the headache. I let out a resigned sigh and fidgeted in my chair.

We all sat in an awkward silence for a minute until Shannon finally spoke up. "What the heck happened at the lighthouse?" She looked directly at Jon.

Owen countered, "C'mon, Shannon. He's probably pretty upset."

"I'm just wondering is all," Shannon said. "I mean, we all are. That's crazy stuff."

"Well, I-I don't really know," Jon stuttered.

"What is your dad saying?" Kendall asked.

"He's just trying to fix as many of the—"

"Are the police investigating?" Hayden interrupted.

Jon started again. "I guess. I think—"

"Good morning, everybody!" Dr. Ross exclaimed as he and Dr. Briggs rounded the corner to the lawn and walked to our circle.

They sat in two adjacent chairs, leaving an empty one between each of them and us. Dr. Ross propped his soft leather case against the leg of his chair. Dr. Briggs had no such case, but he did have a handful of papers inside a manila folder.

"As you are all aware, some rather unfortunate events unfolded at the lighthouse, so we have made a change of venue for the remainder of the course," Dr. Briggs said. "We have been welcomed in by the staff of the Ximenez-Fatio House."

"The final two weeks of the course were devoted to exploring the incredible history of this town, so our location is perfect!" Dr. Ross continued. "We'll be discovering the influences of its unique maritime history, oceanographical location, and marine life played out in a variety of developments, wartime successes, myths, and survival as the nation's oldest city."

Dr. Briggs looked at all of us. "Hmm, hang on—we seem to be short two faces."

"Has anybody heard from the Arch siblings?" Dr. Ross asked us.

We responded with little shakes of our heads, but the question was answered by the flurry of two bodies rushing toward us, backpacks flailing and legs and arms flying. Out of breath, Abigail and Josh came to an abrupt halt next to Dr. Briggs's chair.

"We're so sorry, professors. I told Josh to leave earlier because of parking but—" Abigail started.

"I would have left earlier if Abigail had been able to pick an outfit," Josh said.

"Kids, kids, no problem," Dr. Ross responded. "You are only two point four minutes late. That is only a half-a-grade deduction at most."

Josh and Abigail stared at him as if unsure whether he was joking. A tense half second passed as we waited. The smirk came, and there was a collective sigh of relief.

"I'm only kidding. So serious, these two," Dr. Ross said to Dr. Briggs. "To be honest, compared to the college kids we teach, you guys are the promptest class we've ever had. Even taking Owen's unique sense of time into account." He winked.

We laughed. Owen was nearly always running in just as class was starting.

"And the most consistent in attending," Dr. Briggs added.

"Well, to be fair, *Dr.* Briggs, how many times can you listen to facts about rocks?"

"*Dr.* Ross, rocks are the foundation of our understanding of what happened through time. I believe your choice of study doesn't provide such an important record."

"Well, I suppose studying such intelligent creatures does have its negative points," Dr. Ross replied.

"Intelligent?" Dr. Briggs said. "Did the manatee double its brain gyri and sulci, making two actual ridges and grooves?"

"Some of us just have to fall back on our good looks, then." Dr. Ross laughed.

We all giggled at their banter.

"Okay, now that everybody is here and seated..." Dr. Ross took the stack of papers from the folder and handed them to Abigail. "Take one and pass the rest around. This is the outline of the remainder of the course. We'll be dividing up our time between short lectures and field trips. There will also be one final essay."

Simultaneous moans drowned out the din of insects.

"Really?" Dr. Briggs raised his eyebrow at us.

Dr. Ross continued. "Today we will learn the fascinating history of our host classroom, the Ximenez-Fatio House."

******

The thirty-minute lecture was followed by a tour of the historic home. We were released after making plans for a morning lecture followed by a tour of the Fountain of Youth the next day. Jon and I collected our stuff and headed for the picket fence. As I was about to make a right out of the grounds, back the way I'd come this morning, Samantha caught up to us at a jog.

"Guys! Hey! Phew, glad I caught you." She was slightly out of breath. "I was talking to Dr. Ross, and he said that we could do the final project as a group project if we wanted. Do you guys wanna?"

"Sure," I replied with a glance at Jon.

"Okay," he agreed.

"Yay, cool. So, I was going to walk to Pizzalley's and grab a slice of pizza. Are you guys doing anything?"

Pizza sounded perfect, and I thought the salt would probably help get rid of this stupid headache. "I'm free," I replied.

"I have to get back to helping my dad out with the cleanup," Jon said. "Dad suggested patching, but instead, they're building a wooden representation of a seafloor or something."

"That's creative," I said.

"I suppose," he said, grinning. "Okay, see you guys later."

Jon headed back toward the O'Reilly House, and Samantha and I went in the opposite direction toward St. George Street. A little white bird flew ahead of us as we wandered toward downtown.

CHAPTER ELEVEN
The Song of the Siren

As we neared the pizza place, I recognized the person standing in front of the store, handing out flyers. It was the woman in white who had been ahead of me on my way to class. She had a cute pixie cut with the tips of her hair colored platinum and the rest dark brown.

"Hello, lovely ladies!" She smiled broadly at Samantha and me. "Please, my beauties, take a sample. The wonderful pizza establishment has allowed me to provide samples of their amazing pizza while also promoting my new store on Aviles."

Pizzalley's was well-known for handing out samples of their cheese pizza, and even though we were going to go in and order slices, free pizza was still free pizza.

"What kind of store?" Samantha popped the square of pizza into her mouth.

Good one. If we take longer by asking questions, maybe she'll let us take another.

The woman must have seen me watching because she whispered, "Go ahead—I won't tell." We each took another square as she continued. "The store is part tearoom, part Victorian parlor, part high fashion. Most importantly, it needs you gorgeous ladies to stop in." She smiled.

"Cool, yeah. We'll totally check it out!" Samantha took a flyer, and we went into the restaurant to get our lunch. "Well, she seemed nice," Samantha said as we sat in a booth with our pizza slices. I took off my sunglasses as she studied the flyer. "Beyond the Veil Tea Shop and Emporium. Crystal and tea readings, exotic clothing to fit every style, antiques."

"Sounds very St. Augustine," I replied with a laugh and glanced at the flyer. *Uh-oh. The address puts it right near Paige's shop. Well, this won't go over well.*

Looking up from the flyer, Samantha said, "You're so lucky to live here." She stopped and stared.

"Everything ok?" I asked.

"Well, yeah, but are you wearing one colored contact?"

Sunglasses! "Oh, uh... I just thought it would be fun."

"Cool."

"So, what were you saying?" I asked.

"Just that this is a great town."

"Yeah, I guess." I took a bite of pizza. *If Samantha only knew half of what happens in this town, her mind would explode.* "Do you wanna check it out after lunch?"

"I wish I could, but I have to go meet up with Mom and Dad. Maybe tomorrow after class?"

"Sure." I smiled.

We finished our lunch and headed out. A teenager stood where the woman had been and was handing out the samples.

"Wow, lucky we got here when we did, or we'd never have known about the cool store!" Samantha said as we retraced our steps back toward Aviles.

"Yeah, super lucky."

Samantha smiled when we hit the crossroads. "See ya tomorrow."

"Yeah, bye."

Samantha turned right. I kept on straight. I figured I'd stop in at Paige's to see what she thought about the new place.

******

"What's *wrong*?" Paige exclaimed to Sara, who was leaning casually against the glass jewelry counter. "The witch next door is what's wrong!"

"Really, Paige, it isn't very nice to call people that." Sara slipped a gold bangle set onto her slim wrist.

I froze in place just inside the door.

"I'm not saying anything that isn't already said. Look, it's right here!" She gruffly folded the local paper into fourths and proceeded to read aloud: "Beyond the Veil Tea Shop and Emporium. A new shop has opened on the nation's oldest street. Picturesque Aviles is now the home to Beyond the Veil Tea Shop and Emporium. Its eclectic inventory is like something from a psychedelic Victorian dream."

Paige paused and rolled her eyes then continued reading. "Edwardian-style dresses are mixed in with mini silk chemises. Victorian cameos are paired with elaborate hand-painted scarves and adorned with rhinestones. The shop also carries a variety of home goods, including oil lamps, assorted incense, china cups, and lace-edged napkins.

"The one thing that sets this boutique apart is the emphasis on Victorian spiritualism. You can have your tea leaves read, play with a pendulum while dousing with angel cards, or read about the séances of Henry Flagler's wife, Ida Alice.

"If the 'witchy' thing is not your cup of tea, you can purchase a variety of tea to take home." Paige finished with a flourish and an I-told-you-so eyebrow lift.

Sara reached over and took the paper from Paige and continued reading out loud. "Jacqueline Passerine, the proprietor, explained that spiritualism played a part in St. Augustine's history. It was her goal to pay homage to the time period and not much to the ghosts that seem to haunt these streets. She describes herself as a free spirit who was born in Egypt and traveled around the world, living in exotic locations like New Guinea and Spain. She settled in St. Augustine because of its European vibe. 'It is like a treasure hunt,' Ms. Passerine says of her newly adopted city. 'You never know what you will find.'" Sara laughed.

"This is *not* funny," Paige shot back.

"Stormy," Sara called without even looking back at me. "Don't just stay there by the door. Come here and tell Paige that it is, in all actuality, quite funny."

I inched my way forward, wary of Paige's crazy eyes. Mermaids were unpredictable, and angry mermaids were very intimidating.

"I, umm, I..." *I am in no way going to say anything of the sort.*

"Everyone knows that *I* have the coolest shop in St. Augustine," Paige blurted as she grabbed the paper back and tore it into shreds.

"Well, cousin, I came as fast as I could when you said it was an emergency," Pearl said calmly as she walked in. "But after hearing your little issues, I realize now it was an emergency of ego." She joined Sara and me at the counter. "How's it, Stormy?"

"Good," I replied with a little shrug.

Paige sat atop her tall stool and angrily tapped the air with her one foot.

"Good morning, ladies! I hope I'm not interrupting," a pleasant voice called from the doorway. "I am Jacqueline Passerine, and I'm the proprietor of the shop next door." She smiled brightly and then paused.

No, no... please don't.

"Oh, hi again!" Jacqueline said directly to me.

"You've met each other, Storm?" Paige asked.

"What? I, well, umm, just for a sec." I tried to explain but ended up just wandering over to a rack of wrap skirts and harem pants.

"I'm the new kid on the block, so to speak," Jacqueline continued. "I do hope you will all come over for a cup of tea. I'm not having my grand opening for a few more days but would love a friendly soft opening with my neighbors."

Jacqueline nonchalantly glanced about Paige's store. She looked back at Paige and gave a beautiful smile. Her features were so delicate, almost birdlike in their daintiness. She was only slightly shorter than me, but her petite frame, delicate mannerisms, and distinct enunciation of words defined elegance in my mind.

"Your shop is cute." Jacqueline eyed the shredded newspaper that covered the jewelry case. With another brilliant smile, she said, "Please don't consider my shop competition. I do believe there is plenty of room in this *magical* town for the both of us. We obviously cater to two *very* different clienteles."

Pearl placed her hand lightly on Paige's knee, mostly likely to keep her from pouncing.

Jacqueline then turned her attention to the rest of us and nodded approvingly. "I do hope you will take me up on my offer of a cup of tea before I get inundated with customers. I do so want to get to know all of you and learn more about my new home!"

Then with a small wave, she turned and left. She walked slowly with an unsteady gait.

"Wow, she burned you," Sara blurted.

"How dare she use the C-word!" Paige leapt to standing, both hands on her hips.

"The C-word?" I asked timidly.

"*Cute,* Storm. She called my baby cute! Ahhh!" Paige slammed her palms onto the counter. "I'll show you cute," she mumbled. "How's about a little tour of the inlet while you're on a midnight swim?"

"Are you quite done?" Pearl asked calmly as the raging Paige paced behind the counter.

"Done? I'm not even close to done. She's up to something. That is no ordinary woman. There is something fishy—or rather, *not* fishy—about her. I'm sticking with witch."

Sara shook her head. "I doubt she's a witch, Paige. I mean, when's the last time you saw a real witch? Like, it's been centuries."

"Wait, really? Witches are for real?" I asked.

"Oh, Stormy, what *do* they teach you in school?" Sara said. "Tsk-tsk."

"Well, whatever that thing is, I'm not setting one foot inside its store." Paige sat back down on her stool and air tapped her foot in anger.

"Really, Paige? You're being a baby," Sara said. "You accepting her offer to visit would be a great way to show her you're the bigger person. What is that funny human saying? Keep your friends close but drown your enemies if they get closer?"

I laughed. "Not quite."

"Well, whatever it is, Paige, you should keep her close and drown her if you need to."

"How about we skip the drowning part for now," Pearl said with a chuckle.

Paige looked between the three of us. "Okay, but I'm not going alone."

"Well, then, that's settled." Sara held a pair of gold dangle earrings up to her ear as she examined herself in the countertop mirror. "Pearl and I will watch the shop. Stormy, you go with Paige to check out the 'competition.'" Sara emphasized the word with air quotes.

"Fine." Paige planted both feet on the ground. "Come on, Storm. But fair warning—no promises on the not-drowning-her part."

"Uh, I..." I tried to protest. Being in charge of keeping Paige from killing somebody else didn't seem like a great situation for me. But Paige grabbed my hand and pulled me after her.

CHAPTER TWELVE
Friendly Competition

Jacqueline's store was three doors down from Paige's. Paige pushed open the glass door. I followed her inside and suppressed a gasp of wonderment. A few other shoppers browsed the ornate dresses hanging along the far wall, and another hovered by a table with incense holders, colorful crystals, and brass cups.

We wandered deeper into the store, which was dimly but comfortably lit. The wall opposite the front door was alive with rainbows. I turned from the door to the wall. The enchanting light play was from the sun shining through a mosaic film on the door's glass panels.

"That's cool," I whispered.

Paige gave me a side-eye glare.

"I mean, sorta, like only if you like rainbows, so..." I trailed off meekly.

Jacqueline emerged from a side room with her arms buried in a pile of colorful fabric. She looked up, saw us, and gave a little exclamation of delight. "Oh! You both made it over. How joyous!" She passed by a customer on her way to us and asked, "Are you finding everything to your satisfaction?"

"More than ever! This is the most amazing store I've ever been in," the woman replied happily.

"Wonderful, love. Do tell me if you need assistance of any kind. I hate when clerks hover, so you just let me know." Her dainty voice hinted at time spent in England.

Jacqueline turned her attention back to us as she hung the garments draped over her arm on an industrial-looking metal bar that spanned a large window seat. Beautiful silk shawls hung on hooks next to the window, adding a Middle Eastern feel.

This is where Pearl bought that peacock shawl for me.

"I was afraid these pieces weren't going to make it in time for the opening, but today must be my very lucky day!" She smiled at us both and motioned to the wall. "Even the rainbows have joined us!"

"They're so pretty!" I blurted, avoiding eye contact with Paige.

"I've always loved inviting the sun and its magnificence into wherever I am," Jacqueline said. "And why wait for the rain to make it happen when we can create our own magical rainbows?"

My eye lingered on one dress she had just placed on the rack.

"Oh, yes, this one would look positively radiant on you." She pulled it back off the rack and held it up to Paige and me. "All hand-sewn embroidery on the bodice and the sleeves, and this fabric is so luxuriant, don't you agree? Oh, gosh, I'm ever so sorry, but I didn't catch your names before."

"I'm Storm, and this is Paige."

"Well, Paige, as one boutique owner to another, the details of the silver intertwined with the blue silk are just heavenly. And, Storm, I do believe this color would be absolute perfection with your skin and hair."

"It's super pretty," I agreed.

"It's all right." Paige sighed. "Storm, don't you already have a similar dress?"

"Uh, yeah, sorta," I replied, remembering the beautiful blue dress that Z had gifted to me for the solstice party. It was from Paige's store, and up until that moment, it had been the most beautiful dress I'd ever seen.

"Well, then, we agree the color *is* perfect for her!" Jacqueline smiled. "After I get it steamed and ready for trying, would you be willing to model it? I find dresses such as this one need someone to shine within it to fully appreciate its beauty."

My cheeks warmed. "I'm not a model," I muttered.

"Well, you should be," Jacqueline responded without hesitation. "I'm surprised nobody has asked you to model clothes for them yet. Your shape is ideal." She glanced at Paige and then back at me. "Well, anyway, their loss is my gain, I believe."

"How much are you marking up that little blue beauty for your retail price?" Paige asked.

"Three," Jacqueline replied without missing a beat.

"Three hundred?" I said a bit too loudly.

She laughed lightly. "Yes, quality doesn't come inexpensively."

"Good luck getting a buyer for something in *that* price range," Paige scoffed.

"I've found that items of such high detail and perfection always find the right home, regardless of their price tags. I believe this town is ready for a shop that will cater to the discerning shopper."

"If you say so. Mind if I look around at what you're offering this so-called discerning shopper?" Paige replied nonchalantly.

"Not at all. Please make yourself at home. If you see something irresistible, let me know, and I'm sure I can work out a deal. I even offer layaway."

Paige muttered and wandered off.

Jacqueline watched her go and then turned to me. "Please, have a seat. I'd love to do a tea-leaf reading for you."

"Sure." I shrugged and fell deeply into one of the two oversized chairs placed next to a heavy-looking round wooden table.

Rows of china, linens, teapots, and glass jars of loose-leaf teas lined the wall behind the counter. Jacqueline pulled down two delicate cups and two beige linen napkins.

"Your shop is really cool," I said to Jacqueline as she set the teapot, cups, and linens before me.

"Well, thank you." She took a seat in the opposite chair. Swirls of steam rose as she poured us each a cup, and the scents of raspberry and bergamot filled my nose. "I'm very careful to stay within the era so people genuinely feel transported back in time, perhaps to when the nation's oldest city was just spreading its wings like a young teenager begging to be respected."

"That would be nice," I said with a shy smile. Following her lead, I took a sip of the tea. It was delicious and made me feel sophisticated.

Before we were even half done, Paige strolled back over. "You have some nice knickknacks, but the prices are going to be tough to sell here."

Jacqueline placed her cup lightly back onto the saucer and smiled, though she gave Paige a bird's-eye stare. "Well, that will just be my little challenge."

"Come on, Storm, I gotta get back." Paige motioned to me.

"Oh, yeah. Um, sorry I didn't have time for the reading," I said as I put the cup back onto its saucer—much less perfectly than Jacqueline had—and stood up.

"It's not a problem. Please return anytime you'd like. I don't have many friends here yet, so meeting you all today has been so very refreshing." Jacqueline smiled at both of us.

Paige had just opened the door when Jacqueline hurried beside us and handed me a roll of plastic. "For you. For your own rainbows!" She returned to her other customers.

Once we were outside, I unrolled the rectangle and saw it was the same mosaic pattern that she had on her front door. I rolled it back up and hurried to catch up to Paige.

******

"Well, how did it go?" Sara asked when we got back into Paige's store, which now seemed too bright.

"It was beautiful!" I said. "She had really great dresses and crystals, and she gave me some tea. It was delicious!"

"Looks like an overpriced thrift store to me." Paige made her way back to the counter. "Was like wandering through a musty attic full of trinkets owned by an old person, and now a young person was trying to pawn them off as expensive antiques."

"Are you sure the two of you went to the same shop?" Pearl asked with a laugh.

"That woman is trouble," Paige added.

"No, she's not," I said. "She's new here, like I was. It must be really hard for her. Can I ask Nana if she can come over? Maybe for tea?"

"Tea? So, now you drink tea?" Paige scowled, and Sara laughed.

I looked from them to Pearl.

"Sure. Let's ask Rean what day may work when we get home." Pearl gave a small smile.

"It will be so great!" I exclaimed.

Paige shook her head.

"I'm guessing drowning isn't off the table?" Sara whispered to Paige with a playful nudge.

Paige let out a sigh that sounded similar to a hiss.

CHAPTER THIRTEEN
School Daze and New Friends

I was so excited for Thursday to arrive so, of course, it took *forever* to get here. Nana had said Jacqueline couldn't come over until today because she had some doctor's appointments earlier in the week.

Finally, it's Thursday, I thought happily.

But I was being tortured in the final stretch... by listening to Dr. Briggs discuss the composition of coquina rock. It was used for a lot more than just the fort—and Tressman's creepy cave. *Enough already. I get it. Tiny stuff dies, gets stuck together and voilà, coquina.* Totally ready to get out of there, I sighed and rested my head on my hand.

"Ah, our guest has arrived!" Dr. Ross announced.

"Perfect timing." Dr. Briggs looked at the petite woman and then back at us. "I believe you are all more knowledgeable about the rock on which this town is built. Let's all head over to visit another impressive item on which this town owes its success, the Hurricane Lady, located at the Father Miguel O'Reilly House Museum."

Dr. Ross added, "This is Jacqueline Passerine, a new store proprietor in town."

Huh? His announcement interrupted my daydreaming.

"We met her last night at one of the wonderful local establishments in town, and she mentioned she had yet to visit the Hurricane Lady."

"Thank you very much for letting me crash your class. Oh, hi, Storm!" She smiled and gave a little wave. I smiled back.

"You are most welcome, Ms. Passerine. And you also already know

Ms. Harn. Perhaps she and Mr. Manistar could give you a special behind-the-scenes tour of the lighthouse. Her famous grandmother, Rean Harn, and Mr. Manistar's father, the current head curator, must share a vast amount of insider knowledge."

"Oh, I had no idea," Jacqueline said sweetly. "Well, you are all certainly lucky to have such wonderful and intelligent teachers!"

"You are most certainly correct," Dr. Briggs said.

"Well, at least one," Dr. Ross added.

We laughed.

"Oh, Dr. Ross, don't be so hard on yourself." Dr. Briggs smiled. Jacqueline joined in the laughter. Everything, including her laugh, was light and airy.

"Okay, let's head over," Dr. Ross continued. "You can leave your backpacks, but bring a notebook and something to write with."

"You coming?" Jon asked, notebook in hand.

"Oh, what? Uh, yeah." I lowered my voice. "What're we doing?"

Jon laughed, and with a shake of his head, he handed me a pencil and a notebook. "Seriously, Storm. You could pay a tiny bit of attention."

"I was! It's just I started thinking of other things, and then Jacqueline showed up."

"Yeah... how do you know her?" Jon asked.

"Kind of a long story, but she opened a store right near Paige's."

"Oh, ha. I bet Paige loves that."

"Yeah, not so much."

"Well, we're heading over next door to the O'Reilly House."

"Okay, umm..."

"That's where the Hurricane Lady is." Jon raised his eyebrows.

"Oh, well..."

"So are you going to go? You know, because..." Jon did a little mime of fainting.

"Well, I don't really know for sure it does that to me, right?"

"What about the first morning when I found you on the ground?"

"What about that?" I asked.

"You were right across the street from the O'Reilly House."

"Oh."

"Yeah, oh."

"Well, what should I do? I can't just stay here."

Jon shrugged. "We should think of something."

"I'll be fine."

We filed out of the garden, but as I reached the fence, someone called my name.

"Ms. Harn? Is there a Storm Harn?" A beautiful woman appeared on the path, walking toward us.

Embarrassed because everybody in the class stopped and turned, I shyly raised my hand. "That's me."

"Oh, so glad I caught you. I have your dad on the phone. Inside."

I looked at the professors.

"No problem, Ms. Harn. We'll be just next door when you're done," Dr. Briggs said.

"Well, that works. Catch you later!" Then he stopped and gave his goofy smile, wiggling his eyebrows. "Did you see what I did there? *Catch you later?* Because last time you were near the Hurricane Lady, I had to catch you. Get it?"

I snorted. "Yeah, clever." I gave him a shove toward the group as I turned and headed back to the main building.

The woman was waiting by the open door. She looked familiar, but I couldn't place her. Then I noticed her necklace—it was a silver Lionfish.

"Umm..." I started.

"Shh, wait just a moment until we get inside." She put one bright-pink painted fingernail to her lips, ushered me into the dimly lit parlor of the historic house, and then closed the door behind us. "That was close," she said and tossed her long blond braid behind her shoulders.

"What was?" I asked.

"The Hurricane Lady, young one. I thought you would have learned from the other day."

"The other day?"

"Yes, when you collapsed next to the O'Reilly House. That wasn't a coincidence."

"You're the one who helped me?"

"Yes." She smiled. "That wouldn't have ended well if you'd gone over there today." She sat in one of the antique chairs and admired her fingers. "I've been watching you this past week. I figured they'd plan a trip over there at some point, but I'd hoped you had put two and two together. They told me you were smart." She lifted one perfect eyebrow in a questioning arch.

"Well, I, well..." I stumbled over my words. "I didn't really think the whole Hurricane Lady thing was true. And even if it was, I'm, well, you know, only..."

She laughed darkly. "Only what? A half mer? Well, that's great logic. So you'd only half die?"

"I don't know. Everyone questions me, especially you guys," I replied defensively and pointed to her necklace.

She gave a little chuckle and said dismissively, "Well, please, don't let me stop you. Head on over there."

"No, I... I'm sorry. I didn't mean it that way. Sorry. Can I start over?"

She nodded.

"Thank you for helping me the other day. So, the Hurricane Lady did that to me?" I asked.

"Yes. Her display case is in the room overlooking Aviles. We have to make sure to move quickly past it to avoid the sickness. You apparently decided it was better to have a seat right below her."

This time, I laughed. "No, I tripped. I tend to do that."

She laughed again. This time, it was good-natured. "Okay, well, that makes more sense. I apologize for jumping to conclusions. And I'm sorry—

I never even introduced myself. I'm Suzee. I'm somewhat like the caretaker of this establishment."

The light bulb clicked on brightly, and I exclaimed, "It was you!"

Her eyebrow rose once again ever so subtly, the impish gesture making her perfect face even more beautiful.

"This building... the women who ran it," I said. "I knew that wasn't possible back then."

"Well," she said, leaning back and crossing one leg over the other. "Not *im*possible if you have the right help." Her long nails clicked on the arm of the chair.

"That's so awesome," I replied, putting all the historic stories into perspective now that I knew mers had helped.

"But why did you help humans? I thought your clan didn't do that so much."

"Care about humans? You're correct. I really didn't and don't care about their little lives, but these women intrigued me. They showed a spirit I hadn't seen in humans in all my centuries. It was just a fun project, really. But I admit I enjoyed watching them succeed in a time when the frailer sex of your species dominated so blatantly."

She stood and glanced out of the curtained window. "I believe your class is returning. I'll be seeing you soon, I'm sure."

"Okay. Um, thanks."

"Just be sure to stay away from the O'Reilly House and the Hurricane Lady, okay?"

"Okay," I assured her and turned to leave.

Just before I started down the stairs, she called, "Oh, Storm?"

"Yeah?" I turned back to her.

"You may want to look up once in a while. Always good to know who's watching."

"Thanks," I replied.

Obviously, she'd been watching me. She was the one I'd noticed behind the curtains on the second floor while we were in class. I joined back up with my chattering classmates.

"What was that about?" Jon asked quietly as I blended back in with them in the garden.

"Apparently, the Hurricane Lady *is* bad for me," I whispered and then looked up at the second floor. Suzee gave me a small smile as a little white bird flew past the window and landed on an overhanging oak branch near our class. Suzee melted back into the darkness of the room.

******

"Nana!" I called when I got home.

I walked impatiently from room to empty room.

"Nana? *Naaan—*"

The front door opened, and Nana and Dad came in.

"My gracious, I could hear you from the street," she said with a chuckle. "Everything okay?"

"Yeah, I just want to get stuff ready for Jacqueline to come over, and I didn't know where you were."

"I was just on a walk with your dad. We have plenty of time."

"Pearl should be here in a few," Dad added. "What's so special about this Jacqueline, anyway?"

"I don't know," I replied. "She's just cool."

Nana's cell phone interrupted our conversation. "Hello?" Nana said, walking into the living room. "Yes, thank you. I see." She spoke quietly, but I had no trouble eavesdropping, thanks to mermaid hearing. "Monday? Yes, if you think it's necessary. Yes, morning is preferred. Thank you. Bye."

I scurried around the kitchen, pretending I hadn't been listening.

"Before you ask, Storm, everything is fine," Nana announced as she joined Dad and me in the kitchen.

I guess I'm not such a good actress. I gave her an innocent shrug and a smile.

"I'm just getting something checked out that the doctor spotted on my last mammogram. I didn't want to worry you, which is why I've been keeping you out of it."

Dad handed her a glass of white wine.

"Oh, okay," I said, but then her words registered. "Wait, you mean, like, cancer?"

"An *area of concern* is all," she replied sternly, and with an Oscar-worthy spin of emotion, she immediately switched to a more cheerful mode. "Okay, let's get ready for Jacqueline. I'm excited to meet this intriguing woman!"

******

"Why did we invite her over, again?" Sara asked.

"Storm wanted to welcome her to our town." Pearl gave me a nod of approval.

"Yeah, but since when do we really care?" Sara asked, her gaze following two shirtless men jogging on the beach. "Paige is pretty angry with this newcomer. Do you think it's wise to piss her off further by befriending it?"

"*Her*, Sara, not *it*," Pearl scolded.

Sara switched from the men to Pearl with a sideways feline stare. "Her, it—whatever the pronoun of choice, it's probably not the best idea to piss *them* off before the rematch, is all I'm saying, dearest sister."

I jumped in. "I don't think Paige should be mad. I mean the store is totally different from hers."

"Have you met Paige, Stormy? She'd be jealous of a cardboard shack selling four-for-ten-dollars T-shirts if it was anywhere near her territory," Rowan said.

"I think it's very nice of Storm to arrange this little gathering," Z said as she climbed up the steps from the beach.

"Well, just don't tell Paige," Sara said.

Nana, Dad, and Mr. Humpphrey came out from the kitchen. "I believe our guest has arrived," Nana announced.

Rowan glanced around the corner of the deck and let out a whistle of delight.

That's pretty rude.

"Check her *out!*" He motioned to Dad and Mr. Humpphrey to join him.

Am I really hearing this? I wondered in complete shock.

Dad and Mr. Humpphrey's reaction did nothing to calm me. Like little kids, they all hurried down the stairs and out of sight.

"What is happening?" I asked, my eyes wide with anger and embarrassment. I marched over to the stairs with a gust of sea breeze lifting my hair around me like Medusa. As I was about to let out a flurry of scoldings, I stopped in my tracks. My hair relaxed back down.

All three guys stood next to the burgundy Buick Skylark convertible parked next to our house. Jacqueline, still behind the wheel, smiled elegantly, her hair covered in a canary-yellow silk headscarf. She sported oversized white-rimmed sunglasses.

"Is this a 1954?" Dad asked, his eyes wide with admiration.

"These are original leather seats," Mr. Humpphrey added.

"She is so very beautiful," Rowan said with a slight shake of his head as he caressed the hood.

So, not sexist men but boys drooling over a hunk of metal, I thought with a laugh at myself. *Hopefully, this will be the only embarrassment of the day.*

Rowan glanced back at me. "Stormy, come here! Check this beauty out!"

"Sure, coming," I replied and gave a friendly wave to Jacqueline. Nana, Pearl, and Sara followed me downstairs.

Jacqueline slid out from her seat and closed the door behind her in one fluid move. "Hello, gents. You certainly know how to make a girl feel welcome." She laughed lightly and removed her headscarf with a little shake of her head. The bright tips of her short hair danced like feathers around her face. "Even if the woman in question has four wheels and a steering wheel and is well beyond all of us in age." She smiled.

"Speak for yourself, ma'am." Mr. Humpphrey extended his hand in greeting. "Miles Humpphrey," he said with an easy grin.

"Oh my gosh!" Jacqueline blushed. "Are you Miles Humpphrey, the author?" She held out her hand in return.

"Yes," Mr. Humpphrey replied, matching her blush as he shook her hand.

"I cannot believe I am meeting you face-to-face. Gosh, the author of *Legends Behind the Legends*? You're one of the reasons I had to come here, to St. Augustine. Your stories. They are so fascinating, and well, are they real? I mean, that is bold of me to ask, but so many have captivated me and made me wonder how much we really know. The history, the lore, the... oh, I'm being so rude. I'm Jacqueline Passerine."

"It's a pleasure to meet you, Ms. Passerine," Mr. Humpphrey replied.

"Please, call me Jacqueline." She glanced over at Dad and Rowan, who were still drooling over her car.

"And these gents are Matthew and Rowan," Mr. Humpphrey said a bit louder than necessary to get their attention away from the original leather stitching.

They both looked up. "Oh, yes." Dad walked back around the car. "Great to have you over. Storm has spoken very highly of you and your new store."

"Well, isn't she the sweetest young lady. It's hard to start up a new business as an outsider, especially in a town where there are already so many amazing boutiques. Her invitation here today really means a lot." Jacqueline smiled.

"Hi, Jacqueline," I called with a little wave.

"Hi, Storm," she replied happily.

"So wonderful to meet you, Jacqueline," Nana said as the consort made their way up to the deck. "You already know Pearl and Sara, and this is Z, Storm's..."

"Godmother," Z finished. "Welcome to our little town."

We all took seats around the table under the shade of the umbrella.

"It is such a pleasure to meet you, Ms. Harn," Jacqueline said. "I just learned today from Storm's professors that you are *the* Harn of lighthouse fame and history."

Nana smiled. "Please, call me Rean, and I wouldn't say fame but history, yes."

"Well, then, Rean, I would love to hear about the lighthouse history sometime. It's such a beautiful location. It's a shame part of it is closed. Something about vandals?"

"Yes, it is undergoing some repairs, but hopefully, soon it will be back up and running as usual."

"Do they know who did such a horrendous thing?" Jacqueline asked Pearl and Sara.

"No," Nana replied, drawing Jacqueline's attention back.

"Well, it is quite a shame. Does that sort of thing often happen in this town?"

"No, it doesn't," Pearl replied. "It seemed to be a one-of-a-kind sort of incident."

"Well, that's good to hear."

"Enough about us. Tell us some tales, Jacqueline," Pearl said. Her face looked odd—not quite angry, but there was something that made me feel uncomfortable.

"Yeah, we'd love to hear about life away from here," Sara said with a grin.

"Oh, I don't want to bore you. I have traveled quite a lot, but I just seem to keep searching for the right place to land, you know? Like, everywhere I go, I'm still left wanting." She took a sip of iced tea and smiled. "I'm really hoping St. Augustine will finally give me what I'm looking for."

"And what do you seek?" Z asked.

Jacqueline let out a little laugh. "I suppose I'll know when I find it."

"Well, I know what I want, and I have most definitely found it," Sara whispered.

I followed her gaze. She'd pinpointed the same two runners, now returning from their workout.

"They're twins." She grinned. "I bet they surf. Of course, if they don't, I'm sure I could take them out for a lesson or two."

My face burned with embarrassment. Here Jacqueline was talking about finding a place that called to her soul, and Sara was ogling boys.

"Jacqueline, do you surf?" Rowan asked.

"Oh, no. I'm not a strong swimmer at all. I'm more at home in forests than in oceans."

"Well, I'm sure we could teach you." Rowan smiled. "Haven't met a person yet that I couldn't turn into a surfer."

"Especially the pretty ones, eh, Ro?" Sara winked.

Jacqueline blushed slightly.

This is horrible. They're totally embarrassing me and her.

"Perhaps you would like some more tea," Nana said, adeptly changing the subject.

"Oh, no, thank you. What is it that you're drinking?" Jacqueline asked Pearl.

"It's salt ale, a bit of a local specialty."

Sara added with a sly grin, "And a bit of an acquired taste. Wanna try?"

I started to shake my head to decline for her, but Rowan had already reached into the cooler and was handing the frosty bottle to Jacqueline. She accepted it and took a deep sip of the amber liquid, which immediately led to a coughing fit.

"Oh no," I stammered. "I'm so sorry, Jacqueline!" I handed her the glass of tea and a napkin.

Pearl, Rowan, and Sara stifled giggles. I burned with anger. The wind whipped across the porch in a gust, creating a sudden flurry of chips and unweighted napkins. The three culprits looked at me, and I scowled at their horrible prank.

Rowan regained his composure first. "Jacqueline, so sorry. It is a bit strong the first time. We should have given you proper warning. Let me get you some water." He stood up. "Storm, come on and lend me a hand."

The door had barely closed when I unleashed my anger on Rowan in a spitting whisper. "How dare you guys do that to her? She didn't know anything about salt ale."

"Stormy, relax," he whispered and attempted to hug me.

I burned with anger on behalf of Jacqueline, who was still making little coughs. *Mental note for future me: Not ever in the history of being told to relax did a person actually heed the words and relax. In fact, I'm pretty sure that simply saying the word* relax *makes the person about ten times more tense with a healthy dose of anger as well.*

"Look, it was just good fun, and—"

"Fun? *Fun*?" I glanced at the door and lowered my voice to a hiss. "You call making her choke on a drink only meant for mers because of its salt content—nearly equivalent to drinking seawater—fun?"

"Well, yeah, but also, now we can rule out mermaid."

"We can *what*? What are you talking about?"

"Stormy, we have no idea who Jacqueline is. She just waltzes into town, opens some hippie-dippie store that just happens to piss off Paige more than most, takes an immediate liking to you, and has no real backstory to share. All while you are being forced into a rematch to prove your place as heir to this territory. It's a little odd."

"So, what the heck do you think she is? Can't she just be a regular woman?"

"She might be, but she might not be." Rowan shrugged. "Now at least we can rule out mermaid." He filled a glass with ice and cold water. "Come on. Let's go help her get that taste out of her mouth." He chuckled again but stopped immediately when he saw my expression.

We walked back out to a totally normal scene, aside from a few quiet coughs from Jacqueline as she cleared her throat and sipped her tea. Mr. Humpphrey was just finishing retelling a story from his book.

"And that's the truth behind how the Fountain of Youth treasure came to be. Be this the truth or be me a liar..." Mr. Humpphrey started to quote his famous phrase.

"And I tell you, I ain't no liar," Jacqueline finished in a hoarse voice.

"Well, well, you really are a fan, my dear," Mr. Humpphrey said.

Rowan handed Jacqueline the ice water, and we both sat back down.

"Why, yes! I actually wanted to ask if you'd do me the honor of allowing my store to carry your book."

He smiled brightly. "Of course! I can drop a couple off and see if they sell. I haven't had much of a response when I've asked stores in town to carry it, and I basically stopped trying. The lighthouse, of course, carries copies, but that's mostly because Mr. Manistar is a close friend of both Rean and myself, and my connections with its history are rather, eh..." He glanced at Nana, and she smiled.

"They are rather deeply rooted," she finished.

"Well, all the more reason to get your book into more hands!" Jacqueline exclaimed. "But I won't hear of you dropping off a couple. I will need to buy one hundred from you to start, but I suspect that I will need to up the amount on the next order."

"That will be wonderful," he replied.

Finally back on track to having a nice time, I relaxed. I noticed Zelda sauntering across the dune. She hopped onto the deck railing and strode majestically to us.

"Hey, Zel." I reached out to let her rub her body past me on her journey to be greeted by her subjects.

I turned back and noticed a strange expression on Jacqueline's face.

Looking quickly around to make sure nobody had slipped her more salt ale, I saw everybody just chatting happily about nothing and everything. Everybody except for Jacqueline. She sat as if frozen, only her eyes making minuscule adjustments as she stared just past me. I looked back and saw only Zelda.

Greetings to Zelda could be heard by each person in turn. Zel floated down to the deck and wove between our legs. She sauntered over to the shade next to the house and stretched out. One exaggerated yawn later, she laid her head down on her crossed paws, and her eyes lowered to half-mast.

Conversations continued, but Jacqueline seemed distracted. Z asked about her time in New Guinea, and Jacqueline answered in halting sentences, every few moments glancing over her shoulder at Zelda.

Of course. I broke into their discussion. "Zelda's a Hemingway cat," I said to Jacqueline.

Jacqueline glanced at me with surprise.

"I saw you staring. She looks different because of the extra toes," I said with a little smile.

"Yes, quite true, Stormy. I'm guessing our new friend is unfamiliar with the polydactyl cats," Z said.

Sara added, looking at Jacqueline, "Yeah, sometimes you know something's weird or off, but can't quite put your finger on it."

"Ah, I couldn't, eh, I couldn't quite..." Jacqueline trailed off. "Well, I think I should be heading home. New business and all, lots to still sort out."

"Thank you for joining us," Nana said, surprise in her eyes.

"I hope you can come over again," Dad added.

"I would like that very much." Jacqueline stood up slowly, almost as if she didn't want to disturb a single molecule of air around her. "Storm, would you perhaps like to stop by the store tomorrow after your class? I have some new crystals that I think you'd be interested in."

"Yeah, that'd be great!" I replied, feeling giddy.

"But not too long, Stormy," Pearl said. "You have that study group tomorrow night, remember."

By "study group," she meant more training for the rematch. I now had to practice twice a day.

"Oh." My cheeks flushed with embarrassment. "I'm sure..."

"I won't keep her long." Jacqueline backed away from the table and continued slowly backing toward the stairs, all the while making glances in Zelda's direction. "Thank you again."

And with those words and only a foot or so separating Jacqueline from Zelda, the cat's eyes opened. The tip of her tail did a quick twitch in the air. Her eyes tracked Jacqueline as keenly as Jacqueline's eyes tracked Zelda. A low growl emanated from her feline body, the decibel level slowly building.

Sara looked over. "What's up, Zel?"

"Maybe there are birds nesting in the palm again," Pearl replied. "Sorry, Jacqueline. She's a keen birder."

"Oh, no problem." Jacqueline gave a nervous chuckle and continued toward the stairs. "Good night, all. And I do hope they find whoever caused that horrible destruction to such an important landmark. I mean, before any other place falls prey."

She tucked quickly around the corner.

"Well, that was fun." Rowan picked up glasses.

"Fun in a *what is she* kinda way." Sara popped open another salt ale.

"Did you see how she looked at us when asking about the lighthouse?" Pearl added.

"She was just asking about the lighthouse. Geez." I sighed.

"Storm, she is quite interesting, but we need to be cautious," Z said.

"Not a mermaid," Sara scoffed.

"Vampire?" Rowan asked.

"It's daytime, stupid," Pearl responded.

"And they don't exist." Sara laughed.

"Witch?" Pearl asked.

"Yup, witch," Sara replied.

"Enough with the witch thing," I said.

"Well, Stormy, she's not human," Rowan replied with a shrug.

"She's not... How do you...?"

"Well, I think she has a very good sense about her," Mr. Humpphrey said.

"Oh, Miles, you're just smitten because she likes your book." Nana laughed.

"Like I said, good sense." He nodded.

"Okay, children, till the morrow. We will work on determining if we treat Jacqueline as friend or foe, but for now, her presence doesn't affect our immediate tasks." Z stood and took her leave via the beach.

"Remember, bright and early, Stormy." Pearl gave me a nudge.

"It'll be fun, m'love. Tomorrow, you get to toss me about!" Rowan came back from the kitchen and wrapped me in a hug.

"Do I want to know?" Dad asked.

"No," Pearl replied with a laugh.

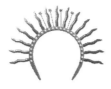

CHAPTER FOURTEEN
Love among the Stars

"I figured I'd find you here, m'love." Rowan sat next to me on the sand, which still held some of the day's heat.

Clever, Rowan, I thought sarcastically. *You found me at the edge of the ocean, where I go almost every night when I can't sleep.* I was still upset about how things had gone with Jacqueline's visit.

"Come on." He nudged me. "You aren't still mad, right?"

I opened my mouth to respond but then closed it. I didn't know what I was. I wasn't happy, but in truth, I also wasn't super mad. I was just tired and confused. I turned my gaze back to the water. A lone tear escaped.

"Oh, hey, don't cry," he said with concern.

"I'm *not*," I shot back and angrily swiped my damp cheek to erase the evidence.

He sighed and paralleled my gaze.

"I'm just frustrated… and overwhelmed… and I'm sucking at being a mermaid, and I'm sucking at being a human… and I'm sucking at being *anything to anybody*."

He replied in a deadpan voice, "That's a lot of sucking. I see why you're upset."

"Rowan, I'm serious. I watch you guys. Like, tonight, you were all just having fun—I get it. But I'm not like that. I don't *just have fun* and act goofy all the time. Laverna's probably right. I'm *not* mer enough."

Rowan nodded slowly. "And the human suckiness you mentioned…?"

"Ever since Vincent, I've wondered how I can protect Jon. And honestly, I don't think I can. I can't protect my best friend, so I've tried to stay away from him so I don't accidentally put him in danger. And then I try to make a new friend, and you guys all bash her! I can't win."

"Okay, let's start with your human failings." Rowan turned to me. I reluctantly met his eyes. "In my opinion, protecting Jon doesn't come down to just you. Jon needs all of us because the truth is, he's in great danger. Vincent has a target now. But honestly, I'm not sure any of us can totally protect him from Vincent. The display we witnessed isn't even a third of his power."

"Wow, Rowan. Thanks for the pep talk. I feel way better." I shook my head.

"Babe, listen. You asked for things not to be kept from you."

I nodded slowly. "Why Jon?"

It was Rowan's turn to give a snort, but his was more of a half laugh. "Sprites have big issues when it comes to humans."

"Like what?"

"Sprites are freshwater beings, and humans—while their treatment of the oceans has been pretty horrific, even I admit it has nothing compared to how they've exploited, polluted, rerouted, and overall just completely ignored natural processes when it comes to freshwater sources around the earth."

"So Vincent hates humans because we—they—*whatever* have caused pollution?" I asked.

"Yes."

"But that's not fair."

"What's not fair?"

"Well, Jon hasn't done that. He's not *all* humans," I said.

"He is when he's dating Vincent's daughter."

"Oh."

"Yeah."

"That's bad."

"Yup," Rowan said.

"What happens next?"

"Jon dies."

"Wow! Thanks, Rowan. You really helped me out tonight. I feel sooo much better, jerk," I said with heavy sarcasm and clenched my fist.

"Whoa, hang on. I'm just saying that Vincent is an admirable foe," Rowan replied with his arms raised in surrender. "But to be fair, Jon died once, and that turned out okay, so…"

I opened and closed my mouth like a fish out of water as I struggled to come up with a nonviolent response. Rowan, seeing my rage build, hopped up and ran into the oncoming waves.

Smart move. I followed slowly, wading into the waist-deep water. *This conversation isn't over.*

I know, he replied in my head. *I just thought it safer if I could be well beyond the reach of my beloved as we hashed out the details.*

Well played, sir, I thought to the dark waters around me.

I swam out and down, found the outgoing current, and let it sweep me away. Of all the troubles in my world, sinking into the depths wasn't one of them. The ocean embraced me and carried me onward in silence.

There you are, my little flotsam. Rowan's arms wrapped around my prone body.

I opened my eyes and saw only the deepest of blue, nearly black, stretch in front of me. I played with closing one eye and then the other. The view was still clear with my eye and blurry with Lilli's.

Floating at the whim of the current felt fabulous. The water washed away my stresses and fears. I became weightless in both body and mind. The problems of the land receded as I drifted farther away. I sighed and wondered why I should even go back. Pearl was there, and now Z. I was pretty much just extra at this point. They would do a much better job protecting Jon and the town with me not there. Laverna wouldn't need a rematch or whatever she was planning to make me do.

Rowan's arms squeezed tightly, and his body copied my curves and subtle movements.

As for Jacqueline, well, that's us trying to keep you safe, Storm.

Can we just float away, Rowan?

No, m'dear, but on the bright side, I think we just sorted out one of the big issues you're worried about.

What do you mean? I asked.

I don't think a nonmer could be doing what we're doing right now.

I chuckled lightly. *Well, yeah, I guess, but...*

Nope, not a single "but," my rainbow fish. You, m'love, are a mer through and through. And can I tell you a secret?

I nodded. My hair mimicked the gesture in slow motion.

I love all of your parts—human, mer, and everything in between. He leaned in and gave me a kiss.

Thanks. I love you too. Now can we just float away?

Rowan gave me a squeeze. *No, m'dear.*

But how come? We could just go away. You and me. No them, no dangers, no responsibility, no... anything. I wrapped my arms around his as they crossed over my chest. *We'd never have to go back. We could just...*

My love. We have more that needs to be done, and you are just the one to help do it.

But why? I asked.

Because you're Storm.

Please stop saying that. Everybody has been saying that since I first arrived here. I've only made a mess of things. And if I go back, I'm bound to make a bigger mess. Trust me.

Why do you think that? he asked.

Ha. Because I'm Storm.

Touché.

I spun in his arms so that the front of our bodies aligned and our eyes were mere inches apart. His were so bright, a blue flame contrasting with the blue-black water holding us in suspension.

I'm not what everybody thinks. I'm half of each, which is worse than just being all of one. I don't fully fit in anywhere! I've had my hand held in everything I've done. Jon helps me in class, Pearl helps me in training. Even the solstice—Laverna's right. Without Lilli's help...

My eyes burned with the tears, which mixed with the seawater. I closed them and slumped into Rowan's arms, defeated by my own negative thoughts.

I can't even polarize without the stupid magnetic rock, I added.

Babe, you are one of a kind... literally. Nobody has any idea what you're capable of or what your limits are. Learning and getting help isn't a bad thing. It means you're listening to those who know more right now, but at some point, the student does *become the teacher.*

I sighed, unconvinced, but his words sank in little by little, and I did start feeling better, despite my best efforts to stay sullen.

Come here. Rowan put a hand behind my head and lifted it back up. He kissed me. Somewhere between ocean floor and surface waves, in the place that was still, two intertwined bodies floated, specks within the embrace of the mighty Atlantic.

He stopped first. I opened my eyes, and he smiled.

Okay, babe. Let's head back before the search party hunts us down.

While no part of me wanted to listen to him, I knew he was right. Running away wasn't an option, but...

On one condition. I looked at him.

Yes?

We do this every day. We escape for a little bit every day. Okay?

Deal.

And we kiss, I added.

Well, now, that would be a second condition. He raised his right eyebrow.

Ah, yeah, okay, you're right, we shouldn't.

But I totally agree, Rowan finished quickly with a flash of teeth then released his hold. *I have an idea!* With a quick kiss, he slid out from beneath me, flipped over with beautiful grace, and shot forward with a powerful kick. *Come on! A little field trip before I tuck you in!*

I sped up to match his pace. *Where're we goin'?*

To one of my favorite places. He gave me a sideways glance and then his famous impish wink.

I shook my head. *This should be good.*

It is!

When we passed Salt Run, I figured we were heading to the fort, but he veered right instead of left. As we got closer to the shoreline, lights from town shimmered below the surface like underwater stars. He took us through narrow Hospital Creek and past Bird Island.

The cross? I thought.

Nope.

Sure enough, when I snuck a peek above the surface, the cross was behind us.

Hey, no cheating, he scolded and pulled my leg.

Okay, sorry. I giggled.

We crossed the basin and then headed up another narrow passage. Rowan slowed, and we hugged the seawall. He motioned for me to wait as he lifted his head above the water. He gave me the okay to join him.

When I broke the surface next to him, it took me a moment to figure out where we were. But then I made out the moonlit silhouettes on the large lawn.

"The Fountain of Youth?" I whispered.

"Yes."

"Why here?"

"You'll see."

We climbed onto the seawall. The thick, humid air, scented with night-blooming jasmine, draped over us. Rowan walked over a few feet to a large wooden lookout tower. He reached behind one of the beams and opened a wooden box. He returned with a small backpack. He unzipped it and pulled out a chamois towel.

"I know." He smiled, handing me the towel. "I would have made a great Boy Scout. What is it they say? Always be prepared?"

"Yeah." I laughed softly. "Something like that."

"But wait, there's more!" He took the towel back and placed a thin piece of black fabric in my hand. I unfolded it and saw that it was a sarong. He had one also. He winked, and we both wrapped the sarongs around our waists. I heard a small pop, and then he handed me a bottle of salt ale.

"A little energy replacement for after the night swim," he said with a smile. "Okay to share one? I have two if you want the whole thing."

"Sharing is fine," I answered but couldn't help taking a long sip.

"Ahem. Does sharing mean something different to a mer raised by humans?" Rowan whispered with a light laugh.

I smiled with the bottle still at my lips and then handed it to him. He finished the rest and then put the empty bottle back into the backpack, closed the zipper, and tucked the bag away. He motioned for me to follow him.

Gosh, there is something so sexy about a man in a sarong. So far, this little field trip is very enjoyable. I smiled to myself. I followed Rowan closely but struggled to keep my mind focused now that I was distracted by him in his sarong.

"Storm, check it out." Rowan's hushed voice brought me back from my fantasy. I blushed at where my mind had been going.

Following the direction he was pointing, I saw them. I closed my mer eye and got a very clear view with Lilli's eye. A cluster of sleeping peacocks and peahens snuggled beneath a low, twisting branch of one of the towering live oaks that speckled the property. I'd only ever seen them in the day as they strutted about the grounds. The birds made little squeaks of contentment while they slept.

"Where are we going?" I whispered.

"To one of the most magical spots in St. Augustine," Rowan whispered back.

"The most magical spot in St. Augustine is at a tourist attraction?"

"This place is so much more than a tourist spot. It's filled with history and stories so amazing that even Miles couldn't enhance them!"

I rolled my eyes. "Okaaay." I laughed and then under my breath said, "I was pretty sure the magical fountain was regular tap water disguised as a spring."

Rowan stopped walking. He gave me a half smile. "I sense doubt, Stormy. Yes, this is a tourist spot, but it *is* founded in magic. The Timucua Indians knew this. And for your information, the water *does* come from the spring that is part of the aquifer below the spring house. Tap water from a hose? Seriously, Storm, this is how rumors get started."

His eyes glimmered with joy, and he picked up the pace. His excitement was palpable, like a toddler on Christmas morning. After we crossed the expansive Settlement Field, he pulled me into the shadow of the mission church. A light bobbed in the distance.

"Night security," Rowan murmured as we crouched low. "Never used to have them, but then these crazy humans started believing there was buried treasure here."

"Seriously? Like pirate stuff?"

He chuckled, deep and soft. "No, more of a treasure hunt. And truth be told, I may have had something to do with people believing the prize was here." He shook his head a little and then, with a shrug, said, "It seemed funny at the time."

"You are definitely going to have to tell me more about that later," I whispered.

The flashlight strolled on, bobbing with each methodical step of the guard.

"Okay, we should be good. It takes him forty minutes to circle the grounds." Rowan stood and brought me up with him.

Peacock-inspired arching metal gates were on our right as we passed the Spring House. *Not there*, I thought.

We passed Discovery Globe. We were running out of Fountain of Youth property. I looked up with questioning eyes. He gave my hand a squeeze. Then, a few yards shy of the picket fence that bordered the tree-laden Magnolia Street and formed the western boundary of the park, he stopped in front of a building.

"The planetarium?" I whispered.

"Yes! Come on! Just wait until you see this!" He pulled me excitedly toward the entrance.

Rowan took a deep breath in front of the door. I had no idea why. All I smelled was brine, wet grass, and dirt. He jiggled the handle a bit, and the door creaked open—the level of security you'd expect for a place nobody would want to break into.

Once inside, he took another deep breath and let out a satisfied sigh. I inhaled, too, but far from satisfied, my nostrils were accosted by stale, moldy air. This building was more of a relic than an exhibit, in my opinion. At some point, it might have been cool, but like the orange wallpaper that hung in our family room in Indiana, it screamed 1970s.

He led me to the center of the dark room.

"Here, lie down. Yeah, right here. Okay, one sec."

He disappeared into the alcoves. I heard some clicks and thunks, and then suddenly, stars appeared overhead. Well, not really stars, but lights made to look like the night sky, all bright and twinkly.

I waited. There had to be more.

Rowan returned and snuggled next to me on the carpeted floor. I tried not to think about the last time the carpet had been cleaned. He let out a sigh of pure contentment.

I waited. After a minute or two had elapsed in silence, and I was pretty sure there wasn't an actual cool thing about to happen, I rolled to my side and faced him. He stared intently at the fake night sky. I glanced back up at it and then back at him.

"So, this is great," I whispered. "Thanks."

His bright-blue eyes glowed in my direction, and then they narrowed. "You don't see it?"

"See what?"

"The magic."

"Umm, I mean, I, well, I uh... think it's pretty." Nana and I often went outside back in Indiana to gaze at the stars, but these weren't real stars. They were lights. I was confused.

I sat up and looked down at his prone body. His ankles were crossed like when we swam.

"Storm, this is the sky of my youth! This is the night sky from the second day of April of the year 1513! We are looking up at the sky I saw when I was a boy. This is a sky of memories. This is a sky of dreams and plans and tales not yet told. This is the sky before the Hurricane Lady existed, the sky before Laverna and Z were at war, the sky before... before I devoted my life to protection."

He spoke so passionately that I had no response. This magical being fascinated by a small-town replica of the night sky from a few hundred years ago literally left me speechless.

"This is the sky of easier times." Rowan sighed.

"Well, not for Ponce or the Timucuans," I said. "This was the last night they had before they were invaded."

He looked at me and then back at the sky. "Who cares about the humans, Storm? Mers, sprites, and all those born into the water existed in peace and clarity. You think Vincent would have it out for Jon right now if he wasn't holding onto a major grudge against the destruction of our serenity—a grudge hundreds of years in the making? This is the one place I can go and pretend it's then and not now. Pretend my life is as free as it was and my goals could be my own rather than revolving around a statue. And at least the Timucuans cared about the earth and this spring."

"Oh, I didn't realize you hated this place and time so much," I mumbled, hurt by his words.

"No, Stormy, it's not that. It's just mers are meant to have fun, and I have to say, all this drama over territory and humans and heirs is getting very heavy."

"Sorry." I started to stand.

"C'mon, rainbow fish." He reached up and grabbed my hand. "I'm trying to show you a time that was simple and fun. You said yourself you wish you could just have fun like we do. Well, one way I do it is to remember! I remember a time when my biggest challenge was trying to outsmart my sisters or see how high I could jump out of the water while trying to catch falling stars."

"I guess this time is hard, and a lot of it has to do with my kind."

Rowan stood up next to me and drew me in for a hug. "Well, only half of your kind, but yeah, a lot has changed in the past few hundred years. But I think we're the ones who can fix it, right? Get us back on track to having fun and maybe have clean water to swim in."

I looked up from his cool, salty chest. "Why did you try to catch falling stars?"

"I always wanted to fly, like up in the sky, and I thought if I could catch a falling star, I could hitch a ride."

"Fly... a mer who wants to fly." I chuckled. "That's as weird as..."

"A human who breathes underwater?"

"Half human," I corrected.

"Well, you always wanted to swim, right?"

"Actually, no, I was terrified of the water."

"Well, once you found out you wouldn't die..."

"Yeah, okay, I kinda see your point. Having mer swimming abilities is amazing."

"And I think flying would be amazing," he said.

"Isn't there some kind of mer that flies? I thought we read about it in mythology."

"I don't think so, but maybe."

"How about when we solve all the problems here, and I win the stupid Laverna challenge thing, we go hang gliding. Then you can be a mer that flies!"

"Deal. So, no more wanting to run away?"

I shuffled my feet back and forth. "No. You're right. We may not have started this mess, but we need to end it."

"What was that?" Rowan asked with a playful look.

"What?"

"You said I was right?"

I laughed. "Yes, Rowan. I did."

"Well, *now* this is a magical night!"

He leaned down and gave me a beautifully slow, warm kiss. And at that moment, I didn't care what year we were in. Time seemed to stand still.

"We can stay a little longer if you want," I said. He smiled, and we lay back down in the quiet with our fingers intertwined. I sighed. "I do wish I could have been here with you when these stars were in the sky."

"Well, I'll tell you a secret." Rowan leaned his head so it touched mine and extended his arm to point at the ceiling. "Do you see that star?"

"Which one?" I giggled.

"The one the big dipper looks like it's pointing to."

"Yeah."

"Humans call it the North Star."

"O-kay," I answered, not understanding his point.

"The other stars and constellations rise and fall and move over the years and centuries, but that one doesn't, at least it hasn't in *my* lifetime, which is a long time. Perhaps Z has experienced a difference, but not me. So, m'dear, that star is the one we share."

I smiled and squeezed his hand. "So it's out there right now?"

"Yes, it is. That's the one to find if you ever need to get back home… to me."

I rolled my head to look at him. He winked and leaned in for another kiss. I didn't object.

Knowing that we couldn't stay all night, we reluctantly disentangled ourselves. Rowan did his entry actions in reverse, starting with turning off the stars and then leading me in the dark out to the exit door. Once he closed the door behind us, we quickly checked for the wandering flashlight. With it nowhere in sight, we started back toward the waterway. I realized I kind of missed the moldy smell of the planetarium.

"Hey, Ro, I get why you like the smell in there. It's—"

Rowan put a finger to his mouth to signal silence. I listened to the night. Mixed with the hum of cicadas and higher-pitched mosquitos, hushed voices drifted out of the mission church.

Rowan's glowing eyes glanced at me. I nodded to let him know I'd heard them too. Like two apparitions, we snuck up to the side of the old church. The aged beams were far from soundproof, but having extra-gifted hearing didn't hurt. Rowan and I crept closer to the corner near the front doors, where we crouched and listened.

A deeply masculine voice, which struck a faint memory, said, "Make it worth my while."

This was followed by a beautifully feminine voice with a hypnotic chime. "I have never wasted your time, nor mine."

Rowan and I turned toward each other and simultaneously mouthed, "Laverna."

"You and I both know my dear sister has failed you." Laverna spoke in a low, even tone.

"You brought me to this filthy human dwelling to tell me the obvious?" the male responded with agitation. A crackling blue light flared briefly out the barely open door.

That blue light, that voice...

"Oh, Vincent, please. Always so prone to dramatic flair," Laverna said.

"Vincent," Rowan and I mouthed to each other. My brain started to spin tales, but I quieted it so I could concentrate on the faint voices.

"I believe we could give each other what we most desire." Laverna's voice moved from left to right. She was probably pacing around the room. "You want Lilli protected and away from that human boy."

"And you...?"

"I simply want my rightful territory returned to me." She sounded so innocent.

"How am I to help with that, and how are you to help with my Lilli?"

"Tell her, Mum," someone else said.

I recoiled back into Rowan's curved form. That voice was as unmistakable as Laverna's. It belonged to her disgusting son, Daniel. I'd known he was up to no good when I spotted him at the drum circle. My belly tightened, and my breathing became shallow.

Rowan's long fingers curled around my arm. I turned back, and his eyes begged me to calm down. He glanced upward and then back at me. I looked up. The once-clear sky had clouded over. Lightning danced between the developing storm clouds. Taking the hint, I took a deep breath and let it out slowly. My heart rate slowed, and my pulse calmed. A ruffle of feathers above us was the only sound that punctuated the air.

"Patience, my beautiful son," Laverna said. I threw up a little in my mouth.

The threesome walked to the front door and moved out into the still night. We remained in position and listened to the mers as they drifted around the far corner.

"Vincent, with your continued help, we can remove the nuisance humans from this area as well as give me back what is mine. In turn, I will help you keep precious Lilli on her correct path. We, of course, know what is best for her."

"Be sure you do, or the deal may not last. I will be watching. I have eyes in many places, and you are not my only proposition," Vincent replied.

"But of course you can trust us. We are each other's means to the end we both desire."

"So you say." Vincent took a step back. There was a sharp *crack*, and light glowed through the gaps in the wood.

"It is done," Laverna said with satisfaction.

"Is it?" Daniel asked. "I thought you said to never trust sprites."

"I did, and you shouldn't. Which is why he is unaware of our other plans and allegiances. 'I am not his only proposition,'" Laverna said, mimicking Vincent. "Well, he isn't ours either."

"Ooh, Mummy, do tell!"

"Come, my handsome boy. I will tell you a tale of flight and fancy."

The two willowy shapes flowed away before we could hear any more. Once we were sure they'd left, we crept forward and peered around the corner of the building. We were back alone in the darkness. Well, except for the security guard, who shouted in the distance, "There is no treasure!"

"Let's go," Rowan whispered, and we ran to the safety of the water.

CHAPTER FIFTEEN
Eyes in the Sky

The merman and mermaid crouched next to the old building. Her view, however, was not from her hiding place among the shadows but rather from far out on a limb overlooking the scene.

Thank the heavens for my second set of eyes. So much had been taken from her and her kind. The insults were compounded by the stupid creatures she'd observed here tonight. Her story, her rightful history, taken over by them... *them!* She frowned in disgust.

But that will change soon, she consoled herself. *I am so very close.* The magic of this land was palpable. Her task did not daunt her. The humans were of no concern to her, and while one should never trust a sprite, she felt confident she could use him properly. And the mers...

Those horrible parasites deserve to suffer after the way they snuck into my story and took it over. They need to be finally given their just desserts and kicked out from the story they stole. I will fly again, and I will reclaim my history. Just wait until they are annihilated and are nothing more than a memory, a sidenote, an oblique reference.

She opened her eyes and squinted at the two crouching figures.

This current situation is quite the trifecta. Sprites wanting to push out humans and mers to reclaim their long-lost spring, mers not knowing the sprites' true desires and—as mers often are—completely absorbed in their own petty squabbles, and me... right in the middle to manipulate them all, like the master puppeteer in my beautifully choreographed marionette play.

She smirked.

Her thin tunic billowed about her pants with a sudden burst of wind.

The merman and mermaid looked at each other, and the wind stopped. A soft ruffle of feathers above her brought her back from her joyful thoughts of destruction. She looked up and saw a shining dark eye on her.

"Sorry," she mouthed and closed her eyes to watch from above.

The scene changed. The sprite who she'd agreed to help with the removal of the mers stood in front of the door, speaking to a merman and mermaid. The mermaid was the one with whom she'd also agreed to remove the sprites and other mers. They didn't know she knew both sides, nor that each side planned to double-cross the other.

Oh, how easy it would be to reveal the two crouching. Just a tiny sound, perhaps that of a strange bird, to draw the attention of the pair just steps away. The eyes in the sky felt her emotions and retreated from the branch's edge. He floated down and landed softly on her shoulder and looked at her with a head tilt.

Meeting his eye, she reconsidered. *You are correct. Now is not the time.*

She and her feathered passenger retreated farther from the building and left the gathering to its own devices. But there was one more thing to be done prior to calling this a good night. She lifted a backpack, reached inside, and pulled out a full amber bottle. She manipulated the bottle slowly between her long fingers.

"These opportunities are just presenting themselves to us. It would be a shame to not take advantage of them. We shall see how they like their vile salt ale now," she whispered to her companion.

The bird hooked his beak onto the bottle cap and easily popped the top off. He leaned into her cheek and fluffed his feathers as he watched her tip the bottle over. The liquid cascaded to the sandy earth. Once it was empty, they retreated silently past the slumbering peafowl.

"Let's go deliver this gift to our little sprite. He will know what to do." She smiled, knowing the mers would pay for their childish behavior. *We will take over this nest.*

CHAPTER SIXTEEN
Picking Sides

You seem distracted, Storm, Pearl commented after I tried and failed at magnetizing the surfboard... again. Rowan sat on top this time because Sara was with Paige downtown. The early-morning light gave the light-green water near the surface a golden hue.

No, I'm fine, I lied.

I *was* distracted. My mind flipped between worries about Nana's doctor's appointment, Jon's danger with Vincent, and my rematch. Also, my head ached.

Why am I doing this again? I asked in frustration.

This is the normal training for all mers, Storm. It's just that you're getting a later start than most, so we have to put in more time than usual. A crash course, so to speak. I'm not sure what the rematch will entail, but it's probably going to be harder than last time since Laverna wants to make a point. And remember, no helpers are allowed.

Rowan's head popped below the surface, and his hair fanned out like a crown. *You're doing great, m'love. You'll totally get this!* He gave a big grin then sat back up. His dangling feet swooshed slowly in small semicircles.

With a sigh, I tried for the hundredth time to move Rowan's board. Step one, rub the black stone down my one arm, palm, and fingers. Step two, raise that arm straight out toward the object you want to move. Step thr—

Guys, come quickly! Sara's voice reverberated in my head.

I spun around, my arm still extended, and bumped into her chest with my palm. She folded in half, let out an *Oomph*, and flew backward through the water.

Pearl swam to me and wrapped me in a hug. *Storm! That was great! You totally did it!*

Rowan ducked under again. *What happened? What was great?*

That was crazy. It was like a current just whooshed through me. Crazy cool, I thought to Pearl and Rowan, a giant smile on my face.

I'm fine—thanks for asking. Sara swam slowly back to us.

Wasn't that amazing, sis? Pearl still had her arm around my waist.

Yeah, really great. Sara's tone implied less. *Anyway, if we can pause on the training for a sec, you guys have to come to the Fountain of Youth. It's mayhem over there. Come on.*

What's going on? Rowan asked from above.

I'll explain on the way, Sara said. *Ditch the board and catch up. Safest if we go by water.*

******

It was high tide when we arrived at the seawall along the edge of the Fountain of Youth property. Holding lightly to the riprap and carefully avoiding the razor-sharp oysters, we hovered at eye level and peered across the expansive lawn. The same peacocks and peahens that Rowan and I had snuck past the night before strutted about in the bright morning light, making mournful cries to one another. Red-and-blue lights flashed in the distance.

Sara motioned with a finger to her ear. We stayed silent and listened to the distant conversations.

A shrill female voice shouted, "This is unacceptable, Officer Rollins! First the lighthouse was vandalized and now the Fountain of Youth. These criminals need to be caught, and we need justice!"

"Ma'am, we are looking into whether there is any connection between the two events. Please be patient."

"Patient? I think I've been patient, and now, despite the fact that we hired a night guard, hooligans have managed to spray-paint the brand-new events hall, leave broken glass around, and molest the peacocks!"

"Ma'am, I don't believe any of the birds were molested. They may have been overfed by perpetrators who filled the hall with peanuts and Tic Tacs, but I believe they are all okay."

I caught Rowan's eye. *We were just here last night. Nothing was weird.*

"What do you mean you guys were here last night?" Pearl whispered and glared at both of us with a look that turned my insides to ice.

I winced and opened my mouth to speak, but no sound came out. I closed it again.

Pearl said, "Come on—we're going home. On the way, you two can explain to me what the hell you were doing because this won't look good for our clan if anybody saw you two."

I suddenly realized that seeing Pearl truly angry was terrifying.

The four of us swam from the inlet in a single file. *It wasn't anything bad, Pearl,* Rowan started. *I wanted to show Storm the planetarium. You know, the stars.*

I know what a planetarium is, Rowan, Pearl shot back.

I was upset with Nana's doctor stuff, and Rowan thought a little swim would help me relax, I added.

Ah, so just a little swim, then, Stormy? You snuck out, and now you both were at the Fountain of Youth when someone vandalized it in a similar fashion to how we covered up our tracks at the lighthouse.

Humans don't know it was us, Sara replied calmly.

No, but mers do, and they weren't pleased that we made such a large demonstration to hide what happened. They understood the necessity and were willing to turn a blind eye, but us existing here safely—all of us— depends on our being able to hide in plain sight. Our little lighthouse stunt, my dearest sister, was far from lying low. And now they will see another one. Eerily similar. This isn't good no matter how we look at it. This all points directly at our clan and right before we're meant to defend our right to remain in control of this town!

Pearl swam the rest of the way silently, or at least she blocked us from her thoughts. The silence was even more horrible than being yelled at. We arrived back in front of the yellow house while the sun was still low and the early-morning surfers were just finishing their sets. We drip-dried our way up the wide beach toward the dunes. Pearl still hadn't spoken to us, with her mind or out loud. When we got close to home, I noticed three figures standing on the deck. They watched us approaching.

"Well, this isn't going to be good." Sara sighed and grabbed her sarong that hung over the railing of the stairs.

"It has been brought to my attention that some damage has been reported at the Fountain of Youth," Z announced before our feet even landed on the top step. On the table behind her was Rowan's backpack.

Pearl spoke first. "I believe there is some kind of mistake happening. It wasn't…"

"So none of you were at the Fountain of Youth last night?"

Z looked every bit of her five-foot, eleven-inch height. Her red hair shone like a flame in the morning sun. I wanted to shrink out of existence. Pearl started to say something, but Z held her hand out in a motion to stop.

"Need I remind you, daughter, lying or attempting to define the truth of others through lies is as draining as swimming at depth too long," Z said.

Pearl didn't reply.

Z turned her attention to Rowan. "Is this your backpack?" She motioned to the bag on the table. It was the same one Rowan had kept our stuff in at the Fountain of Youth.

Rowan nodded.

"Have you noticed it missing recently or perhaps stolen?"

Rowan shook his head.

"That's a pity, because this bag was found in the dumpster by the

Fountain of Youth with two damp towels, two black sarongs, one empty bottle of salt ale, and two empty cans of spray paint."

"What? No, I, we—" Rowan started but Z held her hand out again.

"I was informed by members of a certain clan that two people matching your and Storm's descriptions were seen sneaking around in the dark at the Fountain of Youth last night." Z looked back and forth between the two of us. "You both were there, weren't you?"

Rowan and I looked at each other but didn't answer.

"You should know by now that I never ask a question I don't already know the answer to. Now, I believe you owe me a tale." She sat down in a lounge chair, her white dress wrapped around her long, lean legs. Nana and Matthew took seats at the table. "Let's start, shall we?"

"Ugh, kill me," I muttered.

******

"So that's it, really. I wanted to take Storm's mind off Rean's diagnosis, the competition, and other stuff, so I showed her my stars. We shared a salt ale, but we didn't have any spray paint," Rowan concluded.

Z nodded slowly. "I believe you both, but it certainly puts us in a precarious place. The Lionfish believe our clan had something to do with this new destruction due to its similarities to the first, and they are rightfully concerned. I will try to calm their fears, but for now..." She looked at us slowly in turn. "All. Of. You. Keep your heads low and your hands to yourself." Her gaze lingered on Rowan and me. My cheeks burned.

"Go get changed for the day. Pearl and Sara, I have some calming of angry clan members for you both to take care of. Rowan, I will also be requiring your help. Storm, have a good day at class, and I'll see you this evening for practice."

"Whh... aat?" I stammered. *I'm practicing with Z?*

"Yes, Storm. I thought it was time you and I had some one-on-one time. See you tonight."

We all dispersed in our different directions. Nana caught up to me at the stairs inside. "Storm, please go straight to class and straight back here today. I'm very disappointed in you sneaking out."

My hackles rose. "It was just once."

I already got yelled at by Pearl, then Z, and now Nana has to kick a girl when she's down. I already feel bad about what I did. Can't they all just stop talking about it?

"You need to be smarter than that. This is not the time to—"

"To what? To have fun? To be a teenager? To try to forget for one moment that you might have cancer, that I have to prove myself again to Laverna, that Jon may die... *again*, and that nobody likes a new friend I made?" Hot tears slid down my cheeks.

"This is not the time to be foolish," she said calmly. "Home straight from class today."

"But I'm supposed to go to Jacqueline's store."

"Not today," she replied in her there-is-no-argument tone.

"But..."

Her right eyebrow inched higher than her left, daring me to continue. I responded in the only way I knew how—I stomped up the stairs as loudly as I could.

******

"You're super quiet, Storm. Everything okay?" Jon asked after the professors let us break into groups to work on our papers.

"Yeah... no." I sighed. The morning was extra humid, and my water wasn't salty enough. Even though I didn't feel like what I'd done was that bad, I still felt guilty and angry and frustrated.

"*Ugh*, there's no breeze back here at all," I whined and fanned my thick braid in the hopes that it would provide some relief.

Jon looked around. "I'm sorry. Umm, does it have to do with the uh, the... rematch?"

"Yeah, kinda, but also, well, did you hear about the Fountain of Youth?"

"Of course! I can't believe it! It was so much like the light—" He stopped in midsentence and lowered his voice to a whisper, "Oh my God. You guys didn't..."

"No!" I protested an octave too high. "That's the thing. I guess people think we did because of the lighthouse. But we didn't, I swear."

"Well, good. Folks are really upset. Kinda setting up to be a witch hunt for the people doing these things."

"It's not fair. I mean, it wasn't us, but because Rowan and I were there last night."

"Whoa, wait, did anybody see you?" Jon asked.

"Someone told Laverna, who told Z, but I dunno who."

"Geez, Storm. Be careful. The locals are looking for someone to blame. And well, while your family has been here a long time, you haven't, and I would hate..."

"What? Hate *what*?"

"Well, to have people think you were involved somehow."

Growing more irritated, I said, "I told you, it wasn't us. I think it's Laverna's clan."

"Why would they have done it?"

"To frame us. To mess me up, I'm not sure, but I know Laverna and Daniel are pissed off that I succeeded at the solstice. That's why they're making me do a rematch. I think they're just stacking the cards in their favor. They'll make up some crazy-hard challenge for me but, on the off chance I can do the tests, have a backup of everybody hating me. Like you said—a witch hunt, the result being my clan would get kicked out of here." Tears welled in my eyes.

"No, even if Laverna thought of something like that, Paige wouldn't go along with it," Jon said. "She seems cool, you know? Like she even kinda likes you or respects you or something."

"Well, she did ask me for help with Jacqueline," I answered with a little sniffle. The tears retreated.

"What about Suzee?" Jon nodded toward the upstairs window.

"What about her?"

"Well, she's a Lionfish. Maybe she's setting you up." He shrugged.

"Nah. I mean, well, maybe." My mind spun. *Really? Was Suzee just playing me?*

Before we could discuss more, Samantha plopped down next to us on the grass under the tree. "Hi, guys!" she said happily. "I found a bunch of articles we can use on the Hurricane Lady paper. I went ahead and made copies for all of us." She handed a small stack to me and Jon. "Storm, I know you missed the trip to see the statue the other day. Do you want to go after class to see it in person?"

"Oh, no, I'm good. I've, eh, seen it before with Jon." I nudged him lightly with my elbow.

"Yeah, I took her there to see it earlier in the summer." He smiled.

"Okay, cool. I just think we really need to include a good description of how she looks now compared to how she originally looked, you know, before the restoration."

"Storm, remind me to talk to you about that," Jon whispered.

"What?" I mouthed.

"The restoration—something I found." Then, in his normal voice, Jon said, "I read that they're going to move her in the fall." He flipped through the sheets of paper.

"Oh, I heard the nuns talking when we were over there. The statue is getting switched super soon. That's why I asked if Storm wanted to see her."

"Switched?" I asked.

"That's what they said. I figured they meant her location, but maybe they meant her dress," Samantha replied without raising her eyes from her article. "So yeah, Jon, you may be right. Maybe they aren't moving her but just switching her outfit."

I looked up when a movement in the window of the main house caught my attention. Suzee's bright-green eyes glowed through a slit in the intricate antique lace curtain. Then they dimmed as she slipped back into the darkness of the room.

We left the lawn at the end of class, and I walked with Samantha and Jon north down Aviles toward the town center. They had parked in the parking garage, so they said goodbye and made their way across the square. The scooter was back in the opposite direction, but I didn't want to go there yet. Nana had said to come straight home, but I had to at least tell Jacqueline that I couldn't hang out.

"Hey there, Storm," Paige called, startling me. She laughed. "Didn't mean to scare you."

"I, uh, no, my mind was somewhere else," I stammered and walked across the narrow street to where she sat on a mosaic bench.

Even though I hadn't been technically doing anything wrong, I felt like I'd been caught in a lie. I wasn't supposed to be going where I was going, and Paige had just seen me. But she didn't know I was grounded, so this strange anxiety wasn't based on anything real.

"Were you heading to the store? We got in some rather fabulous new dresses."

"I was heading back to the scooter. Class just ended," I said, which was a half-truth.

"Okay." She stood up. "Well, stop by soon."

I smiled as she walked back across the road and went into her store. My heart pounded, and my temple throbbed. *Geez, Storm. Get a grip.*

With an eye roll directed at myself, I also crossed the street, but I continued past Paige's store and stopped at the mosaic glass door three buildings down. I glanced behind me. The only observer was a small white bird preening its feathers while sitting on a palm frond.

I opened the door and ducked inside.

CHAPTER SEVENTEEN
Truths and Lies

"I'm excited to spend time with you this evening, Storm," Z said as we made our way to the water's edge. "Pearl tells me how well you're doing with magnetism, and once you've mastered that, the rest is so much simpler."

The evening was warm, but for some reason, I shivered. I smiled and concentrated on subduing the anxious fluttering in my belly.

I am practicing in front of Z. I've never practiced in front of her. Z is Z! Oh my God! my mind yelled. On the outside, I continued to smile. And nod. And walk, putting one foot in front of the other.

I've got this. I took a deep breath.

I haven't got this. My shoulders slumped in defeat as I exhaled.

I followed Z through the froth near the shore, and then we floated over some low waves. Z shook her long red hair behind her shoulders. Her bikini-clad body cut easily through the water. She looked just like a normal, albeit beautiful, young woman enjoying a sunset swim. This was the first time I was seeing Z as anything other than the formidable and intimidating leader that she was. Watching her smile and float in the chest-deep water, I thought she could have been any young woman playing in the setting sun.

Z, the matriarch of my clan, hundreds of years old—if not older, I thought. *Hmm, speaking of older, who is older, Z or Laverna?*

Her chest-deep water became my head-deep water since she had a good few inches on me, so I dove first. I swam forward on my own, unsure what the plan was but instinctually heading out to where it was deeper, like Pearl, Rowan, Sara, and I often did. Z joined me, looked over with a big grin, and tilted her head toward the left to indicate the direction we should head. She wasn't speaking or thinking—or maybe she was, but she wasn't letting me listen. All I could hear was a soft chime, a soprano note, long and beautiful. Pearl and Sara often did that, and I'd heard Rowan's deep tenor before, but I hadn't yet figured out how to...

Hide your thoughts? Z asked.

I jumped in surprise. *Uh, yeah. Umm, how much did you hear?* I asked with some embarrassment.

I'm seven minutes older than my sister, if that's what you mean, and I appreciate that you can see me as more than just the—what was it?—"formidable and intimidating matriarch" tonight. She laughed. The sound was absolutely enchanting.

I half grimaced. *I'm glad she doesn't get offended.*

If I got offended by every thought I heard, I'd never get out of bed, she responded. *Now, on a more serious note, you must learn to guard your thoughts. Thoughts kept secret can make the difference between victory and defeat in our world.*

I've tried. I just don't understand how it works.

She laughed again. *Have you tried thinking of your favorite song?*

What do you mean?

Your favorite song. Sing your favorite song.

Despite feeling silly, I started singing a song in my mind.

After a few bars, Z asked, *Are you sure that's your favorite?*

Well, all my friends sang it back home. It was the most popular.

Ah. But is it your favorite?

I guess not. I thought again and tried another, but my thoughts kept interrupting.

Okay. Try this. What's the song that you turn to when you are sad or upset or exhausted? Z asked.

Oh, that's easy.

I hummed the first few bars, and the lyrics flowed. It was one of the songs my dad played in his office when he was writing. I would crawl into the aged brown leather chair, its arms worn shiny by years of hands absently caressing them. I'd sit in there for hours, content to be close to him while he worked, listening to the music he loved. This song always came on, and when it did, he'd hum along.

Singing the song now transported me back to the room. The lighting was dim, except for a desk lamp that illuminated Dad's computer. The familiar loud clacking of his typewriter-style keyboard soothed me. Dad's fingers moved as quickly as his thoughts, and he hummed off-key to his favorite song, which played softly in the background. A faded oriental wool rug covered the hardwood floor, and the overcrowded bookcase was filled with a menagerie of volumes. The chair I curled up in was opposite the mermaid painting. I knew now that those mers were Z, Pearl, and Sara. But back then, I only knew I loved it and that my mom, whoever she was, had painted it. The office was my safe place, my comfort, and where I somehow knew that everything would be okay.

That's your song, Z said softly in my mind. *You are an A minor.*

I'm a what? I stopped singing.

Your chime. Remember hearing the chimes? Each mermaid and merman has their own chime.

I thought back to that night training before the solstice when Sara had gotten me to find her using only my senses. That was when I learned about the mer chimes. I hadn't known if I even had one since I was only a half mer.

So I have one? I asked.

Of course you have one. And a beautiful one at that.

Can you only hear it when I block my thoughts?

No. Our chimes are always present. On land, they aren't audible, but you may have noticed how humans like to be around us.

Yeah! Pearl and Sara said it had to do with our vibe.

Z laughed. *Yes, I suppose you could call it a vibe. It's our chimes creating that vibe. In the water, we can hear them as they radiate out from us.*

But I don't always notice the others' chimes.

Do you always think about breathing?

No.

Same idea. Unless you really concentrate on it, our chimes are just another one of those sounds that fade into the background and usually get buried in the louder noise of our shared thoughts. But once you learn to hide your thoughts, your mind can be your own.

I nodded. *How did you know the first song wasn't my favorite?*

It didn't begin with A minor, and a mer's song always matches their chime. Keep singing it, my dear. The A-minor chime has a special place in my heart.

I did as she suggested, and we swam in a large arc. I couldn't hear Z's thoughts, and she couldn't hear mine. Night had fully descended by the time the seafloor rose back up under us. We rode a wave to shore and stood up once we reached the shallows.

Z turned to me at the water's edge and said with a grin, "Great job!"

"Great job at what?" *All we did was swim.*

Z answered my unblocked thought. "Oh, little one, we did much more than swim. We swam while keeping our thoughts our own, and that is a precious time indeed."

"There were so many sounds out there!"

"Yes. The ocean's creatures—and that includes us—are never silent."

"Oh, I never thought of it that way."

Z smiled and placed her hand lightly on my shoulder. She leaned down and whispered in my ear, "You are one with the ocean, Storm, as much a part of it as the rest of us. Don't ever let anyone try to convince you otherwise. Even when our other senses may fail, our chimes link us together. They keep us from losing each other."

I smiled back. "Thank you."

We made our way onto the hard-packed sand, and Z turned away.

"Aren't you coming back to the house?" I asked.

She slipped her white smock dress over her head. "Not tonight. I have a few things I need to take care of. Good night." She leaned down and kissed my forehead.

"Good night," I replied.

Z turned and made her way along the water's edge. Her dress flowed around her slender form. I continued to watch her retreat up the beach. She casually put her hair in a single braid that trailed heavily down her back.

So much strength inside a body that doesn't look like more than a beautiful twentysomething woman. And by strength, I mean power, magic, and wisdom, all at unfathomable levels. Their breadth and depth can't be quantified any more than you can figure out where outer space ends. But with the figure walking away from me at this moment, no sign of that power is revealed. Looks really can be deceiving.

Yes, they can be, Z responded.

I looked down and saw the thin layer of water underneath my feet from the previous far-reaching wave. *Seriously?* I thought with mock anger.

A short burst of breeze carried her lighthearted laughter back to me. I couldn't help but laugh with her.

Keep practicing, Storm.

I turned with a smile and headed up to the warm embrace of the yellow house.

CHAPTER EIGHTEEN
Hiding in Plain Sight

"I'd better get going," I said reluctantly to Jacqueline when she returned from the back room of her shop.

I sipped the last bit of the tea before gently setting down my china cup. I'd been observing Jacqueline and remembered not to gulp the last sip. I knew I wasn't supposed to be there ever since the completely unfair grounding after the equally unfair blaming of Rowan and me when we hadn't done anything wrong. But nobody was the wiser, and I only stayed thirty minutes each day.

"Okay, Storm. Don't want you to get in trouble." Her smile was coy. She opened the door to one of the many antique metal birdcages she had for sale in the shop.

"Why do you always open the doors to the cages?" I asked.

"I don't believe in keeping birds in cages. So it's a symbolic gesture, I suppose, but I believe these should be places of rest and refuge, not jails for our feathered friends." She stroked the thin metal of the bars lightly with the tips of her fingers and then came over to the sofa where I sat.

"Hmm. I don't know much about birds."

"Oh, they are my favorite animal by far. They're intelligent and skilled in so many ways."

"I know parrots can talk, so that's pretty cool," I said.

She laughed. "Yes, that's cool. But you want to know my favorite bird?"

"Sure."

"The cuckoo."

"Wait, like on those old-fashioned clocks?"

"No, you silly little thing." She smiled. "The cuckoo pulls off the cleverest of deceptions. A female will secretly lay her eggs in the nest of another species of bird. And unbeknownst to the nest's owner—often a bird of lesser intelligence—they will incubate the egg until it hatches. The mother raises it and nurtures it as her own. The newborn cuckoo, however, doesn't want to share, so it pushes any other babies out of the nest so it can get all the food from its surrogate mom. It's the perfect Trojan horse of nature. The cuckoo just infiltrates the nest and uses another's resources until it is able to go off on its own."

"That seems super mean."

"I suppose, but it's not that dissimilar to hiding in plain sight, no?"

I watched her, waiting for an explanation.

She sat next to me with a concerned expression. "It must be hard for you, being who you are and still being treated like a little girl."

Does she know who I am? I didn't know how to respond, so I stayed quiet.

"It's okay, Storm. You can trust me. I won't tell anybody that doesn't know. You and your family's secret is safe with me." She winked and took a final sip of her tea.

So she does know? "Umm, thanks," I mumbled.

"I think what your family does for this town is wonderful. Too bad *they* don't think you're ready to really help." She made a sound of disapproval. "From what I've seen, you are stronger than most."

"Well, I'm still learning. I mean, this is all new to me."

Should I be talking to Jacqueline about this? I don't know. Jon used to be my somebody, but since that encounter with Vincent, I really don't want to involve him in my world's troubles.

She folded a leg under her and shifted sideways to face me. "So is it true what I hear about the Hurricane Lady?"

"True in what way?"

"That she has some kind of power."

"That's what I've been told."

"Do you know the story of her? I've heard a bit about how she got here, and it's really quite fascinating, don't you think? Especially because of similar stories I learned while traveling through Spain. She was quite a legend over there as well!"

"I didn't know much about her before she was here. I'm actually doing my final paper for the summer course on her, but there isn't much published about before she arrived."

"I'm guessing you have to stick to quote-unquote 'facts' for that one, eh?" She gave me a wink.

I laughed. "Yeah, the professors don't like it much if I talk about magic and mermaids." I stopped suddenly.

"I totally get it," Jacqueline replied, not missing a beat. "'Tis a shame, though, as the origin story of her is so very fascinating. I especially found the mystery surrounding the ill-fated artist spellbinding!"

She knows who the artist was, I thought with excitement.

We both sat a moment longer than a comfortable natural silence allowed. I finally asked the inevitable question. "What was the story you heard?"

Jacqueline leaned in like she was about to tell the most delicious secret, but before she could speak, the door opened, and a group of customers wandered in.

"I'll be right back." Jacqueline sat back and, with a smile directed at the newcomers, stood up to greet them.

I stayed put and looked around the store, which was filled with unique items and beautiful clothes. I glanced at the group as they wandered from the display table of crystals to the incense to the carved wooden figurines and around to the hanging dresses. The door opened again, and three beautiful women walked in. I immediately recognized their silver pendants—all Lionfish.

Uh-oh, I thought.

I turned my back to them as much as I could without looking obvious and leaned forward toward the round coffee table. My hair draped like a curtain and partially blocked my face. I flipped the pages of the fashion magazine that was on the table.

"I heard the same thing," one of them said quietly.

"They've never belonged here, and now it's just worse with that little orphan showing up and claiming power," a second said.

"I didn't really care until they threatened to expose us with their destruction. First the lighthouse and now the Fountain of Youth. Not exactly hiding in plain sight," the third one said.

"I heard it was the orphan and her man," the first one added.

"Not *orphan*—she's a halfling. She *belongs* to them," the third one corrected.

The second one replied, "Whatever. We were better off before she got here. And I wouldn't mind keeping *him* company in her absence."

"You and me both," the third one agreed.

"Well, no matter—I heard that Laverna has a plan. She should be gone soon enough."

"Hopefully, they all get out of here."

"Agreed. A few more weeks is all, and then hopefully, they'll be gone for good."

"Well, Rowan can stay... as my guest."

"Only if you'll agree to share."

The second and third started giggling. The first one changed the subject. "This is a cool place. No wonder Paige's tail is in a twist."

They wandered toward the back. A hot tear rolled down my cheek. But it wasn't sadness—it was anger. The sky outside responded. The rainbows disappeared from the wall opposite the door.

"Hey, guys, look," the third one said.

No no no no... calm down, calm down, calm down, I thought.

The three mermaids were quiet. The other shoppers chatted to

Jacqueline about a brass statue of Buddha. I took slow breaths and continued to turn the pages of the magazine. I sang my song in my head. The rainbows reappeared on the opposite wall.

"Hmm. I guess it was nothing," one of the mermaids said.

"Ready?"

"Yeah."

I followed the three through my hair veil as they completed their browsing circle. With a sigh of relief, I watched them leave. The other women finished making their purchases and left, chatting excitedly to themselves, their arms laden with bags.

"Well, that was wonderful," Jacqueline said as she returned to the couch. "Nearly a one-thousand-dollar sale between all of them!"

"Great," I answered, still following the three as they walked away down the street.

"What's wrong?" Jacqueline asked.

"Oh, nothing, really, I guess." I sighed. "It's just, well, they were talking about me." I motioned with my head toward the door.

"Those girls?"

"Yeah. it was just about... about... this stupid competition thing I have to do," I blurted.

"Ah." Jacqueline sat back on the couch. "I've heard some talk about that. Do you want to talk?"

"Not really."

"Okay. Well, for what it's worth, I've heard mostly positive things from others. There was this one who seemed to not feel your chances were so good, though."

"Oh yeah? Who?" I asked.

"Oh, goodness, I never caught her name. She stopped in here only once with another woman. The one I overheard had a long blond braid and the most beautifully painted nails."

Suzee? I wondered, and my stomach lurched uncomfortably. *I thought she was helping me. But of course she's not. Stupid me. Way to be super gullible.*

"Doesn't matter. I don't care," I said. *Not true, I totally care.*

"Where were we?"

"You were going to tell me about your story of the Hurricane Lady." I wiped my sweaty palms on my shorts.

"Yes! Such a crazy thing. Well, I don't want to keep you. I know you have to hurry home so you don't get in trouble. But let's just say that it seemed that the artist who made that statue met a rather untimely watery death. An old local man in Spain told me the story his mother had told him, which her mother had told her. He said, '*Un hombre, Diego, llorando llevado a la fuerza al mar por la bruja con llamas en lugar de cabello*' which roughly translates to, 'A crying man, Diego, forcibly taken to sea by the seawitch with flames for hair.'"

"Oh." I fidgeted with confusion.

Diego? His name was Diego? And she's saying a mer killed him? And not just a mer, but a mer with flaming hair, as in red hair, as in Z? Z didn't say anything about that, just that she'd gone to see him about the mer sickness that surrounded his statue. Z wouldn't kill a human, would she?

My mind spun uncomfortably with the ramifications, and my stomach joined the pain party. I felt the onset of cold sweats and knew I had to get out of there.

"Gosh, I've definitely kept you captive way too long today. I love our little afternoon chats, and don't you worry—they are our little secret." Jacqueline smiled.

I smiled weakly back, but my mind was far away. I struggled to ignore the pain while I frantically compared what Z had told us about the Hurricane Lady with Jacqueline's new information. *Did Z really kill the artist? Has Z lied all this time about what happened?*

"Thanks." I stood up to leave. *I don't feel good at all.*

"Hey, Storm..." Jacqueline met me at the door and handed me a scrap of paper. "Here's my address in case... I don't know, in case you need to get out for a bit and talk. You know, whenever. I'm here for you."

"Thanks," I repeated and tucked the paper into my pocket.

******

"Hi, Stormy," Nana called as she came out from the kitchen and met me by the stairs. "You're late."

"Sorry. The scooter was acting weird. It took me a bit to get it going."

She looked me in my eye a bit longer than usual but ended with a slow nod. "Okay. I'll make sure your dad checks it out tonight. The scooter seems to be acting up quite a bit lately. I can always drop you off and pick you up tomorrow."

"I'm sure it's fine. It's just temperamental sometimes."

"Are you okay? You look a bit pale." Nana put her hand to my forehead.

"I'm fine," I replied more curtly than I probably should have. "I'm just kinda tired."

"Okay, if you're sure," she replied, but her tone wasn't as accepting.

I turned, made my way upstairs, and flopped down on my bed. I really didn't feel good. I was clammy but also kind of flushed and exhausted.

"Hiya!" Pearl said a few moments later and bounced onto the bed next to me.

"Humph," I replied, still facedown on the comforter.

"Ready to go?"

I turned my head to the left and saw her bikini-clad body. Then I turned back. "No," I mumbled, facing down again.

"Come on—we have to practice. It's only a few weeks until the challenge, and I want to be sure you can—"

"I can't do anything," I whined.

"Oh, come on—of course you can," she said, trying to reassure me, which was exactly *not* what I needed.

"It doesn't even matter. Laverna won't let me win. I don't want to do this anymore."

"Whoa, what do you mean? Stormy, she can't stop you from winning. The challenges have to be agreed to by both clans. You'll be great."

I sat up, angry. "No, I won't be great because I'm not great. Everyone hates me, and they also think I vandalized the Fountain of Youth, and I didn't. Even *you* think that. I'm tired, I don't feel good, and I don't want to be an heir. They were right—you guys were all better off before I got here."

"What are you saying? Who said they hate you, and who said we were better off? Don't you remember it's because of you that I have my braid back? Because of you, our clan can continue staying here."

"Yeah, and about that, why are you here? This isn't your territory. Why is Z protecting the Hurricane Lady now? I mean I get that you had to stay to find your braid, but you have it now. Shouldn't the Sea Stars go back to the South Atlantic?" I had no idea where this outburst was coming from, but I couldn't stop the words from spilling out.

"Stormy, what's going on? Who have you been talking to?"

Knowing I couldn't say anything without getting in trouble on at least a dozen different levels, I sighed and said, "Nobody. I just don't think Laverna will play fair, and I'm not stupid—I hear the whispers around town."

"Well, first, Z won't let Laverna pull anything underhanded, and I don't think—"

"What do you know about Z and the Hurricane Lady?" I asked abruptly.

"What do you mean?"

"Well, you know how she said that she went to speak to the artist?"

"Yes."

"Is that all she did?" I asked.

"Stormy, what are you saying?"

"I... I don't know. I was reading some articles on the Hurricane Lady for the paper I'm writing for the class, and there was an account of an artist in Spain named Diego drowning right around that time."

"Hmm. I heard the artist died. I didn't hear it was from drowning, and I never heard of his name. All I know is what we all know—Z followed him shortly after he delivered the statue to the ship, and then she was summoned by her mother to join the mers on the journey when there was news of some falling ill."

"Okay. I just wondered, is all. Seemed a weird coincidence."

Pearl sat silently, but I knew her mind was weighing the information I'd just shared. She rubbed her temples with her index fingers. When she resolved whatever inner debate she'd been having, she said, "Come on, get dressed. We have to get you ready."

Her tone was not one I could argue with. I pushed myself off the bed and put on my suit.

******

Voices climbed over each other as we filed back to the lawn after our latest outing to Ripley's and the rotunda inside Flagler College.

"I think our paper is pretty much ready," Samantha said to Jon and me. The three of us hung toward the back of the group.

"I agree," Jon replied. "Thanks for getting all of those articles together, Samantha."

She smiled. "You're welcome. Hey, if you guys aren't doing anything after class, wanna grab some food?"

"Sure," Jon replied.

"Sorry, I gotta get home," I said.

Dr. Briggs broke into the conversations. "All right, everybody, hope you enjoyed that as much as we did. As we head into our final week next week, I'm sure everybody has been working hard on finalizing their papers on the history and influence of the Hurricane Lady. Reminder that they are due Wednesday at the *beginning*"—he looked at each of us to emphasize his point—"of class."

Owen raised his hand, but instead of calling on him, Dr. Ross just said, "The beginning of class as per our class start time, not the time you may decide to show up, Mr. Beller."

We all laughed.

"Any other questions? No? Okay, then, we have a few for you," Dr. Briggs continued.

The white bird that always hung in the overhanging oak branches fluttered away. The movement made me look up, and I saw the curtain in the upstairs window flutter. Suzee's words from the previous week resonated: "Also, you may want to look up once in a while. Always good to know who's watching."

Dr. Briggs said, "Who can tell me...?"

I partially listened to his question about Ripley's and heard the giggles about the rather risqué anatomically correct Michelangelo statue, but most of my focus was drawn to the second-floor window. Suzee materialized and motioned for me to come to her. I turned back to my class. Shannon was telling them about the history of Flagler Hotel. I hesitated but then raised my hand.

"Miss Harn. Something to add?"

"Oh, sorry, not really. Shannon said pretty much what I had in mind." I smiled at her. "May I please run to the restroom quickly, Dr. Briggs?"

"Yes, but, Storm..."

Shoot, is he mad at me for leaving class?

"Don't run. Walking is fine." He smiled.

"Thanks," I said, relieved.

The discussion continued before I had even cleared the circle. I always forgot how differently these professors ran their class. We were treated like college students, and from the little I'd learned over the past weeks, college was really cool compared to high school—at least, if the professors were anything like these two.

I walked into the house, climbed over the sisal rope blocking the stairs with the Staff Only sign, and went up to the second floor. I saw Suzee in the captain's room and went in.

"Hiya," she said from the antique winged chair next to the fireplace.

"Hey, what's up? Is everything okay?" I tried to sound casual. *Is she playing me?* I wondered with anger.

She examined her bright-purple nails, frowning. "For me, yeah. All's grand except for this nail. Just had it done, and already there's a chip." She shook her head. "But that's not your concern. You and your clan have some pressing issues."

I looked past her out the window to where the class was still animatedly in discussion. "What do you mean?" *Can I trust her?*

"Well, for starters, word around town with the locals"—she touched her Lionfish pendant—"is that you all are endangering our staying discreet with those recent actions at the Fountain of Youth."

"We didn't—"

She held up her hand in peace. "I don't really care, but seriously, probably not the best timing what with the lighthouse incident so recent, you know? Anyway, there's that little mess, but that's not why I called you up here."

I waited.

"I shouldn't say anything, but I've never been a fan of not playing fair. I mean, what's the point of winning if you cheat, right? Although the fact that she's supposedly up to a potential cheat makes me think she's not so confident with winning, so that's a bit telling." Suzee stopped to contemplate a private thought. She concluded by simply saying, "Interesting."

"What is?" I asked, getting a bit impatient as my internal clock was counting down an appropriate time for a bathroom absence.

"Your challenge, Storm. Be careful."

"Well, yeah, I'm practicing. I don't really have a choice in what happens."

"I know, but something's up, and the problem is, I think the solution isn't in winning but in losing in order to win."

"Huh?" *What the heck is she saying? Maybe she* is *just messing with me. Seems like the favorite pastime of Lionfish mers these days, anyway.*

"I need you to consider that Laverna may be setting you up to win in order for you to lose," Suzee said.

"I totally do *not* understand," I replied. I was also blatantly reminded of how bad I still was at solving riddles. *Ugh. Yet another thing on my list of mer shortcomings.*

"I know. Just keep it in mind." She went back to her flawed nail, and I knew I'd been dismissed.

I made my way back to class, where we'd broken into our writing groups. Jon and Samantha were discussing our paper when I sat down.

"No, look, it's right here." Jon showed Samantha a paragraph from one of the papers she'd copied for us.

Samantha read the passage he pointed to aloud: "The darkened sky began to dance like she-devils. The wind howled like wild banshees. The water poured across the deck. Unnatural sounds could be heard from the bowels of the ship. In the middle of this chaos, the waves threatened to swallow us whole. I spotted the angels of the sea. I knew at that moment, even as the captain ordered us to jettison everything we could to add buoyancy, that we'd be saved. And because of their protection I felt it right to tell the captain of the discovery of the Virgin Mary statue. For there was no way my heart would allow me to throw her likeness overboard to succumb to the dark depths of hell below us."

"See?" he said.

"Well, yeah, that was when the sailor discovered the statue, mistaken for the Virgin Mary but now known to be Saint Barbara," Samantha replied.

"No, not that part. Oh, hey, Storm. Do you remember this?" He pointed to the same passage.

"Yeah. The sea angels." I smiled at him, and he smiled back.

"Ohhh!" Samantha exclaimed. "The siren reference, like the *Odyssey*. Yeah, that would be cool. We could do a reference to that."

The Odyssey, I thought happily as the light bulb lit on the memory I was trying to tell Rowan about at the planetarium. *That's where there were mers who could fly. The sirens.*

Jon stopped her. "Not sirens—mers."

"Well, yeah," she replied. "Same thing."

"No, totally different."

Both Samantha and I looked at him with confusion.

"Well, I've been doing some reading about this." He glanced at me sheepishly, and I suppressed a giggle. "Sprites, mers, sirens—they're all unique, but unfortunately, modern literature has combined their historical attributes. Specifically, mers and sirens are super different! Sirens are part bird, not fish." I cringed at his *fish* reference, and he mouthed, "Sorry."

"Seriously?" Samantha said.

"Yeah. So these were definitely mermaids, or at least, that's what the sailor thought."

"What about sprites?" Samantha asked.

"Freshwater only," Jon and I replied in unison.

Samantha looked between us, perplexed.

"I-I think it was," Jon stammered as he flipped through the stack of papers.

"Last paper, we read about them, or maybe it was one of the chapters in crazy Mr. Humpphrey's book," I replied in support.

"Oh yeah," he quickly agreed. "Anyway, just thought the reference to mers was cool."

"Well, I still think it would be a cool comparison. I'll look up more about sirens versus mermaids tonight," Samantha said. "Wanna meet up next week after class Tuesday just to finalize everything?"

"Yeah," Jon said.

"Sure." I smiled.

"Awesome," Samantha said, packing up her stuff. Class had just ended. "See you guys Monday, our last week! Eeek! I can't believe we've basically completed a college class!"

After Samantha left, Jon asked, "So, what are you up to? I haven't seen much of you."

"Well, nothing really. Just this class and training and home. Grounded, remember?"

"Oh yeah. But just to double-check, you guys didn't...?"

"No!" I said too loudly and then calmed. "No, I already said that."

"Okay." Jon held up his arms. "I didn't think so. I just—I don't know. Lilli was saying..."

"Lilli said *what*?" I asked defensively.

"Nothing, just that..."

"You aren't supposed to be seeing her, Jon. Vincent made it very clear that—"

"Yeah, yeah. Don't say anything okay?"

"Me? No, I won't. I can keep a secret, but it's not smart," I replied and knew just how hypocritical I was being.

"I know. Thanks, though. So, you really are doing okay, Storm? Don't take this the wrong way, but you don't look so great. I'd be happy to help out with anything you need."

I sighed. "It's just..."

"Just what?"

"Nothing."

I made the decision to not tell him about my afternoon meetings with Jacqueline, the information about the Hurricane Lady and Z, the mermaids who had come into Jacqueline's store, or Suzee's weird warning.

"You can tell me, Storm," he prompted.

"No, really, it's nothing. I'm good," I lied.

I'm really not good. God, I'd love it if my head would stop hurting for, like, a second, and more than that, I'd love it if I could ask my best friend for help, but I can't. I can't put him in danger again.

"Okay," he said, but *I* knew *he* knew I wasn't good.

"Okay," I parroted.

"Oh, hey, your friend Jacqueline stopped by the lighthouse a bit ago."

"Really?" *Subtle, Jon. Way to change the subject.*

"Yeah. She asked my dad about your family."

"What?" I was shocked.

"Your *human* family," he clarified.

"Oh." I relaxed a bit. "Probably just from talking about the connection in class the other day. What did she ask?"

"I'm not sure. I didn't hear all of their conversation. Had something to do with your nana and that old hurricane... what was its name...?"

"Dora."

I remembered the partial story Nana told me. It was a warning, of sorts, about our kind—*my* kind—mixing with humans.

"Yeah! Dora. Anyway, something about that. She seems nice."

"Yeah, she does," I replied, but I felt confused.

"See you later?"

"Sure." I walked toward the front gate. Then I turned. "Hey, Jon?"

"Yeah?" He looked up from his backpack.

"Please stay safe."

"I will, Storm."

"Thanks."

"Oh, hey, Storm?"

"Yeah?" I asked.

"You too."

I smiled. I wanted so badly to talk to him about everything. But instead, I walked away alone.

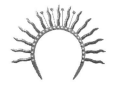

CHAPTER NINETEEN
Tales and Wings

"Hi, Nana." I dropped my bag by the front door and walked into the living room.

"Hi, Stormy. How was class?" Nana asked, looking up from the TV with a smile. The weather station was announcing tropical storm watches and warnings for the Caribbean.

"Fine. What's this?" I gestured toward the TV.

"Looks like a storm is brewing down south."

"Is it going to come here?"

"Hopefully not, but it's worth keeping an eye on. I'm hoping the protection St. Augustine generally enjoys will keep us safe." She laughed. "Interestingly, this one is named Matthew."

"Dad's a hurricane?" I sat next to her on the couch.

"Well, only a tropical storm at this point. I can't believe we are already up to *M* names, but at least we've been fortunate to this point this season."

"When do we make the jokes about him always being full of hot air?" I smiled.

"Now is a good time to start." She laughed again.

"Does it make you worried?" I motioned back to the weatherman pointing to a graphic of the storm's projected path.

"Not particularly."

"Well, what about if Laverna tries something with the Hurricane Lady?"

"I would like to think that all of us, humans and mers, have learned our lesson in regard to that statue."

"Do you think Laverna has? I mean, learned her lesson?"

"That's a tough one to answer, but the last time she tried, it was more than just a bad result for your clan. Lionfish members were also harmed in the fury Dora unleashed on this town. Paige was even missing for a time following the storm."

"Really?" I asked with surprise. I'd never heard that.

Nana nodded. "Yes. It turned out she was trapped in her old store when the roof partially collapsed around her. I think that made Laverna second-guess any overt attempts to use the Hurricane Lady in that way again. Kinda like realizing you can't always put the genie back in the bottle. While mers can guide weather and to some extent control it, Z has told me time and again that they are limited when weather reaches a certain size and strength. At that point, it becomes critical to have all mers working together. Nature's power requires more strength to shift than any one mer—or sometimes even one clan—can muster. Even then, control isn't guaranteed."

I gave a snort. "I can't imagine the two clans working together."

"Rare indeed," Nana agreed.

"Can I ask you something else?"

"Sure, sweetie." She hit the mute button on the TV remote and shifted in her seat to look at me.

"What really happened during Hurricane Dora—like, with you and Mr. Humpphrey and the Hurricane Lady?"

Nana sighed and stood up. "I suppose you have a right to the whole story. It's not one I enjoy sharing, but come on." She opened a drawer in the end table by the front door and pulled out a worn-looking book. She motioned me to the deck, pausing on the way through the kitchen to get me a salt ale from the fridge and a glass of wine for herself.

We settled into chairs in the shade, with nothing but the sand and ocean stretching before us beyond the sea-oat-covered dunes. Sunscreen and brine permeated the afternoon air. My head still pounded. I reached for the cold salt ale and took a drink.

This is nice, I thought with a contented sigh. Sipping cool drinks on the deck with Nana reminded me of my much simpler existence from a few months ago. It felt like a different lifetime. So much had happened since the last time Nana had shared a cryptic description of her interaction with the Hurricane Lady that ended with Dora smacking into St. Augustine. She'd said to me, in regard to including Jon in our search for Pearl's braid, "Sometimes the greatest burdens are the ones of choice. Take it seriously and choose wisely."

It was a warning I didn't heed, and Jon had paid the ultimate price, just like Mr. Humpphrey's daughter during Hurricane Dora. Unfortunately for little Sophie Humpphrey, there had been no Lilli to bring her back. That night, Nana had learned that not all mers could be trusted.

My mind jumped to Jacqueline's story about a mer killing the creator of the Hurricane Lady. *That mer's description bears a striking resemblance to Z... but Z can be trusted, right? Most mers can be trusted, right? What about Suzee? Is she lying to me?*

"This view is mesmerizing, isn't it?"

Nana's question brought me back from my spiraling thoughts. "What? Yes." I pushed those last thoughts as far away as possible.

"You were somewhere else, dear," Nana said with a small smile.

"Yeah, sorry. I was just remembering sitting out here when you told me a little bit about Hurricane Dora and being tricked." I brought the bottle back to my mouth and took another sip.

Nana sipped her wine then put the glass on the table. "Hurricane Dora was a direct hit on St. Augustine *and* a direct result of actions taken by Miles and me. Those actions almost cost Z her life and your clan this territory. I shudder to think what that would have meant for Pearl since, as you know, her braid's location wouldn't be found for many decades to come."

I sat up a little, faced Nana, and curled my legs under me.

"It started with the pure enough intentions of two eager teenagers determined to be the ones to solve the mystery of the braid. Miles and

I researched. We spent time with the old records of my ancestors and of Tressman—anything that made even the odd mention that might link mers to St. Augustine. We, of course, read a lot about the Hurricane Lady and its mysterious arrival on our shores. I wish I could find more on the artist after hearing Z's account of the statue's origins. What was his name? Did he have other works of art? What happened to him?"

Should I say something? How would I have heard it? I wasn't supposed to be seeing Jacqueline, and she's the one who used his name and *the one who told me about his death. Okay, no. I'll just stay quiet.*

"Anyway, I digress. Where was I?"

"You were teenagers with good intentions," I replied.

"Oh yes. And we certainly were on the path that good intentions lead to. Years passed, and our teenage fantasy of solving the old riddle and finding the secret location of Pearl's braid changed into young adult obsessions and then eventually became too heavy a burden. At least Miles found a productive outlet for our thousands of hours researching and treasure hunting by putting all the lore—and more importantly, the discrepancies in historical accounts he'd discovered—into his books. It led me to do just the opposite and flee this town. I felt like a failure. The weighted reality of so many wasted hours and years nearly crushed me. So I left."

"What?" I asked with surprise.

Nana just nodded. "It's true. I felt like a failure to the mers, to my family, and to myself, so I packed a bag one night and walked to the bus station near State Road 16. I didn't know where I was going or what I would do, but I knew I needed to get out of here for a while."

"Where did you end up?"

"Key West." She smiled, clearly lost in memories—and, by the looks of it, good ones.

I laughed. "Seriously?"

"Yup. Those few years were amazing and crazy. I felt like I was living at the end of the earth, where there were no rules. Those of us living on

Storm and the Hurricane Lady

the rock full-time stuck together. Waitressing work wasn't hard to get, and fresh fish was always cheap if your friends were the ones catching. I figured Key West was my new forever home... until one of the treasure hunters came in from a wreck with a piece of rope he'd recovered."

"Why would a treasure hunter bring back rope?" I asked.

"Because it happened to be rope apparently woven from hair, intertwined with gold-and-silver strands in one of the most intricate patterns ever seen."

"A mermaid's knot?" I reached for my own.

"Yes. It wasn't exactly the same as yours—I'm guessing it was from a different clan. I'm not even sure where the shipwreck he was exploring originated from or what century it was from, but it was a jarring reminder that my duty was here in St. Augustine. I left the next morning to return home."

"Wow, Nana. That's amazing." *Nana felt overwhelmed. She even ran away like I wanted to.*

"Thanks." She laughed. "I suppose it is odd to picture your old nana as a young woman living the nomadic lifestyle, but yes, it happened."

"Well, yeah," I admitted. "But also, hearing your emotions makes me feel better about mine."

"It's hard, Stormy. Don't let anybody tell you differently. Our lives are not for the faint of heart. And you are doing wonderfully." She smiled.

"Thanks. I'm trying, but I still get super overwhelmed."

"Well, you wouldn't be half-human if you didn't." Nana winked.

"Fair." I laughed. "So, what happened when you came back?"

"As soon as I set foot back in this little town, I knew I'd made the correct decision. Z and my family welcomed me back with no hard feelings. Apparently, it isn't that uncommon for the Harns to need a break from the hunt, according to what my mother told me. I had a similar look of amazement when she told me of her years away."

"What about Mr. Humpphrey? Was he mad at you?"

"No, he wasn't. But he was one of the few things that *had* changed while I was away. Miles had gotten married, and he had a baby on the way!"

"Was that weird?" I asked.

"Why weird?"

"Well, you two... I mean, you guys were together, right?"

"Oh! No, we were just friends."

I scrunched my face in disbelief. "So you two neveerrr...?"

"Never. Just friends."

"Okay, *whatever*. If you say so." I overexaggerated a wink.

Nana cleared her throat. "Anyway, to my surprise, Miles had continued collecting clues about the braid's possible whereabouts. His wife, Victoria, even got in on it, but she never knew the truth about what he was looking for, just that it was a treasure meant to be somewhere in town. We didn't waste much time once I returned, venturing out to our old haunts and retracing possible locations. It was after one such hike behind the Mystery House that we first met Daniel."

"Wait. Where?" I asked.

"The Mystery House, a strange attraction that helped put St. Augustine on the tourist map as folks traveled south along A1A. It took advantage of an interesting magnetism of the site and, of course, some sleight of hand, but basically, it was a madhouse where nothing stood straight or had right angles, and it appeared that gravity reversed itself. Now, many folks discounted it as charlatan maneuvers to play with people's perceptions, but Miles was the one to realize there really was a magnetic anomaly on the spot, and it also tied into the ley lines."

"The ley lines! Lilli felt those. That's how we found the tunnel at the lighthouse."

"Exactly! Of course, we didn't know about the tunnel, but Miles and I would visit the spot frequently to try to glean some kind of clue. In the summer of 1964, we happened to cross paths with Daniel in those woods.

He introduced himself in a most charming manner, as you know mers are quite capable of."

Anger rose in me at the thought of Daniel manipulating Nana. *I hate that merman.*

Nana continued. "We were both taken with him and his charm. He told us how impressed he was that we'd discovered the magic at the spot. He'd thought that knowledge was only for mers. He said if we needed anything to just ask. We thanked him, and I remember thinking on the drive home that night just how great it was to be able to work together with the mers. I felt so special to be accepted by such wonderful, magical beings." Nana scoffed. "More like, played like puppets." She took a sip of wine.

"Over the next few weeks, the three of us would meet at different places, sometimes discussing the search, other times just hanging out. It was at one of these times that Daniel mentioned the need to move the Hurricane Lady. He said he hated to ask us, but he feared for the safety of a particular mer named Suzee who had long resided at the Ximenez-Fatio House. Since the Hurricane Lady had been moved closer to her residence during the restoration, she'd been getting very ill. He said he discussed it with both Laverna and Z, and they had agreed that the best place to move the Hurricane Lady would be the mission church at the Fountain of Youth."

"Wait, did you say Suzee?"

"Yes, why?"

I am being played.

"Sorry, nothing."

"I should have known right then that he was lying to us. Laverna and Z agreeing on anything, let alone something to do with the Hurricane Lady, was absolutely ludicrous. But again, human ego is a fascinating blindfold that hides the obvious. The date was set to move the statue the first week of September. We'd heard news about a storm brewing in the Atlantic, but we didn't concern ourselves with it since no storms ever hit St. Augustine." Nana gave a sad smile.

"We almost didn't move the statue because the weather conditions had deteriorated so badly by the end of the first week. But Daniel beseeched us, saying the mers needed our help by moving the statue immediately to help them redirect the weather. We, of course, believed him. I picked Miles up at ten o'clock at night on September 9. I remember sitting in my blue Corvair and watching Miles kiss little Sophie on the head as Victoria held her. The family was backlit from the living room light. I heard Miles say to Sophie that it was *definitely* time for bed now and Daddy would be back soon. He hopped in next to me and"—Nana's attitude changed from matter-of-fact to angry—"we left to *save St. Augustine.*"

She let out a big sigh and finished the remaining wine in her glass. "Refill?" she asked with a slight break in her voice.

"Yeah, thanks." I desperately wanted her to continue but figured she needed a moment, and I did need more salt ale. My headache persisted even though I'd drunk the whole bottle, and I still felt clammy. I hoped I wasn't getting sick.

Waiting for her to return, I thought about the ending I already knew. The storm had raged and ravaged the town with ten-foot seas crashing over the seawalls and flooding the streets. The hurricane winds tore roofs off buildings and toppled the mighty oaks. There was, of course, only one death. It was so fortunate there weren't more, the articles would say. Sadly, the death was of a girl a mere three years old. The old oak branch crashed down on the roof of her bedroom a few minutes after midnight on September 10 as the storm made landfall.

Sophie. I wiped the tear from my cheek.

"Here we are." Nana returned and handed me the cold bottle.

"Thanks." I half smiled. This had to be really hard for her, and I hated to ask, but I really wanted to know, partly for personal reasons and partly because of a morbid fascination with this statue's power over my kind.

"Z mentioned that the half-mer boy on the sailing ship died because of the Hurricane Lady being on board, and they all talk about how dangerous it is to mers, but what happened when Z got close to it with you? Like, what did it look like was happening to her?"

Nana leaned back in her chair and held the wineglass with one hand while she rested a finger lightly on her lips. "Are you sure, Stormy?"

"Yeah, I want to know."

"Well, we heeded Daniel's instructions. Miles and I retrieved the statue easily from the nunnery. The two of us drove her to the Fountain of Youth. The sheer force of the wind caused trees to bend, and huge oaks began to snap apart like twigs. Multiple times, we had to swerve out of the way of falling branches. Struggling against the wind, we climbed the coquina wall and then went over the short picket fence. We stopped abruptly, though, when we heard water. The ocean seemed much closer than it should have been. And it was. The waters had risen many feet above regular high tide, and waves lapped halfway up the lawn. Seeing this, we became more determined to accomplish our task. We had to get the statue to the mission church. Daniel said it was imperative. We believed that putting the statue in place would be like some sort of key to help the mers shut everything off. We couldn't have been more wrong. We took shelter on the lee side of the church to catch our breath. The statue was cradled under Miles's rain jacket. The sound of wind, rain, thunder, and lightning was pure power and anger all tied together. I crept forward and looked around the corner. The full brunt of the wind hit me, but I squinted to see Z standing tall in the field. Her red hair blew wildly around her, and her clothes danced manically. In front of her was pure darkness—no grays or storm hues but a sky of the purest black. Her arms were raised, and it was as if she and the darkness in front of her were in a stalemate of wills. Once I caught my senses again from this insane vision in front of me, all I thought was that we could help. We had the Hurricane Lady!

"I motioned to Miles to come quickly, which he did. We pushed forward through the gusts, and we probably got to within twenty feet of Z when it happened. The blackness started winning. Z staggered back a step and then another. She fought back, but something was wrong."

"It was the Hurricane Lady," I said.

"Yes. We were breaking Z down without realizing it. Z then fell to her knees. I rushed forward and caught her in my arms. I crouched in the foot-deep water, cradling the most powerful mer in existence. She didn't even have the strength to lift her head. Salt crystals clung to her long lashes, and a trickle of something shimmery trailed from the side of her mouth. Her eyes were wild, glowing bright amber but unfocused. I told her I was there, Miles too, and we had the Hurricane Lady like she'd requested. At that, her eyes struggled to focus on mine. She whispered, 'No.' I shook my head, not understanding, still trying to comfort her, like an idiot. The wind raged, and Z and I slid backward. Miles stopped our slide by pressing into my back. The Hurricane Lady was on the ground next to us, still wrapped tightly in the jacket. Z's skin, despite the darkness and rain, looked dry and sunburned. She just repeated, 'No.' Her eyes darted to the package on the ground. It was Miles who put it all together. He yelled in realization and grabbed the Hurricane Lady and ran away from Z and me. I stayed on the ground, holding Z, and the blackness overtook us."

"Oh, Nana," I whispered.

She wiped her cheeks. "I awoke to a dim morning light and an eerie quiet. Every bone in my body hurt. I realized I was on the floor of the church, in a corner. Z was wrapped around me. Roles reversed this time— she protected me. A service I certainly didn't deserve."

"There's no way you could have known."

"Perhaps not, but that night can never be taken back. It was my fault."

I stood up and gave Nana a hug from behind. She wrapped her arms over mine and rested her head on them.

******

The clock next to my bed taunted me with its red glowing numbers.

My body was exhausted, but my mind wouldn't stop. Z's story about the Hurricane Lady and Nana's experience churned relentlessly in my mind. Then, just for fun, my brain tossed in Jacqueline's story and worried about Suzee playing me like Daniel had played Nana.

Yeah, sleep just isn't going to happen. I sat up. The red numbers said *2:28.*

I slipped on shorts and a tank and tiptoed downstairs. While I was technically still grounded, a little walk on the beach was surely okay. It wasn't like I was going to go far.

The sand had finally released its heat from the day and felt cool to my naked feet. The night was dark with only a sliver of moon. The metronome of the waves soothed my active mind, and I sat just beyond the rush of water. Every wave reached higher on land, trying to reclaim more territory, only to stop, pause, and then retreat.

How far can it reach before it has to turn back? I leaned my head back, closed my eyes, and inhaled deeply. The delicious salt air filled my lungs. I was so exhausted, probably from lack of sleep, but I also felt off somehow. It wasn't just my overactive mind—something inside me felt drained. I hoped the ocean's proximity would replenish whatever I lacked.

Up the beach, I noticed a shape—probably another insomniac out for a midnight beach-therapy session. I sat still and watched the shape draw closer. The person was high up on the beach, in the soft sand. Their progress was slow.

I quickly lost interest in the stranger and turned my attention back to the expanse of water. *How am I going to compete in this new contest? What is Laverna going to do? And what about Nana and her tests? And what is the deal with the Hurricane Lady? And Jacqueline? How does she know about us? Could she help me? Why don't the others trust her? And then there's Suzee... and Vincent. And Jon. Ugh, Vincent wanting to kill Jon and Jon risking his life to still see Lilli. I miss Lilli so much. She'd be able to help me figure this all out. She has a way of knowing things even if she* doesn't realize she knows. She has such a way of helping my brain connect the free-floating thoughts.

I let out a snort of humor and frustration. Stretching and spreading my toes, I let them dig into the damp packed sand. Water rushed forward and gave their tips a light kiss of foam.

I spoke to the oncoming waves with a pure sense of being overwhelmed. "And of course let's not forget about a stupid tropical storm or hurricane or whatever it ends up being. Seriously, universe?"

"Storm?" a quiet voice asked.

I turned in surprise and saw a slim silhouette backlit by the dim red porch lights of the homes beyond the dunes.

"Hello?" I asked.

She gave a light laugh. "What are you doing out here? I thought I was the only one who came to the beach when I couldn't sleep."

Jacqueline walked toward me. Her long, loose pants and top rustled around her slight form. Her stride was slow, and she grimaced as she struggled with the uneven, yielding terrain.

"Oh! Hi." My heart rate recovered from the surprise. I smiled. "I thought I was the only one too."

She sat down next to me, adjusting her pants around her legs. "Well, great minds, I tell you. I've always found the sound of the waves very soothing. You?"

"Yeah. I guess for the past few months, anyway."

"Oh, that's right. You didn't grow up here."

"No, I only came here for the first time this summer..." I hesitated. "It's when I found out about my family."

"That's probably why we get along so well—two newbies trying to fit in." Jacqueline smiled.

"Yeah, probably." I smiled in return.

Memories of the past few months flashed behind my eyes—seeing the ocean for the first time, meeting Rowan, taking my first swim. I thought of my first kiss, Z telling me tales, and Pearl putting my Sea Star on. I absently touched my necklace, the cool metal tingling on my fingertips as I moved the pendant between them.

Then came the memories of the night at the lighthouse and the braid... and then Jon. I inhaled sharply.

"Everything okay?" Jacqueline asked.

"Umm, yeah, sorry. Just a crazy few months." I snorted.

"Well, tomorrow night—" She stopped and let out a small laugh. "*Tonight* technically, the woman who owns the house I'm renting a room in is having some folks around. They're a very interesting bunch—I think you'd really like them. Maybe you'd like to join as my guest? You know, we outsiders have to stick together sometimes."

"Oh, wow, that would be great! I'll have to ask," I replied, already guessing the answer everybody would give me. It wasn't yes.

"Great! With that, I should be getting back home. I'm sure sleep will be easier now that I breathed in the salt air." Jacqueline stood up slowly and made a soft sigh of discomfort.

"Did you hurt your legs?" I asked, looking up at her.

"A long time ago, yes." She frowned. "Still bothers me sometimes. Maybe there's a storm on the way." She watched the horizon. "It tends to act up before big weather events."

I remembered the distant tropical storm Nana had mentioned. *Hopefully, not actually on the way, if we have anything to do with it.*

"Good night, Storm," she said.

"G'night."

"Let me know about being able to join me later."

"Okay, thanks. I will."

I watched her slow retreat up the beach. Then I stood and walked back to the yellow house. *Outsiders. Huh.*

CHAPTER TWENTY
To Tell or Not to Tell

My mind awoke before my body wanted to get up. After only a few hours of sleep and a fruitless twenty minutes trying to get more, I gave in, got up, and padded quietly downstairs.

If I'm awake, I might as well watch the sunrise. St. Augustine has some of the most amazing sunrises. Too bad they're so early in the morning.

I made myself a cup of rooibos tea with lemon and salt and went out on the deck to watch the light show. Zelda jumped into my lap, no doubt after a busy night of dune hunting, and demanded a chin rub. It wasn't long before her contented cricket purrs vibrated through my belly. I rested my head against the lounge chair, breathed deeply, and watched as the dark night sky yielded to the morning's display of bold magentas and vibrant blues.

"How's my favorite girlfriend?"

I turned and smiled. Zelda let her displeasure of my movements be known by a sharp flex of her claws.

"Daaad!"

"What? Are you too old for me to be calling you that?"

"No."

He came over and planted a kiss on the top of my head. I gave Zelda a reassuring pet. She relaxed back into her purring slumber.

"Why are you up so early?" I asked.

"I had trouble sleeping, so I thought I might as well enjoy the sunrise. St. Augustine never disappoints." He smiled at me and sat in the adjacent chair.

Like father, like daughter, I thought. The smell of cinnamon wafted up from his insulated mug. "Mmm. You got a honey badger from Kookaburra?"

He nodded and took a slow sip.

"Did you know one of your classmates works there?"

"I didn't," I replied with a shake of my head.

"Her name is Shannon."

"Oh, yeah! I think she mentioned she works there in the summers."

Dad took a slow sip of his steaming drink. "So I hear Pearl has a day planned for you! You know, it took some serious talking to Z and Nana to let you go."

"Dad, you know we didn't vandalize anything." I sighed.

"I believe you. But parents *always* want to believe the best of their children, so my belief doesn't carry much weight with the others. Unfortunately for you and Rowan, someone did vandalize the property, and you both were seen there right around that time."

"Purely circumstantial."

He chuckled and looked toward the sunrise. "Yes, circumstantial indeed."

We sat in silence as the sky morphed.

Dad smiled. "The water looks pretty good. I think I'll go see what these old bones have left in them and try to catch some waves." He stood and walked down the stairs to the sand. After grabbing his board from under the deck he turned back. "Have fun today, Stormy. Don't do anything I wouldn't do."

I laughed. That phrase was as common from him as "How's my favorite girlfriend?" Fortunately, his directions really didn't limit me all that much.

I placed a reluctant Zelda on the deck and headed inside to get ready. I passed Nana on the stairs. "Thank you." I smiled.

She hugged me and shook her head. "You'd better get going before I change my mind!"

I danced up the stairs before she could say another word. I showered quickly and with no idea what Pearl had planned for the day, I tossed on my favorite green sundress over the white bikini. I gave a quick brush of my damp hair and then wove it into a long braid, making sure my mermaid's knot was well hidden within my locks.

A scooter honked below. I grabbed my small bag, flew down the stairs, and blew a kiss to Nana, who sat on the couch, watching the news.

"Storm, don't slam the door," she called after me as the door slammed.

Oops.

"Where are we going?" I asked as I sat on the scooter, my arms wrapped around Pearl's waist.

"I have a little surprise for you."

She accelerated through the traffic toward the Bridge of Lions. We parked on Cordova, near Scarlett O'Hara's. I still had no idea where we were going.

"Hmm, the scooter seems to be running fine," Pearl said offhandedly as she leaned it into the kickstand. "Rean said you'd been having some trouble with it."

"Oh, right, umm, it's nothing. I must have just done something wrong with starting it. Probably flooded it or something. So, what're we doin'?" I asked, hoping to change the subject. It worked. A smile lit up Pearl's face as she gave a little nod behind me.

Confused, I turned around. Nothing. I then looked across the street to the corner where Scarlett's was.

"Lilli!" I called with excitement and ran toward the small bouncing white-haired body. We met in the middle of the street, and I grabbed her and swung her around.

Pearl joined us as I set Lilli back on her feet. "It's just a little something I thought you'd like," she said.

"It's perfect! Lilli, where have you been?"

Before she could answer, a car honked. *Oops.* We were still in the middle of the street. The three of us giggled and scooted to the side of Scarlett O'Hara's.

"I've been here and there, mostly there, but oh goshes, sometimes here, but I had to be there a lot more because of Papa and his crazy notion about humans and Jon."

"I missed you, Lilli." I smiled and bent down for another hug.

"Oh, I've missed you all so much!" she replied excitedly. "Papa just doesn't understand he's targeting the wrong problem. I know there is a problem, and I have to talk to you guys about it because it's a big problem, and she is trying to make it a bigger problem, and it needs to be taken care of, but I haven't been able to…" She swiped at an errant piece of hair that had fallen over her forehead, just like Jon did—the trait she'd taken from him when she returned his soul.

"Whoa, whoa, what are you saying?" I asked.

Lilli looked left and right in a secretive manner, and then, before she could say anything, a voice called from above us, "Is this a private party, or can any mer join?" Sara was leaning over Scarlett's balcony.

"Sara!" Lilli squealed and clapped her hands. Sara sauntered across the restaurant's balcony to us. She brushed aside the half dozen men offering her drinks.

"Come on. We don't have all day," Sara said, peeling Lilli off from her hug. "Well, we do, but you know, at some point, someone is bound to worry about… Storm." She laughed.

I laughed, too, because it was true. Whatever Lilli meant to tell us was pushed aside. I was sure we'd get back to it.

The first place we stopped was Schmagel's Bagels. The salt bagel with vegetable cream cheese hit the spot. Pearl and Sara went with lox—a different salted treat. Lilli, our little sweet-toothed sprite, had a chocolate chip muffin, which I happened to know was also Jon's favorite.

"Okay, ladies, where to?" Pearl asked.

Sara smiled and motioned with her arm, like a game show host, to a shiny black stretch limousine parked across the street. "I'm not sure, but we'll get there in style!"

As if on cue, the sunroof opened, reggae music filled the street, and Paige popped up like a rock star. "Need a ride?" she called.

We hurried across the narrow street and piled into the limousine's luxurious interior. A man in uniform closed the door behind us and slid into the driver's seat.

"How did you get this?" I caressed the flat-screen television hovering above the engraved glasses set neatly in their holders next to the full ice bucket.

Sara winked at me. "Let's just say we know people!"

Pearl stifled a giggle. "I swear you are more siren than mer!"

"I resent that, dear sister! Sirens are so not glamorous, and in addition, no one died!"

Paige, Sara, and Pearl burst into fits of laughter.

I didn't understand their siren reference, but my human side poked its boring head up, and I asked, "Are we going to get in trouble? 'Cause I'm on pretty thin ice, and I also seem to be a magnet for trouble recently."

Sara stopped laughing. "Relax, human Stormy. No harm, no foul. No one will get in trouble tonight. You only need to worry about your *other* magnetic challenges."

"Not funny," I said.

"Kinda funny," Sara replied with a laugh.

I looked over at Pearl for help, but she just smiled and nodded. "It's really okay, Stormy. Last night, Sara and Paige met the owner of this limo company at Jack's. He was bragging about being an expert free diver."

"I can hold my breath longer than anybody in America!" Sara said in a faux man's voice.

"In the world," Paige corrected.

"Oh, right." Sara laughed. She waved her arms in a flourish. "In the world!"

"Hang on," Paige said with a finger to her lips.

She leaned toward the open division between us and the driver. After a short conversation, she sat back and pressed a button to her right. A dark glass divider rose up and sealed our side from the front seats.

"Carry on," she said with a coy smile.

The car pulled away from the curb, and Pearl popped open salt ales for us and sparkling water for Lilli. Sara continued the story. "I challenged him to a breath hold in the pool. If he lost, he agreed to let us use the limo today for free! If he won, I'd have dinner with him."

"I guess I know how it ended," I said.

Sara shrugged and sipped her salt ale.

As we drove through downtown, I felt like a movie star behind the tinted glass. All the people on the streets watched us go by. They pointed and were probably trying to guess who was ensconced within such luxury.

"Why did you call Sara a siren?" I asked Pearl.

She turned from staring out the window and smiled. "Oh, nothing really. Just an inside joke. Sirens are bitter creatures of old that thrive on causing misery to others." She stopped as if a stray thought had passed through her mind. "They were once thought of as magical creatures that escorted souls to the underworld, but that's a tale for another day."

"But aren't mers sometimes called sirens?" I asked.

"Only if you want to insult them. Thanks for that, by the way, sis." Sara glanced at Pearl.

Pearl laughed lightly. "If the wing fits."

"Stop," Sara said.

Before I could ask what wings had to do with anything, the limo pulled into the parking area of the Casa Monica, and two men in black shorts and polo shirts opened our doors. We exited and walked up to a marble entrance, where a smiling woman greeted us.

"Welcome, ladies. Right on time! Please have a seat and enjoy the refreshments while Lana prepares your rooms." She motioned to a tufted couch. In front of it on a wooden table was a silver tray holding tall perspiring blue-tinted glasses. Each was filled with an opaque liquid and slices of cucumbers. The rims were encrusted with salt. "I believe they are just as requested."

She walked back to the entrance, and we all sat and picked up glasses in turn. I sipped and looked around. I'd never been inside the Casa Monica and had definitely never been pampered at the Poseidon Spa.

Pearl smiled and, with her glass held high, announced, "Today is our day to reenergize. All work and no play makes for very dull mermaids. Cheers, my sisters!"

Glasses clinked, and happy chatter ensued. Spa attendees led us to a room dimly lit with salt lamps and smelling like lavender and sage. After placing our shoes in cubbies, a woman in a white uniform directed us to a wall of colorful polishes with instructions to pick out our favorites.

Pearl gave a girlish giggle. "Paige, no need to lick the lamps."

Paige looked up in midlick like a kid caught with her hand in the cookie jar. She sheepishly shrugged and met us at the rainbow wall of polishes. Lilli pointed for colors beyond her reach to be brought down to her. I handed her five different options then replaced all five. The sixth one, though, drew out her classic happy Lilli bounce, and she hugged the bottle to her chest.

"I know, I know, I know! A game!" she squealed, still bouncing on her toes. "When we pick our colors, keep them secret. Then everybody else tries to guess the name of the color you picked when you show them the color! And if someone gets it right, then you owe them a secret."

"What if they guess wrong?" I asked.

"Hmmm..." Lilli pondered.

"They owe *you* a dare!" Sara said with a wink.

"Sounds fun to me." Paige smiled and waved her hand in front of a row of polishes. Her other hand coyly reached behind and took one of the hidden bottles.

Sara followed Paige's lead in taking a bottle and hiding it in her palm.

Lilli bounced and clapped some more. She pulled one more color down from a low shelf and twirled away from the wall. With our polish bottles hidden, we each took seats in the large massage chairs. They were arranged in a semicircle, so we could all talk easily to each other. The warm water felt great as I submerged my feet in the shallow basin.

"Okay, who wants to go first?" Lilli had moved her seat all the way forward but still barely reached the water with her feet. She looked tiny in the massive chairs.

Pearl smiled. "Let me add a few rules. You pick one person to guess your color choice. If they guess correctly, you must reveal a secret. If they guess wrong, you can give them a dare. All answers must be true!" Pearl held up her arms as if holding court. "Let the games begin."

Lilli bounced up and down in the chair. "Okay, me! Me first!" With a quick smile, she added, "I'm choosing Storm to try to guess my color!"

I laughed and without hesitation said, "Violet! Just like the color of your *and* one of *my* eyes!"

"Yes! But what is the name?"

"Hmm..." I tried to remember the names I'd read as I looked through the colors. "I think it was called Ultraviolet?"

Lilli jumped up from her massage chair, her feet leaving wet prints on the tile, and hugged my neck. The nail tech was not amused as she motioned to a male attendant to wipe up the slipping hazard.

Sara stifled a yawn. "Okay, little Energizer Bunny, tell us your secret!"

Lilli hopped back into her seat and resubmerged her feet into the cauldron-like basin of steaming water. "Okay, I have two, but one is kind of a secret, and one is a *big* secret."

I smiled. "Tell us your *big* secret!"

"Well, Papa would kill me, but..." She looked around and then whispered, "I love Jon!"

Paige rolled her eyes. "That's your big secret? We all know that, Lilli! Can we ask for another secret?" she asked the rest of us.

Lilli's smile instantly turned upside down. "Really? You all knew that?"

Pearl shot Paige a silencing glance. "Lilli, no, we didn't *all* know. I think that was a brave secret to reveal!"

Lilli's mood lifted again. "Okay! Since you didn't like my secret, I choose you, Paige, to go next."

Paige smiled slyly and tapped the tips of her fingers together. "Okay, my pretties, who wants to have a go at my color? Sara...?"

Sara let out her beautiful nonmalicious laugh, rarely heard, which sounded like harmonic chimes blowing in the wind. "Okay, let me talk this one through. Let me see... you love color and the whole hippie vibe. Back in the day, you dated Jerry Gar—"

"Dear cousin, I was a hippie, and yes, hanging out with Jerry was a blast, but as you can clearly see, this decade, I'm rockin' more of a gypsy Stevie Nicks vibe!"

"Who's Stevie Nicks?" I asked.

"You aren't serious," Paige replied, her eyebrows nearly on the ceiling.

I looked around. "Sorry, but, uh, yeah."

Pearl, once again, calmed the room. "Baby, I'm sure you heard your dad play 'Blue Denim'?"

I shook my head.

"'Dreams'?" Paige asked.

I shrugged.

"'Go Your Own Way'?" Sara hummed a few bars.

"Oh! Yeah. From *Forrest Gump*." I smiled. "Dad and I did watch that. Got it."

The three of them exchanged glances. "This new generation..." Paige shook her head slowly.

"Does make you feel the centuries," Pearl agreed. "But okay. Now, back to the game. I believe, Sara, you need to figure this out."

Sara laughed. "You are not going to throw me off on this one! I say you are going to go for a Grateful Dead reference!" She looked at me and, in a mock whisper, said, "I'll tell you who they are later."

I laughed. "Duh, Sara. I totally know them. They sang 'Accidentally in Love.'"

"Do you want to tell her?" Sara turned to Pearl.

"No, I'm good," she replied.

"Cool." Sara nodded.

"Okay, Paige, I saw a color over there that I really believed you would pick. I think you went with Uncle John's Brandi Copper!"

Paige held out her hand to reveal the color.

Sara did a little chair dance. "I knew it! Okay, spill a secret!"

Pearl warned, "Remember, it must be true!"

Paige held a hand to her heart. "Pearl, you think I would lie? We all know what lies do to each other. I would never."

Pearl tilted her head.

"Okay, I wouldn't anymore," Paige said. "I like you guys, ya know? And besides, if we win, I want it to be fair and square. No need to cheat by weakening you with lies."

I had no idea what they were talking about.

Paige's tone grew serious. "I'm afraid my mom and my brother are up to something. I'm guessing it has something to do with Storm's challenge. I'm not sure exactly what they were talking about, but I heard Daniel and Mum discussing a *switch*."

"A switch?" Pearl asked.

"Yeah. I don't know. That's all I heard."

There's that word again. I remembered Samantha saying something about how the statue was getting "switched."

"Paige?" I asked.

But before I could ask my question, a handsome man appeared with a tray of salt ale, sea salt caramels, a card, and a bouquet of flowers. "Ladies, I was instructed to deliver these to you!"

"Were you, now?" Sara said alluringly.

Pearl laughed lightly. "Thank you. Please ignore my sister—she doesn't get out much. You can put it over here by me."

He did as directed and stood to leave.

"Oh, do you have to go so soon?" Paige smiled sweetly. The man's jaw went slack.

"Stop," I whispered to Paige.

"What?" she asked innocently.

"Stop doing *that* to him." I glanced at him awkwardly. He stared at us with glassy eyes.

"Storm, manipulating people is a skill just as important as weather manipulation or magnetism," Sara replied. "Trust me."

I sighed. "That doesn't have to mean I like it. What does the card say?"

Pearl plucked it off the colorful bouquet and read it silently. Then she read out loud. "Have a wonderful girls' day out! Enjoy these treats. XOXO Jacqueline."

We all looked at each other.

"How does she know we're here?" Paige asked with a scowl. Her mood change released the man from his trance, and he gave a brief smile and left.

"Well, who cares. She has great taste in both presents *and* delivery instruments." Sara winked. "Anyway, I believe it is now my turn." She reached down to the basket between her and Pearl, picked out a caramel, and popped it into her mouth. "Hmm, who shall I pick to lose this challenge?" She looked around at each of us, and then her gaze settled. "Pearl! Since you think you know me so well, dear sister, I dare you to guess my color!"

Pearl smiled. "This is too easy! I've known you for centuries, and your go-to color has always been red!"

"Okay, red is correct, but you must be more specific."

Attempting to hide a smirk, Pearl continued. "Well, there was that time in Massachusetts. You caused quite a stir. So I am guessing Scarlet Letter Red!"

Sara pretended to look hurt. "No, sister, it's called Vamp Red!"

Lilli giggled. "Tell us why?"

Sara bared her teeth. "Because I am really a vampire!"

Paige threw a piece of chocolate at her. "Wrong story!"

Sara laughed. "I'm just kidding! I was thinking about that time in Salem, and that's why I chose Scarlet Letter!" Opening her hand, she revealed the color.

Pearl nodded in satisfaction.

Lilli giggled again. "Okay, you gotta spill a secret, and as Pearl said, it has to be true!"

"Lilli, you know we always have to tell the truth."

My stomach was in knots with all the truth talk. *Is it really that big of a deal? I mean, people lie all the time. I can't believe mers don't.*

"Okay, my secret is... Stormy has really grown on me. I do believe her heart is in the right place, even though her mind doesn't use the best judgment."

"Wow, Sara! That is the nicest thing you've ever said to me."

"Well, don't get used to it," Sara replied gruffly.

"Okay, I choose Stormy to pick my color." Pearl smiled at me.

I knew immediately the color she chose.

"Pearl of Wisdom!"

"Well, we all know it is my namesake." She held the bottle in her open hand.

"Boring!" Sara faked a yawn. "But go on—reveal your secret."

Pearl began quietly. "I was named after a human's grandmother. She helped us a long time ago, and Z wanted to make sure she was honored!"

Lilli squealed. "What? Tell us more, please, please, pleeeeze?"

"That tale, my dear Lilli, is for another time!"

"What about you, Stormy?" Pearl asked.

Before I could answer, the nail techs came in. "Ladies, let's get started."

"Wait! We didn't get to guess Storm's color! And there weren't any dares," Lilli said with a pout.

I breathed a sigh of relief. I really wasn't in a good place to be telling secrets—or the truth come to think of it. "Don't worry, Lilli," I said. "We can always play this again!"

She gave a little smile and nodded.

We all quieted into our massage chairs' rhythms and melted into our overdue pampering.

******

After leaving the spa, the driver dropped us at the fort for the sunset firing of the cannons. We sat in a row along the seawall to the side of the barracks.

"It is most definitely not a good idea, Sara." Pearl laughed.

"You, my dear sister, are without a doubt the most boring mer on the planet," Sara responded, shaking her head in disappointment.

"I don't believe *not* wanting to sink the pirate ship counts as being boring."

"Depends on who you ask."

"I just think it would make the cannon firing that much more believable for the tourists."

"Oh!" Lilli exclaimed. "I've gotta go."

"Aw, you sure?" I asked.

"Yes, very sure." She looked at the sky, which was clear except for some distant thunderheads that made low grumbles. The calm weather wasn't going to last much longer. "Storm?" She beckoned me to stand with her.

I got up. "Everything okay?"

"Not really, but I want you to know I love you like a sister, like my bestest friend."

"Okaaaay," I replied, not sure what Lilli was going on about.

"So, that's all. I just want you to remember that, okay?"

"Sure. I never thought anything other than that!" I smiled.

"Right, yeah, never, okay, so just remember that."

I nodded. Lilli looked over my shoulder at the sky again.

"Lilli? Do you need to tell me something?"

"Well, yes, but no, but well, yes. But I can't. But you should know, you know? But he said you had to figure it out. But I want to help you, but he said no, so I'm not sure." She bit her lower lip and pouted.

I wasn't sure what she'd just said. But that was pretty normal when listening to Lilli, especially when she was conflicted about something. So I tried a little trick I'd learned with her.

"Okay, so he, whoever *he* is said not to tell me. So don't tell me. Maybe show me." I winked.

Her pout disappeared instantly. She did three tiny bounces and then pulled me across the lawn.

"I'll be right back," I called to the others.

Lilli stopped pulling and motioned for me to stay. She jumped in front of me and then started a little show. It began with her walking a few feet and falling down. I shook my head, unsure what she meant. Then she pointed to me.

"Oh!" I laughed. "You're being me. Got it."

She nodded happily. She repeated the walk but this time collapsed, looked up toward the fort, and then lay flat and still.

"Right, I get it. I'm clumsy. Not so much breaking news, Lilli."

She stood up and gave me a disappointed look, shaking her head. She repeated the dramatic scene and sprawled on the ground as if dead.

"I'm dead?"

She nodded at me.

"Why?"

She looked back up toward the fort.

"The fort?"

She shook her head then made more dramatic writhing, death-throes motions.

"Oh, you mean when I collapsed by the Hurricane Lady—I could have died?"

She nodded with a smile.

"Okay, yeah. It's real. I get it now," I said.

She hopped back to her feet and then did the same walk and glanced up at the fort but this time didn't collapse.

I shook my head, all confidence gone. "I don't get it now."

She started over again and did the same walk, look, and no collapse.

"The Hurricane Lady won't affect me?"

She shook her head with a little shrug.

"And now I'm super confused," I said.

She ran over to me and wrapped me in a hug. "You'll understand if you watch closely," she whispered. "I'm sorry. I super-duper have to go now."

As she left, I closed my normal eye, for fun, and watched her retreating form with just my purple Lilli eye. She was so clear even though she was already across the street. A small white bird flew past her. I could see the details on the bird, even the black tips of the flight feathers.

"Seriously a bird's-eye view," I said quietly, completely amazed by my vision from this eye. "Too bad it didn't also come with a Lilli decoder." I started back toward the seawall and tried to make sense of Lilli's little performance.

The Hurricane Lady can kill me, except now it can't. But... Something niggled in the back of my mind.

"I'm just not sure what to do about my baby," Paige said to Sara as I walked back to them.

"You really have to stop calling it that," Sara replied.

"What? It is."

Sara was about to respond but stopped as I rejoined them. She turned to me and asked, "What was that all about?"

"No idea." I shrugged, feeling frustrated.

"Well, what should we do?" Sara asked.

"Let's go shopping," Paige suggested as she hooked her arm in mine.

I looked at the darkening sky. "I should get back. I want to get all my school stuff done before this week so I can focus on winning."

"Wow, Stormy, you sure?" Pearl asked, surprised. "We have the limo all night."

"Yeah." I smiled. "This was a great day."

"It sure was!"

Pearl gave me a hug. "And don't worry too much. I'll try to figure out what Lilli was going on about."

"Yeah, okay, thanks." I stood up and walked away from the fort alone. A dull throb started behind my eyes.

******

By the time I reached the scooter, my stomach hurt, and my headache pounded vigorously. "You know we always have to tell the truth." Sara's words echoed behind the pain. *I shouldn't have lied to Pearl. I'm not going home, and I'm not going to study.*

I almost turned around. Almost.

CHAPTER TWENTY-ONE
Stolen Moments

The last light of day was swallowed quickly by the night as the scooter bounced slowly down the uneven streets. Each turn brought me closer to the old town and, more specifically, to historic Lincolnville. In class, we'd learned that at one time, the area had a thriving African American community with shops and a real sense of inclusivity. Due to gentrification in recent decades, families that had been generational slowly moved out. Many of the original homes fell into disrepair. Land opportunists moved in, snapped up these places, and refurbished them but also divided them into efficiency rentals, often pricing out longtime locals. Other homes were purchased by young professionals looking to settle in. But few of the original descendants of the Lincolnville glory days remained. I supposed—for a change—this tale was not unique to St. Augustine.

I pulled up to one of the many rambling Victorian houses with ornate gingerbread trim and a wide spacious porch overflowing with plants. The owner was a former ballerina named Ariana. She rented to students, artists, and writers. Jacqueline had assured me I would love her.

I double-checked the house number, 1022, and parked the scooter. And in case I had any doubt about being at the correct house, there were two ornate birdcages, like the ones in Jacqueline's store, balanced on the wide railing. Their doors were open. I smiled and walked up the path toward the stairs. Before I reached them, the front door opened, and Jacqueline's form was framed in the soft light from within.

"You made it!" she called with enthusiasm. "I wasn't sure they'd set you free to come and play tonight."

I laughed nervously as I walked up the cement steps. "Yup. I already feel like I'm on borrowed time."

Jacqueline held her arm dramatically for me to come inside. She wore a beautiful flowing green tunic over a pair of matching loose pants. She reminded me of an exotic bird in full plumage with her brightly tipped pixie hair and the green and gold of her outfit and jewelry.

"Whoa," escaped my lips before I could reel it back in as I glimpsed the room behind her. *What century am I in?*

I'd never seen a home like this. Wide-plank hardwood floors shone in a variety of brown hues, heavy wooden side tables were draped with colorful velvet scarfs, and Tiffany-style reading lamps provided a romantic, soft glow. And the oddities only began with the decorations.

Soft jazz played in the background as two people chatted in tall-backed leather chairs next to the lace-draped windows. Another pair was intent on a board game involving small black-and-white discs. Just as the quartet looked up at Jacqueline and me, a woman entered the room from a side hallway carrying an ornate silver tray that held glasses, a crystal bottle filled with amber liquid, and a plate piled with little sandwiches. She smiled at us standing at the door and placed the tray on the mantel above the empty fireplace.

"You must be Storm." She made her way to us and kissed me on both cheeks. "Jacqueline has spoken so highly of you. Welcome to my home. I'm Ariana."

"Hostess extraordinaire," one of the men playing the game said with a smile.

"Oh, please." Ariana waved her hand in friendly dismissal. "Come in, come in." She took my hand and drew me from the doorway into the heart of the room. "Storm, some quick introductions for you. This is Paul." Ariana motioned to one of the disc-game players, a man in jeans and a black T-shirt. "He's a rather distinguished artist. And the woman kicking his butt in backgammon right now is Kev. She's a poet."

"Wouldn't you know it!" Kev said with a laugh. Paul rolled his eyes.

"Your move, Emily Dickinson," Paul replied.

What's backgammon? I wondered.

But before I could watch any moves, Ariana motioned to the man and woman in the chairs. "And these two are Kathleen and Doug."

"Hi, Storm. Great to meet you." Kathleen smiled and gave a little half wave. A black-and-white dog lay at her feet.

Doug stood up and extended his arm to shake hands. I accepted it, and he smiled.

"Kathleen is a potter, and Doug is a singer-songwriter," Ariana continued.

Okay. I guess this is what it's like to hang with grown-ups. I'm feeling pretty much like a fish out of water here. Nana and Dad didn't have any friends like this.

"I only have a bit more time before I have to get to my next gig," Doug said with a slight tip of his green felt hat with a red feather tucked in the strap.

"Were you playing downtown earlier today?" I asked.

"I was!" His smile brightened. "Did you happen to hear me?"

I nodded shyly. "You're good!"

"Well, I aim to please, ma'am," he said with an exaggerated bow. "May I?" He looked at Ariana and then at the food on the mantel.

"Oh, of course, Doug. Nobody can play well on an empty stomach."

He went to the tray, poured himself a sizable glass of the amber liquid, and lifted it, giving an air toast to the room.

"Or if they're parched," Kathleen said. The room of people laughed together.

"Please, everybody, help yourselves." Ariana sat next to Kathleen in Doug's recently vacated seat. She turned to me. "Jacqueline collects the most interesting people to have over. I learn something every week."

"Do you play?" Kev asked me, bringing my attention back to the room.

Seeing what had to be a look of confusion on my face—a poker player, I was certainly not—she smiled and glanced down at the backgammon board.

I shook my head. "No, never tried."

"Oh, well, that's going to change." Jacqueline nudged my arm.

"Please, take our spots, ladies." Paul stood. "This game is pretty much determined. And if I ever figure out Kev's tricks, I'll be sure to let you know."

"No tricks, Paul—all skill."

"Yeah, yeah." Paul said. He and Kev each poured a glass and then walked out the still open front door.

"All right, ready to learn a new game, Storm?" Jacqueline sat in Kev's seat.

"Sure," I said. "But first, can I use the restroom?"

Ariana quickly answered, "Oh, of course. It's the door just under the stairs there." She pointed toward the twisting staircase.

"Thanks." I walked over to what was, indeed, a door slotted into the wood that enclosed the underside of the rising stairs.

I opened it and tentatively entered the dark space. I reached toward the nearest wall and fumbled around for a light switch. My fingers found one and flipped it up. The walls were roughly spackled and painted a rich blue. The toilet had an old-fashioned pull handle that had been attached to the modern handle. A vanity inlaid with colorful tiles had an inset ceramic-bowl sink. Next to the sink, a miniature lamp with an ornate blue stained-glass shade softly illuminated the room. I closed the door behind me and enjoyed the moment of quiet.

I'd never seen such an eclectic group of people all in one place. Check that—I'd never seen such an interesting gathering of *humans* before.

They are humans, right? Yeah, duh, Storm. What else would they be?

In the back of my mind, I heard my family discussing the possibilities of other magical creatures. I chuckled inside and shook the silly thoughts away.

The pull handle was fun. As I turned one of the small silver faucet handles to wash my hands, I noticed that the drain didn't have a plug. Having learned from a previous time when I'd almost lost my moonstone ring down a drain, I slipped it off and laid it carefully on the back of the sink. Though just a pretty ring, it had once been a rather rudely enchanted ornament meant to show my heart's desires. However, it hadn't just changed its appearance—it had physically burned. I chuckled softly to myself, remembering the night it had burned my finger to the bone, all because Pearl was nearby. I hadn't known then that she was my mom, but a mom was the thing I'd wanted most. Thanks to Rowan removing the enchantment, the ring no longer did much more than reflect the light in its beautiful milky whiteness.

"Storm, would you like something to drink? Perhaps iced tea?" Ariana called in through the door.

I quickly dried my hands and opened the door. "That would be great, thanks." I really wanted to ask for a salt rim, but I didn't dare.

"Ready?" Jacqueline asked after Ariana left.

"I guess." I smiled and joined her at the game table.

"Okay, first thing is to set up the board, like this…" Jacqueline took the small discs and started to arrange them on the felt board.

I watched with fascination. Kev and Paul returned from outside and grabbed some sandwiches. They sat on the couch and started discussing people in power I'd heard of but had no real knowledge about. Ariana and Kathleen talked animatedly about a new art exhibit opening, and Doug gave his farewells while picking up a guitar case that I hadn't noticed sitting upright by the front door.

"So you will join us for the Frida exhibit?" Ariana called to Doug as he opened the door.

"You bet." With a little tip of his hat, Doug left.

"Who's Frida?" I asked Jacqueline.

"Frida Kahlo is a very intriguing Mexican artist."

"Oh yes, Storm." Ariana picked up a large book from the table. She brought it over and held it out for me to take. "She was an amazing painter who explored the themes of identity, the human body, and the inevitability of death."

I opened the coffee-table book. Colorful self-portraits filled the eleven-by-seventeen pages. "Wow." I was unsure what else to say. I'd never really paid much attention to art.

"She was crippled by polio that she contracted at a young age and later nearly died in a horrific bus accident. She spent years enduring one surgery after another and in constant pain, but she didn't let that stop her from becoming one of the most influential artists of the time." Ariana glanced at Jacqueline.

I handed the book back. "Thanks."

"They are doing an exhibit of her works downtown next week. You should join us."

"Yeah, I'll try," I replied. Ariana went and sat back down.

"Ready to try *this*?" Jacqueline asked.

"Sure." I shrugged and looked down at the game board.

I played backgammon—albeit not well—listened to the intricate jazz riffs, and watched the surrounding interactions. This experience was so odd, certainly not what I'd expected. But I was pleasantly surprised at how relaxing it all was. There were no food fights, talks of competitions, or end-of-the-world issues to figure out. Nobody pointed at me or talked about me or mentioned the fact that I was *Storm*.

Huh, I thought with a sigh. And then a further thought followed. *But I guess these people doing this is because of all the stuff my people have done behind the scenes.*

I suddenly felt homesick. I missed the beach house. *I shouldn't be here, and I certainly shouldn't have lied about it.* The pounding in my head intensified, and my stomach churned.

I need to go home, I thought and stood up quickly.

"Everything okay?" Jacqueline looked up with concern.

"Oh, yeah, sorry. I should get back home."

"Ah, the clock striking"—Jacqueline mocked looking at a watch on her wrist—"nine o'clock, Cinderella? Better hurry before your chariot turns back into a pumpkin, right?"

My cheeks heated up. *That was kinda mean.* I gave an uncomfortable chuckle to cover my hurt.

"Oh, hey." She stopped smiling. "I'm just kidding."

"Yeah, I know." *But I don't really know, and now I definitely want to leave.*

"Before you go, I want to give you something I think you might like. We got it in the store yesterday, and I immediately thought of you. Do you have just one more minute?"

"Okay," I mumbled because I didn't want to seem rude.

"Come on—it's upstairs, in my room." She stood up from the table. We walked slowly to the wide, curving stairs. I followed her up as she climbed stiffly to the top of the staircase.

"This is me," she said as we crossed the hall and she opened the second door on the left.

Her room was in the front corner of the house and had tall windows that filled two of the four walls. The nonwindowed walls were covered in deep-green striped-velvet wallpaper. A four-poster bed draped in white netting took up most of the floor space. The bedspread was an intricate embroidered pattern of leaves and long-tailed birds in greens and blues. A floor-length mirror stood in the corner next to a closet whose door had been replaced with a pink-and-red silk tapestry. A single painting hung on the far wall above an antique-looking secretary desk.

Jacqueline went straight across the room to the desk and opened the many tiny drawers. "I know I put it in one of these," she mumbled.

"Is that what happened to you?" I stood in the doorway.

"Is *what* what happened to me?" Jacqueline asked without looking up from her search.

"Polio. Your legs. Is that what happened to you? Like Frida?"

"Oh, no, nothing as glamorous as that. But since learning of her art and her story, I have felt something of a connection," she replied with a glance at me. "Not giving up on goals, that sort of thing. I suppose some might call me tenacious. Once I set my sights on something, I don't ever stop until I get it."

I nodded and fidgeted with my shirt.

I was about to walk to her when she exclaimed happily, "Found it!"

She moved back to me, but my attention was now fully on the painting. It was entrancing. I had trouble looking away. Jacqueline was at my side and must have noticed my distraction because she suddenly pulled me to head back out of the room.

"Oh, sorry. That painting is really amazing." I craned my head to try to take more of it in, but it was hard with the distance... and being ushered out. I planted my feet. "Wait, can I check it out?" I asked with a little laugh, unsure what the sudden rush was.

"Oh, that thing? It's nothing. Just a cheap knockoff print. *This*, though, is what I want to give you!"

She held her hands out, palms closed and facing down, and bounced each one slightly. I smiled and pointed to her right hand. She flipped it over, and when she opened her fingers, her palm held a small silver birdcage with an open door.

"Wow, it's beautiful." I picked up the intricate silver miniature.

"I remembered how you noticed the cages in the store, and we got these in, and I thought you should have one. Just in case you ever need a reminder that nobody should try to hold you back or keep you locked from your potential."

"Thanks." I closed my fingers around the metal figure.

And that was when two things happened very quickly. The first thing was that I looked back at the picture but focused on it with Lilli's eye. Her crazy eagle eye revealed details as if I were mere inches from it. I immediately noticed the brushstrokes—layers of paint added to previous layers, like hills and valleys on a raised-relief map.

It isn't a print. This is an original painting. The stormy sky was all grays, off-whites, and dark blues overlaid with a thick, rough layer of sunset—or sunrise—colors, like fire burning the horizon in red, orange, and pink. A woman in white stood atop a cliff that overlooked a very angry sea. Her dress billowed away from the edge. A small bird hovered above her just beyond the cliff. Lilli's eye also gave me a chance to read the inscription on the bottom right: *Un Canto de Sirena, J. Diego, 1849.*

Diego? 1849? Didn't Jacqueline say someone named Diego made the Hurricane Lady?

As my mind tumbled these strange ideas, I looked back at Jacqueline, and that was when the second thing happened. The way she stood in front of me, the image in my mind of her walking along the beach in her loose pants and top, the wind blowing, and the figure in the painting... they were identical. *And something else, one more detail...*

I inhaled sharply and turned my full attention back to Jacqueline. She blinked.

Her dark eyes, her features...

"Well, you'll have to come again. Have to strengthen your backgammon skills." She smiled. Then my arm was hooked into hers, and she escorted me out of her room.

"Oh, yeah, right." I forced a smile. "It will take a lot to get those going." I tried to sound as natural as possible.

What was it she said about the cuckoo bird secretly taking over a nest?

"Nearly as much effort as weather manipulation, huh?"

Her comment caught me off guard. I blurted, "How do you know about us?"

Without hesitation or surprise, she replied coolly, "I just make it a point to pay attention to my surroundings. And this town has a lot to pay attention to. I like to know who I can trust, you know? Like, I know I can trust you, right, Storm? Just like you can trust me. But I believe I would be remiss if I didn't warn you."

"Warn me about what?"

She sighed. "Well, I'm afraid I would worry about Z. She is keeping some very bad secrets from you... specifically about the Hurricane Lady. And don't get me started on Suzee..."

"I have to go," I said bluntly and rushed down the stairs. Acid rose from my stomach and burned in my throat. My head threatened to burst open.

"Are you heading out, Storm?" Ariana asked when I got back downstairs.

"Yes. It was nice meeting you. Thanks." I gave a fake smile.

I hurried to the scooter and took off down the narrow dark streets. My heart beat hard, and my mind spun. I wasn't paying attention and nearly crashed into a garbage can that had been left half in the street. I was near downtown by that point, so I decided to park by Flagler College and take a little walk to clear my mind and try to calm my belly.

Was that painting by the *Diego? Why would Jacqueline have it? Not a print but the actual painting. Is she telling me truth or lies? Who do I trust? I am going to be sick.*

I walked down St. George Street and willed myself not to throw up. But I left a garbage can between Lincolnville and St. George full of some unpleasantness. *What is going on with me?*

It was nine thirty on a summer Saturday night, so a lot of people were still walking around, finishing dinner, getting drinks, and shopping. Fortunately, walking in the humid night air calmed me. I inhaled deeply as I walked by the Earthbound Store. The heady incense-laden scents soothed me further.

"Storm?" a familiar voice called.

I looked up and saw Jon and his dad standing on the other side of the street, eating slices of pizza. He waved and walked over to me.

"Hey, stranger, how's it going?" he asked.

God, I miss hanging out with him. "It's, umm, it's good."

"Liar." He laughed then turned serious. "Storm, you really don't look so good. Seriously, what's up?"

I sighed.

"Wanna talk?"

Yes! my inner voice screamed.

"I'll be fine," my outer voice answered.

"Storm..." He raised an eyebrow.

I just looked at him. I didn't know what to say.

"Okay, how about just hanging out a little. We don't have to talk at all. Like, not even one word." He mimed zipping his lips and throwing away the key.

I laughed. "Yeah, I'd like that."

"Okay, one sec. Oh shoot, I already messed up." He furrowed his brows.

I laughed again. He then acted out, charade style, that he just had to let his dad know. I nodded and, with more laughs, watched him jog back across the road, weaving between people. After a few moments of conversation, a wave from his dad to me, and a smile and wave back from me, Jon came back, dodging new groups passing by.

"We can talk about normal stuff," I said when he returned.

"Oh, phew. My sign-language skills are rudimentary so... yeah, thanks." Jon put the remaining bit of his pizza into his mouth and wiped his hands on the sides of his jeans. "So, where to?"

"I don't know," I replied with a shrug.

"I have an idea! Come on." He took my hand and led me down the street toward Hypolita. We stopped in front of a two-story building. The sign hanging overhead read Medieval Torture Museum.

"Seriously?" I asked.

"I've wanted to check this place out. I heard it's super cool, and there's even a miniature museum too."

"A what?"

"I dunno. Let's find out!" He grabbed my hand again and, grinning like a little kid, pulled me inside.

******

After a rather gross adventure through the torture exhibits, during which Jon and I each took turns being the most squeamish, we made our way to the miniature museum next door which was cleverly called Micro Masterpieces Art Gallery. And just as advertised, every piece of art was to be viewed under a microscope. Floor-to-ceiling windows let us overlook the Columbia Restaurant across the street and all the foot traffic passing between the cars that attempted to wind through the too-narrow road.

"So, spill it, Storm." Jon spoke with one eye at a microscope, examining an image of a scorpion etched on the head of a pin.

"Spill what?" I feigned stupidity and wandered over to the Statue of Liberty image. We had the whole place to ourselves, probably because they would be closed in a few minutes.

"I knew what I was getting into with you when you shared your secret."

"I thought we weren't going to talk about real stuff." I crossed over to another microscope.

"Would you prefer I mime again?"

I looked over to him. "No. I just know I can't protect you."

"You don't have to. This time won't be like last time. This time, we are prepared for all outcomes."

I stared at him. "Really? Like dying?"

He laughed. "Okay, I'd prefer not to do that again. But even knowing that's a possibility doesn't stop me from wanting to help. I *can* help. You *need* my help."

God, I do. "I just don't want you getting hurt again, and now, with Vincent, I just—"

"*Just* don't worry. You need to keep getting ready to compete, but I can help in other ways. I've been looking more into the Hurricane Lady, much beyond our paper for class. I've found some pretty cool things that could possibly help with the competition."

I couldn't help it—I had to ask. "Did you happen to read about an artist named Diego?"

"No." Jon shook his head, and the small curl popped down in front of his forehead. He swiped it back into place.

"Okay, it's nothing."

"Storm," Jon scolded.

I didn't know whether I should fill him in. He essentially remained safe by not knowing anything beyond stuff he'd read. Even Vincent couldn't get mad at him for that. If I told him what was going on with Z's story, Jacqueline's story, Lilli and Suzee's cryptic messages to me, and what I'd found tonight in Jacqueline's room—well, he'd be right back in the middle of everything. He and all of his fragile humanness.

I couldn't protect him last time. How would I be able to this time—especially if the Hurricane Lady is involved in the endgame?

As I waffled about what to do, something—or rather two *some-ones*—caught my eye on the street below. I closed one eye and looked only with my Lilli eye. The two people were off to the side of the main foot traffic but still blended with the passersby. They stood and talked, which was not overly unusual, except this pair was unique. He was shorter than she was, and his long hair was as bright white as his beard. She was slim and wore flowing green pants with a matching tunic. The tips of her pixie haircut reflected in the glow of the streetlights.

She handed him something. He nodded.

"What the *hell*?" I muttered.

And then I immediately slapped my palm to my mouth and backed away from the window. Vincent's head tilted, and I saw Jacqueline question him. I turned around. I didn't need to see more. We all made choices. Last time, neither Jon nor I had fully understood the consequences of our choices. But now that we'd experienced the extreme penalty, we both understood. I needed help from my friend, and he wanted to help me. I didn't have much time to fill him in. But once I did, I also needed to make sure neither one of us ended up dead.

How hard could that be, right?

CHAPTER TWENTY-TWO
Strike Two

I talked nearly as fast as Lilli. Jon and I hurried back to the scooter, and boy, it felt so good to finally let it all out. The pounding in my head that had been a constant companion of the past weeks subsided. The more I talked, the better I felt.

"And then tonight, when I saw the painting in Jacqueline's room, it really made me wonder. I mean, she's the only one who ever mentioned the artist's name, and then to have a painting by someone with the same name was super weird. But the problem is, I can't ask anybody about it because I wasn't supposed to be there. I feel way bad about lying to Pearl, and now I am trapped by the lie." I dumped the entire tale on Jon, forgetting to take a breath.

We reached the scooter, and he leaned on the seat. "Okay, I'm going to do some research to find out about this Diego guy and the painting. I have a hunch that might tie things together. And you may not like this, but I agree with the others. I don't think Jacqueline being here is about opening a cool new shop."

I sighed. "I know. I feel pretty stupid. Seeing her meeting with Vincent tonight makes me agree something is going on. But even that, I can't tell anybody because I wasn't supposed to be there either." Frustrated, I cried out, "Ugh! I can't flippin' win!" Anger rose inside me. "I should have listened to the others. I'm so stupid." I kicked the scooter's tire, which hurt, but I deserved the pain... I deserved a lot worse.

"Hey, relax. I'll help. And I know you were just trying to keep me safe by not talking to me, but I think this time we'll make it work. Eyes wide open and all of that." He smiled. "It felt really good to tell you about Lilli. It's been super hard not having my best friend to talk to as I've been trying to avoid being electrocuted by my girlfriend's father."

I snorted. "Yeah, that's a tough spot."

I thought about Lilli's truth from the game before. She loved Jon, and based on his silly expression when he talked about her, the feeling was mutual. I had to help them. Vincent wasn't being fair... not to mention that if he was up to something with Jacqueline, he didn't even deserve a say in how Lilli lived her life.

"Are you sure about the Hurricane Lady?" I asked, referring to what he'd told me about when the nuns refurbished the Hurricane Lady a few years back.

"Yup, totally sure. Just not sure how it helps or hurts—or maybe doesn't even matter."

"Well, I definitely think it can help, but I'm not totally sure how yet. But I do think it changes the game a bit, depending on Laverna's angle." I remembered Suzee's cryptic advice about Laverna setting me up... but then I worried about whether I could trust anything Suzee said.

"What're you up to tomorrow?" Jon asked.

"Probably getting my butt kicked by Pearl, Sara, and Rowan in training. I have such a hard time with the magnetism thing. I still need the training rock Pearl gave me weeks ago. And based on how much time we're spending on it, I'm guessing they're pretty sure it will be important for the competition."

"Have you tried getting angry? That worked pretty well for you before," Jon said with a smile.

The image of the final challenge at the solstice party flashed in my mind. They had used Jon as the bait and Rowan as the challenge of wills to overcome. My anger about that had been pretty effective.

"I suppose, but that's a hard one to just *do*, ya know? Like, how do I just get angry on cue?"

"Maybe you don't have to get angry but just have to remember the feeling it brings. Once you remember what happens when you get angry, you can just skip the anger part and harness the results. Like with those funny abstract drawings that you have to bring the picture super close to your face and stare at the two dots to make your eyes cross and then slowly bring the paper away in order to see the hidden three-dimensional image."

"Oh, yeah," I agreed. "And once you get it—like the feeling of it—you can just make your eyes do it automatically."

"Exactly. So even with the rock, focus on what it feels like, then maybe you can just do it by remembering the feeling. But if that doesn't work, maybe try crossing your eyes."

"Gee, thanks, Jon." I laughed.

"Or just throw the rock at the thing or person you're trying to move."

I rolled my eyes. "Just a wealth of advice you have."

He smiled. "Thanks."

"Do you need a ride?" I asked.

"Nah, I can hoof it. Talk to you tomorrow?"

"Yes."

"Promise? No more leaving me out. I can help, and I promise not to die... again."

"Well, that's good. I'll hold you to that," I said.

"Or if I do die, I promise to stay near my body so Lilli can put me back together again."

"Right, let's stick to plan A on this one—you know, the *not* dying part."

"Cool, yeah. Night, Storm."

"Night, Jon. And hey..." I looked at him for a long second as he stood in front of me. "Thanks."

"*No problemo.* That's Spanish, by the way, in case I confused you," he said with a wiggle of his eyebrows.

I got on the scooter and, with a laugh said, "Night, Jon."

"Oh, Storm?" he said after I'd started it up.

"Yeah?"

"Purple looks good on you."

I laughed at his obvious reference to my Lilli eye. "Thanks."

I put up the kickstand and headed toward the Bridge of Lions. I got caught at the light, but as I waited, I realized how good I felt. Hanging out with Jon and sharing all the stuff I had bottled up inside was exactly what I'd needed. Finally, I felt a little lighter, back on top of the water rather than sinking with my burdens. I felt so...

Oh no... My breath caught in my throat. To my right, I saw Sara and Paige at a table on the porch of the Martini Bar. Before I could even think of a plan to not be seen, Sara lifted her drink in a mock toast to me.

The light turned green, and all I could focus on was trying to come up with an excuse to tell Sara when she asked why I was still downtown. I'd very clearly told her and Pearl I had to go home. I turned the corner and noticed a short man with strikingly white hair and a beard standing in the shadows of the lion statue to the right of the bridge. I quickly gave the man another look, realizing who he was.

What the heck is Vincent up to? And is that spray paint?

******

"How'd it go, Stormy?" Nana asked as I came onto the deck. Nana, Miles, and Dad sat together at the table. The food was long gone, but drinks and mosquito coils were still going strong. "Glad they got you back before dawn." She smiled.

"Pearl with you, hon?" Dad asked.

"Uh, no, she had to go," I mumbled.

"Everything okay?" he asked.

"Yeah, it's fine. I had a lot of fun. Lilli joined us too," I said.

"Oh, good. How is she?" Nana asked.

"She's okay. I guess Vincent is being pretty heavy-handed with her, so she has to be careful where she goes and when."

"Sounds like a regular father to me," Dad quipped.

"Daaad. No," I scolded. "He has it in for humans—for *all* humans, not just the bad ones destroying our planet. Like Jon, for example. Jon hasn't done anything wrong except for being human."

"Well, that and catching the eye of his daughter," Mr. Humpphrey said.

"Yeah, but seriously? No excuse," I replied.

"I don't know. I'm sure I would have purchased a shotgun or two for when my Sophie would have started dating," he answered.

Dad chuckled. I smiled awkwardly, unsure whether to be sad or glad that Mr. Humphrey could talk so openly about her.

"So everybody behaved?" Dad asked me.

"Yeah, of course," I said a bit rudely.

He held up his hands in a *don't get mad at me for asking* gesture.

"Well, Dad, come on—you know we discussed this. We didn't vandalize the Fountain of Youth."

"Stormy, you did sneak out and end up there with Rowan. You haven't exactly been fully truthful with us."

"Yeah, but we didn't do anything wrong."

He raised an eyebrow. "Tone…"

I took a breath. "Okay. I mean, I'm sorry. I shouldn't have snuck out. But I didn't destroy anything, and neither did Rowan or Pearl or Sara."

"I'm just saying you have to be careful. If you didn't—"

"We didn't!" I stomped my foot in frustration. My thumb absently reached to fidget with my moonstone ring, except something was wrong. I glanced down at my hand, and I wasn't wearing the ring.

"Okay, okay, if it wasn't you, then somebody—or *bodies*—wanted it to look like you. Do you see what I'm saying?"

I did understand and reluctantly mumbled, "Yeah."

Where is my ring?

"I love you."

"Love you too," I said.

"Who's my favorite girlfriend?" he asked with a smile, his way of offering a truce.

"Me," I answered with a little laugh, accepting his offer.

"Time for bed?" Nana said.

"Yeah, good night." I kissed Nana and Dad each on the cheek and told Mr. Humpphrey good night.

I probably never put the ring on today, I figured with some conviction.

I overheard Mr. Humpphrey say, "That's quite a special young woman you both have there."

"Indeed, Miles," Nana replied.

"Vincent may have something to his electrocuting Lilli's young loves," Dad said.

"Never too late for that shotgun," Mr. Humpphrey said.

The three laughed quietly, and then Dad asked, "So, Mom and Miles, what are your thoughts on Tropical Storm Matthew's current path?"

******

The ocean looked like glass as the four of us left the yellow house at sunrise. The air felt extra heavy, as if a weighted blanket had been placed over everything.

"Z said not to worry," Pearl said to Sara. "It's nothing so big it can't be redirected. We'll just have to be on call this weekend."

"You know I don't work weekends, dear sister."

"I think you may need to make an exception this one time."

"I'll see if I have any openings in my calendar," Sara retorted.

"What about the competition?" Rowan said, interrupting their bickering.

"Shouldn't be a problem. If we need to multitask while Stormy's kicking some challenge ass, so be it," Pearl replied.

Rowan squeezed my hand. "That's right, my little ass kicker."

"Yeah, sure." I rolled my eyes. "That's me, all right."

He chuckled, swept me off my feet—literally—and ran into the water. He splashed his way forward as I laughed. We fell into waist-deep water, stood back up, and waited for Sara and Pearl. They joined us with much less splashing. The lakelike water stretched before us, reflecting the golden light of morning like a mirror. The four of us dove forward and swam side by side into the green-tinged depths. The tan sand dropped away and left us somewhere between the ocean floor and the surface, surrounded by nothing but the deliciously warm and salty Atlantic.

I thought about my time practicing with Z and decided to give my thought blocking a try. I went to my song and started humming it. I kept it up until it stayed there without me even trying.

Lookee who's practicing her block, Sara said, breaking into my mind.

That's really great, Stormy, Pearl added.

So it's working? I asked. No one answered. *Uh-oh, not sure how to turn it on and off. Hang on... so if I stop the song, hmm, think of some different song...?*

So it's working? I tried again.

Yes, my little secretive rainbow fish. Rowan flipped around and swam directly beneath me. He grinned up at me. *It's really sexy to not know what you're thinking. Was it about me? It was about me, wasn't it?*

All right, Romeo, let her be, Pearl said.

Rowan gave a kick and swam ahead.

Pearl continued. *Keep practicing it, Stormy. That's a really important skill. You'll need to stay as private as possible during the competition so you can't be tracked.*

Okay. I looked forward to Rowan's body cutting effortlessly through the water. He was hot. *Man, his legs, thighs, butt...*

We can hear you, Storm, Sara said.

Oops.

Rowan winked back at me.

Since Stormy has made so much progress with her thoughts—Pearl smiled back at me—*let's all block our thoughts during this practice. See how long we can remain out of each other's minds.*

Just like the quiet game when I was little, I thought.

Exactly, Pearl responded. *But this will be harder than just keeping your thoughts private because I need you to stay silent* and *polarize. Also, you won't be able to get any help from us.*

So you're pretty sure I'll need to do something along these lines? I asked.

Yeah. Laverna's trying to say you aren't mer enough. Due to our internal salt concentrations, only a strong mer can magnetize. But staying silent, while a good indicator of being a mer, is more of a tactical advantage in the event of spies.

Well, then, good luck staying in your own heads, Sara said.

At least you'll have all of your different personalities to keep you company, Sara, Rowan said.

Sara made a rude gesture.

I laughed. Pearl glared. They swam off.

One by one, beautifully harmonic tones, high and low, sang in my head. It was so melodic and soothing. *So very...*

Rowan raised an eyebrow at me as he circled slowly in front of my face and held one finger to his lips.

Oh, right. Oops again. I started my song up in my mind.

The next couple of hours were spent with me feeling like I was trying to rub my belly while patting my head. As soon as one of the trio came at me to make me magnetize and repel them, I would forget about my song and send out my thoughts. And then I'd remember my song but not be able to repel them. The strange part was that Pearl, Rowan, and Sara also seemed off, as if they were exhausted. Or maybe they were just tired of trying to teach me. Anyway, I was more than happy when Pearl called it a day.

As the sand rose to meet us, I surfaced and took on the form of an early-morning beach swimmer. Using my arms in the freestyle motion felt so good. I stretched and reached and enjoyed the warmth of the morning sun on my back. The waves still hadn't picked up, and there was no wind. It was as if someone had taken all the moving air and put it somewhere else.

"The storm," Pearl said with a sigh, answering my unspoken thought as we walked out of the water.

"You okay?" I asked.

"Yeah, just a bit drained. Not sure why. I'll be fine." Something in her tone made me doubt her confidence. "Why the big sigh?" Pearl asked.

"Nothing," I answered.

"We'll all be fine."

"Yeah, okay."

Rowan and Sara emerged from the water, in a full-blown discussion over whether vampires could swim. *Leave it to these two to come up with the strangest arguments.*

"And what was up with you today? I've felt better repelling from a fridge magnet!" Rowan said to Sara.

"Just not into it. I've had a headache the past few days," Sara said.

"Funny you mention it. Me too. Salt ale when we get back?"

"Most definitely! Breakfast drink of mer champions everywhere!"

"That's never good," Pearl said quietly to herself, though of course we could all hear. I looked up and saw her reason for concern. Z stood on the deck, both arms braced on the rail. She stared intently at us.

Sara gave a soft whistle. "I hope everybody has their escape plans ready."

Nana and Dad also stood on the deck. Something deep within my body screamed at me to run very far and very fast, but like a lamb to slaughter, my legs proceeded forward despite the prominent warnings of danger ahead.

Z simply said, "Sit."

We did.

"How was your day downtown, ladies?" Z asked calmly... too calmly. Like the calm before the storm.

"It was... great," Pearl replied cautiously.

"I heard tales of a limo making quite the attraction around downtown," Z added.

"Yeah. Whew, that was something," Sara said. "See, there was this guy at Jack's, and he—"

Z held up her hand. "And Lilli? She's good?"

"Yes," Pearl said.

"Did she say anything about her father?"

We all shook our heads.

Z just nodded slightly.

Where the heck was this going?

"And when did you get home?"

Uh-oh. How am I going to account for my missing hours from leaving Pearl and Sara to when Dad and Nana saw me?

"I don't know. Not late," Pearl responded.

"And you, Storm?" Z asked.

I stuttered, "Yeah, umm, not late."

"You were all together the entire evening?"

"No," Pearl said as I blurted, "Yes."

"Perhaps you would like to discuss among yourselves to get your stories straight," Z replied curtly.

"We were all downtown," Sara said. A droplet of sweat slid down her inner arm.

Pearl and I remained quiet.

"I believe it would be of some interest to you all that one of the lions was vandalized last night. A ring was found at its base. I was told it was a moonstone ring."

My thumb unconsciously reached to touch my ring, which should have been on my middle finger.

"I will return exactly four hours from now, and you *will* tell me your tale. Need I remind you, one of the most sacred things we have as mers is truth, both our own and respecting that of others. In truth we find strength."

With a quick turn on her bare feet, she left the way we had come up and walked north up the beach. The sky had clouded over, and what had been an oppressively calm morning suddenly looked like it was about to break into thunderstorms.

"What the hell was that, Sara?" Pearl shot a glare at her sister.

"What the hell was *what*? Don't look at me like that. Save your glares for our little dearest over here." Sara motioned toward me.

"What are you talking about? Storm went home early last night to study," Pearl said.

Dad and Nana looked at me questioningly.

"Yeah, she did. You did, right, Storm?" Sara asked pointedly, raising her eyebrows. "Go home early?"

"I, uh, I…"

Dad frowned. The worry lines between his eyes became more pronounced, which was never a good thing. "Storm, we talked about this. You looked me in the eye and…"

"I know, I know," I shot back defensively. "Sorry."

"Sorry?" Pearl asked.

I looked at Pearl. "Sorry, I lied." I stared at my sandy toes.

"Where did you go when you left us at the fort?"

"I…I…" My voice caught on itself.

"How long have you been lying?" Pearl asked.

"Based on my headaches, for the past couple of weeks," Sara said.

I looked between the two of them, thoroughly confused.

"Storm?" Pearl's tone suddenly softened.

My face felt hot, and the pounding behind my temples returned with vigor.

"How have you been feeling lately?" Pearl continued.

The subject change confused me, but I was able to answer honestly at least. "Not good."

"Me neither. Been feeling pretty tired and getting headaches," she replied.

"Awful headaches," Sara added.

I was super confused.

"Lying, Storm," Pearl said. "Lying has a terrible effect on mers. You may not have known that, but it is a sure way of draining your own strength, and when you share a lie, you define a false truth for the one you share it with, and so it drains that mer as well."

"Oh." I sighed. "I didn't know that."

Rowan spoke softly. "Remember how I couldn't tell you anything about your true nature because that would be defining your truth and cause an overall weakening of you? Well, it would have been even worse if I'd lied about your truth. Defining your truth with a truth is not ideal, but defining your truth with a lie is like a slow, tortuous death sentence."

"How long?" Pearl asked.

"A few weeks," I answered.

"Told you," Sara said. "I'm getting some salt ales." She stomped inside.

"Wanna tell us what's been going on?" Pearl looked back at me.

"Not really," I said.

"But you're going to," Dad added.

I nodded and wiped a salty tear from my cheek. I started with my visits to Jacqueline's store and the things she'd told me.

Sara returned and handed out the bottles. "Defining your truth with a lie."

I mentioned Jacqueline's story about the Hurricane Lady.

"Ooh, she's good," Sara said.

"She knows how to hurt us, all right." Rowan shook his head with displeasure.

"What else?" Pearl asked me.

I told them about the party and the painting and Jon and how I'd seen Vincent and Jacqueline through the window of the miniature museum.

"I bet she didn't expect to be seen since you were meant to have gone home," Pearl said.

"Yeah, just like Storm didn't expect to be seen," Sara said with a sneer.

I ended by telling them about Vincent at the lion statue. I waited.

Pearl spoke first. "Well, you screwed us."

"What?" I was caught off guard by her harshness.

"Sorry, but it's true. You fell for the first temptation that came your way. We told you to be careful of her until we could figure her out. But you didn't listen. Jacqueline pulled you in with nothing more than a smile and some shiny trinkets. And worst of all, you lied about your actions to us, which hurt us all."

"But I..."

Sara rolled her eyes. "But you what, Storm—you didn't know? Yeah, cool. Good one. Let's hope we don't all end up dead because you didn't know."

I used all my strength not to cry. My face reddened, and the wind blew my hair into my face.

"Stop, Storm," Pearl said coldly as she tucked her wayward hair behind her ears. "This isn't new. Get a hold of your emotions. *Now*."

I inhaled sharply at her deep, powerful tone. I looked over at Rowan for some sort of comforting words or glance or gesture.

He just shook his head. "Storm, mers can't lie to family. Lies weaken all they touch, liar and deceived alike. Believing a falsehood can create illness."

"Why didn't you just tell us?" Pearl walked toward the railing and looked toward the ocean.

"I... I thought you'd be mad," I mumbled.

"Ha!" She huffed and spun around to face me. "Really. You thought I'd be *mad*? Wow. Well, how's it working out for you now?"

I bit my lower lip to stop it from quivering and swallowed hard.

Rowan stepped between Pearl's dagger glare and me. "It's so much more now than just you keeping secrets or lying. So much more is at stake."

Sara shook her head. "Every day, we're doing nothing but training you in the hopes of getting you strong enough, and here you go and basically sabotage our efforts."

"What do you mean?" I asked, not trusting my voice with anything above a whisper.

"You've poisoned our clan from the inside out," Pearl replied. "You've weakened us all. Your actions—your secrets and falsehoods—affect us all, Storm, and now I just hope you didn't doom us."

Forget about stupid Tropical Storm Matthew—I had just been hit by a Category 5 hurricane right in the middle of my chest. I sank back with the force and thought about the cuckoo bird. Jacqueline had turned me into one. My actions were destroying my nestmates. I was her secret weapon. I looked from face to face. No one returned my gaze. I was alone. I had screwed up in my silence, in my weakness about facing my wrongdoings, and in my attraction to the false promises of Jacqueline. Pearl was right. I'd fallen head over heels for the first temptation that came my way, without a second thought for what my actions might do to my family.

"And not to beat a dead horse, but it also doesn't explain your ring," Dad said.

I couldn't hide my frustration and embarrassment. "I didn't *do* anything to the statue." A flash of me taking my ring off in the bathroom at Ariana's house popped in and out of my mind.

"Except you did lie about where you were… again," he said.

"Matthew, give her a break," Nana interrupted. "She's sixteen. I could share a few less-than-honorable instances from you at that age."

"Mom, that's not the point," Dad snapped.

"What I'm saying is we all make mistakes in our lives, and our teen selves make a rather large proportion of those."

Dad shook his head. "I'm still disappointed. And how do I know you aren't still lying?"

The sky had darkened significantly since we'd come back from training, and the wind had picked up in gusts. I took both of these trends as bad omens because I wasn't causing this weather tantrum. Things were going wrong beyond our little porch.

"Okay, look, let's all take a break," Nana said. "Z won't be back for a few hours. How about you all get dried off, take a rest, and meet back here in two hours."

Everyone nodded and silently departed.

"See you all in a few for one hell of a party! There may even be fireworks!" Sara winked.

Nana stood up with a sigh. "Go on, Stormy—upstairs."

I took a steaming-hot shower, covered my body in the lotion from the green bottle, and inhaled deeply as the soothing scent wafted up from my warmed skin. I dressed in my off-white cotton shift. It had been my favorite dress, but now the tiny pink flowers mocked me.

I don't deserve anything pretty or cute. I sullenly brushed my hair in front of the mirror.

"So I hear you're back in, Jon," Nana said from downstairs.

I stopped midbrushstroke.

"Yes," he replied.

"Please be careful. Things are—well, let's say things are going to be very challenging over the next few days."

"I promise I'll be careful."

"Storm's upstairs. Storm?" she called up.

I popped to the top of the stairs, hairbrush still in hand. "Yup, I'm here. Can Jon come up?"

Nana nodded.

I motioned to Jon. He smiled and hopped up the stairs two at a time.

Once in my room he asked, "So, what's going on? Your dad and Nana seem pretty serious downstairs."

"Yeah, well, that's my fault."

"What? Why?"

"Ugh. Z found my moonstone ring at the lion statue."

"Oh, Storm. The whole town is pissed about those statues. But we were together."

"I know, I know. And I saw Vincent at the statue. And Jacqueline gave him something when I spied them from the museum. I bet it was my ring. I think I left it in Ariana's bathroom. But I wasn't supposed to be out then, remember? Anyway, I finally told them all the truth—well, not to Z yet because she had already left—but I don't know what to do now. They're all super mad. And even though everybody knows everything now, I don't know if they believe me. They think I'm lying even when I'm not."

"My dad used to tell me the reason not to lie was because it broke apart a special bridge between people that took years to repair."

"Gee, thanks, Jon. I feel way better."

"Well, do you know a good thing about the mers?"

"What?"

"I don't think they're known for holding grudges past, like, a minute. So at least give them a second, maybe two, to process it all and, you know, rebuild."

I thought about that. He was right.

"Hey, wanna go for a walk?" Jon asked.

"Okay." I sighed.

******

The beach was mostly empty, thanks to the threatening skies. Even surfers had called it quits because the waves were mushy with the unpredictable gusts. We wandered slowly in the damp sand near the high-tide line. Every few minutes, one of us would spy some beach treasure, like a shell shaped like a heart, a cool mermaid's purse—which, as we learned in the summer course, was another name for egg cases of sharks and skates—and a piece of weathered green sea glass. I picked up the glass and rubbed it between my fingers like a worry stone.

"Nice!" Jon said as I handed him the treasure. "I love sea glass."

"It's pretty cool."

"It's more than pretty cool. The ocean literally got hold of a piece of trash, and not just trash but something sharp and potentially dangerous, and then rolled it around, smoothed it out, and voilà! A transformation into a coveted treasure. The ocean is magic, like you!"

"I'm not feeling so magical right now. Kinda more dangerous trash than coveted treasure."

Jon handed the sea glass back. "So, things are rough with your family, huh?"

"Yeah. I didn't talk to them because I was worried they'd be mad with me. And now I talked to them, and they're even more mad at me because I didn't say anything earlier."

Jon chuckled. "Yeah, sounds about right. My dad's the same way with stuff."

"I'm just always worried about disappointing them."

"Have you?"

"Have I what?"

"Disappointed them a lot?"

"Well, now I have." I shuffled my feet through the sand.

"Right, but, like, before...?"

I thought for a moment. "No, not really."

"Then why are you so worried? You are anything but disappointing, Storm. I mean, you're really kind of amazing."

"I don't feel amazing."

"I get that, but you need to start seeing yourself that way," he said.

I shrugged.

"No, really. You're like the person that was out of shape but then got in really great shape but still thinks of themselves as out of shape."

I nodded. "That pretty much sums me up."

"Okay. Well, Storm, I hate to break it to you..." Jon stopped walking and looked at me. "You're in really great shape."

I rolled my eyes.

"No, really!" he said. "Show me the magnet stuff you talked about."

I shook my head. "I don't know. I've never tried it on land."

Jon stepped in front of me with his arms outstretched to the sides. "I'm ready!" He squeezed his eyes shut.

I walked around him without breaking stride.

"Hey!" he shouted and jogged to catch back up. "Come on. Give it a try."

"What if I can't do it?"

"Well, better to figure it out now than during the competition."

"Why are you so logical?" I asked.

"It's my special talent. We all have one, you know. Like, you can live underwater. I can say practical things. You and me, we're basically twins."

I laughed. "Okay, okay."

"Woo-hoo!" He jumped back in front of me in the same silly wide-armed stance.

I took the magnetic rock from my dress pocket. Like my swimsuit, which I wore under every outfit, my rock had become a fixture of my going-out attire.

"Ooh, that's cool," he said, looking at the black stone.

"Yeah, would be cooler if I didn't need it."

I moved it slowly down my arm and my hands. I felt the familiar tingling inside, somewhere between a tickle, an itch, and a light muscle tension—not unpleasant but something that wanted to be released. After the sensation ran fluidly down both arms and pulsed in my palms, I held my arms up to Jon's chest and felt the transfer of energy from my fingers.

"That tickles," he said with a laugh.

I smiled at him and then shoved the empty air between us. He flew backward and failed to catch himself before falling onto the sand a few feet away. I walked to where he'd landed and gave him my hand to help him back up.

"That was *so* cool, Storm!" he exclaimed, getting back to his feet and wiping the sand off the backside of his shorts. "So the stone does that?"

"Well, sort of. It aligns my polarity so I'm like a big magnet, but I'm supposed to be able to do the alignment without it."

"Give it a try!" he said.

"Okay. But nothing's going to happen."

I gave the rock to Jon to hold while I attempted to make the tickle itch happen with my mind. I closed my eyes, exhaled slowly, and imagined the positives and negatives aligning within my body. Then I opened my eyes and pushed the air.

Jon looked up at me. He'd been busy examining the rock. "Oh, sorry. Was that it? I wasn't ready."

I rolled my eyes and held my hand out for the rock. "Yeah." I sighed. "Told you I couldn't."

"No, no, try again."

"No, just give me the rock."

"No, come on. Let's keep trying!" he said.

I swiped for it, but he was too quick and backpedaled a few steps.

"Come on, Jon." I closed the gap.

He tossed the stone from hand to hand and backpedaled more.

"Jon, really not in the mood," I half scolded, half laughed and ran at him.

He grinned and turned. He ran a zigzag pattern toward the soft sand.

"Seriously?" I called. "Am I an alligator now?" His running pattern was what was posted at the Alligator Farm for how to escape a charging alligator. *The things Florida kids learn.*

He laughed and doubled back to me. I laughed too.

What is happening? This was so stupid, but funny. A crazy game of keep-away. The more he ran and dodged me, the more I laughed, and as I laughed, I noticed my arms getting tingly. As I laughed more at his pretend wide-receiver maneuvers of tucking the rock in his arm like a football, I turned quickly around and felt my palms itching, so I went for it. I shoved the empty air. He was at least five feet from me, and all of a sudden, he flew backward and landed on his back in the sand.

"Whoa!" I exclaimed and ran to him.

"There's my girl." He smiled up at me. "And remember, if all else fails..."

"What?"

"Throw the rock." He tossed the rock at me. It bounced lightly off my belly.

I doubled over with laughter, and he rolled to his side in equal hysterics. After we calmed down, I dusted the sand off the rock and tucked it back in my pocket.

Still sitting, Jon said, "Looks to me like you just needed a good laugh."

"That's so weird."

"Yeah, except your manipulation of weather is tied to your emotions also."

"Anger," I said.

"Yeah. So I guess magnetism is tied to laughter."

"I guess."

"You know what?" he asked.

"What?"

"I'd totally rock at this mer stuff. Sign me up!"

"I wish I could. You could take my place."

"Aw, no way. You're the coolest mermaid-human I've ever met!" he said.

"Oh yeah? How many have you met?"

He pretended to think for a moment, and then we both laughed again.

"Thanks," I finally said. "I needed that."

"What? To toss a human around a bit with your crazy powers? Glad I could be here to help out."

"No. I needed someone to get me out of my head. You did that, and it really helped."

He smiled. "I'm here for you, Storm. Always."

"I know that. Thanks."

We turned around and started back toward the beach house. "Do you know what you're going to tell Z yet?" he asked.

"No, not really. I'll tell her the truth about what I've been doing, but I don't know how much to say about Jacqueline. I don't have any proof, and the stuff Pearl and everyone told me about lying and defining other mers' truths makes me not want to say anything I don't have proof for. The last thing I need is to weaken Z somehow. I mean, that would just be great, right? First, I'm blamed by everybody for messing up our cool secret-gig thing in town, and then I'd be nailed for hurting Z. Thanks, no thanks."

Jon absentmindedly kicked a piece of driftwood toward the oncoming froth. "I did find some stuff out about your Diego. But I'm not sure if it's enough to tie him to Jacqueline."

"He's not *my* Diego."

"True, but he did seem to be a pretty interesting guy. Nothing much about him until nearly the mid-1800s, when his paintings caught the eye of a local from his seaport city."

"Really?" I asked.

"Yeah. He had some special technique with his brushstrokes. I didn't really understand, but I guess it made his work sought-after. He was also popular with the ladies, or his *muses*. And he did die strangely but not from drowning, or at least most likely not since his body was found at the base of a cliff that overlooked the ocean but wasn't *in* the ocean. So I guess he either jumped or was pushed." Jon shrugged.

"Hmm, okay. Anything about him making the Hurricane Lady?"

Jon shook his head. "No, nothing. I can't find anything that ties *anybody* to making it. Her origins really were kept secret, like Z said. But I guess, based on what Jacqueline told you, what Z said may or may not be true."

I sighed. "Yeah. I know the name on Jacqueline's painting was Diego, but I guess that name is probably common enough in Spain. There could have been multiple Diegos. And Jacqueline's been messing with me from the very beginning, so I don't know what or who to believe."

Jon shrugged. "Although, a great way to tell the truth and have no one believe you is to dilute it within a bunch of lies."

"Hmm. I guess."

"Diego was also known to be quite superstitious. Like, he had lots of talismans to ward off evil. His workshop was guarded by an evil eye, he had salt in every corner, and then there was this one other weird thing."

"What?" I asked.

"Bird feet."

"Bird feet?"

Jon chuckled, "Yup. Dried bird feet."

"That's what Z mentioned when she told us the tale of the artist who made the Hurricane Lady. He cursed it with bird feet. So that may be the connection between Diego the artist and the creator of the Hurricane Lady. How many people kept dried bird feet around, ya know?"

"Good point." Jon kicked a pool of water left behind by a retreating wave. "I looked up some stories about the powers of dried bird feet, and the one that struck me was the old practice of cutting off the feet of birds of paradise, just like Z mentioned."

"Yeah, that part of her story I didn't get. I thought a bird-of-paradise was a type of plant."

"It is, but it's also a real bird. Super pretty too. And sadly, quite a collector's item back in the day. But people didn't want them just wandering around, so they'd cut off their feet, and the bird would just live, sitting inside a small cage."

"That's horrible. How come they didn't die?" I asked.

"The interesting thing is because of bird anatomy and the way their blood vessels work, the wounds would just heal."

"Still horrible." I frowned at the idea of torturing animals.

"Yeah, the more I read, the more I got mad at humans. We really do a lot of sucky things."

"Well, not *all* humans."

"No, not all, but those that don't act like that really need to be more vocal against the ones that do."

"You should tell Vincent that. He'd like it." I jokingly bumped his shoulder with mine.

"Uh, yeah, I'm sure I'd get super far telling him before he electrocuted me," Jon said with a laugh.

"Point taken. Anyway, back to the poor birds."

"Yeah, well, the birds became attractions, and the feet, well, they would be dried and sold as magical items that could be used as protection and to destroy your enemies. Except the magic of the bird-of-paradise feet wasn't real. It was just a con."

"Oh. But something *was* different about these feet, Z said."

"Yeah. Maybe it was from a magical bird of paradise." He laughed and gestured like he held a wand.

"Yeah, a *magical* bird," I repeated. The niggle niggled again. I reached for it, but it slid left and then right and eluded me once more.

"And aside from his creepy obsession with animal good-luck charms, there was something else he was known for."

"What?"

"Creating wooden dolls." He looked at me and waited.

"Wait. What?" I perked up.

He smiled. "Very special ones."

"Why special?"

"All of Diego's carvings had articulated limbs."

"Like the Hurricane Lady."

"Yup. And that technique was way ahead of its time."

"Jon, you could've led with that! That totally ties him to the Hurricane

Lady. Diego the artist *is* Diego the doll maker! Or else just a really huge coincidence."

He nodded slowly. "Yeah. But I'm still trying to find the painting that would prove it and be a reason to suspect Jacqueline isn't as nice of a woman as you thought she was."

I sighed. "Paige and Sara were right—she's probably more of a witch than a woman. I was so stupid."

"No, you weren't. She was just very manipulative. You said the painting was called what, again?"

"*Un Canto de Sirena.*"

"That's Spanish. I'm pretty sure it means song of the siren, or maybe siren's song."

"Wow, really? I didn't know you *really* knew Spanish."

Jon smiled proudly. "It's nice of you to start appreciating my intelligence and not just my good looks."

I shook my head and laughed. "Anyway, Einstein, what does this painting have to do with everything?"

"It was a woman on a cliff?"

"Yeah. A seaside cliff, angry sky, and sea. And there was a..."

"A what?"

I turned quickly, grabbed his shoulders, and stood in front of him. "Oh my God, Jon. I *am* stupid."

"What?" he asked in surprise.

I let go of his shoulders and took his hand in mine. "We gotta go back."

"Wait, *we*?" Jon pulled back slightly.

"Yes, I need your help. You have the exact information we need."

"But you said Z was crazy angry."

"Oh, yeah. She's super scary," I said.

"Right, well..."

"Jon Manistar, you aren't backing out now."

He gave my hand a little squeeze and sighed. "Ugh. Fine."

We let go of each other's hands and started jogging back to the house.

******

We got back to the house with still time before everyone was meeting back but recognized a petite form standing on the porch. Her white hair blew around her face as the wind came in short gusts.

"Hey, Lilli!" I went to give her a hug, but she backed away from me. Shocked by her rejection, I asked, "Whoa, what's up?"

Jon stood behind me in silence.

"How could you?" She spoke in a menacing whisper.

"How could I what?" I felt defensive because I had no idea what I was being blamed for this time.

"Spray-painting the lions!"

"What? No, I didn't do that," I replied, shaking my head emphatically.

"Papa said you did. He said he saw you there." Her eyes were black as coal. "*And* he saw... you." She switched her gaze from me to Jon.

"No no no," Jon replied with hands raised. "I didn't... we didn't..."

"He said he saw you both." She was tiny, but her voice was strong, and her presence seemed magnified with her anger. There was an unnerving electrically charged glow surrounding her. Her white hair shimmered as miniature lightning bolts danced between the strands.

"Well, he may have seen us both downtown because we went to the torture museum together, but we didn't do anything to the lions," Jon answered.

"Don't lie." Lilli spat the word *lie*. "Dad said how humans lie all the time, and now you're destroying things, too, just like he said."

"No, Lilli, you're wrong," I replied with a touch of anger I couldn't hide. "It was Vincent who did that to the lions, not us."

She laughed. But it wasn't a normal, happy Lilli laugh. This was a nasty, scary laugh that made the hair on the back of my neck stand up.

"He said you'd say that." She glared at me. "You're no better than him."

She nodded toward Jon. "Dad was right about you too. More one of them than one of us. More of the land than of the water, he said."

"Lilli, come on, you have to believe me," I pleaded.

"Believe *you*?" Her eyes turned the color of the inside of a flame, and I heard a crackling behind me.

My hair lifted off my shoulders, just a minuscule amount but enough to make me take notice. I dove to the right and took Jon along with me. The crack of light struck with a sizzle between where Jon and I had been standing mere seconds before. The sickly-sweet smell of ozone filled the air.

"Lilli! Stop!" I shouted from the ground, where I covered Jon protectively.

She looked down at us. "That was a warning." Then she vanished.

Jon and I stayed where we were for an extra minute, both of our hearts pounding too loudly behind our ribs. Then we separated our limbs and stood up slowly.

"So, that went well," Jon said in his usual way to try to lighten the mood.

"I've never seen her like that."

"I'm guessing my plan B wouldn't work out so great at this moment," Jon added, referring to how he'd promised that if he did die, he'd be sure to have Lilli put him back together.

"No, I'd say we shouldn't count on that at this moment."

I looked out toward the water and the cloud-filled sky. A white bird took flight from one of the palm trees nearby just as the local nanday parakeets started squawking.

CHAPTER TWENTY-THREE
A Bird in the Hand

Jon and I helped Nana and Dad unpack dozens of bags of groceries after they returned from a run to the market to quote-unquote "pick up a few things." I wasn't sure if I should tell them about Lilli's freak-out or not. I chose not to. Beyond the bags of food, there appeared to be plenty of bottles. Nana insisted we should have drinks and snacks because, apparently, food solved any crisis and people with full bellies and glasses of bubbly drinks were less likely to be aggressive.

Good to know, Nana. I snickered inwardly as I arranged the sliced meats on the wooden board. *This is the perfect time to test this theory since my mer family hates me and Lilli tried to kill Jon and me.*

"*Olé*!" Dad announced with a flourish after he popped the cord on a bottle of champagne.

I narrowed my eyes at him. "Dad, why do you always say '*Olé*' when you open champagne?"

"I don't know. It just seems like the right thing to say."

I walked my tray to the deck. Jon followed with his.

"Hiya!" Pearl skipped up the steps from the beach. She seemed rather chipper for what was about to happen.

"Hi," I replied hesitantly.

"Oh, Stormy. Don't look so glum. You screwed up. Get over it because we have serious work to do," Pearl replied curtly. "Thank goodness you didn't keep that lying up much longer, or else we all could have been weakened to the point of not being able to recover."

"I'm so sorry, Pearl. I really am."

"No point in dwelling. Feeling better?" Her voice was cold.

I didn't like it. Her words said to move on, but her tone made me feel like she was still mad. But to be honest, I hadn't thought much about how I was feeling. Since my confession and walk with Jon, I hadn't been fighting back the pressure behind my eyes or the general feeling of nausea. And I'd done that amazing magnetism work without the rock.

"Really good, actually," I said.

"Good."

"But I have to tell you about Lil—" I started, but she stopped me.

"One sec. Let me go in and see if Matthew needs help."

"Oh, okay, yeah, sure," I replied, feeling brushed aside.

"So, do you think it's okay if we have some?" Jon asked, motioning to the copious amount of food already on the table. And this didn't even count the snacks Nana had heating in the oven.

"I don't think anyone will notice a few pieces missing," I answered, watching Dad, Nana, and Pearl smile and laugh in the kitchen.

So she is fine but just not with me.

Jon made a stack of meats and cheeses on a small round of garlic bread. He had just put the monstrosity into his mouth in one bite when Rowan showed up.

"Hey, Storm," Rowan said.

No "m'love" or "cutie" or "rainbow fish." Huh. I frowned.

"Good to see Jon is keeping up his strength." He gave Jon a pat on the back.

"Mmm-hmm," Jon mumbled as he chewed.

"Did we miss any of the fun?" Sara walked arm in arm with Mr. Humpphrey up the beach steps.

"Just some snacks, from what I can see," Rowan responded.

Jon shrugged and smiled.

So this is how it's going to be. Everybody acting cool with each other but not with me. Great, just great. Totally glad I told the stupid truth. I slumped into a chair that was off to the side.

When Sara reached Rowan by the table, she whispered, "Is she here?"

"Yes." Z's deep voice resonated clearly from the base of the beach steps.

"Oh, good!" Sara looked up and smiled awkwardly. "Every time," she said to nobody and shook her head.

The kitchen crew filed out, and everybody except Z filled plates with food. I stayed in my chair.

Z opened with an uplifting, "We have a problem."

Yeah, me. I looked out at the ocean.

Z continued. "It appears that Storm was taken advantage of, and in her trusting, she unknowingly betrayed our family."

Yup, cool. I suck. I get it.

"But I believe she has admitted her wrongdoing, or at least most of it, which has allowed some healing and strengthening to begin. Which is extremely important now because of both the upcoming competition and the impending hurricane."

"It's a hurricane now?" Jon asked.

"Yes," Z replied.

"So it's coming here?" Nana asked.

"Yes, Rean, unfortunately, it is. But I still have hopes that we will have the unified strength..." Z looked at me, and I looked away. "To protect the town."

Discussions continued about the competition. It was taking place on Saturday regardless of the hurricane. But if the storm continued to strengthen and threaten St. Augustine, everyone made clear I'd be even more on my own than I already was supposed to be because the rest of the clan would be needed to deflect the disaster. Interestingly, nobody brought up the even bigger elephant in the room until...

"So who—or more importantly, *what*—is Jacqueline, and what is her part in all of this?" Sara asked.

"Storm? Would you like to share what you know about your friend?" Z asked.

I stutter-mumbled, "I... I'm... not totally sure." I nervously cleared my throat. "I think she's been spying on us through this small white bird I've noticed for a few weeks. I only connected them after seeing a painting she had at the house where she's renting a room. There was a white bird in it, and it made me remember this white bird I keep seeing. So I think they are connected maybe. I don't know..."

"Anything else?" Z asked.

"I think Jacqueline's behind the vandalism except not her directly. I saw her with Vincent."

"I met with Vincent after I left here. He said he saw both of you at the lions." Z looked at Jon and me. "Have you asked Lilli about her father's whereabouts?"

"Uh, that didn't go so well," I replied.

"She tried to electrocute us," Jon added.

"Seriously?" Sara replied with a little laugh. "Crazy little sprite."

"Pissed-off little sprite," Pearl corrected.

"Her dad told her the same thing he told you, so she thinks we did the lion vandalism," I said.

Z just nodded. "Did you?"

"No!" I replied too forcefully.

She nodded again.

"So, what now?" Rowan asked.

"Keep a low profile. I will talk to the clans and hopefully calm them both," Z answered. "Storm, focus on your competition. Everyone else, know that we have a lot of work to do this weekend."

"What about us?" Nana asked.

"I'll need the four of you—yes, Jon, you too—to keep an eye on the Hurricane Lady's movements. I'm unsure what Laverna has planned, but I worry she will play with fire."

"Do you really think she'd risk something with the Hurricane Lady?" Mr. Humpphrey asked.

"No idea. Laverna is running this game, and your guess is as good as mine. But I do believe she is playing for keeps." Z stood up, wished us a good night, and left.

Everybody started chatting about everything and nothing. I sat quietly. Jon came over to me, another meat-cheese stack in hand.

"Hey," he said.

"Hey," I replied.

"It's going to be okay." He smiled.

"Yeah."

"I trust you, Storm. Just let me know what you want me to do, and I'll do it."

"Thanks." I half smiled.

******

That night, I tossed and turned and was never able to find a comfy position to welcome the escape of sleep. It was probably for the best since I certainly didn't trust my dreams to provide any respite from the hell that was my life at that moment. I'd managed to hurt my family *and* make everybody distrust me, all in one fell swoop.

Way to go, Storm, I thought with self-malice.

The worst part was that I did have an idea of what to do, thanks to what I thought was an important message from Lilli at the fort. Her demonstration—combined with what Jon had told me about the statue, Jacqueline's painting, and what I'd observed around me during class—started a plan in my mind. I sighed loudly and rolled to my left side for about the millionth time.

This is so stupid. I sat up and threw my legs off the bed. I looked out to the distant ocean. It was too dark to see the water without a moon. I needed to go out there... knowing who I'd meet if I went.

If I'm right in my thinking, and if I go, I can probably start my plan with or without the others helping me at the end. If I was wrong about my thinking, though, I may actually end up dead.

But heck, that may just be an added bonus for everybody, right? Kill two birds with one stone, I thought blackly. *Or a bird and a fish? Ugh.*

I padded softly downstairs, out the kitchen door, and down the steps to the soft sand. I held the magnetic rock tightly in my palm. I was being watched by small black eyes, but the difference this time was that I knew it. And if I was right, nobody else knew I knew, so for the first time, the hunted could be the hunter. That was, of course, if I was right in my many, many assumptions.

I guess I'm about to find out. I plodded toward the sound of the lapping waves. The time was somewhere between the middle of the night and first hint of an approaching dawn—it was difficult to tell with the thick black clouds that had taken up residence overhead.

I sat in my usual place at the high-tide line, buried the rock in the sand next to me, drew my legs close to my chest, and waited. The wind sprayed fine, salty mist from the choppy water onto my skin.

"I totally get it," I said out loud to the darkness.

And as if on cue, a voice said, "Storm?"

I smiled to myself and then turned and feigned surprise. "Oh my gosh! You scared me, Jacqueline. I guess you really do have insomnia as much as me."

Jacqueline approached me, navigating her way cautiously and somewhat erratically across the sand. "Yes, I suppose I do. Tonight is so dark I had trouble making you out from higher up. But I am so glad it allowed me to run into you." She took her hand from her pocket and held something out to me. I reached up, and she placed a cold metal object into my open palm.

I brought my hand back and looked. "My ring!"

"Yes! I found it in Ariana's downstairs bathroom." She smiled and sat down next to me, arranging her long linen pants loosely around her legs. She looked around as if confused but then refocused on me.

I put the ring back on my finger and absentmindedly twisted it back and forth with my thumb. My mind snapped into focus. *Laverna is the one who told Z about the ring. And I saw Vincent with Jacqueline and then Vincent at the Lion. So Jacqueline is working with Vincent* and *Laverna? The connections keep pointing back to Jacqueline. It's been her all along.*

"So, what's keeping you up on this rather dreary evening?" she asked.

"Just some family issues."

"Oh yeah?"

"Yeah. I had been kinda lying about hanging out with you, and well, I came clean, but everybody's mad at me."

"Oh my gosh, Storm. I'm sorry to hear that. I hate that I'm part of the reason for your family discord. Is there anything I can do to help?"

"No, not really." I drew small circles in the sand with my fingers. "Although I'm not quite sure if I should also come clean about something else."

"Oh, well, if you'd like to talk, I'm happy to be your safe space." She smiled at me.

I noticed how elongated her features were. Her face was narrow with high cheekbones, and her nose and lips were thin. Her loose clothing billowed around her slight form when the wind decided to make itself known for brief moments. She shivered after a gust, made a little fluffing motion, and then settled back to stillness.

"Hmm, well, it's kind of a secret."

"Okay. I can keep secrets."

"Well, it's about Paige," I said.

"Ah. Yes, she doesn't like me very much."

"No, she doesn't. But to be fair, she doesn't like many people. Anyway, do you know who her mom is?"

Jacqueline answered after a slight pause, "I believe I do."

"Okay. Well, then, you know she is not a fan of half mers," I said with a little head bob.

"Oh, I see. Like you."

I snorted. "Yeah, like me."

"But Paige is a full mermaid," Jacqueline stated.

"Yes, she is. But..."

"But...?" Jacqueline coaxed.

"Her unborn child may not be."

"Oh! Are you saying Paige is carrying a half mer?"

I shrugged. "I overheard her asking Pearl for advice on her baby."

"So Laverna doesn't know."

I shook my head.

Jacqueline looked beyond me in thought and then back. "Well, this is quite the heavy secret to be carrying, Storm."

"Yeah. I'm worried about what's going to happen."

"Ah, I see. Well, I don't know if I've ever spoken to her, but I bet she would find a way to understand. It's her daughter and all."

"Maybe, but I'm not so sure. I'm kinda hoping she doesn't find out for a while, at least until after this weekend. I really don't need her in any worse of a mood. Anyway, thanks for listening. It was really eating me up inside. I guess I should head back to the house now." I stood and offered her a hand up.

"Oh, thanks, but I think I may just enjoy the night air for a bit longer."

"Okay." I turned and walked up the beach. When I'd gotten about halfway between Jacqueline and my house and felt comfortably hidden in the shadows, I turned and watched.

Jacqueline stayed seated for a moment longer, but then she started the process of standing. It certainly looked painful. After she made it to standing, she shook her body again in that same fluffing move I'd seen her do before. She turned a full, slow circle as if unsure about the correct direction to head in. She took a few steps toward the water then gave a little shake.

After looking around again, she turned back north and walked away slowly. A small white bird hovered above her. The two created a familiar silhouette. The bird landed lightly on her shoulder. She limped up the beach along the water's edge, caressing the bird with one hand.

"Siren's song," I whispered to her retreating form.

I returned to our spot once she was far enough away, retrieved the rock from the sand, and held it once again in my palm. One question had been answered, and one remained. Rowan's words echoed in my mind: "Believing a falsehood can create illness."

I hope Laverna believes the news Jacqueline thinks she knows and will undoubtedly share. I think it's time the cuckoo *got pushed out of the nest, for a change.*

CHAPTER TWENTY-FOUR
Sleight of Hand

Wednesday arrived after not much more than a blur of Monday and Tuesday, which consisted of class, training, and worrying, not specifically in that order... but as a bonus, I also enjoyed the silent treatment from my family. Jon came home with me each afternoon under the pretense of finalizing our paper, but really, we were researching the Hurricane Lady, Juan Diego, and the siren's-song painting. I told Jon my plan and asked him to get my family to join in. I doubted they would listen to anything I had to say. I'd really messed things up by lying and by trusting the wrong person. But I had no choice but to see things through... even if it meant *I'd* be through.

"Hey, don't be so hard on yourself." Jon nudged my arm as we walked across the lawn to class.

"I'm..." I started to deny it but realized there was no point. "Yeah," I finished lamely.

When we made it to the circle of chairs in the shade, I looked at the second-story window for the millionth time, desperately hoping to see Suzee watching over us. But for the millionth time this week, the curtain didn't reveal a shape behind it in the darkened room.

Jon and I had spent most of the night alternating between researching the painting and making final adjustments to the Hurricane Lady essay. Samantha said she would print out the final paper and bring it to class with her. The rest of our class wandered into the courtyard in ones and twos, their chatter echoing between the buildings that surrounded us.

As each new person joined us, I would glance up to see if it was

Samantha. So far, she hadn't arrived. *No problem. We're still early. I mean it isn't as if Owen is here yet, so...*

"Am I late?" an out-of-breath Owen exclaimed as he raced into the garden with his backpack in tow and one shoe untied.

A deep, pleasant voice answered him from the edge of the garden near the white fence. "Well, now, this is a surprise, Mr. Beller." Dr. Briggs walked up the stone path with Dr. Ross.

Dr. Ross took an exaggerated glance at his watch. "Are we late, or is it possible Mr. Beller is on time for the first time?"

Dr. Briggs smiled. "Way to go, Owen. On time for the last day of class."

We laughed, and Owen grinned broadly as he sat heavily in his seat, still obviously winded. I nudged Jon with concern, though, because one seat remained empty—Samantha's.

"Good morning, everybody. What a sad day it is—our last day together," Dr. Briggs said. "I hope you will all miss us as much as we will miss you."

"Fortunately, for us," Dr. Ross continued, "we will have your in-depth and exceptionally well-written final reports to keep us company following our departure."

The class let out quiet chuckles and a few groans. I glanced at Jon. He looked back with concern and shrugged.

"If one member from each writing group could place the papers in a stack over here"— Dr. Briggs motioned to his leather crossbody bag, which lay flat on the grass under the large oak—"we can move on to our last lecture."

"Yes, Mr. Beller?" Dr. Ross motioned to Owen, whose arm was raised.

"Umm, sir, don't we get to read them out loud or anything?"

"Well, Mr. Beller," Dr. Ross said, "while that would be fantastic, I'm afraid we won't have time for everybody to do that. However, I'm sure your group's paper will be an extraordinary read. We will, rather than read the papers in class, spend time discussing some of the highlights you learned during your research of the Hurricane Lady—interesting or perhaps unusual facts you discovered—and also do a small recap of all we have managed to cover in these few short weeks this summer."

Owen smiled, seemingly satisfied, most likely having only heard Dr. Ross say that his paper would be extraordinary. Individuals then stood to drop their papers off. Others rummaged in their bags and pulled out neatly stapled stacks of printed paper with cover sheets. Jon and I just looked at each other and stayed in our seats. The professors didn't seem to notice who stood and who didn't, except Dr. Ross looked at the empty chair next to Jon and asked about Samantha.

"I'm not sure," Jon answered.

Just then, we heard someone running down the brick street, and Samantha raced into the courtyard. She dropped her backpack and rushed over to where Dr. Briggs was standing. Waving the papers frantically, she exclaimed "I'm here! Did I make it? Am I late?"

He smiled, shook his head, and pointed to the bag on the ground. She added our paper to the others and began to try to explain the reason for her tardiness. Dr. Briggs held up his hand.

"Ms. Watson, I didn't think I'd see the day that Mr. Beller beat you to a deadline, but I guess today is that day."

Owen gave a big grin. Samantha looked devastated.

"But no worries. While cutting it quite close, you and your group will be pleased that you did, indeed, make it. Please take your seat, and we will begin."

Class flew by. Afterward, hugs were given, hands were shaken, and numbers were exchanged. It was weird to be done. So much had happened since that first day I'd walked into room C. Jon and I lingered behind to wait for Samantha, who was saying her lengthy goodbyes to the professors.

I guess some things stay the same, I thought with a laugh.

She came back to our chairs and flopped down. "Oh my gosh. I can't believe I was almost late."

"Yeah, what happened?" Jon asked.

"It was crazy. I turned down Aviles to get here, and the whole thing was barricaded. So I had to backtrack all the way and then go totally around the other way. I ran most of it. Man, that was horrible."

"That's super weird," I said.

"Well, it *is* St. Augustine." Jon laughed.

"True," I replied. "Where was it?"

"That's the thing," Samantha replied. "There was no warning before I got to it. And I was already by the O'Reilly House. I saw some nuns by the big gate and called to them to see if they would let me dart through. They acted like they couldn't even hear me. I know they heard me. It was pretty rude. There were two women that were trying to go to the museum, since they were supposed to open for visitors. They were pretty upset as well. I eventually gave up, and I backtracked all the way to Marina Street and went around."

"A barricade by the O'Reilly House? Blocking the street?" Jon asked.

"Not just Aviles but all the nearby streets too. Come on—I'll show you." Samantha picked up her books. "I hope you guys didn't park on that side of town. It's a long walk around."

We left the garden and turned onto Aviles. "Storm, do you want to...?" Jon started, but I shook my head.

"I'll be fine. If I need to turn back, I will."

"Oh, do you have to go somewhere?" Samantha asked.

"Uh, yeah," I said to cover for the fact I would pass out if I got too close to the Hurricane Lady.

"Okay. It'll be fast. I mean it's right—"

We all stopped short. Ahead of us was a perfectly clear Aviles Street. No wall, no blockade, not even a brick out of place to impede us.

"What the heck?" Samantha exclaimed incredulously. "Where did it go? I had to walk *and run* all around, and now there's nothing here?"

Jon and I looked at each other. "That's pretty weird," Jon said.

"Good job making it to class," I said to try to cheer her up. She looked as if she was going to cry.

We walked a little farther, and Jon motioned discreetly to the Hurricane Lady's window. I nodded. I was pretty sure if I chose to take the next few steps, I'd know whether Jon's discovery was correct and whether my plan had a chance of working.

******

"Nana? Dad?" I called.

"In here, Stormy," Dad called from the living room. He and Nana sat on the couch, watching an update on the storm.

"The official track is still uncertain this far out, but what we do know is Hurricane Matthew will have time to continue strengthening before coming into contact somewhere along the east coast of Florida," the weather forecaster explained.

"Whoa, it looks pretty big," I said as I came to a stop next to the couch.

"Yup, Z was right," Dad replied.

"And seems to have its sights set on Florida," Nana added.

"How bad?" I asked.

"Right now, it's only a Cat 2," Dad answered, "but the predictions don't look so good. Hot water, low shear, very little land to get in its way—could easily blow up to a three or four or even a—"

"Matthew, no," Nana said. "They won't let it."

"Mom, *they* are a bit distracted, don't you think?"

Nana glared at Dad and then softened her gaze as she turned to me. "Nothing to worry about, Stormy. Your dad never did have the stomach for these types of things. We'll be just fine. Why don't you head upstairs and relax a bit before dinner?"

I nodded, feeling numb inside. It wasn't fear or worry but more of a cold recognition that whatever was going to happen had directly to do with not only how well I did on Saturday but also how *quickly* I got it all done.

CHAPTER TWENTY-FIVE
READY OR NOT

Neither I nor the weather woke up in a good mood on Saturday morning. I sat sullenly on the deck, looking at the ominous clouds. Strong gusts bent the sea oats in half and flung sand so hard it stung my skin while the humid ocean air formed salt crystals on the hairs of my arms. Hurricane Matthew was still hundreds of miles from the coast, but it appeared to be heading right at us, based on the latest models from a weather channel that Dad had on nonstop. I hadn't slept well—surprise, surprise—and the more I tried to sleep the farther sleep retreated. Tonight was the challenge, and I had no idea what to expect. I felt very out of my depth.

"Not much of a sunrise," Nana said quietly.

I just shook my head and mumbled, "Nope."

I smelled Nana's coffee. Her new favorite was French pressed with a dash of cinnamon, oat milk, cayenne, and a pinch of salt. I usually loved the fragrance, but this morning, it might as well have been dirty bathwater.

"Did you figure out the riddle?" Nana asked.

I replied without emotion, "I think so."

The riddle was my clue about that night's event. An envelope had appeared on my pillow Thursday morning. I'd found it after I came out of the shower. It was a thick ivory envelope with a gold interior. Inside was a folded paper, but it wasn't really paper—it was more of a woven linen with ornate script in emerald-green ink that said,

Find your first 3 prize keepers standing watch
with Fiel and Firme.
When darkness puts the town to rest

they will put your tracking skills to the test.
Tag 1 then 2 then 3.
Return to the spot where stars shine during the day, and
this time, 3 more are ready to play.
Tag 1 then 2 then 3.
2 sets down.
1 to go.
9 prizes in total if you must know.
This challenge will end when you reach the base.
Only then will you be allowed to end the chase.
-L

A riddle, I thought with despair. *Of course Laverna would start with a stupid riddle.* I read it a dozen times.

"Morning!" Jon called as he climbed up to the deck from the beach. He had on his usual frayed khaki shorts, but over his T-shirt, he wore a thin green unzipped rain jacket. A gust caught the sides and blew them backward. He quickly grabbed at them and finished climbing the stairs.

"Great day, huh?" he said with a little laugh.

"Not really," I sullenly replied.

"Well, no, I know. I was just… oh, right. Sorry. Not talking about the weather. Come on—I thought when I left last night you were feeling pretty good about tonight."

"I guess, but that's when today was tomorrow. Now today is today, and the competition is tonight, and it seems that much more horrible."

"Ah, yeah."

"Storm, Rean—just who I needed to talk to," Z said as she strode around the corner. "Good morning, Jon. Glad you're here also."

Z's deep-purple dress blew sideways as she walked. The way it flowed and pulled gave the illusion of her swimming toward us.

"This storm is making a beeline for us. We need tonight to go smoothly and"—she looked at me—"quickly. Laverna has given us all jobs during the competition, which will make it that much harder to fend off this weather. No doubt that's also part of my sister's plan," Z said in frustration. "Nevertheless, Storm, I have confidence in your strength and your wits. Just stay true and do what you need to finish. Unfortunately, we will not be able to help beyond our required actions assigned by Laverna. As soon as each of us completes our task, I have asked all available Sea Star mers to head toward the hurricane for the difficult task of diversion. I wish we could be of more assistance to you, but I know you are ready, little one."

I nodded.

"Rean and Jon, are you ready?"

They both nodded.

"Good." Z looked at each of us in turn. "Rean, can you join me for a moment?"

After Nana and Z left, Jon smiled. "Storm, that's the good news I wanted to share! I talked to Rowan, and he thinks he can convince the others to help with the plan."

"He *thinks*?" I asked with concern.

"Well, nobody's sure how many will be around with this crazy hurricane."

"Okay." I sighed.

"Hey, it'll work." Jon patted my shoulder.

"Yeah." I stared at the angry gray froth-covered waves pounding the shoreline. "Oh, here. I almost forgot." I handed him the magnetic rock.

"You're sure you won't need it?"

I shrugged. "No idea. But for the plan to work, you need it more than I do."

"Right. Well, I bet you'll do just fine. And I'll make sure this gets to where it needs to be."

"Thanks, Jon."

"You're welcome."

We stood in silence for a moment.

"I'm going to head out." Jon reached over and gave me a light punch to the shoulder. "Please call if you need anything between now and sunset."

"I will. Thanks, Jon." I mustered a partial smile, straightened out the riddle, and reread it. I was pretty sure I knew where to start.

"Can I get you some food, Stormy?" Nana asked as she returned without Z.

I shook my head.

"Jon filled your dad and me in on your idea. I think it's a good one. And I think you're correct about Jacqueline. I guess that must be hard, though. It always is when someone you trusted turns out to not be who you thought they were."

"Like Daniel?" I looked up at her.

"Like Daniel." She sipped her coffee.

"Well, it won't really matter if I don't get to that point."

"You will. You've never given yourself enough credit."

I sighed.

"Okay, okay, no lectures," she said. "Just please trust your instincts. You've already proven yourself once. I have every confidence you will do it again. And not only that—you will possibly force others to show their true colors as well."

"Thanks."

Nana gave me a hug, and I hugged her back.

"Nana?"

"Hmm?"

"Are you going to be okay—I mean, with the doctor and if they find something?"

Nana gave me a comforting look. "Yes, I will. Like you, I may have to face some scary stuff, but also like you, I'm a fighter. We Harns should never be underestimated by our enemies, visible or not. So if you promise me you'll keep fighting, I promise you I'll do the same. Deal?"

"Deal." I smiled. "I love you."

"I love you too, Stormy."

Nana went back in the house, and I went back to wishing I could freeze time.

******

The weather deteriorated further as the hours ticked by. From my bedroom, I stared at the dark-gray clouds and strong squall lines that expanded over the water. This was so different from the first challenge. No beautiful dress. No clear sky speckled with stars.

I put on my tank top and bike shorts over my bikini. I reread the riddle one more time and then tucked the linen document into the pocket in the waistband. My hair was tied back in a bun with my favorite scrunchie, for good luck. With a sigh and glance at the clock, I turned from the darkening scene outside and walked downstairs.

It was eerie to not be able to see outside. Earlier, I'd helped Dad put up most of the shutters and move the porch furniture inside. It was a nice distraction. Even though it wasn't night yet, all the lights were on as I wove my way around the lounge chairs and stepped over the umbrella on the floor.

The meteorologist's voice was a constant companion now. The channel had been on all day, and Nana and Dad would pop in at irregular intervals to watch the progress of the hurricane and then continue with their house preparations.

"I think we're as set as we can be," Nana said.

"Yeah, I'll head up to finish Storm's window as soon as she goes, and then we'll make our way downtown," Dad said.

"Well, she's going," I said.

They both turned.

"Don't look at me like that," I scoffed with every ounce of false bravado I had. "How tough can it be, right?"

"That's right." Nana gave me a tight hug. "Your dad and I know you've got this. And we'll be with Jon to make sure our part goes as smoothly as possible."

"I don't want you guys getting hurt," I said softly.

"You just get through those challenges. Don't you worry about us." Dad kissed my head. "You're not the only superhero in this family!" Smiling, he threw an invisible cape behind him and proudly put his hands on his hips.

I giggled. "Okay, Super Dad."

"That's right, and besides"—he motioned to Nana, pretending to whisper—"she won't hear of any of us getting hurt, and you certainly don't want to mess with that one."

I smiled. "Thanks."

Nana smiled back. "We love you. Now, go show Laverna just who she's dealing with."

"I will. So, you guys are all set?"

"Yes, we've got this," Dad replied. "You just bring your best acting skills."

"Yeah." I snorted. "Who'd have thought our future would depend on those?"

A house-rattling gust of wind interrupted us. I knew I'd been procrastinating, but still, I was having a hard time bringing myself to leave. I just wasn't sure when... if...

"We will all get through, Stormy," Dad said in answer to my unspoken worry. "I'm going to finish the last of the house prep. You be careful getting downtown. Are you going by land or sea?"

"Sea. Safer, based on the sound of the wind out there."

"Good choice. Now, get going so we can get going," Nana said sternly but kindly.

After one last group hug, I pushed the door open and went into the blustery evening.

Meghan Richardson and Tina Verduzco

******

    I recited the riddle, still tucked in my bike shorts, in my mind as I swam through the churning coastal waters. I was glad the riddle was written on linen. This way, I could bring it with me and didn't have to memorize it all, even though, by obsessing over it so much, I had learned it by heart. I was pretty certain Z had something to do with the riddle not being on paper. *Thanks, Z.*

    I made the turn in the inlet, fighting the sloshing waters of the confused sea, the high tide, and my increasing nerves. *Fiel and Firme*, I repeated as a mantra with each powerful push of my legs. Upstroke, *Fiel*. Downstroke, *Firme*. My first location clue was the Bridge of Lions. I knew this because Jon had told me their names back on the night I told him I was a mermaid. We walked downtown and ate ice cream, and when we passed the marble lions, he referred to them as Fiel and Firme. So to the lions I swam. What awaited me when I arrived was still a mystery.

    The milky green water churned with small cresting waves that crashed and bashed into the ones before and after. Sailboats moored in the harbor near the bridge bobbed erratically. They looked like a line of racehorses tugging at the bit to get out of the harbor. I swam past them staying just below the surface so as not to be spotted by any liveaboards who might be on deck, checking their lines. Maneuvering closer to the seawall, I stole a glance above the surface and spied three figures near the lions. One sat cross-legged on the grass. One leaned against the lion with a leg pulled up and a foot pressed behind him on the marble pedestal, and the third stood as lookout, facing my direction, hands on hips. I slipped back under and finished the short journey to the sandy cove where the bridge met downtown.

    The stormy evening made telling the exact time difficult. I was pretty sure the sun had set but it was still early evening. I waded through the shallow water and pressed myself up onto the seawall. The light had just turned green for cars turning onto the bridge, and the air had a mist-like feel from the wind picking up some water from the bay. I walked toward the trio.

"You owe me a tenner," Rowan said to the lookout, who I now saw was Daniel.

"I didn't say she *wouldn't* show. I just doubted she'd make it on time," Daniel replied.

"Well, she did both!" Pearl stood up from the grass.

"Umm, hi," I said hesitantly, looking at each of them.

"Lovely night, huh?" Rowan pushed off from the statue and gave me a peck on the cheek.

"Oh, please," Daniel said with a mock gag. "Can we get on with it without the public display of affection, please?"

"So that's what you call affection, huh?" Rowan mocked. "You really should get out more, cuz."

"Don't start with me, Ro—"

"Boys, please." Pearl shook her head in disapproval. "Can we not?"

"He started it," Daniel whined.

With a sigh, Pearl continued. "Storm, you've discovered the first location. As you must have determined, tonight's challenge will take you to different locations as well as require you to showcase a variety of skills." She spoke as if reading from a script. "Each group determines their own game and skills needed to obtain a prize. All the prizes are the same." She held up a small white sphere between her thumb and index finger and gently rolled it back and forth. "This, Storm, is a prize. There are nine in total, and you need to collect them all to win."

Rowan looked toward the water, which was still churning in the increasing winds. "We don't have much time to waste. Let's get going."

"Ooh, Rowan," Daniel said. "So stern with the halfling. Did you two have a falling out? Tsk-tsk." He shook his head. "Young love, such a shame to see it get washed away so easily."

My stomach lurched. *Is Rowan still mad? Are Pearl and the others* still mad? Jon said they'd help in the end, but there's no guarantee. What if they don't help me with my plan? *Well,* I resolved in my mind, *that's fine. I will finish this one way or another. I've got this, even if I am on my own. The plan will still work—I just may not survive to enjoy it, but my family and friends will, and that's what matters now.*

"No," I replied to Daniel coolly. "Rowan's right. We don't have much time. Can we just get on with it?"

Daniel's left eyebrow rose, and Pearl's head cocked ever so slightly. I thought I detected a smile on her face.

"Storm, as I was saying, this"—Pearl held out the sphere—"is your prize. It's a pearl, and there are nine to collect."

"How do I get them?" I asked.

"You have to tag us," she said.

"I—"

"Have to tag us." Rowan dramatically dropped to a knee. "Oh, no," he said in a fake-sounding whimper. "I seem unable to move. I sure hope Storm doesn't try to get the pearl from me now."

I looked at him then at Pearl. She rolled her eyes. Rowan stopped moaning for a second and motioned with his head for me to come over to him. I walked slowly over to where he knelt. He shrugged one shoulder higher and held it there. I turned to the others.

"Are you kidding me?" Daniel threw his arms wide in exasperation.

"Umm," I said with uncertainty and then tapped Rowan's arched shoulder with my hand.

"*Ahhh*, she got me!" Rowan exclaimed with mock disappointment. "Here you go." He handed me a white pearl and then stood back up. "Dang trick knee. Ever since the cannon incident at the lighthouse when *Danielle* cheated, it just gives out."

Pearl gave a laugh but quickly recovered her game face. "Well, so that was an example of getting a pearl. I'm afraid they all won't be that easy.

For example, here." She held out her hand and revealed the pearl resting in her open palm.

I walked over and reached for it, but my hand shot backward as if shoved away. I looked at Pearl. She just stared back. I tried again, and this time it was as if my entire body was shoved back, and I stumbled, struggling to keep my feet underneath me.

Magnetism. If I couldn't get to Pearl, I couldn't tag her. She was repelling me.

"How do I change it?" I asked.

Daniel scoffed.

Pearl continued to stare. I reached for a third time and felt the energy repel my attempts. Magnets could either repel or attract. *How do you get magnets to attract?* I thought back to the hours of underwater training. I pictured the rock in my palm. I'd made it hover during repelling, but then, I'd also made it stick to me by...

I looked up. Without saying a word, I spun around and backed quickly toward Pearl. When I got close, I felt it. She was pressed against my back.

"Well done, baby girl," she said. I turned back around and smiled. She handed me the pearl.

A slow, methodical clapping interrupted the happy moment. Daniel stood at the edge of the seawall, making his mocking clap. "Wow. The halfling understands magnets. I'm so very impressed. Maybe for her next trick, she can show us the breaststroke."

"What's your problem?" I spat.

"My problem is you don't belong here. You certainly don't belong as heir to anything. So far tonight, you have once again gotten out of doing anything real. Rowan just let you tag him, Pearl displayed a wonderful use of her skill, and you, *halfling*, simply used an infantile understanding of magnetism to obtain your objective. And I hate to break it to you, misfit, I don't plan on letting your spoiled little princess self get me without a proper skill test."

"Oh, like the time she outsmarted you after you dragged her to the depths?" Rowan walked next to me. "Can you do that same squeal again, Danielle, like after she bit you? I've not been able to match that high a note since before puberty."

Daniel's face darkened. "And the longer you will inevitably take once you have to truly *do* something, the closer the hurricane can come to this horrid little town. Maybe this time, it will finally get destroyed. So without further delay of the inevitable outcome for your clan and this town, you're it." He turned and dove off the seawall.

I sighed.

"Go get 'em," Pearl said encouragingly.

I looked at her and blurted, "I'm so sorry!"

She softened her gaze and walked closer to me till her forehead almost touched mine. "I know, darling Stormy."

Confused by her change in demeanor, I asked, "So you aren't mad?"

"No. We've been good since you told the truth. Of course, I was upset, but everybody makes mistakes. I've been watching Jacqueline since she arrived, so I kinda knew what she would try."

"The shawl!" I finally connected Pearl with the shawl from Jacqueline's store. "You were spying on her."

"Yes."

"Well, if you knew she'd do something, why didn't you warn me?"

"You tell me."

I thought for a moment. "Oh, defining truths again?"

"Bingo. Unfortunately, I had to let you figure it out."

"Sorry it took me so long."

She laughed. "I admit I did underestimate your strength at weakening us."

I slumped in embarrassment.

"Stormy, look at me." Pearl lifted my chin so I looked her in her eye. "We all make mistakes, and now you are that much smarter and stronger for having gone through them. We all are. Also, Rowan filled us in on your plan, which Jon shared with him. I'm impressed. It is quite clever! So, to make sure it goes as you hope, we all have roles to play. We can't appear to be on your side. I pray tonight you will finally succeed where others have failed and bigger truths and deceptions will be revealed." She gave me a brief smile then stepped back.

I'm not on my own. I smiled.

"Now, go. And remember, while truth to others is important, truth to yourself is imperative. Your strength lies in who you are, Stormy. And who you are is unlike any other."

I stepped back to her and hugged her tightly. "Thank you, *Mom*."

"Meet you on the flip side, rainbow fish," Rowan said with a wink.

"Yeah, thanks." I smiled again and let go of Pearl.

"Okay, Rowan, let's get to work." Pearl took his arm.

"Slowly... my knee." Rowan feigned a limp.

"Really?" Pearl laughed.

Rowan chuckled and stood up straight.

I turned in the opposite direction, toward the harbor. Rain hit my face, and the wind blew some escaped locks of hair behind me. Both pearls were securely tucked into my waist pocket. *Two down, seven to go.*

Without hesitation, I dove in and swam toward the open waters of the Atlantic. *Ready or not, Daniel, here I come!*

CHAPTER TWENTY-SIX
Tag! You're It

I swam near the seafloor to avoid the surface swells created by the hurricane. The downward slope leveled out at around sixty feet from the turbulent surface. The hurricane's center, while still distant, was already making its increasing strength known. Even at this depth, I was at the mercy of the surge as it alternated its direction. Half the time, it was to my benefit while the other half, I had to work very hard not to lose ground. Rowan and Pearl would hopefully be nearing the storm's center. They'd have to return for the finale, but I hoped they could create some steering currents powerful enough to shift it more out to sea in the time they had.

Clusters of coral heads rose suddenly in front of me in the darkness. I was nearly pushed headfirst into them by an unexpectedly strong surge. To give me time to make out shapes in the unfamiliar terrain, I swam slower, fighting against the surge regardless of its direction. I decided to take a quick rest in the lee of an enormous brain coral. Nighttime fish gathered around its base while the daytime ones were tucked into surface crevices for their rest. An octopus crept out from beneath, its long tentacles acting as legs to walk it along the seafloor in a mesmerizing fashion. From the other direction, a lobster marched proudly, antennae at full height, toward a neighboring coral ledge. *Ha!* I laughed to myself. *This is like the start of a cheesy joke. An octopus and a lobster walk into a bar...*

And the bartender says, "Why the long faces?"

I spun around to the intrusion of Daniel in my mind. My sudden action caused phosphorescence to light up around me. The tiny glowing animals dispersed in the current and faded back into blackness. I couldn't see anything beyond a few feet. I pushed off the seafloor and wove cautiously between the coral heads shaped like giant anvils.

Colder, Daniel's steely voice said.

I paused and rested my fingertips on the edge of one of the coral outcrops that made up the head of the anvil shape. Soft sea whips caressed my skin as they swayed with the swell. I timed my push off with the swell and floated with it to the right.

Colder.

I dropped lower again and swam left around the base of the second anvil-shaped mound.

Warmer.

How do you see me? I thought in frustration.

Laughter rang in my mind. *You may as well just hand me a map with you as a glowing red dot on it.*

Confused, I continued forward.

This really is going to take all night, isn't it? I can't believe I even considered that you might have had a slim chance of succeeding. Daniel chuckled.

I stopped. I peeked through an archway. Nothing.

No worries. I have nowhere to be while you play in the rocks. You, however, have a bit of a deadline to meet. As does your silly family trying to stop the inevitable destruction. Oh well. I wonder what your precious little town will look like after this storm.

Ugh! How the heck...? And then I stopped to think. Z and my swim came into my mind. *Daniel knows where I am because I'm not blocking my thoughts, and he's listening to my observations.*

I closed my eyes and started my song. Memories of my dad flooded my mind, but I pushed them aside and focused on the music, the tune, the notes. Thoughts were pushed back, and the song took center stage. I opened my eyes and kept the song in front. I swam slowly forward and thought of only the beautiful minor key, soulful and slightly sad. I purposely ducked through another small arch of coral to change my location, backtracked a little, and then angled off from my original course for about a hundred feet. I listened to the nighttime ocean—the clicks, scrapes, crunches, and soft rustlings, the deep rumblings of a large ship, and... the chime of a merman.

With my thoughts hidden by the veil of my song and my little redirection, I turned back toward where Daniel had last said I was getting warmer. But this time, I'd be approaching from a direction different from what he would be expecting. His chime got louder.

I'm doing it! I continued forward, trying to make out shapes in the blackness. Then all of a sudden, a burst of green exploded in front of me. The water was lit up like the sky on the Fourth of July. I blinked quickly, blinded by the sudden light. The water swirled around me. I spun in quick circles and then was flipped head over heels, at the mercy of the angry water. I felt like I was caught in a whirlpool—up was down, and down was up. Then just as suddenly as the churning had started, the water went still, and I floated like a rag doll somewhere between the seafloor and the surface with nothing but darkness around me. My heart raced, and my head spun. I sank slowly and calmed myself. Then I noticed it—Daniel's chime was gone.

What? No! I cried to myself.

Did you really think it was going to be that easy? Daniel asked.

But I was doing it, I whined. *I was hiding my thoughts.*

Wow, well done for hiding your thoughts. Do you want a gold star? It certainly won't earn you a pearl.

Okay, Storm, don't let him get to you. He obviously already knew where you were, and you didn't do a good enough job sneaking up, I thought.

The song was easy to get going again, and I swam in a random direction for a few yards, settled down, and then listened. No chime. I turned to the left and swam in that direction for a bit longer and then listened. I turned left again and swam longer. I was purposely spiraling outward to listen for where Daniel might have ended up. That third turn did the trick, and I picked up his chime. It was faint, so I figured he wasn't super close, but I was at least heading in the correct direction. I continued swimming slowly in long zigzags to determine a better location. Once again, his chime grew louder, and this time, I never let my thoughts reach him. This was obviously proving I could hide them. I smiled, confident I had beaten the challenge, and pushed a bit faster.

Nice try! Daniel's voice rang loudly in my mind at the same moment that I was roughly pushed backward by a black shape. I hit an outcrop and scraped my side against fire coral. I grabbed my skin and winced as the burning sensation tore through me. I pushed away from the coral and spun to catch a glimpse of him, but the phosphorescence was already a wide swath, giving only a general indication of where he'd gone.

I don't get it, I thought. *I'm doing it right. I'm hiding my thoughts.*

That doesn't mean I can't hear you.

Well, yeah, you can hear my chime, but that's not fair. I can't turn that off—that's not a skill! Why would this *be the game? Isn't it about testing my skills? This should be about my skill of blocking my thoughts. I'll never catch you if you can just move away by tracking my chime.*

I rubbed at the angry red welts the fire coral left on my side. My breath was heavy from the exertion. The depth and darkness were catching up to me.

Ah, well, I heard something about me picking a place and staying there if your thoughts didn't give your approach away, but well, who's going to know, right? And yeah, at least you've finally gotten something right. You won't ever be able to catch me. How you feeling, by the way? Getting tired yet? We're pretty far from the surface and it's nighttime. Tsk-tsk. Not so sure how long you can keep this up, but my guess is it shouldn't be too hard to play keep-away from you long enough that you may just never return.

But that's not fair! I protested.

He just laughed.

Even as my anger rose, I knew that he was right about my endurance limits and that nobody would learn of his cheating unless I made it back.

I was starting to feel the effects of the night and the depth—my limbs felt heavy, and I shivered in short bursts. With no sun to recharge me, I wasn't going to be able to last much longer. I had no idea how to win at a game that Daniel made impossible. I'd proven my skill at blocking my thoughts, so that wasn't an issue anymore. Unfortunately, it also wasn't going to be enough to tag him. There was no way to hide my chime—it was always there, so it would always be heard. You couldn't hide a sound.

Anchored by my fingertips in the sand, I drifted forward and backward as I surrendered to the surge like a sea whip. I closed my eyes and tried to think. My song played in my mind, and I was transported once again back to Dad's study. He was writing, and I was curled up on the leather chair, watching his fingers move rhythmically on his keyboard. But during this memory, the distinct clacking of each keystroke was missing. The music was loud enough to cloak the sound his fingers should have been making on the keyboard. It was fascinating to watch because I knew the clacking should be there each time his fingers moved, but the music overpowered it.

Wait a sec. The music overpowered the clacking! My mind jumped back to the present. *How do you hide sound? With a louder sound. Oh my gosh, that's it!* I quieted again and listened. Daniel's chime was audible, and I had an idea which way he'd gone, so that part was good. Then I listened for another sound. *Please, please, please,* I wished at the rumble of the ship that was somewhere overhead. *Be headed this way.*

Have you given up yet, Storm? Daniel asked.

I didn't reply. I wanted to wait to see if I had a chance.

I still hear your chime, so I guess you haven't faded completely. No rush, halfling, I have nowhere to be.

The rumbling was definitely getting louder. *Thank goodness St. Augustine is along a major shipping route,* I thought. *Now it's just a matter of timing, deception, and luck that I'm guessing his location correctly. I'll only have one shot.*

I floated up slowly from the seafloor.

I'm not feeling so good, I thought to Daniel.

I'm not surprised. You were never cut out for this life. This was almost too easy, Storm.

As he spoke, I drifted higher, closer to the surface and the approaching barge. The ship's reverberating rumbles were louder now. I concentrated through the sound to hear Daniel's chime. I needed to get as accurate a location as possible before his chime was lost to me behind the ship noise.

Pearl should really take responsibility for putting you in this situation, Daniel continued. *She should have been honest with you that you aren't mer enough. But I suppose no surprise on her questionable judgment, being that she chose a human over me.*

The ship was nearly overhead, and I rose until securely within the sound bubble of its engines. On the plus side, I was audibly invisible. On the downside, I couldn't hear Daniel's chime through the deafening reverberations. My insides vibrated with the deep rumble. I matched the pace of the ship and hoped I'd made a correct guess for my next move.

And Z, she has absolutely no excuse. When my mother regains control of this territory, everything will be sorted properly. A restructuring is way overdue.

Daniel's annoying monologue droned on in my mind. At least he didn't suspect anything yet. I just needed another minute.

Storm? Uh-oh. Did you fade out already? That was quicker than I thought.

My next move had to be quick.

Storm?

I angled my body downward and took a large gulp of water in the hopes that it would energize me enough for this last push. With all I had, I kicked and shot toward the seafloor. I'd guessed pretty well. I picked up Daniel's chime. It was loud. I was close.

A large coral ledge took shape. That had to be it. I bore down at the speed of a torpedo.

Yes, Daniel? I replied.

A sudden burst of green exploded from under the ledge. Daniel's dark shape bolted away. I stayed with him, closing the gap. Tracking him was easy with the neon trail of phosphorescence in his wake.

He dodged left around a mound and then wove between too long ledges. I followed his desperate attempt to flee. A burst of adrenaline filled me, and I kicked harder than ever before. I held the high ground as he hugged the seafloor. He swerved once more, and when he swam up to clear a giant brain coral, I dove onto him from above at full speed. He squealed in shock. We flipped and twisted out of control, ending up in a tangle on a round patch of sand surrounded by tall corals.

Tag! I announced, staring into his eyes. I rolled off him and held out my palm.

He shook his head in dismay and handed me a pearl from his pocket. *Well played, halfling.*

Thanks.

I doubt you'll survive the night.

I guess we'll have to wait and see. But I do have a question.

What? he asked.

Did it hurt?

Did what hurt?

Getting beat by a halfling.

I left before he could answer, heading back toward what I hoped was the direction of town. *Three pearls down, six to go.*

******

Uh-oh, I thought. The seafloor wasn't angling up, meaning the water wasn't getting any shallower, meaning I wasn't heading back to shore… meaning I was… lost. I fought the urge to just give up. *All right, don't panic, Storm. Let's go up and take a peek around.*

With a quick tap of my pocket to make sure I still felt three pearls and the folded riddle, I swam up. The water pulled and pushed me as I reached the surface. I rose and fell multiple feet with the surface swells amid choppy cresting waves. The conditions were deteriorating badly. I guessed Rowan and Pearl weren't having any luck steering the storm away.

Okay, still okay. We'll be okay. I just need to get to shore and finish this stupid game. Then we can all work together to shift this monster.

Sloshing around in the turbid water, rising and falling and trying to avoid the breaking waves, I desperately tried to orient myself. I knew I had to head west to get back to St. Augustine, but which way was west? The sky was dark with clouds. There were no stars and, of course, no moon, and a 360-degree spin didn't offer me any glimmer of lights near the horizon. Just the angry sea and me. No one to help or guide me. No one. My chest tightened, and a wave crashed over me. I tumbled and then righted again with my head above the water. I coughed and wheezed in the air. Hot tears slid down my cheeks.

I doubt you'll survive the night. Daniel's words stung in my belly.

"Help!" I cried to the wind and spun again in a fruitless circle as waves crashed on top of me. I hit the water with my fists closed in frustration and kicked erratically.

My little tantrum did nothing to help me. *Okay. Stop it, Storm. You have to figure this out. Think,* I scolded myself.

Another wave crashed over me, and that did it. Something snapped inside me. I yelled with all of my might, "Stop hitting me!"

The water around me immediately calmed. Waves veered left and right of me. I was no longer being tossed like a rag doll but simply treading water in the middle of a calm circle of water.

Water manipulation. Of course. Duh, Storm. You are a mermaid after all. I laughed a bit hysterically and then was happy no one was with me to witness my partial mental breakdown. The laughter stopped as suddenly as it had begun, and I looked around again. Then I looked up.

My mind replayed my conversation with Rowan at the Fountain of

Youth planetarium: "Well, I'll tell you a secret. Do you see that star? That's the North Star... while so many of the other stars and constellations rise and fall and move over the years and centuries, that one doesn't, at least not in my lifetime, which is a long time. So, m'dear, that one is our star... the one to find if you ever need to get back home... to me."

The North Star. That's how the original Spanish sailors landed in St. Augustine. That's how I can get home. The only problem was no stars were visible behind the storm clouds. I exhaled slowly and closed my eyes. Then I opened them to the sky, took a big breath, and on the next exhalation, mentally pushed the clouds apart. The water rippled around me with the energy, but the waves didn't dare to come close.

The clouds fought me, but I kept breathing and pushing. I broke through the first layer and the second, then the towering thunderheads gave way. I spotted the inky sky studded with a million twinkling lights. The clouds were getting harder to push as they seemed to pile into each other and build resistance out of sheer mass, like a plow pushing against piles of the deep snow during Indiana winters. My breath was coming in short bursts, and my heart pumped hard. My legs got weak and tingly as they struggled to kick. I stopped pushing. The clouds tumbled back into the small hole I'd fought so hard for.

Flopping onto my back and floating within my calm oasis, I caught my breath. *Okay, that didn't totally work out. I can't clear all the clouds. This is a freakin' hurricane and all. So... I need to be strategic. I need to clear just enough to get a direction from the North Star. But if I knew where the North Star was, I wouldn't need the clouds cleared. Great, Storm. Now what?*

I scanned the sky for some hint. I noticed that as bits of seaweed entered my circle, they drifted past me quickly, following a steady current. Some of them wrapped around my arm, and while they were trapped by my body, the tendrils still reached like kite ribbons in a strong wind.

"The Gulf Stream!" I shouted at the darkness. *While I calmed the effects the storm had on my little circle of water, I didn't stop the mighty*

Gulf Stream on its journey. I can use the current to orient myself as I make clearings in the clouds in ninety-degree increments. I'm bound to spot the dipper and the North Star, and I won't have to clear more than a small circle at a time.

"I can do this," I whispered and started with the seaweed floating past me from right to left, some of it continuing to wrap around my arm, helping with the visual of the current's direction. After not finding the dipper to help me locate the North Star, I rotated ninety degrees to the right. I repeated the clearing of the clouds.

Nothing.

Another ninety-degree turn to the right.

Nope.

Again, I made a turn. Still nothing.

Swallowing my fear about completing my circle and having my theory busted, I made another rotation, with the current now at my back. *Bingo!* My beautiful, bright North Star appeared at the edge of the gap I'd created.

"Hello, lovely." I sighed with relief.

I oriented myself to the west and felt the angle of the current against me. I just had to keep the current hitting me in the same spot and swim. At best, I'd reach St. Augustine. At worst, I'd have to make adjustments once I got close enough to land to see where I'd ended up. But at least I knew I was heading back to the correct continent.

Sighing with relief, I dropped a few feet into the water. I aligned myself with the current, so it still pushed me from the same direction as it had at the surface, and started my journey back. I rose above water every ten minutes or so to check on my star and make sure I wasn't off course. Finally, after what felt like an endless cycle of surface checks, I was rewarded with lights on the horizon. And not just any lights—a beacon calling to all wayward seafarers. I grinned until my cheeks hurt because my best-case scenario had come true. That lovely, recognizable beacon belonged to the St. Augustine Lighthouse. Her light was guiding me home.

I made it, I thought and rolled onto my back. I calmed the surrounding water again and floated for a moment, rubbing my aching legs. The three pearls were still secure in my pocket. Smiling, I couldn't help but feel proud of myself. I wanted to savor this feeling but knew time was getting short.

What was the next part of the riddle? Oh yeah. "Return to the spot where stars shine during the day, and this time, three more are ready to play." I rolled back onto my belly, oriented myself, and ducked beneath the surface. *Fountain of Youth, here I come.*

I approached the narrow channel and made my way to the seawall. The tide was very high, and water splashed onto the grass. That was a bad sign with the storm still so far away.

I saw a dim flickering light in the distance. As I strode across the lawn, past the sleeping peacocks and hens, I noticed it was coming from the Spring House. I took a calming breath and marched bravely toward whatever awaited me.

"Sara? Suzee?" I exclaimed with surprise when I entered.

"Stormy! Perfect timing." Sara winked.

"What are you guys doing?" I asked with confusion and stared at the sight before me. Sara was lounging in a deck chair down in front of the Fountain of Youth's trickling spring, while Suzee held a metal drink shaker under the water stream. A full ice bucket was snuggled into the sand between their chairs, and salt-rimmed margarita glasses sat on a table.

"They always taste better with this," Suzee said with a nod toward the stream of ancient spring water.

"Umm, you... what?"

"Margaritas, Storm." Sara took the now-full glass from Suzee. They clinked their glasses, and Suzee sat down in the other chair.

"But I..."

"Oh sorry, do you want some?" Sara said. "We only have the two glasses, but there are plastic cups by the entrance."

"No, I—what is happening right now?" I looked between the two lounging beauties in the sandpit by the park's namesake.

Sara smiled. "Really, Stormy, you should go and get a cup."

"Okaaay..." I walked to the plastic cup dispenser and pulled down the bottom cup. In it was a small black pearl. I smiled back at Sara.

"Told you."

"Thanks!"

Suzee took a sip of her drink and tilted her head. "For the record, I don't agree with this redo challenge. Laverna took things too far and with that siren, no less."

"Wait, you know about Jacqueline?" I asked with surprise.

"Yes, little one. Of course. And I agree with your cute plan. Sara filled me in. Serves them both right, I say."

My stomach did a little happy flutter. *They are on my side. I'm not on my own.*

"But with that said," Suzee continued, her shimmery purple nail tapping her chin in thought.

Uh-oh, I thought.

"A game is a game, and who can pass up a chance for fun? So my pearl is outside. Specifically, it is in the pocket of the night security guard, who is patrolling the grounds as we speak. Good luck!"

The happy flutter disappeared. I sighed and turned to go.

"Hey, Stormy," Sara called.

"Yeah?"

"You've got this."

I nodded and went to find the security guard.

CHAPTER TWENTY-SEVEN
FULL CIRCLE

The flashlight bobbed with each step he took. He passed the mission church and stayed on the path as it led out toward the blacksmith hut. I tracked him quietly by cutting across the grass. Eventually, I got ahead of him. I didn't really have a plan, but I'd figure it out when he got to me.

I hopped up, sat on the blacksmith booth's wooden counter, and waited. The guard's whistling got louder, and the beam of light swayed left and right with his plodding steps.

He was nearly in front of me before he noticed my shape.

Not the most observant. I laughed to myself.

He jumped, coughed, then regained his composure. "Who's there?" he asked in a gritty voice that revealed a heavy smoking habit.

"Oh, hi!" I said in my sweetest tone.

He ambled forward a bit and then blinded me with a direct hit of his light. I instinctively held my hand up to shade my eyes. Then I remembered my role.

I recomposed my smile. "Please put the light down."

He did.

I swear, manipulating human men is one of the silliest and easiest abilities of mermaids.

"You look really tired," I said.

"No, I'm..." He yawned.

How is this even considered a skill? I wondered with an internal eye roll. But I remembered Sara's advice that it *was* a skill and one I needed to succeed.

"Come over here. There's plenty of room to sit and rest up a bit." I tapped the table next to me.

"I really shouldn't," he replied but walked toward me.

"I won't tell a soul," I said quietly.

He sat down, and I hopped off.

"Here, more space. Relax for a few minutes. I'll wake you."

"I am pretty beat." He yawned again and lay on his side.

"There you go. Close those eyes."

He was snoring before I could count to three. *All right, then.* I felt his chest pocket and was rewarded with a small bump. I reached in and pulled out another black pearl. I added it to my growing collection. I started to leave him but had a moment of guilt. I didn't want him to get fired.

Leaning to his ear, I whispered, "Open your eyes in ten minutes and forget everything you saw."

He moaned softly from his sleepy land.

That should give me time to get the next pearl and head to the final destination.

I jogged back toward Suzee and Sara. As I reached the doorway, Lilli popped onto the path in front of me.

"Gah!" I jumped. Swallowing my heart back down to where it was supposed to be, I smiled. "Lilli! I just want to say—"

"Here." She dropped a black pearl at my feet. It bounced and skittered to the side.

"Lilli, please, I need to talk to you about—"

"I'm good." And she walked away.

"Geez." Suzee whistled. "Never piss off a sprite."

"No kidding," Sara agreed.

Fighting back tears, I bent down and picked up the pearl.

"Where next, Stormy?"

"Huh? What?"

"Next. The next place you need to get going to. We need to be done with this game so we can save this silly town... again," Sara sighed.

"Oh right. I, umm, I..." The tears started as I fumbled for the riddle in my pocket.

"Stormy, stop. You're fine. You're doing great actually." Sara stood up and walked over to me.

"But Lilli—she's so mad."

"I've learned that sometimes things aren't what they appear." Suzee took a sip from her glass.

I had no idea what she meant, but I also didn't have time to ask more questions. Sara was right—the longer I took, the closer the storm got. Laverna seemed determined to destroy us and this town one way or another.

I recited the final lines: "This challenge will end when you reach the base. Only then will you be allowed to end the chase."

"Ah, that's so clever of Laverna—a poetic full circle," Sara said as she peered over my shoulder at the riddle.

"Yup, the lighthouse," I replied without emotion. "But what is she going to do?"

"No idea," Sara replied. "Suzee?"

"Let's say it will be interesting to see how Storm's plan works," Suzee replied. "I like you, Storm. You remind me of me. But we have *got* to do something about your nails."

I half laughed and shook my head in disbelief. *Mermaids.*

"Okay, go for it, Stormy. We'll see you there," Sara said.

"Time for one more drink?" Suzee asked.

"Of course!" Sara gave me a wink.

I turned and sprinted back to the water to make my swim to the final destination... Laverna's idea of closure.

******

I kicked up the speed and made it to Salt Run in record time. I still hated swimming in there after the whole Jon incident and just wanted to get past the cave and to the beach as fast as possible. As I was thinking about that, I heard a chime. I slowed.

Hello? I called to the dark waters.

The chime grew louder. I didn't recognize the tone. It wasn't one of my family's.

I swam forward with some hesitation. The water was so churned up that my eyes weren't at all useful.

Hello? I tried again.

I passed by the cave and began to turn for the shore when an arm grabbed my leg.

"Eeek!" I screamed and drew my leg in tight while I spun around to see who was there. Paige swam into view and smiled.

Paige! That was mean, I whined.

Oh, little one. That was too easy is what that was. She laughed lightly. *Why so jumpy?*

I shook my head and regained my composure. *Oh, I don't know*, I replied sarcastically.

Oh, right. She nodded toward the cave.

I rolled my eyes at her feigned surprise.

Well, I have a little something for you. She smiled, her teeth a ghastly green in the murky water.

I didn't dare to be too hopeful that she'd make it easy by just handing the pearl over to me.

More laughter from her. *No, Storm, not easy, sorry.*

Stupid thoughts.

So, do you want to know where it is or what?

Where is it, Paige?

Just there. She nodded back toward the cave.

Inside? My heart sank.

Nope.

Really? Just over there? That was unexpectedly nice.

Yup.

What's the catch? There had to be a catch.

She shrugged and turned away toward shore. *Oh.* She stopped and looked back.

Yeah?

I've gotten used to you. Don't get dead... again. And then she swam into the darkness, leaving me alone.

Right, well, as far as Paige goes, that was a pretty nice compliment. I chuckled to myself.

I turned toward the cave and scanned the wall and sand. Then I swam slowly, feeling my way around its wide curving surface. *Did she stick it in the coquina? There are endless nooks and crannies to place a pearl. Or did she just drop it in the sand? Talk about needle in haystack. This will take all stupid night.* I sighed. *And seriously, here? Here, where I hate to be, I am now stuck for who knows how...*

Hey! You're back!

Yay!

We missed you!

Oh my goshes! She said you'd play with us again!

She was right, I told you.

Oh no, I thought. *No no no no.*

What's wrong?

Come on and play!

Is Jon with you? We miss him too.

This was a nightmare. Like, *actually* one of my nightmares. I flailed my arms wildly in an attempt to get away. *No no no no.* I shook my head while my arms and legs propelled me awkwardly toward the channel.

The water-soul voices faded. The pounding in my head didn't. I was gulping water like a goldfish. My stomach lurched, and I threw up. Food particles floated in front of me before being carried off in the current.

Gross, I thought and swam away from the vomit water. *What the hell am I going to do?* I wondered in desperation.

Okay. Okay. It's okay. Okay. My mind spun. *I just need to swim over there and ask them where the pearl is. They like me. Yeah. It's fine. I'm fine.* My internal motivation wasn't fooling anybody, but I had no other choice. *And really, what's the worst that happens? I die... again. Ugh.*

I took a slow inhalation of water, closed my eyes, and steadied my nerves. I reopened my eyes and swam back toward the cave.

Girls? I called quietly. This was going against every ingrained sense of self-preservation. My entire being was shouting alarms to swim away, but I pushed them down and continued my forward progress.

Girls? I called again with slightly more conviction.

I listened to the water around me and picked up hushed chatter and whimpers. *Aw, man. Now on top of being scared for my own life, I feel bad because I scared the girls by freaking out.*

Hey, girls, I tried again. *It's okay. It's me, Storm. I'm sorry I acted like that. I wasn't expecting you.*

Silence. Maybe they were listening, so I continued. *I was looking for something my friend dropped. We're playing a little game, and I need to find it to win.*

Soft sniffles were followed by, *Why did you yell at us?*

I'm so sorry, girls. I just was surprised is all.

The water was too churned up with sediment to pick out their milky cloud, so I had to hope they didn't sneak up on me silently. *Will you help me with the game?*

I like games, one girl shyly answered.

Me too, the second agreed with a touch more enthusiasm.

Great! I replied with every ounce of cheerfulness I could muster. *I'm looking for a small pearl that my friend with dark hair dropped. You probably saw her over here.

I saw her! the third girl said excitedly. *She swam around the side of the cave. She was pretty, like you.*

Thanks! Yes, she is pretty. Are you around there now? I asked. *The water is too murky for me to see you girls.*

What's moorky? the first girl asked.

Murky, I repeated slowly. *It means not clear.*

Oh! I like that word. the third girl replied.

So I'd like to find the pearl, but I can't swim around the cave if you girls are there.

Why? all three tiny voices asked in unison.

Hmm, I thought. *How do I tell them they could kill me without hurting their feelings?*

Remember when you girls tried to play with me before, and I got very sleepy? I asked.

Yeah, but then you became not moorky!

What? I asked.

You became clear, but you left before you could play.

Oh, right. When my soul had left my body, they'd seen me become not murky.

Well, being not murky isn't good for me, I explained.

Why? the second girl asked.

I need to stay murky so I can help other people. And you girls, when you get too close to me, make me not murky, and that hurts me.

We didn't mean to hurt you.

No! We like you!

Well, I like you three also. How about this? I promise to come play with you girls every week if you promise to keep me murky when I'm here. And all that means is you can't come too close. Okay?

Okay! they all said.

So, now can I come around to look? I asked.

Yeah!

Yes!

We moved.

Thanks! I swam around the far side and searched for the pearl. It didn't take long to spot it nestled in the coquina wall. I couldn't tell the color of it with the tinge of the water, but I eyed it proudly in my hand. I sank to the seafloor to take a breath. The adrenaline was leaving me, and I felt suddenly weak. I couldn't believe I'd done it. I felt so proud but so exhausted.

It's so pretty, the first girl said.

My eyes opened wide, and I fought the urge to scream and dart off. They were just kids. They would learn, and I would teach them as long as I didn't die trying.

Very calmly I replied, *Yes, it is. Thank you. But remember about not making me not murky?*

Yeah.

You're making me not murky right now.

Oh! I'm sorry. She giggled. *Too close?*

Too close, I replied softly.

How about now?

I started to feel my energy return. *Better, thank you.*

You're welcome! Now what?

Well, I have to go to shore to show that I won the game against the other mermaid. But I promise to come back, okay?

Yay! Okay.

Bye! they shouted slightly out of sync.

Bye, girls. Thank you again. And remember, I can play as long as you promise to keep me murky.

Yes! We'll remember.

I promise!

Me too!

Meghan Richardson and Tina Verduzco

I smiled and pushed off from the bottom. A cloud of silt billowed in my wake. I swam toward the beach and the final step of this challenge. I had no idea how the end of this tale would be written, but for the first time, I felt like I had a voice, and I was ready to be heard.

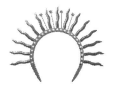

CHAPTER TWENTY-EIGHT
Busted

My pocket contained seven precious spheres. I darted across the grass toward the lighthouse visitor center but stopped at the tree line, by the gravel parking lot, to get a sense of what awaited me. My position was protected by the pitch-black of the new moon and the impending storm. The only illumination was the slowly revolving lighthouse light guiding us wayward souls back home.

Here I am. Full circle. This town is my home, and this is where my family and I belong. I am no outsider.

The wind gusted at my back, and thunder grumbled. I scanned the buildings. A movement caught my attention. A shape rocked slowly in one of the many rocking chairs on the brick porch of the Keepers' House. Her deep-amber eyes met mine. She nodded to me.

Busted. I guess my hiding skills aren't so ninja-like against Z.

I stepped out into the open and made my way over.

"Have a seat," Z said in a hushed voice when I hopped onto the porch. She patted the rocking chair to her right.

I sat on the edge and faced her. She, however, kept her eyes on the darkness of Salt Run.

"You are making short work of this game, Storm. Very impressive! I especially liked how you handled Daniel." Z chuckled softly.

"You were there?" I asked.

"Oh yes. I've been near you each step of the way. I will have to have words with Sara and Suzee, however. Margaritas are not appropriate." Despite her words of admonishment, her eyes smiled. "And you showed such compassion for the girls. They deserve that, you know. Compassion. Something they weren't shown in their tragic, untimely deaths."

Z turned to look at me. "You really are one of a kind, Storm. And you possess the ability to do more than either your human or mer family ever accomplished. Your empathy toward others is quite unparalleled in our kind. With that and your strong will and clever mind, I think you will really accomplish extraordinary things."

My cheeks warmed with the familiar embarrassment I got whenever anyone complimented me. I struggled not to look down. "Thanks," I mumbled.

"I speak the truth." She smiled and winked at me.

"I also do that now."

"Yes, you do. And now, I believe it's time to have others do the same." She held her hand out, palm up. In it rested a pink pearl. I reached out and picked it up.

"Now, go. They are waiting."

I took a deep breath and let it out slowly. My heart pumped with adrenaline. I stood up, tucked the new pearl with the rest, let out my bun, and hopped off the porch. I knew I had to get to the courtyard without the luxury of going through the gift shop. I jogged around the far side of the building. The bells on my mermaid's knot, finally able to be free, sang hopeful chimes as my mane blew wildly in the wind.

"I've got this," I whispered. *I hope...*

I hopped easily over the low fence and stopped just short of the courtyard. Quarter-sized droplets of rain splattered onto the bricks.

This is it. I took a deep breath, ran my fingers through my wild hair, and held my braid for a moment. So many things flashed through my mind—catching my first view of the ocean, climbing the tower with Nana and Jon, floating at sea with Rowan, Pearl stroking my hair, sitting with all my family, human and mer, on the deck, Lilli bouncing happily, Z telling me I could do what others couldn't.

She didn't say the dreaded phrase, but you know what? I can do this because...

"Because I'm Storm," I declared and willed my legs to move forward.

Wind howled, and the large, heavy raindrops continued. I entered the courtyard cautiously, unsure what I would find. Low murmurings led me in, but once I crossed the threshold of the entrance, all talking ceased, and hundreds of glowing eyes turned to me.

The courtyard between the lighthouse tower and the Keepers' House was dimly lit with yellow light. The circular path of the beacon made the area light up brightly for a brief moment on each rotation. I walked to the center and looked up.

The balcony of the Keepers' House looked like a packed standing-room-only concert venue. Mers were pressed against the rails, and rows of bodies were stacked against the walls, with heads popping up intermittently to see past those in front.

"Whoa," I whispered and gave a little wave.

Some mers chuckled. I finally located familiar faces in the front row. Z stood next to Laverna. Pearl and Paige stood to the sides of their mothers. Daniel was next to Paige, and Sara was next to Pearl. The balcony was divided into Lionfish and Sea Stars. Rowan stood in the packed second row with other Sea Star mers. I also spotted Suzee. I scanned more faces, a few of which I recognized. Some looked excited, and others looked bored.

"It took her long enough to get here, don't you think, T?" one mer said.

I scanned the crowd to locate the voice. It was on the Lionfish side of the balcony. A mermaid with long blond hair stood on tiptoes in a gap between a mermaid and a merman in the front row. She was speaking to a mermaid next to her.

"Yeah, Meg," a mermaid with striking white hair responded. "It feels like we've been waiting for years! Thought she'd be quicker getting to this point, but at least she *finally* made it!"

"Wonder what's going to happen?" Meg asked.

"No idea." T shook her head.

The mermaid in front of them shushed them.

Meg stuck out her tongue, and T stifled a laugh.

"Ahem..." I refocused on Laverna and Z. "I've completed all but the final challenge." I reached into my pocket, pulled out the eight pearls, and held them in my open palm for all to see. "Could somebody tell me what to do to get the last pearl and finish this?"

My heart raced. I worried everybody could hear it pounding.

"I told you she'd make it," a mermaid on the Sea Star side said.

"Well, Rose, she isn't done," another responded.

"And I don't trust Laverna to play fair, so it definitely isn't over," a third added.

A fourth laughed. "Laverna playing fair would be like Rose not starting a fight when she gets cut off."

Rose laughed. "Hey, Paulette, they saw that merge lane at the same time I did."

"Ladies, shh," a fifth in their little cluster said.

"Sorry," the four replied in unison.

I worked hard to not laugh at them. They did have something right. This last part wasn't going to be easy. But one thing they didn't know was that I'd banked on Laverna not playing fair. And turned out, I didn't necessarily play fair either.

"Well done, Storm. I believe you had to prove yourself in both mental and physical skills that only a mer could complete. Is that true, sister?" Z turned to Laverna.

"Well, yes," Laverna said, but her voice lacked its usual velvet tones. "Storm was able to complete the games. But she is not simply claiming to be a mermaid—she's claiming to have the matriarchal rights of your clan. This status requires her to prove beyond all doubt that she is capable of not only being a mer but also of leading your clan." She coughed lightly.

Z glanced at her sister. "She stands before us, does she not?"

"She does. But I wouldn't want anything to threaten your ability to continue our mother's final bequest to you, which is to protect our clans from the evils of the Hurricane Lady. That *is* the only reason your clan exists outside its rightful boundaries of the South Atlantic. Correct?" Laverna leaned against the rail as if needing its support. It might have been the lighting, but she really didn't look well.

This may work after all.

Z responded, again, in a neutral tone. "Yes, sister. Our mother requested I protect the statue from falling into the wrong hands and, by default, the town where it landed. This statue is an evil force that has devastating consequences to our kind."

"Ah." Laverna motioned broadly. "Devastating consequences to our kind. So glad you and your clan are here in *our* territory to help protect us. Or should I say, to protect the humans." Lionfish clan members mumbled to each other.

Anger rose within me that Laverna spoke so sarcastically to Z. I opened my mouth to give a rebuttal but closed it quickly when I caught Z's glance at me.

"Laverna, we protect all, mer and human," Z replied. "*We* have never hidden our intentions. The Hurricane Lady was made with positive intentions as a protector for our half brother. Unfortunately, evil took over. I will not forsake our mother's wishes."

"So, not like Hurricane Dora, then?"

I used every ounce of strength to not lash out. I stood motionless.

"The final challenge, sister," Z responded.

"What's the rush?" Laverna asked as the wind noticeably picked up around us.

Z gave an exasperated sigh.

"Fine, fine. It's probably too late to save this miserable little town, anyway." Laverna smiled and called, "Storm!"

"Yeah?" I replied as nonchalantly as possible.

"Your final pearl is awaiting you on that table." She motioned to a table on which sat a tall object covered in a dark cloth. In front of the wavering cloth was a tiny pink pearl that glowed brightly with each revolution of the beacon.

"That's it?" I asked, unsure.

"That's it," she replied with a salesman's smile. Her hands gripped the railing.

"Okaaay," I said.

"That's it, Sharon?" Paulette asked the mer with dangling turtle earrings.

Sharon shrugged.

"We've been waiting this long for her to pick up a pearl from the table?" Meg asked T.

"Li'l punkin may not make it," T said.

Rose glared at T.

"Bless her heart," Meg replied.

Paulette replied, "Seriously?"

"I'll bless their li'l punkin hearts." Jen, standing next to Paulette, glared across at Meg and T.

Another mermaid shushed them.

"Mary, I'm just sayin' they need to shut it," Jen replied.

I looked from the audience to the table. I took a few steps toward the table and stopped in midstep. I looked at Z. I looked at Pearl and Sara.

Then I found Rowan's eyes. He mouthed, "I love you."

I inhaled, exhaled, then took one more step.

"What's happening?" Sharon asked.

"Is she stuck?" T asked.

"Get the dang pearl," Rose said.

I dropped to one knee.

"Ooh!" Meg exclaimed. "She's down!"

Gasps filled the night. I looked back at my family. Z nodded. I crawled forward.

"Z, what's happening?" Pearl asked with obvious concern.

"Laverna. What are you doing?" Z turned and confronted her sister.

Laverna's face was contorted in anger. "No!" she shouted. "What is she doing?" One of her hands went to her temple, and she slumped slightly.

"No, Laverna. What did *you* do?" Z said angrily.

All eyes turned to Laverna. She looked sickly under the harsh yellow lights. The fingers of one hand still pressed her temple while the other held the rail.

"I didn't do anything," she replied. "Storm, she... it's not..."

"Real?" someone said, and a form emerged from around the tower and stood next to the table with the covered object and the pearl I so desperately wanted to reach. The voice belonged to Jacqueline.

She tilted her head and looked at the balcony with one eye. "You said to put the Hurricane Lady here, Laverna." Jacqueline whipped off the cloth, and there she stood—the four-foot-tall wooden Saint Barbara likeness. Each revolution of the tower's light reflected off her pointed silver crown. Her white dress gave her a ghostly appearance of hovering just above the table rather than resting on it. The Hurricane Lady. Not behind glass, not up in a room in the far corner, but right in front of me.

"No!" Laverna cried out. "I said to bring the replica to make it look like Storm wasn't a mermaid."

Gasps from both sides, Sea Stars and Lionfish, echoed in the courtyard.

Z bellowed, "You planned deception?"

"No, yes, well, it's for the best," Laverna stammered. "She doesn't deserve... she isn't..."

"Stop!" The Keepers' House shook. "You dare use the Hurricane Lady against one of us?" Z bellowed. "*Again?*"

"Again?" Suzee asked.

Laverna turned sharply to her and then back to Jacqueline. I was on all fours a few yards from the table. I shifted forward another few feet and collapsed.

A small white bird landed softly on Jacqueline's shoulder. She petted it absently. "Yes, again. Dora, was it? Something with Daniel tricking some gullible humans into bringing it to Z. Isn't that what you told me, Laverna?"

From my sideways view on the ground, Laverna looked frozen. Mers from both sides watched her, none of them happy. A cacophony of chatter ensued.

"Oh, she did *not*," Rose said.

"Oh, she *did*," Jen responded.

"So it wasn't Z's fault?" Mary asked.

"Or the humans'?" Sharon asked.

"It was Laverna," Paulette said.

"No!" Meg shouted from the other side. "It was Daniel!"

"*And* Laverna," T added.

"That's low," Suzee said.

I glanced at Daniel. He looked like a deer in headlights.

Laverna shouted above the rising din, "No! Forget Dora. Tonight, I directed Jacqueline to put the replica of the Hurricane Lady here, and when Storm approached, it would appear she was unaffected! Ugh!" Her legs faltered, but she caught herself.

Silence fell for two beats. All eyes were on Laverna.

Rowan broke it. "So, a trick? You meant to make Storm look like she wasn't mer enough? With a fake? With a... lie?"

All the mers gasped.

"Well..." Laverna backed away from the rail. She pushed against Daniel, and the two of them slid toward the door.

Jacqueline's voice stopped them in their tracks. "It appears I may have messed up." She laughed. "You foolish mers. Laverna, you asked me to reveal Storm for what she is. I believe I have held up my end. I have revealed she is a mermaid. Sorry it wasn't the answer you were hoping for. I also

Storm and the Hurricane Lady

promised Vincent I'd rid this land of as many of you as possible. I feel this will accomplish the task."

Laverna inhaled sharply. "You were working with Vincent?"

Jacqueline laughed. "One cannot pass up opportunities that present themselves." She then looked down at me. "Like your silly backpack and ring. My gosh, handing candy to a baby."

"I don't think that's the saying," Rose said.

"No," Paulette agreed. "It's…"

"Hush!" Jacqueline scolded.

"She did not," Jen said.

"She *did*," Sharon replied.

I glanced at the balcony and then back at Jacqueline. "Please, we can help you," I pleaded, barely lifting my head. The rain fell harder all around me.

"That time has long passed us by, Storm," Jacqueline replied.

The white bird fluttered to the table and picked up the tiny pearl in its beak. He flew to me, dropped the pearl on the wet bricks next to me, and returned to perch on Jacqueline's shoulder. The pearl bounced and then rolled into an expanding puddle a few inches away from my prone hand.

"Thank you." She smiled at the bird. It fluffed and then smoothed its feathers. Jacqueline turned back to us, "I am here to reclaim what is well past my time to have."

"I have to get Storm out of there," I heard Pearl say.

"Go," Z replied.

"I'm coming too," Paige said.

"No," Laverna scolded weakly. "Paige, you mustn't go in your condition." She tried to hold Paige's arm, but Paige easily swiped her away and continued after Pearl.

Other Lionfish mers started moving toward the doors of the balcony.

"Mother, come." Daniel took Laverna's arm. There was a commotion as the two forms pushed through the crowd.

"It was meant to be a fake. Paige, *no*!" Laverna shouted amid the growing discontented chatter.

"While you hoped a fake statue would prove your point, I felt there was no substitute for the real deal. You know? You are both very welcome." Jacqueline looked between Laverna and me. "Seems we have answered the question. Congratulations, Storm. You are 'mer enough.' Shame you won't get to live long enough to celebrate."

Pearl and Paige ran into the courtyard only to drop to their knees a few feet before reaching me.

I looked over at Pearl. She mouthed, "I'm sorry."

"Oh dear. Like swallows hitting a glass window. And a little one to boot. Sorry, Paige! Sorry, Laverna!" she shouted up to the balcony. Laverna was deathly pale. Jacqueline turned back to me with a smug smile. "Stormy, I may have spilled your little secret about Paige to Laverna."

Both Laverna and Z screamed in anger.

Jacqueline motioned for silence. "You have sung my siren's song long enough. I have been searching for centuries. The most recent attempt at reclaiming what is rightfully mine was undermined by a stupid human and a stupid mermaid. I was so close. I almost had it, and then it was gone. Why?" She motioned to the statue. "This vile creation. Well, I finally have it, and I will take back what is mine. My feet, my tale, my magic."

Mary spoke from the balcony. "Her feet?"

Jen shrugged.

"Oh!" Sharon exclaimed. "She's a siren!"

"Umm, isn't that another name for a mermaid?" Rose asked.

"Yeah, mermaid... siren... same," Mary added.

"No, they're—" Sharon started but was interrupted by a cry that could be heard for miles.

"Aargh!" Jacqueline exclaimed and spread her arms wide. "No! Sirens are not mermaids!" The tern on her shoulder took flight.

"Half birds," Sharon concluded.

The mers around her nodded in their new knowledge.

Jacqueline continued in a calmer voice. "You stole our siren tale, and others stole my feet. The feet are in this stupid idol that you hold in such reverence. I will reclaim my feet. But I will also reclaim my history. You mers have always been such a stupid breed. I will do you all a service and only destroy this damn doll after the storm destroys the town and also after my sprite friend is at hand to take control. You don't deserve this kindness, but I feel it is unduly cruel to take advantage of your small brains more than I have. From this day forward, the story of the sirens will be what is told."

Looking up, I spotted Laverna and Daniel. Suzee had them pushed back against the wall.

"It's your daughter down there," Suzee said.

"I have no strength. The statue," Laverna responded.

"Paige is trying to protect our clan." Suzee was angry.

"Good luck." Daniel pushed Suzee away and grabbed Laverna. They ran out the side door.

Looking back, I saw Jacqueline pick up the statue. "Jacqueline, no," I pleaded.

Jacqueline laughed.

I glanced back at Pearl and Paige. They both nodded.

I looked up at the balcony. Z nodded.

Looking Jacqueline squarely in the eye, I rose smoothly to my feet. There were a few gasps. I pushed my wet hair aside. "No. It's over," I said firmly.

Jacqueline stopped laughing. Her face showed confusion as her brain had trouble processing what her eyes were telling it. She looked at the statue and then back at me. I took a confident step closer.

"What? How?" she stammered, holding the statue in front of her like a shield.

"Jacqueline, it's over," I said with a hint of sympathy, my arms extended, palms up, in a peaceful gesture.

Her eyes glimpsed something behind me. I sensed Paige and Pearl were also now standing.

"No!" she exclaimed, and for the first time, I saw fear in her eyes as reality washed over her. "No!"

Hugging the statue to her side, she ran into the lighthouse. The bird soared and circled. It rose toward the top of the tower on invisible currents in the pouring rain.

I raced into the lighthouse after her and started the dizzying climb.

CHAPTER TWENTY-NINE
Strike Three

Adding two hundred nineteen steps to my already exhausted legs, I rounded the final curve of steps. I caught a glimpse of Jacqueline as she darted out to the balcony. She didn't know the statue she held wasn't the real one. I had to tell her, or she'd go to a place that she couldn't come back from.

"Jacqueline?" I called, catching my breath just inside the doorway that led to the balcony. I peered out just as thunder rumbled overhead and an impressive light show illuminated the sheets of rain falling at angles matching the erratic gusts of wind.

"Storm?" Jacqueline asked. "Are you looking for a death sentence? Go back. This doll hurts your kind, and despite my feelings toward you all, I do not wish to be the one to kill you. Let me get what is mine, and the rest of the story will rewrite itself."

"Jacqueline," I repeated. "That's not the real Hurricane Lady."

Thunder rumbled. I stole a glance out the door and saw Jacqueline backed against the railing with the Hurricane Lady held tightly to her body. Rain pelted her from the side. Her clothes blew wildly. The lightning, in coordination with the beacon, created an uncomfortable strobe effect. With each bright flash, her hunched form looked like a trapped, extremely dangerous animal.

I timed my entrance onto the balcony with a clap of thunder and flash of lightning. I sprang toward Jacqueline.

"No! It's the real one!" she shouted and threw the statue to the ground. It shattered into a dozen pieces.

I stood still. She looked at me triumphantly and then back at the broken pieces that littered the grated walkway. After an awkward moment that lasted a full rotation of the beacon, she screamed in realization.

I shrank back against the rounded concrete of the tower. Jacqueline pushed aside the pieces of fabric and wood that had very recently been a lifelike statue of Saint Barbara. She turned to me and then back toward the ruins. She picked up a small black rock and held it out to me.

"It's not the real statue," I repeated meekly.

"But mers can't lie," she replied.

"No, we can't. And we didn't. You assumed it was the real one. Probably because the magnetic rock distorted your perceptions... like magnets do with birds. Jacqueline, we know what you're after, and we can help you if you let us."

She laughed and backed into the rails. "Are you kidding me? *You* can help me? I don't think so. You, Storm, are the problem. Your kind—*both* of your kinds—are the problem. Clever with the magnetic rock to throw me off. Someone's done some research, huh? Jon, perhaps? Don't worry. I'll find him next and make him pay, just like Diego."

"So you killed Diego?"

"Of course. After he sent my feet away, I made sure he knew what it was like to try to fly without wings."

She went to throw the rock over the edge, but I dove to stop her. I grabbed her arm and brought her body down on mine. The rock fell onto the grate and tumbled to a stop next to us.

"You are the dumbest of all," she said. "I was willing to let you survive tonight."

"Survive tonight, Jacqueline? For what? To have my family and friends die? No, thank you."

I reached and grabbed the rock, but then she rolled us to the side. My back hit the rough cement wall. Jacqueline kept me pinned there and pried the rock away from my tenuous grasp.

"No!" I screamed in anguish.

She pressed into me to trap me against the wall and lifted her hand, which held the rock triumphantly, to the sky. "Good try."

But then something happened. Her hand that held my magnetic rock was empty. The rock lay a few feet away, near the railing. We both looked around, completely confused.

"Stormy!" a little voice called.

"Lilli?" I asked the darkness.

A giggle. "Of course."

Jacqueline jumped off me and leapt to the right. I stood quickly, unsure of what was going to happen. *Is Lilli here to help me or kill me?*

"Give me the real statue," Jacqueline said.

"Hmm." Lilli sighed. "No. You aren't nice at all."

Jacqueline's reply, nothing more than a guttural sound, made all the hairs on my arms rise. Without thinking, I dove and tackled her. She fell hard on the metal grate. We were both drenched as the rain continued to pelt us. I rolled her over and reached for the rock. If I could get that, I could magnetize and then overpower her. *I just need the—*

"Rock?" she whispered to me. "Never."

I clawed at her hand. We were so tightly bound there wasn't space to really fight. Then I thought about my very first battle.

"Ouch!" She pulled back. "You bit me!"

I smiled and snatched the rock. Unfortunately, she anticipated my move and hugged me close. So I had the rock but couldn't use it to help myself while in a bear hug. I struggled a moment more. Then I remembered what Jon had joked about: "When in doubt, throw the rock."

Jacqueline's eyes were black pins. With only my hands free to move, I lamely tossed the rock at her. It bounced lightly off her hip and landed with a *clang*.

She laughed triumphantly.

I laughed genuinely because this was ridiculous.

Lilli laughed at me laughing.

I laughed more at Lilli laughing. Jacqueline stood up, thinking she'd won.

"You stupid little..." Jacqueline continued with a bunch of degrading phrases. But I didn't pay close attention to them. I only focused on my laughter and the tingles that grew within me.

Jacqueline moved toward Lilli. The sprite tried to sidestep her, but Jacqueline grabbed Lilli by both arms and pushed her nearly over the rails.

"No!" I shouted and stood.

"No? Then give me the real statue! Now!"

"It's not here!" I cried. I felt the tingles. I knew I could magnetize, but I didn't want to do it while Lilli was also at risk of being stunned.

"I will fly again!" Jacqueline shouted at the night and pushed harder on Lilli. I caught Lilli's eye. She winked. I understood.

I extended my arms to Jacqueline and pushed with everything I had. Lilli disappeared, and Jacqueline's eyes widened as she stumbled forward in the space where Lilli had been. I'd only meant to throw her off balance, but I'd underestimated my magnetism and pushed too hard. She teetered half over the balcony rail.

"No!" I screamed and grabbed her right leg just as she fell.

She cried out in fear or pain—I wasn't sure which.

"Hang on. I'll get you back up!" I pulled with both arms.

I caught a glimpse of Jacqueline's face. She looked defeated. All the anger that had once propelled her was gone. She was just a frail-looking creature teetering between life and death. The rain made her skin so slick that it was hard to hold onto.

"Come on—I've got you!" I shouted.

She looked up at me, gave a little shake of her head, and twisted. I lost my grip, and her leg started to slide through my hands. With my hand on her boot, I thought I had her, but she didn't stop. I let go of the boot and reached for her foot. But where her foot should have been was nothing more than a stump, and my hands closed on empty air.

"No!" I shouted.

A bolt of light flashed from the balcony to Jacqueline's falling body. The light lifted her, and she hung, seemingly weightless, in the air beyond the balcony. Her clothing billowed in the wind, and she raised her arms out wide. For one moment, she was a beautiful bird surrounded by light. She smiled at me and, with a little nod, closed her eyes. And then she was gone.

Vincent approached my side. The storm raged around us. Lilli reappeared next to me. A single black feather floated gently among the erratic air currents.

"It was what was needed. There was no saving her. But despite herself, she deserved to fly one last time," Vincent said.

I looked at him and back at Lilli, who nodded solemnly. The white tern soared into view and scooped up the floating feather in its beak. It circled once and then flew away toward the ocean.

CHAPTER THIRTY
Home

"Can you take this tray, Storm?" Nana asked.

"Sure!" I met Nana at the screen door and grabbed the full tray of food from her hands.

Dad, Pearl, Mr. Humpphrey, and Nana followed outside with more trays of food. The table was already pretty full, but there was apparently no such thing as too much. This was, after all, quite a celebration and a good use of our hurricane supplies.

We'd cleared the deck of the fallen palm fronds, and a quick survey of town showed it had escaped with only minor damage. There were a few downed trees and some flooded low-lying neighborhoods, but the consensus among the locals was that it could have been—and based on predictions, should have been—much worse. The last-minute shift to the east and increased sheer were godsends.

"I saw Mrs. Todd from two doors down, and she was so thankful we skirted another storm." Nana set down her tray on the table. "She, of course, wasn't worried because of the protection afforded by the Hurricane Lady, but this one did seem to cut things a bit close in her opinion." Nana winked at us.

"Hurricane Lady, shmurricane lady. Always taking our glory," Sara replied.

"You can say that again," Pearl said with a shake of her head. "I'm exhausted!"

"Speaking of exhausted, I volunteered us all to help her clear the debris in her yard."

Moans echoed around the deck.

"Of course," Dad answered. "Least we can do. She's nearing on eighty-eight, I think."

"That young?" Rowan asked.

Dad laughed. "She's a human."

"Ahh." Rowan grinned.

"Well, technically, we did already save her house and every other one in town, so..." Paige said.

"Should have saved her oak also." Mr. Humpphrey laughed.

"No good deed, I tell you," Rowan said.

"These humans are never satisfied," Paige said with a sigh.

With our volun-*told* duties established for the afternoon, everybody filled plates and poured drinks. Sara laughed with Paige, while Pearl snuggled close to Dad as they listened to the story Rowan and Suzee told them. Nana, Z, and Mr. Humpphrey sat at the table and sipped their drinks. Jon stuffed his face with a too-big sandwich, and Lilli and I laughed at him. The sun had already ducked behind the house, and the evening sea breeze kept us cool. Thanks to the clans working together, the storm hadn't been a disaster.

Rowan popped open another salt ale. "I'm still impressed, ladies."

"What, we don't need to hate each other *all* the time, you know," Paige said. "And, Rowan, your speech was quite empowering."

I immediately thought of *Braveheart*. Rowan had pulled at his Scottish roots when he'd made his speech.

"What was it, again, that you shouted?" Paige asked.

Rowan stood tall, cleared his throat, held his salt ale bottle high, and exclaimed to the dunes, "Get your fecking shite together already! We are on the same fecking team. And if you aren't, *feck off*." He sat back down with a bow.

"So, not quite *Braveheart*." I laughed.

Pearl smiled. "Not quite, but the sentiment was there, and his words struck a nerve. He reminded us we're all family. We might disagree, but heck, if someone or something tries to attack us..."

Paige laughed. "Hurricane Matthew didn't stand a chance with us as a united front."

"And neither did Jacqueline," Pearl added.

The three of them toasted each other with a clink of salt ale bottles. I joined in but didn't feel joy. Jacqueline had been evil and manipulative, but she'd also been hurt. She'd been wounded on so many levels. I fiddled with the metal trinket in my pocket.

"I'm impressed with Storm's quick thinking on the magnetic rock," Mr. Humpphrey said to Nana.

"She said that once she realized Jacqueline was a siren, she and Jon looked up bird facts and realized they are guided by magnetics. She thought it could also be used to confuse them," Nana replied.

I smiled. "Yeah, once we figured that out, and I saw her odd reaction at the beach when I had it with me, I asked Jon to put the magnetic rock inside the replica. I wasn't totally sure it would confuse her enough, but I guess it did!"

"I didn't even know there *was* a replica statue," Rowan admitted.

"Neither did we until we did our research paper for the summer course," Jon replied. "They created it when the real statue had to undergo extensive repairs. The sisters wanted to make sure the town kept believing, so they created a near-identical one to keep on display."

"Yeah, Samantha told us about overhearing the nuns say they planned to switch out the statue early," I said. "At first, I thought they just meant they were moving it, but the fact that Samantha said 'switch' made us curious. And then Paige mentioned that weird conversation between Laverna and Daniel about a switch, and then Lilli did a weird mime thing for me. Basically, it all came together that there were two Hurricane Ladies. But it wasn't until this past week that we knew for sure."

"Samantha was almost late for our last class, which is totally not like her," Jon said.

"Right?" I agreed. "I thought she was going to collapse after the professors teased her."

"But the reason she was late was what intrigued us. She said there was some commotion blocking the entire street near the O'Reilly House. We were curious about what was going on so close to the competition, so we wandered down there after class."

"What happened?" Pearl asked.

"Nothing," I replied with a little shrug. "I stood below the window of the Hurricane Lady. I could see her. And nothing. That's when we figured out that the switch had been made and the one on display was the replica."

"Well done," Z replied.

"Yes." Dad sighed. "My little girl." He shook his head and met my eye. I half smiled and walked over to him and Nana.

"Then it was just a matter of getting the rock in it so Jacqueline would be confused. Well, that and everyone else playing their parts."

"So the thing about Paige being pregnant...?" Rowan asked.

"I thought it was time Jacqueline weakened someone else, for a change, by defining their truths. And to be honest, I never said Paige was pregnant. I just said her unborn child may not be a full mer. I mean, that's possible in the future, ya know? And I did hear her talking to Pearl about her baby, so..."

Paige laughed. "Yeah, I did use that word when I asked Pearl about my store. My store is my baby."

I smiled and shrugged with innocence. "Oops."

"That was smart, Storm," Sara said with an approving tilt of her head.

"I have to admit, I wasn't sure if Jacqueline would pass along the information. But I hoped she'd be unable to keep it a secret. I figured if Laverna felt weak, she'd believe Jacqueline's claim that the statue was the original, forcing Laverna to confess her plan to trick me. Thank you, everybody, for trusting me. I know I didn't really deserve your trust after all the lying and sneaking. I'm sorry."

"I don't know about everybody else, but I accept your apology. You are doing the best you can. Please remember, you are still learning, as we all are." Nana looked around the table. Dad, Mr. Humpphrey, and Z nodded.

"Always." Z raised her glass. The others followed.

"So where is the real statue now?" Rowan asked.

"Back in storage, where we found her," Mr. Humphrey replied. "We didn't want to take any chances that Jacqueline would realize the one she had was the replica, so we took the real one to the old Mystery House spot. Again, those magnets really provide great camouflage. Oh, and we brought you this." Mr. Humpphrey handed a small oval porcelain object to Z.

"Oh my goodness," Z whispered and stared at the miniature painting. "Mama."

"We figured you'd want to have that. Also, without all three objects together, we hope the Hurricane Lady is less of a weapon and more of what she was meant to be."

"Thank you, Miles, Nana, Matthew, and Jon."

"But... if the Hurricane Lady isn't as dangerous, won't Laverna say we don't have to be here?" I asked.

Paige smiled. "Unfortunately, my mother and brother were last seen heading out into the Atlantic. I'm not sure what they're up to, but I don't plan on telling them anything soon after their little stunt. They didn't even try to protect me or my unborn baby!" Paige rubbed her belly mockingly.

"Thank you, Paige," Z replied. "Perhaps while the magic may no longer be in the statue, the belief in the statue can still be magic!"

Paige chuckled. "And what my mother and brother don't know won't cause anybody any harm. In fact, it may just keep everybody a tiny bit safer."

"Oh, shoot, what about the replica?" I said, suddenly worried. "Jacqueline smashed it on the lighthouse balcony. What are the nuns going to do when they realize it's missing?"

Storm and the Hurricane Lady

Pearl winked. "Never fear, Storm. Sara and I fixed her right up! She is back on display, and none are the wiser."

"Well, I wouldn't take her dancing anytime soon. Not sure how well we did on the joints, but... as long as no one touches her, I believe she'll pass," Sara said.

"So, has anybody talked to Lilli?" I asked. "I know you guys were pretending to be mad at me during the competition, but I don't think Lilli was faking it. I mean, she tried to electrocute Jon and me."

Laughter drifted to us from the stairs. It was followed by a bouncing Lilli, who held Vincent's hand. Jon slid behind Rowan.

"I didn't try to kill you guys." She giggled as she and Vincent walked toward us.

"You kinda did," I replied. "I mean, you only missed us by inches."

"Oh, Storm, you're funny." She laughed. Then she became serious and said in a deadpan tone, "I never miss."

I swallowed loudly with the new understanding.

"Never piss off a sprite," Sara said.

"Cheers to that," Paige added and clinked bottles with Sara.

"Papa," Lilli said sternly. "Don't you have something to say to Jon?"

Vincent looked down at his daughter and sighed. "Jon..." He took a breath and then mumbled, "Mmmsory."

"Papa," Lilli scolded.

Vincent cleared his throat and repeated his mumbled words more clearly, "I'm... I'm sorry." He nodded in Jon's direction.

Jon poked his head out from behind Rowan. "Umm. Thank you." Then he ducked back.

"No, Jon, it's okay." Lilli bounced over to him and took his hand. She dragged him over to Vincent. "Papa knows you are one of the good humans. And of course, I knew you guys didn't vandalize anything."

"You did?" Jon asked.

Lilli looked between me and Jon. "Of course it wasn't you two—it was Papa. He did it to help."

I opened my mouth but closed it again. *He did what to do what?*

"That's correct," Vincent said. "Jacqueline came to me with her plan to destroy you all, and after discussing with Lilli, she filled me in on all the good your family does. But I had to play along, so I came up with the best option."

"What was that?" I asked.

"Well, to provide you hints for the challenge, Storm."

Lilli bounced and clapped with glee. "Isn't he so clever?"

I didn't know how to respond.

"Yes, you see, the places I vandalized were the exact spots you had to visit for the challenge." He nodded with pride.

"Ah, yes," I replied hesitantly, thinking of all the trouble I'd gotten into because of his *help*. "Thank you?"

"You are most welcome," he replied with a smile. "And, Jon..."

"Yes, sir?" Jon replied quietly.

Vincent held out his hand. Jon looked at him then at Lilli then at the rest of us. I shrugged, and Lilli nodded excitedly.

Jon slowly extended his right hand. Vincent immediately grabbed it, pulled him close, and pressed his left palm to Jon's chest. Jon gasped, and we all lurched forward, but before we even made it a step, Vincent released him and smiled.

"There. The tracking is removed."

"Oh!" Jon exclaimed. "Thanks."

"Vincent," Z said. "I believe you will find that we can once again have a good relationship with these humans. Like you had with the noble Timucuans. These humans are hoping to improve this land."

"I hope so," Vincent said.

"Yes, Papa," Lilli said. "Jon is even going to study environmental policy and law after high school!"

"Please, Lilli and Vincent, join us for some food and drinks." Nana motioned them to the overflowing table.

"Speaking of school," Dad said. "I'm happy to announce that I've decided to sell our Indiana house and come back home to St. Augustine for good. So, Storm, that means we just need to get you enrolled in school here."

"Oh. Wait, what?"

"Storm, you may be a mermaid, but you're still only sixteen."

"You aren't serious. After everything this summer—the competitions, the magic, the trainings, the near deaths—now I have to go back to high school?"

"Yes," Dad replied.

"Yes," Nana echoed.

"But..." I looked at Pearl for help. She shook her head.

"Aw, Storm, it won't be that bad," Jon said. "I mean, I'll be there, and also I bet you're a shoo-in for the swim team."

Everyone laughed. I sat back in my seat, knowing this was one battle I was not going to win. Rowan came over and stood behind me.

He leaned down and kissed my head. "I love you, rainbow fish."

I looked up. "I love you too. But I do have one question."

"Anything, m'love."

"Do you still want to fly?"

He laughed. "You know what? I think I'm fine with my own tale."

I nodded. He wrapped me in a hug and then went back to talk with Jon and Sara.

I reached into my pocket and pulled out the tiny silver birdcage Jacqueline had given me. For all her evil, she was also a victim. She'd never asked for what had happened to her. She and I were kind of similar in that way. And part of me felt bad for her. I hadn't been able to help her in the end. Vincent was probably right—nobody could.

But going forward, I don't want this pain or suffering to have to take place. I will find a way to help those lost on their journeys. No, not find a way... I am the help. I am Storm. I am the lighthouse beacon for wayward souls. This is my purpose.

I swung open the tiny silver door and placed the little cage on the table in front of me. A Frida Kahlo quote popped into my mind. Jacqueline had told it to me as she limped through her rounds of opening all the birdcage doors: "Feet, what do I need you for when I have wings to fly?"

I hadn't understood it then, but I did now. Rather than focus on our limitations, we needed to soar with our strengths. Sadly, Jacqueline had forgotten that beyond individual strengths, love and family were an unbreakable power. *I wish we'd met her earlier. I wish we could have helped her. I wish she could have seen us not as the enemy but as the family she had been so long deprived of. Maybe at least now she is at peace.*

At just that moment, a line of pelicans dipped low over the water and then played follow-the-leader as they climbed back up into the sky. I smiled and lifted my bottle of salt ale to them... and to her.

I turned my attention back to the conversations surrounding me and recalled Mr. Humpphrey's description of St. Augustine as a small town with big secrets. Big secrets indeed, but St. Augustine meant so much more to me now. It was where I'd found a community that welcomed me. It was where I'd discovered an extended family I hadn't known I had. It was where I'd learned of my true nature and become comfortable being me.

It was home.

Author's Note

Like you, we weren't sure how Storm's tale was going to continue! Thank goodness she believed in us and insisted that we keep writing until we got it right. Also, thanks to our dedicated readers for returning despite the short... ahem, okay, excessively long wait after leaving you with *Oh Jon. We need to talk.* Honestly, we didn't think it would take this long. If you are new to the Mermaid's Knot series, consider yourself lucky to have been able to experience immediate gratification.

We have been working on Hurricane Lady for years. Unfortunately, those years included quite a few false starts, many stops, and some life events that pulled us in various directions. Tina is still a cat mom, but now her kitties are Luna and Soul. Meghan and family have traded the boat life for solid ground, and her kiddos have grown up and are off on their own adventures. Our real kickstart to completing Hurricane Lady, though, came during the pandemic. With not many things to distract us, aside from making bread and growing celery and green onions, we committed to weekly phone calls with each other. At first, it was awkward discussing the second book but over time, awkwardness became forgiveness which became brainstorming which became paragraphs and chapters. Storm and all her family and friends began to speak to us again, trusting us to continue telling their tale!

This whole process taught us a valuable lesson in the strength of friendship. We were there for each other during the ups and downs, times of inspiration, and times of empty minds. We continued to talk and support each other. Storm's latest story came naturally after that. We are very proud of the result and are excited to share it with you. Cheers to Storm and cheers to you, our readers!

Meghan and Tina
October 2022

Acknowledgments

Our first thank-you goes to you, our readers, for being patient with us. We know it's been a long time between books, and we appreciate your continued support. We also are excited to acknowledge the local St. Augustine Haunts that welcomed our mers in this sequel: Bridge of Lions, Casa Monica Resort and Spa, Castilo de San Marcos National Monument, Father Miguel O'Reilly House Museum, Lincolnville, Medieval Torture Museum, Micro Masterpieces Art Gallery, Pizzalley's on St. George, Scarlett O'Hara's, Schmagel's Bagels, The Fountain of Youth, The Tini Martini Bar, and the Ximenez-Fatio House Museum. A special thanks to our early readers for sifting through the coarse sand and providing valuable feedback: Kevan Breitinger, Jess D'Ascanio, Samantha Eide, Paula Grasel, Shannon Pitchford, and Mary Williams. And thanks to our amazing editor, Sarah Carleton of Red Adept Editing, for bringing Storm's story to the next level. Thank you to the tribe for always being supportive, to Jennifer Woida for always making sure the champagne was cold, and to Mary "Sunshine" Williams for making Tina get her bottom out of bed to enjoy the inspirational St. Augustine sunrises. Thank you, Joe, of "Yes It's Real Sterling Silver Jewelry 925" for the inspiration of the Sea Star clan's symbol. Thank you, Dean Richardson, for making vision become reality on the cover painting. A shout-out to John Bolen and JP Bolen for their full investment into the Storm conversations during Meghan's weekly family calls, and to Jonathan Pitchford and Owen Pitchford for making Meghan (aka mom) feel like a superstar for completing a second book. And finally, there is no way we could have published this book without the incredible help of David Bolen. Thank you!

About the Authors

Meghan, the youngest of four siblings, grew up in New Jersey. She received a Marine Biology degree from Eckerd College in St. Petersburg, Florida and after graduation, stayed to study the Florida Manatee for the Florida Fish and Wildlife Conservation Commission. In 2006, Meghan, her husband, and her three children moved to St. Augustine, Florida.

Tina, an only child, grew up in Iowa, where she had a career as a radio DJ. Fleeing the cold, she moved to St. Augustine in 1984 where she met the love of her life, and future husband, Paul. The two became essential to the St. Augustine art scene.

Meghan and Tina met when Tina tried a Yoga By the Sea class taught by Meghan. The two women hit it off immediately, becoming fast friends, and eventual co-authors.

While writing their first novel, Meghan traveled with her family aboard their sailboat for several years, finally settling in Marathon, Florida. Tina served as a guide for GhoSt Augustine hearse tours and eventually started her own firm.

Meghan currently works for Habitat for Humanity of the Middle Keys, and Tina creates a variety of art out of her home studio. They continue writing books together.

For further information, visit:
LunaSeaPublishing.com